A CLASH OF WILLS . . .
AND A TRIUMPH OF DESIRE . . .

"Your little displays of defiance are annoying, though understandable. But this time you've gone too far. It seems you are quite adept at playing the wanton, but I should have known that from the kisses we shared."

"Kisses?" she rasped as he pulled her closer, so roughly that she lost her hold upon the blanket. To her horror, it slid from her body, leaving her naked within his arms. "Let me go!" she demanded, panicking. "I remember no kisses!"

"I do," Rurik said huskily. Splaying one large hand over the small of her back, he drew her so close that her breasts swelled against his chest. "Warm, eager kisses that fooled me into thinking you were accustomed to a man's touch. I remember how you parted your soft lips for me, Zora . . ."

"I would never have done that! I'm no wanton!" she cried, trying to twist free and realizing it was hopeless. As his hand slid slowly up her back, a strange, unsettling warmth radiated from some deep, mysterious place inside her to the ends of her toes and the tips of her fingers. Every time she moved against him, she felt a catch in her throat. To her dismay, she realized she was trembling.

"See how your body betrays you, Princess?" he taunted. "You don't have to be a wanton to possess the passion of one. But why try to convince you with words when actions speak so much more clearly?"

Zora gasped aloud as his mouth came down hard upon hers . . .

The Pagan's Prize

Miriam Minger

JOVE BOOKS, NEW YORK

THE PAGAN'S PRIZE

A Jove Book / published by arrangement with
the author

PRINTING HISTORY
Jove edition / January 1993

All rights reserved.
Copyright © 1993 by Miriam Minger.
This book may not be reproduced in whole
or in part, by mimeograph or any other means,
without permission. For information address:
The Berkley Publishing Group, 200 Madison Avenue,
New York, New York 10016.

ISBN: 0-515-11014-0

Jove Books are published by The Berkley Publishing Group,
200 Madison Avenue, New York, New York 10016.
The name "JOVE" and the "J" logo
are trademarks belonging to Jove Publications, Inc.

PRINTED IN THE UNITED STATES OF AMERICA

10 9 8 7 6 5 4 3 2 1

For
Bebe Walker, my Norse Nana,
and
Catherine Wicinski, my Slavic Grandma.
Two great ladies
whom I infinitely love and admire.

Author's Note: In the eleventh century, the country known today as Russia was called "Rus" by its inhabitants, and so they referred to themselves. The Rus called the Norsemen who came as mercenaries and traders to their land "Varangians," meaning "pledge men," for these fierce warriors obeyed an inviolable oath to defend their sworn leader to the death. The word "viking," a name given to the Norsemen in later centuries, described a favorite activity of these bold and fearsome Varangians . . . "adventuring in search of wealth."

For now brother said to brother: "This is mine, and that is mine also," and the princes began to say of little things, "Lo! this is a great matter," and to forge discord against themselves.

"The Lay of the Host of Igor"
(S. Cross's Translation)

The Pagan's Prize

PROLOGUE

Novgorod, Rus Land,
April, A.D. 1024

"No, you cannot go! You stay with Semirah!"

Rurik Sigurdson smiled lazily at the pouting, sable-haired woman straddling his hips, her wet warmth sheathing that part of him that only moments before had throbbed in thunderous climax.

Of his six concubines, he favored this tempestuous Khazarian slave with her long white limbs, lilac-stained nipples, and flashing agate eyes. But he would never allow her to know his mind, or permit his attraction for her to grow beyond lust. He had learned long ago to put no faith in women, seeking only the carnal pleasure they could provide him.

"You have no say in the matter," he said huskily, caressing Semirah's slender thighs. Her pale skin, a startling contrast to his deeply bronzed hue, was as soft as swan's down beneath his large, callused hands. "I leave at dawn."

The woman's chin jutted, her expression growing determined in the glow of an oil lamp placed near the richly carved bed. She touched her fingers to her breast as she leaned over him, her silky hair enveloping them like a gossamer ebony cloud. She laid her hand over his heart. "I go with you."

Chuckling at the absurdity of her statement, Rurik drew her against his chest and rolled with her to one side, her lithe, coltish body molded to his powerful frame.

"Greedy wench." He nuzzled her throat, her spicy citrus scent of bergamot and cedar exciting his senses. "Isn't it enough that I summoned you to share this last night with me rather than one of the others?"

"Those women are cows," came her petulant reply. "How could you not choose Semirah?" Draping a smooth leg over his thigh, she softened her voice, almost purring. "Take me with you, Lord Rurik. I want to please you, yet how can I if you go so far away?"

"Enough," Rurik said firmly, his patience ended. He raised his head to look into her face. As his newest concubine, this exotic desert woman with her thick, honeyed accent had apparently not yet discerned what his other women already knew and accepted. He treated his concubines equally, granting none special favors. "Fetch us more wine, Semirah, and plague me no more with your demands. You will remain here like the others and wait patiently for my return."

Despite the disappointment shining in her eyes, the slave woman said no more. Extricating herself from his embrace, she rose with athletic ease from the bed and sauntered across the room, her body gleaming white as alabaster, her trim bottom swaying with provocative exaggeration as if she wanted to emphasize what he would soon be missing.

By Thor, she was impertinent. Rurik smiled and felt his good humor return. Yet it was tempered by the memory of his meeting that morning with Grand Prince Yaroslav, his sworn lord, at the *kreml*, the citadel overlooking the city of Novgorod. Without the distraction of a warm, willing woman in his arms, his thoughts turned easily to the gravity of the times and the secretive mission to which he had been entrusted.

"Not only has my brother Mstislav laid claim to my throne and invaded my realm with his warriors," Yaroslav had blustered, the short, barrel-chested ruler pacing restlessly in front of Rurik, "he has now conquered Chernigov, one of my most prosperous trading cities, and established there what he calls his temporary throne! His arrogance knows no bounds! Does he truly believe that he can defeat me, the grand prince of all Rus Land?"

"Perhaps so," Rurik had commented dryly. "It is rumored that Mstislav boasts of victory before the winter brings ice again to the rivers."

"Never! He was nothing but a boy and a weakling when our father Vladimir sent him as viceroy to Tmutorokan. I always thought that southern city founded upon stinking swampland a fitting place for him to rule!"

"A weakling no longer, my prince, but a bold and calculating warrior who lusts for more than a swamp. While you fought your brother Sviatopolk for the Rus throne after your father's death, Mstislav made no move but harbored his forces during those four long years of battle."

"Yes, the coward! And while Sviatopolk, may his putrid corpse writhe in hell, murdered three of our brothers, Mstislav hid behind his palace walls among his women—"

"Shrewdly waiting," Rurik interrupted, knowing that in his position of friend and trusted adviser, Yaroslav would not take offense. "He planned his strategy during these last five years of peace since your victory to strike against you now."

"And so he has." Yaroslav faced Rurik, who towered almost a foot above him. "You must go to Chernigov under a merchant's guise and discover the strength of Mstislav's forces. I've already sent a message to my northern allies, your King Olaf of Norway and to my wife's father, the king of Sweden, asking them to send more Varangian mercenaries to bolster my army. When they arrive, we shall make our move, but until then I must know how many enemy warriors we face to better plan our attack. And if you can find out Mstislav's battle plans without jeopardizing your guise, do so."

"I will leave at first light tomorrow," Rurik assured him, eager to serve again the Rus prince to whom he had sworn a sacred oath of allegiance eight years ago.

"Excellent. My steward will see that you have everything you need." The energetic man resumed his agitated pacing. "What goods will you sell, Rurik?"

"Furs," he replied. "The perfect ruse. Easy to transport both by river and on land. Anything else would only hinder my pace. I want to inspect the entire region and return to Novgorod by June."

"Such a journey will take at least that long." The grand prince stopped to stare at Rurik thoughtfully. "I chose you because you know a merchant's life well. I am only grateful you returned in time from your latest trading ventures to fight for my cause."

As if this reminded him of his brother's foul ambitions, Yaroslav cursed vehemently. "Go now, Rurik Sigurdson, and make your preparations. And take a few of your men with you as fellow merchants. I will sleep better knowing you travel with friends to guard your back. I do not want to lose the most famed warrior in my senior *druzhina* to those vermin dung-eaters. May Christ protect you!"

"And Odin," Rurik said grimly to himself, his baptism into the new faith shortly before he entered Yaroslav's service unable to wash away pagan beliefs engrained in him from birth . . .

"Are you thinking of Semirah, my lord?"

As Rurik focused upon the beautiful woman who stood beside the bed holding two silver goblets, her lilac nipples hardened temptingly from the early spring chill pervading the room, his reverie faded into sharp reality. The days ahead would bring many dangers, but for now he wanted only to enjoy this night.

"Now I am," he said thickly, paying no heed to the wine sloshing upon him and the soft furs as he grabbed her and sat her astride him, Semirah squealing with delight. Taking both goblets, he slowly poured what wine remained down the front of her body. His desire flared like molten heat as the scarlet liquid slicked her small pert breasts, her belly, then caught and glistened in the lush sable pelt between her legs.

"Rurik Beast-Slayer, will you drink now?" she taunted, using the name he had earned during a hunt by saving the grand prince from a charging bear.

"Lie back, woman, and let me slake my thirst."

The wine was sweet upon his tongue as he first suckled at her breasts, Semirah's throaty moans fanning his lust like the hottest wind. Then pushing her down upon the furs, he cupped her taut bottom and lifted her to taste the intoxicating nectar he craved.

No one should trust the words of a girl or what a married woman says. Their hearts have been shaped on a turning wheel, and inconstancy dwells in their breasts.

Poetic Edda, Havamal
The Sayings of Odin, the High One

CHAPTER
1

May, A.D. 1024

Zora swept from her tent and brushed past the tall, pallid-faced chief eunuch, wrinkling her nose in distaste at his pungent scent of myrrh.

"But, Princess, will you not ride in the litter my mistress has sent for you?"

"I prefer to walk, Phineas." She drew her cloak tighter against the damp chill that hung like a mist in the air. "It's hard enough being confined upon a riverboat much of the day without having to be carried here and there once we make camp. I long for any chance to use my legs."

"You will surely soil your slippers and the hem of your gown, fair one," warned the eunuch, his voice effeminately high and nasal. He signaled for the four bearers supporting the drapery-shrouded litter to follow as he hastened to catch up with her. "It grows dark and the ground is muddy from recent rains . . . you could slip and fall, perhaps injure yourself. Certainly you would not wish that to happen only a fortnight from your wedding day."

"Since when have you or your mistress ever been concerned about my welfare?" Zora muttered, pretending not to hear him. And why the sudden invitation to join Hermione in her tent? Zora could count on one hand the number of times she and her half sister had exchanged words since they left Tmutorokan weeks ago, which was no different than the icy distance they had maintained in the *terem*, the women's quarters of their father Prince Mstislav's palace.

Skirting murky puddles and quagmires of mud, Zora proceeded undaunted through the torchlit maze of striped tents toward the largest one erected at the very heart of camp.

Her own tent was always pitched on the edge, another not so subtle jab on Hermione's part to ensure that Zora never forgot her place as a bastard daughter. But Zora didn't mind. She liked being apart from the hubbub created by countless slaves, eunuchs, and guards who made up the bulk of this ponderous caravan. The number of retainers required by two Rus princesses, several concubines, and the wives and children of Prince Mstislav's highest officials was astonishing.

Yet she did mind abandoning the deliciously fragrant supper of spit-roasted pheasant her cook had prepared for her. Zora's stomach was growling irritably.

She had been tempted to refuse the unexpected invitation, but why incite Hermione's anger? Soon they would be separated. In a little less than a week they would arrive at Chernigov, their father's new capital city, and within another week Zora would marry and become the mistress of her own household. No longer would she have to endure Hermione's imperious slights and petty jealousies, for they would rarely see each other except for court functions. That arrangement would suit Zora perfectly.

"Allow me to announce your arrival, beauteous one," Phineas insisted, overtaking her just as she reached the guarded entrance to Hermione's tent.

Noting his labored breathing and mud-splattered tunic,

Zora felt a small ripple of satisfaction. She had always disliked this eunuch's smooth and haughty ways, which so mirrored those of his mistress. It pleased her to have upset his composure, even a little.

"If you wish."

As the guards pulled aside the flaps, Zora followed Phineas through a small antechamber and then into the sumptuous interior, which was flooded with golden light from shining copper lanterns and wax candles as thick as a man's arm.

"My mistress, Princess Zora has come."

"Thank you, Phineas. You may leave us."

The eunuch bowed deeply and retired from the tent, leaving Zora standing alone just inside the entrance. Her gaze settled upon the lovely young woman ensconced upon a cushioned divan, dressed in amber silk, her smooth dark hair pulled back and coiled on either side of her head in the Byzantine fashion, the tight spirals interlaced with shimmering strands of pearls. Zora's own thick hair had never accepted such a style and she fingered a long, unruly strand as she waited.

"How gracious of you to accept my invitation, dear sister," said Hermione in a silky yet cordial tone. She gracefully waved a marble white hand at another divan placed opposite from her own. "Please. Come and sit."

Lifting her chin, Zora coolly approached. Her life would have been truly miserable at the hands of this intimidating half-Greek princess if their father had not accepted Zora into his family. Bastards without paternal acknowledgment counted for little in Rus. But Prince Mstislav's enduring favor and fatherly affection had given her courage, and instead of growing into womanhood cowed and meek, she carried herself with pride and met any insult with determined defiance.

"Have you eaten?" Hermione inquired as Zora took the seat offered to her.

"I have supper waiting for me at my tent," she replied,

giving her half sister a pointed hint that she did not intend to linger.

"Oh, but you must be hungry." Hermione clapped her hands before Zora could object, and a moment later female slaves appeared from a side entrance bearing trays laden with food and drink. "I haven't eaten either," she said as the ivory-inlaid table between them was quickly set with plates of chased silver, savory dishes were uncovered, and enameled goblets filled with vermilion wine. "Join me."

Annoyed by her sister's presumption, Zora reluctantly accepted a brimming goblet from a slave and watched as Hermione dipped her silver spoon into a steaming lamb stew laced with leeks and tiny onions. Stubbornly resisting her gnawing hunger, Zora took a healthy sip of wine to ease the hollow pangs in her stomach.

"Umm, it's wonderful." Hermione pushed the bowl of stew toward her. "You must try some."

"I'd rather wait, thank you," Zora said firmly, although her mouth watered at the wonderful aroma of fresh-baked honey and poppy seed bread. "Perhaps if you told me why you invited me here, I could return to my tent. It's been a long day and we have to rise early tomorrow."

Sighing resignedly, Hermione set down her spoon and regarded Zora with stunning cobalt-blue eyes, their only shared feature other than their like age of seventeen years.

"I suppose I'm to blame for your hostility toward me, my sister, but I hope that after tonight we'll begin to find more pleasure in each other's company. I invited you because I never congratulated you upon your betrothal to Lord Ivan. I would like to make amends for that oversight . . . and my callous mistreatment of you in the past, and present you with a gift."

Zora blinked, incredulous.

"I know this comes as a surprise, but I've been thinking that since you and I will be separated soon by your marriage, it doesn't seem right that we should part as enemies. We're starting new lives in Chernigov. Father wouldn't have sum-

moned us to his new court if he wasn't certain of his ability
to wrest the Rus throne from Grand Prince Yaroslav. So in
honor of Father's approaching victory, I think we should rec-
oncile our, shall we say, differences, and start afresh."

Thoroughly stunned, Zora stared at her half sister. Did
Hermione really believe that years of insults and unkind-
nesses could be so easily forgiven and forgotten? It had been
Hermione's bitter resentment that had first driven the ugly
wedge between them.

As the silence lengthened, Hermione arched a slim dark
brow. "Have you nothing to say? I hoped my words would
have pleased you."

"Pleased me?" Zora asked, finding her voice at last. "No,
I'm merely puzzled. You speak of reconciliation, yet my tent
remains on the outskirts of camp almost to the forest—"

"The slave manager's oversight, I can only suppose
through force of habit," Hermione broke in, dismissing the
comment with a wave of her hand. "But it won't happen
again, I promise you. Tomorrow night your tent will be
pitched next to mine." She lifted her goblet in salute. "I
drink to your coming marriage, my sister. Receiving news of
your betrothal to Lord Ivan must have brought you great joy.
He's handsome, wealthy, a landed boyar, and a member of
Father's senior *druzhina*. Fortune has indeed smiled upon
you."

Although highly skeptical of her half sister's sincerity,
Zora joined in the toast. She was content with Prince
Mstislav's choice for her husband.

True, she didn't love Ivan—and his arrogant, imperious
ways sometimes grated upon her—but she had agreed to the
match knowing it would please her father. She could do no
less for the honored place he had given her within his household, even though she was born out of Christian wedlock to
a Slavic concubine.

Yet it was strange that she would be the first to wed, Zora
thought, licking the tangy wine from her lips as she lowered
her goblet. Lady Canace, Hermione's Greek mother, would

never have allowed such a thing if she were still alive. After all, Hermione was older by a few months and a trueborn princess. Zora imagined that Prince Mstislav must have someone else in mind for his eldest daughter, most likely some foreign monarch's son who would befit her status.

"And now for my gift." Hermione's eyes were curiously alight as she again clapped her hands. Two slave women hastened to a great carved chest and while one held open the lid, the other withdrew a large oblong bundle wrapped in gray linen.

Despite herself, Zora felt excitement flare as the slave knelt before her and placed the heavy bundle in her lap. She glanced up at Hermione, whose smile seemed fixed upon her face.

"Open it, dear sister."

Taking a small knife from the table, Zora slit the twine binding the linen and hastily unwrapped her present. Her breath caught as a bolt of iridescent cream silk was revealed, the thin, tissuelike material striated with sparkling threads of gold.

"It—it's beautiful," she murmured, astonished that Hermione would give her anything, especially a gift so fine.

"For your wedding gown. Do you remember those Byzantine fabric merchants who visited our camp last week?"

Zora nodded. She draped a glittering length over her arm, the fabric feeling wonderfully cool against her skin.

"I bought the entire bolt for you. I knew the moment I saw it that the color would accent your tawny hair and golden skin to perfection."

For the first time since Hermione had said she wanted to make amends, Zora dared to believe that she might have meant it. She met her half sister's gaze, and although it felt strange to do so, she smiled at her, her gratitude heartfelt.

"Thank you, Hermione. I'll wear it proudly."

"I know you will." Hermione took a long sip of wine, then set her goblet upon the table. Delicately dipping her spoon into a silver bowl filled with glistening black salmon roe, she added, "The food grows cold. Dine with me."

"If you don't mind, I still wish to retire," Zora murmured, rewrapping the bolt of silk. Indeed, she did feel tired, her eyelids strangely heavy. "As you said, this has come as a great surprise. I need time to think—"

"I understand," Hermione interrupted, wiping her full, red mouth with an embroidered napkin. She rose with Zora, calling, "Phineas?"

The eunuch must have been waiting in the antechamber, for he appeared as if in an instant.

"Princess Zora would like to return to her tent. Will you escort her?"

"Of course, mistress, the litter is waiting outside."

"I'd rather walk." Zora wondered why her legs felt so sluggish as her taller half sister led Zora to the entrance. She hadn't drunk much wine, but her weariness seemed to have quickened its effect.

"Walking will not be possible, fair one," said Phineas. He cast a covert glance over her head at Hermione. "The rain has begun again."

"Yes, you wouldn't want that lovely silk to be ruined, Zora, and you do look exhausted. Please take my litter."

"Very well," she said, suddenly feeling disinclined to argue. Clasping her gift to her breasts, she turned to Hermione. "Good night . . . and thank you."

Hermione's tight smile did not reach her eyes. "Good night, dearest sister."

As Zora entered the antechamber, she stumbled, but Phineas caught her arm, preventing her fall.

"I don't know why I'm so tired," she said as he helped her into the litter that was drawn right up to the tent.

"The journey from Tmutorokan has been a long and taxing one, Princess," he said smoothly, closing the heavy curtains to leave her in darkness. "Do not trouble yourself. Rest."

Zora obliged him by sinking gratefully against the plush

cushions, but when the litter was hoisted into the air she was assailed by a wave of nauseating dizziness.

"Phineas?"

Her weak cry went unanswered. Outside she heard the bearers' sandals squelching in the mud and rain beating upon the litter's canvas roof, but not a sound from the chief eunuch.

Mother of Christ, what could be wrong with her? she wondered dazedly. Every pitch and sway of the litter heightened her sense of light-headedness. Her tongue felt thick and as dry as wool, and try as she might, she could barely open her eyes.

Overwhelmed by a terrible drowning sensation as her body sank deeper into the cushions, Zora could swear that they should have arrived at her tent by now, but the slaves kept on walking. Where were they taking her? Was it possible she had lost track of time and they had not yet reached the camp's outskirts?

Suddenly the litter pitched to one side as if a slave had tripped and lost his footing, then it felt like the world dropped from beneath her. The conveyance hit the ground with a jarring thud. Through the cold numbness enveloping her body she heard sounds of struggle—and muted screams?—then Phineas's ragged whisper.

"Grab her and be gone! And I warn you, tell your master Gleb not to forget his sworn agreement. This concubine's tongue is to be cut out, and she's not to be sold until you reach Constantinople! My mistress has paid much gold to ensure that her wishes are met. Tell Gleb if they are not, she will gladly spend a thousand times more to have him found and punished."

Zora moaned in horrified disbelief. She'd been caught in a treacherous web. She gasped as the curtains were torn aside and rough hands wrenched her from the litter. But it was so dark she could not see her assailants' faces. Nor could she move her limbs to escape them.

"No, please . . . my wedding gown," she whimpered almost incoherently, glimpsing the cream silk lying like a bright beacon upon the muddy ground.

In the next instant a dank, fetid cloth was stuffed in her mouth, and limp as a rag, she was flung over a broad shoulder, the wind knocked painfully from her lungs. She felt her captor running, his breathing hard and labored, and when he abruptly stopped, she heard as if from a great distance the rush of water and oars scraping. Then all consciousness receded and pitch-blackness engulfed her.

Hermione waited several hours—enjoying a leisurely bath and the ministrations of her slave women as they massaged her with fragrant oils and dressed her for bed—before she sent all of her attendants away and summoned a rain-soaked guard. Reclining comfortably upon a divan, she didn't deign to look at him, but toyed with a filigree gold and glass perfume bottle.

"Go to Phineas's tent and wake him. I wish to speak with him at once."

As she expected, the guard returned to inform her that Phineas had not yet been to his quarters.

"Then search the camp and find him!"

And, as she expected, a short while later a great hue and cry of alarm was raised, echoing throughout the camp. Within moments a grim chief of the guards came rushing into the tent. Feigning panic, Hermione rose to meet him.

"What has happened?" she demanded shrilly. "Why all the shouting?"

"Princess Zora has been abducted, my lady! We found the empty litter near her tent and Phineas lying senseless beside it. Three of the bearers were strangled, while the fourth hovers near death."

"No, this can't be true," Hermione objected with suitable disbelief while inwardly she fought the urge to laugh aloud in triumph. "It can't be! How could such a thing have happened? Where were the guards?"

"Those assigned to your sister's tent were murdered, their

throats cut. The rest in the camp heard and saw nothing. The rain was so heavy, dousing the torches, and with no moonlight—"

"Did Phineas say anything when you found him? Did he see his attackers? Holy Mother Mary, I sent him a good while ago to escort Zora back to her tent after she and I had finished our supper. I thought him long abed!"

"When we managed to rouse him, he said only that he and the bearers were almost to the entrance when he was suddenly struck from behind on the head. He remembers nothing more. As for the slave, we will have to wait until he regains his senses . . . if he does."

"Have Phineas brought to me." Wringing her hands, Hermione began to circle the divan in distraction. "My women will care for him here."

"Very well, my lady. I am ordering a search to begin at once for your sister—"

"No!" Hermione hysterically rounded upon him. "I forbid any guards to leave this camp!"

"But, my lady, Princess Zora's abductors already have a good lead upon us. If we don't set out soon—"

"I said no! We could be attacked again, and if your elite guards could not prevent this terrible event"—she glared at him accusingly—"what makes you think half their number will be enough to protect the camp? This could be some evil plot by Grand Prince Yaroslav . . . taking hostages to use against my father. Next, they might be planning to come after me!"

"Calm yourself, my lady. I will post a double ring of well-armed guards around your tent—"

"Yes, at once! But I still forbid any of your men to leave! You can blame the element of surprise for this unfortunate night's work, but you will have no excuse for my father if we suffer a second successful attack!"

His sweaty face paling, the chief of the guards reluctantly acquiesced. "As you wish, Princess Hermione, but at first light I insist upon sending out some of my men. Prince

Mstislav's wrath will be fierce if we do not search for your sister."

Sensing his stubborness and accepting begrudgingly the truth of his words, Hermione decided it was wise to humor him. At least no guards would be sent out until morning, long hours away.

"Very well, that much I will allow," she said shakily. "And though Chernigov is almost a week's journey away, we shall make all haste and alert my father. If your guards fail to rescue my poor sister, his men surely will." She bowed her head and covered her face with her hands as if about to weep. "Leave me."

But no one would find her, Hermione thought smugly, watching the man through laced fingers as he strode from the tent.

The slavers who had captured Zora were miles down the Desna River by now, and would travel all night to put distance between themselves and the camp. They had been paid well to do so. Their ships would be past Chernigov and on their way south to Kiev long before word of the abduction ever reached her father, no matter how swiftly the caravan traveled. And even if the chief of the guards insisted upon sending messengers ahead with the grim news, they would still be too late.

Alone again, Hermione poured herself some wine and raised the goblet in a silent toast to Phineas. Her loyal chief eunuch had done his job well. It had taken him weeks to find a slave merchant to suit their purpose, but two nights ago while visiting a trading town not far from camp, he had finally succeeded.

A wily old trader bound for Constantinople with over one hundred slaves had readily agreed to have his men abduct a woman described as a concubine fallen into disfavor with her master's wife. Apparently Prince Mstislav's invading forces had killed both of the merchant's sons, and he was only too eager to win his own brand of vengeance against the royal upstart from Tmutorokan. He believed he'd be depriving some arrogant boyar of his pampered whore. Gold grivna had changed hands and arrangements were made. All Hermione had to do was find some way to drug Zora, and that had been easy.

"Gullible little bitch," Hermione muttered, disgusted by the conciliatory role she had had to play. She took a draft of wine, but her throat was so tightened that she could barely swallow.

Poison would have proved simpler—and she would have resorted to it if the right slave merchant hadn't been found—but mute servitude suited a bastard daughter born of a common slave better than a quick death. A bastard who had usurped Prince Mstislav's affection and become the favored one, the much beloved golden child. A bastard betrothed to Ivan, the man Hermione secretly loved and hoped to marry. That final indignity had forced the plan she had long nurtured. Tonight, vengeance was hers at last . . .

Hermione's attention was drawn by a sudden commotion at the tent's entrance. She glanced up to find Phineas suspended limply between two burly guards, his soaked tunic muddy and torn, his shaved head lolling upon his chest. How convincingly he played his part!

"Bring him here," she ordered, gesturing to a divan that she quickly covered with a blanket. "Be careful, I tell you, or you'll only cause him more pain!" When Phineas was settled, a warm blanket thrown over him, she asked one of the men, "Has the bearer been taken to the healer's tent?"

"He is dead, my lady. A few moments ago."

Absorbing this news, Hermione dismissed the guards with a nod. She held her breath, waiting until they were gone, then she exhaled slowly, a smile curving her lips.

"We're alone, Phineas."

The eunuch's dark eyes opened, but he made no effort to rise. "I have pleased you, my mistress?"

"Infinitely, faithful one. You have secured my happiness. Lord Ivan's bride will not be a bastard, but a true Rus princess with the blood of Byzantine emperors in her veins."

Kneeling beside the divan, she lifted his head and brought her own goblet to his lips. As he drank thirstily, she asked, "Did you give Gleb's men my warning?"

Laying his head down, Phineas met her eyes. "Yes, mistress, but I have one fear. If Princess Zora tells them who she is before they can silence her tongue forever—"

"It will make no difference," Hermione assured him as she refilled the goblet. "You said this Gleb burns for vengeance for the death of his two sons. Whether his captive is princess or concubine, he will follow my bidding and sell her with pleasure in the slave markets of Constantinople."

"But if he becomes convinced of her royal parentage, he could find his revenge in giving her to Grand Prince Yaroslav."

"You also told me that Gleb was a shrewd man," Hermione reminded him. She had already considered this possibility and yet deemed her plan worth the risk. "To believe Zora was a princess, he would also know that he had not dealt with a rich, embittered wife as you described me to him, but someone vastly more powerful. I'm sure he would realize defiance of my orders would cost him his life." She rose to her feet. "Enough talk, Phineas. I will summon my women to care for you. Remember, you've been struck violently upon the head. Now close your eyes and rest."

Turning her back to him, Hermione went to the side entrance that led to her personal slaves' tent. After sending one of the guards standing sentry outside for her women, she deftly pulled a small enamel vial from the tight sleeve of her sleeping dress and poured a measure of fine white powder into her goblet. The poison dissolved quickly and she returned the vial to her sleeve.

"I imagine you've heard about the tragedy that has befallen my sister, and that Phineas was injured," she said quietly to the first slave who entered. "I put you in charge of his care." She handed the somber-faced woman the goblet. "See that he drinks this wine. It will calm him."

"Yes, mistress."

Glancing at the divan, Hermione felt a twinge of regret. Yet she couldn't allow Phineas to live. He knew too much, and it would seem suspicious that the four bearers had perished but not him, however convincing his charade. He would expire of a sudden seizure within the hour, a development easily blamed upon his injury.

"Is there anything you need, mistress?" inquired another slave woman who followed Hermione to her curtained sleeping area at the rear of the tent.

"No," she answered as the brocade draperies were drawn for her privacy. "Go and tend to Phineas with the others." Turning away, she smiled to herself. "Tell him I said to sleep well."

CHAPTER
2

Zora awoke to the sound of snoring. Her ears buzzed from the loud rumbling noise and her head pounded viciously. Dazed, she opened her eyes, her blurred vision gradually focusing upon a canvas wall only inches from her face.

She wondered who could be making such a racket. Her brain ached at the effort to think. Surely not one of her slave women, and if a guard was sleeping at his post outside her tent, she would have to report him for his laxness. Yet she wasn't inclined to leave her bed to discover the culprit. Besides her terrible headache, she felt dizzy, and it was comfortable lying here, the furs so soft beneath her—

"Furs?" she breathed, confused. Her bed had never been covered with animal skins, but a fine silken quilt. And she slept between linen sheets, not under a prickly wool blanket like the one pulled up to her shoulder.

Filled with sudden unease, Zora winced as she slowly raised herself on one elbow. Massaging an aching temple, she looked around the small, shadowy interior.

This wasn't her tent! The space was empty but for this low

pile of furs and some wooden barrels stacked against an opposite wall. A strange roughly dressed man slumped on a
bench near the entrance, his arms crossed and his chin resting on his chest. Another snore shattered the stillness and
she realized he was fast asleep, his mouth hanging open and
drool trickling from one slack corner.

Her confusion mounting, Zora thought to rise, but suddenly uproarious laughter sounded just outside the tent.
Gasping, she fell back upon the furs as if she had been struck
and rolled onto her side, squeezing her eyes shut. Her companion snorted awake, the bench creaking as he shifted his
stout bulk and rose.

"Damned Varangians," he grumbled, coming to stand
over her.

Zora fought the urge to stiffen as the man nudged her bottom with his toe. She heard him grunt and, to her disgust,
break wind as he scratched himself, then he turned abruptly
as the tent flaps were thrown aside.

"Still asleep?" The voice was gruff and gravelly, like that
of an older man.

"Aye, Gleb. Hasn't twitched a muscle. Whatever that eunuch used to drug her, he must have given her a double dose
to knock her out for this long."

So she had been drugged, Zora thought wildly, the dense
mist gradually clearing from her brain. But how? When? She
had gone to Hermione's tent, had drunk some wine . . . Oh,
God! Vague memories crowded in upon her and became
more vivid . . . her strange weariness, the litter crashing to
the ground, Phineas's whispered voice, brutal hands seizing
her—

"It's just as well. I've no time for her right now. This trading camp is swarming with eager buyers. Foreign merchants,
too. I want to make more sales before we set off again. The
journey downriver will be swifter with a few dozen less
slaves."

"But, Gleb, do you think we should risk another hour's
delay? We've already been here since midafternoon and it's

nearing sunset. Guards could have been sent out to look for the wench."

The older man gave a dry laugh. "For a concubine? I doubt it, but if they are, we've managed a good day's lead on any search party. Why do you think we kept our ships so hard to the river until we stopped here?"

She was no concubine! Zora screamed silently, her thoughts reeling. She forced herself to take steady breaths, knowing both men now stood over her.

"Pity she has to lose her tongue, a fine beauty like this," the younger one muttered. "As a mute, she won't fetch but half the price in Constantinople."

"To hell with your sentiments! The great Prince Mstislav's soldiers showed no mercy when wielding their knives, accursed butchers! They did the same thing to my sons before both were slain as supposed spies, hacking out their tongues, chopping off their fingers, noses, ears . . ." Falling silent for a moment, Gleb's roughened voice was bitter when he added, "That eunuch's mistress paid me well to carry out her orders, and I'll not invite her wrath. Call me when the girl wakes. I'd cut out her tongue now but she'd choke on her own blood."

Horrified, Zora feared her pounding heart would give her away. Holy Mother Mary, please tell her that this was a terrible dream!

Yet Phineas's urgently whispered words came back to her with bone-chilling clarity—*"Grab her and be gone!"* She knew the nightmare was real. Hermione had finally engineered the cruelest offense of all, staging a reconciliation while treachery seethed in her breast.

Zora banished her sister's hateful image from her mind as the two men, engrossed in a discussion, moved away from her toward the entrance. She half opened her eyes to take a peek at them.

The older one, Gleb, wore a purple silk caftan over his gaunt frame, a stark contrast to the stout guard's coarse woolen shirt and trousers. A close-cropped graying beard covered Gleb's jaw. He looked shrewd, his features angular and pinched, and she stifled her irrational impulse to jump up and tell him that she was no mere concubine but Prince Mstislav's daughter.

If this slaver's sons had been killed by her father's men, any such revelation would place her in greater danger. Who knew what Gleb would do to her then? Maybe kill her on the spot!

Zora shut her eyes as Gleb left the tent and his stocky subordinate retook his seat. It seemed her traitorous sister had chosen her abductors with care. Her only hope lay in escape.

Interminable moments passed while Zora lay upon the furs, her body tense beneath the blanket. She heard the bench creak each time her captor shifted his weight, but she didn't dare look at him, certain that he was watching her. She couldn't have been more astonished when a short while later, a loud, gargling snore burst from his throat. After a third such noise, she dared to raise her head. He was stretched out upon the bench, sleeping again!

Seizing her chance, Zora pushed back the blanket and rose shakily to her feet, fighting the lingering dizziness. For the first time she noticed that her silken clothes had been exchanged for a plain linen tunic and she was barefoot, her slippers gone. Why, those bastards must have seen her naked! And her a princess!

Refusing to dwell upon the indignity, Zora swallowed hard as she took a few cautious steps to test her wobbly legs. When she felt certain that she wouldn't collapse, she edged steathily across the tent, all the while keeping a cautious eye upon her prone captor.

She almost jumped through her skin when he snorted and smacked his lips, but he did not waken. Carefully she lifted the flap, peering outside, and was dismayed to see that the camp was abustle with activity, traders haggling everywhere over various goods while groups of silent slaves, mostly women, were being led here and there. She also heard muffled male laughter emanating from several tents and occasionally high-pitched squeals that were decidedly female.

But there was one clear advantage. Although the tent was pitched near some larger ones, it was also close to the trees. If she could reach the forest, she could hide near the river and wait for the caravan to pass. The merchant had said there was only a day's lead between any search party and the trading camp. But if she couldn't escape through the front entrance, fearing that she might be seen . . .

Zora's gaze fell upon the knife protruding from the man's leather belt. Dare she?

Another resounding snore startled her, spurring her into action. With shaking fingers, she crouched beside him and eased the weapon from its sheath, then moved quickly to the rear tent wall. Fortunately the razor-sharp blade slashed through the canvas as silently and smoothly as if the fabric were butter, and falling to her knees, she slipped through the narrow opening.

Her heart beating in her throat, Zora lifted her tunic above her knees and fled, looking neither to the left nor right but dashing straight for the tree line. She was nearly there when her left heel glanced off a jagged rock and, grimacing in pain, she had to hobble the rest of the way. She was almost crying with relief when she safely reached the dense woods. She leaned upon a trunk and paused for a brief instant to catch her breath and inspect her foot.

"By the blood of Odin, where are you flying to, my pretty bird?"

Gasping in fright, Zora glanced up to find a huge Varangian trader fastening his breeches as he stepped from behind a tree. Her heart sinking, she realized she had been so preoccupied with her injury that she hadn't noticed the man relieving himself against a gnarled trunk only a few feet away.

"Stay away from me!" she cried when he took a step toward her. Brandishing the knife she still held, she glanced beyond him to the darkening forest and freedom, then met his leering gaze. In the fading light filtering through the leaves, his eyes appeared a pale, chilling blue, and the deep scar bisecting his sparsely bearded cheek only heightened his air of menace. His hair was white-blond and coarse, and he was dressed in fur skins like a barbarian.

"Have you flown from your master's nest?" Ignoring her poised weapon, he advanced another step. His gaze roamed over her, lingering uncomfortably on the rapid rise and fall of her breasts. "I don't remember seeing you among the other women. If I had, I swear I would have sampled you first."

Craning her neck, Zora felt as if she faced a giant. She had seen these massive Norsemen before in Tmutorokan's marketplaces, and her father himself was a tall man, descended from fierce Swedish warriors who had settled in Rus two centuries ago. But now she was alone with the large Varangian, with only a knife to protect her.

"Stand back," she warned shakily. "I am Zora, princess of the Tmutorokan Rus and taken captive against my will—"

"And I'm the king of Denmark," he mocked her, drawing closer. "Sheathe your talons, pretty bird, and come back to the camp with Halfdan Snakeeye." His arm, strangely tattooed with serpents devouring each other, suddenly shot out as he lunged for her.

"No!" she screamed, swiping at him with the knife. As the blade sliced into his flesh, his harsh laughter filled the woods. He easily knocked the knife from her hand, and catching a fistful of tangled hair, he yanked her hard against his massive chest. Crying out from the stinging pain, Zora thought her scalp would be ripped from her skull.

"I said come to Halfdan. I want to find your master and strike a deal."

Zora fought him with all her strength as he lifted her in his arms, but he only laughed harder, enjoying her struggles. Nor did it seem to make any difference to him that blood trickled from his wound. When they stepped from the trees, a curious crowd began to gather and Halfdan smiled broadly, enjoying the attention.

"Look what I found while I was pissing in the woods! A golden bird, a daughter of Freyja, goddess of desire and beauty! From whose nest has she escaped? I wish to speak with that man!"

Zora twisted wildly in his grasp, but the giant's muscled arms were like bands of steel and thick as small tree trunks. Torn by cold fear and outrage, she demanded, "Let go of me, you vile, disgusting—" A beefy hand clapped over her mouth abruptly silenced her, and she was jerked even harder against his chest, pinned so tightly she couldn't move. Her stomach roiled from the Varangian's acrid stench of sweat and filth.

"Who owns this woman?" Halfdan bellowed, now almost to the center of camp.

"I do! Release her at once!" came an indignant reply. Gleb rushed forward with his stout guard. "She is not for sale!"

"Not for sale?" the Varangian trader echoed incredulously.

"I'm saving her for a better market . . . Constantinople," added Gleb, his gravelly voice raised in anger. He halted right in front of the Norseman, who loomed over him, then he shot a dark glance at his wide-eyed companion. "My man here was watching her, but she managed to escape. Release her, I tell you—"

"My silver grivna are as good as any Greek's!" With one swift movement Halfdan yanked a gleaming broadaxe from his belt and lifted Gleb's pointed chin with the well-honed blade. "Will you stop me from sampling her now, little man? Maybe she will displease me and then you can have her back! If not, I will buy her. Those are the rules of the trade!"

Answered by stunned silence, Halfdan snorted in triumph and shoved the ashen-faced Gleb aside, then strode to a nearby tent. As he stormed inside the stuffy lamplit interior, Zora was assailed at once by the overpowering smell of sex, cloying and primal. She gaped in horror at the sight before her.

Everywhere she looked naked slave women were being

bedded by potential buyers, upon the floor, on crude benches, against the tent walls, a wild, sweaty tangle of rutting bodies. But she heard no cries of protest, some women laughing throatily, some moaning in pleasure, others mutely bearing what must be a slave's lot . . . dear God, and this barbarian thought she was a slave!

Suddenly realizing the Varangian's lustful intentions, Zora sank her teeth into his callused palm and his hand fell from her mouth. "No! You can't do this!" she shouted hoarsely, her throat constricted with fear.

"Silence, woman!" Halfdan threw her down upon the nearest vacant bench and held her there, despite her wild flailing, with one massive hand pressed between her breasts. Wrenching at his breeches, he released his huge, swollen member and Zora froze, her eyes widening in terrified disbelief. "Frey the Fruitful has blessed me well with the means to please you," he said, coarsely fondling himself. "Now spread your plumage and enjoy the god's bounty." With a harsh laugh, he ripped her tunic from collar to hem, exposing her trembling body to his gaze.

"Stop . . . no, oh, no!" Zora cried as he straddled the bench and lowered his bulk down upon her. In wild desperation she brought her knee up sharply, catching him in the groin. As the Varangian doubled over, sucking in his breath and cursing, she wrenched herself from beneath him and fell hard to the dirt floor. An instant later she was scrambling on hands and knees toward the entrance. As she clambered to her feet and dashed outside, Halfdan's bellows of rage resounded from the tent.

"Help me!" she screamed, seized by hysteria. She took refuge behind several traders only to have them dart away in fear as the Norseman burst through the tent flaps, brandishing his broadaxe. Spying Gleb, she ran to him but he, too, backed away, the sight of three hundred pounds of enraged Varangian stifling any protest he might have offered.

Clutching her torn tunic against her body, Zora spun in terror. Halfdan looked like a vengeful behemoth as he slowed his mad dash to a relentless stalking, his pale eyes gleaming almost silver in the torchlight illuminating the camp.

"You cannot escape me, pretty bird. I will have you . . . here, now, in the dirt in front of everyone. And when I make you scream with pleasure, you will wish you had surrendered sooner to Halfdan Snakeeye."

"Mother of Christ, protect me!" she begged in a daze, shock enveloping her like cold, creeping fingers. Stumbling backward, she turned and fled toward another tent, her eyes nearly blinded by tears. She didn't see the tall, broadshouldered man stepping outside until it was too late and she ran headlong into him, jolting the breath from her body. She would have fallen if he hadn't caught her, his grip strong and sure.

"Help me! Please help me!" she pleaded almost incoherently, swiping her hair from her eyes. "A reward . . . I promise you a reward! You must help . . ." Her entreaty died in her throat as she stared up into the bearded face of another Varangian trader, a gaze of intense blue meeting hers. "Oh, God . . . no!"

Pushing away from him in horror, she staggered back the other way, everything around her becoming a swirling blur. As Halfdan bore down upon her, his triumphant laughter ringing in her ears, she heard her own voice as if from inside a deep well, crying, "You can't do this to me! I am—"

"Silence, bitch!" Halfdan's sudden openhanded blow to her cheek sent her reeling into a pile of stacked goods, jagged flashes of light bursting before her eyes. Without a whimper, she crumpled amid overturned casks and crates, escaping into sweet blackness.

CHAPTER
3

"So what will it be, man? Do you want the wench or not? I've two other traders waiting to try her if you're not in the mind to buy."

Rurik did not waste a glance upon the fat Bulgarian merchant or the nude slave being thrust toward him, a voluptuous, almond-eyed beauty who had eagerly opened her legs for his pleasure moments before the commotion that had drawn him outside the tent. His gaze was riveted upon the young woman lying on the ground like a limp cloth doll only twenty feet away, and the Varangian trader who stood above her.

"Didn't you hear me, friend? Time is money and you're wasting mine. Now what's your answer?"

Again ignoring the merchant, Rurik tensed as the huge Norseman bent down and grabbed one of the woman's delicate ankles, clearly intent upon dragging his quarry from the debris scattered around her.

He had witnessed many abuses at trading camps, but never anything that had so turned his stomach as seeing that fur-clad oaf striking down a woman who appeared almost a child to his massive bulk. A woman with the most incredible blue-green eyes Rurik had ever seen, and a face and form rivaling Freyja herself. A woman who had begged for his help, mumbling frantically of a reward, only to recoil from him in terror. A woman whose refined accent marked her as no common, illiterate slave. Yet he knew the wisest thing for his guise and secretive mission was not to become involved, however strong the temptation, and by Odin, he already had enough women at home.

"Well?"

Rurik turned at the insistent tug on his arm and fixed a dark glare upon the presumptuous merchant. The man withdrew his pudgy hand as if stung and stepped backward in surprise, his eyes round with fear.

"You risk much to impose yourself so upon a stranger," Rurik said in a low warning. "Take your slave and be gone."

"V-very well." The affronted merchant grabbed his crestfallen chattel's forearm and pushed her back into the tent. "Just the same, you're passing up quite a bargain," he added as the flap fell behind them.

A female slave was the last thing he needed on this journey, Rurik told himself again, watching grimly as the Varangian dragged the fine-boned woman back to the center of camp, her torn tunic trailing behind her and her exquisite body bared to the gathered crowd's gaze.

He and his three men had stopped to trade furs for supplies for their trip downriver to Chernigov, nothing more. Sampling slave women was part of their ruse as merchants, a pleasurable one to be sure, but indulged in only to satisfy lust, not with any intention to buy. So there was no logical purpose in challenging the Varangian for his golden-limbed captive.

"Rouse yourself, woman! Feigning a swoon won't save you!"

Rurik felt disgust tighten his throat as the Norseman

roughly shook the young woman's prone body. The dullard hadn't even noticed that his vicious blow had rendered her senseless.

When he received no response, the trader spread her legs wide with his foot and went down on his knees between them, dropping his broadaxe near her head. He stroked her upturned breasts with huge, thick-fingered hands, then, grinning, cupped the golden mound at the apex of her thighs and squeezed.

"I said I'd take you in the dirt, pretty bird, and I meant it. When you feel Halfdan's Frey-wand deep inside you, you'll wake soon enough and cry out for more."

"By Thor's hammer, enough! What kind of dog are you to rut on the ground with a woman who lies as if dead?"

All eyes turned to Rurik in astonishment. A charged hush filled the air. The Varangian trader did not rise, but his grin tightened perceptibly as he appraised Rurik.

"You addressed me, stranger?"

Rurik nodded, his hand moving to the bright silver hilt of his sword. Although acting upon impulse was foreign to him, he felt strangely glad.

"Get up. You heard the wench before you struck her down. She doesn't want your attentions."

"This slave's wishes are none of my concern, nor are they yours, if you value your neck—"

"But they are mine!" A well-dressed Slav merchant pushed his way to the front of the silent onlookers, though he and the stout fellow who stood at his elbow remained a good distance from the kneeling Varangian. "That woman belongs to me and she is not for sale until we reach the markets of Constantinople." He eyed Rurik shrewdly, then his gaze shifted back to Halfdan. "I offer ten gold grivna . . . no, twenty, to any man who will wrest her from this barbarian, Halfdan Snakeeye. He refuses to release her to me of his free will."

As the Varangian trader cursed and rose to his feet, speculative conversation surged among the crowd but no other man stepped forward. Surprised that a merchant would pay gold for a slave's behalf, even one as fine as this lithe, tawny-haired beauty, Rurik's curiosity flared hotter. The man would hardly recoup such a sum once they reached Byzantium's capital; the most sought-after slaves sold for much less, and usually in silver. This one woman was obviously valuable to him. Strange.

"My lord Rurik, surely you do not plan to fight this trader!" whispered the urgent voice of one of his men.

Leif Einarson's ruddy face was flushed an even brighter shade of red, his light blue eyes wary. "The woman is beautiful but just look at her captor, my lord! Almost a head taller even than you and as big as an ox, no doubt with the strength to match."

"The wits of an ox as well, Leif. The man is ruled by lust instead of brains."

"True, but big, dumb, and well armed could prove a dangerous combination, and we have much at stake—"

"Is it two of you who conspire against me now?" Halfdan blustered. He swung his broadaxe menacingly in front of him. "Come on, you dung-sniffers, and let's have done with it. When I've cut out your beating hearts"—he glanced fiercely at Gleb—"next there'll be a merchant's blood staining my blade."

"Go back to the ship, Leif." Rurik's voice was grim as he kept his gaze trained on the Varangian. "If I don't return shortly, you, Arne, and Kjell sail without me."

No protest came. Rurik hadn't expected one, for as their sworn lord, the right of command belonged to him. Yet he could sense that the seasoned warrior wished to remain by his side, ready to fight to the death for him if necessary.

"As you say, my lord." Scowling at the huge trader, Leif stalked away.

"I accept your offer of twenty grivna," Rurik announced, noticing the merchant's look of relief. His instincts told him that the man had something more important at stake than simply regaining possession of a female slave, and he in-

tended to find out what it was, if Odin the all-powerful
deemed him the victor. Let the wily slaver think Rurik was
fighting for gold. In truth, he wanted to know more about the
woman, yet that was impossible until this belligerent Varangian was brought down.

"So your copper-haired friend is afraid to fight Halfdan,"
the Norseman jeered, his extreme height enabling him to see
above the crowd. "Look how he hastens toward the river
with his tail dragging between his legs."

"Hardly afraid." Rurik stepped forward as he pulled his
sword from the leather scabbard hanging from his belt. His
lips curved into a taunting smile. "Why use two men where
only one is required?"

His insult was met with a violent oath from his opponent,
who suddenly rushed at him, moving amazingly swift for
one so large. Halfdan wielded his heavy, long-handled
broadaxe with both hands. Possessing no defensive shield,
Rurik barely had time to raise his sword before Halfdan's
flaring blade, a full twelve inches across, came crashing
down toward his chest.

Steel sang out against steel, Rurik's sword deflecting the
death blow as he dodged to the left and whirled, aiming a
low, swinging stroke at the Varangian's legs in hopes of sev-
ering a limb. But Halfdan must have anticipated the tactic
for he leapt aside, the tapered end of Rurik's blade barely
scraping his knee.

As they circled each other, the clamoring crowd began to
press closer, sputtering torches held high to illuminate the
deadly contest. Fearing that the woman might be trampled,
Rurik shot a glance in her direction to see that the merchant
and his stocky companion were dragging her from harm's
way. Halfdan must have noticed, too, for he shouted, "You
cannot hide her from me, you stinking Slav! The moment I
find her will bring your death!"

Rurik took advantage of the Varangian trader's fleeting
inattention. With a bloodcurdling cry, he grasped his sword
with both hands and swung the gleaming blade in a heavy

blow across his opponent's stomach. To his surprise, a loud thwack met his assault and not the sensation of polished steel slicing into flesh. Cursing, Rurik leapt backward just in time to elude a retaliatory strike, now aware that the Norseman wore a padded jerkin beneath his fur clothing.

"Reindeer hide and bone plaques," Halfdan rasped through clenched teeth, the ferocity of Rurik's blow nevertheless having doubled him over. "As good as any rich man's mail-coat." Glaring at Rurik, he drew himself to his full height. "It appears you and I are well matched, stranger. I would swear a hardened warrior hides beneath that merchant's garb. Pity you are soon to be a corpse."

The Varangian had hit perilously close to the mark, but Rurik had no time for concern over possible spies in the crowd. Halfdan charged at him, roaring in rage and swinging his broadaxe.

Ducking a blow aimed at his head that could have split his skull like an eggshell, Rurik twisted to get clear, but the Varangian's raised knee caught him under the chin. Smashed backward, his sword knocked from his hand, Ruril sprawled in the dirt, stunned. In the next instant Halfdan landed on top of him and pinned him, his broadaxe hovering directly over Rurik's heart.

"Pray to Christ or Odin, stranger, but pray quickly for now you die—"

The Varangian's words were cut off by the zinging flash of a sword, his blond head severed from his body and sent flying into the crowd. As warm blood rained down upon Rurik, the broadaxe falling harmlessly from a lifeless hand to the ground, Halfdan's twitching body was kicked unceremoniously to one side and Rurik hauled to his feet. Still slightly dazed, he stared into Arne Flat-Nose's grinning face. Rurik was never more glad in his life to see the grizzled bear of a warrior.

"Must I forever rescue you from scraps, my lord? It's a good thing your father granted me the right to disobey your orders if necessary, and aye, this occasion was surely one of them."

"*Forever* rescuing me?" Rurik wiped the blood and sweat from his face with his sleeve. "A fine exaggeration. In all the years I've known you, Arne, I could count on two fingers—"

"Three now, my lord, and well timed, wouldn't you say?"

At the glint of seriousness in Arne's eyes, Rurik could only nod, all semblance of joking put aside.

"You have my thanks, friend."

"That is all well and good"—Arne glanced pointedly at the curious onlookers and lowered his voice—"but the best thanks would be to walk with me to our boat and forsake any idea of rescuing some slave wench in distress. I'd say we've drawn more than ample attention to ourselves for one day. It's time we sailed."

"Not yet." Rurik's senses were now back in sharp focus. Ignoring Arne's look of disapproval, he picked up his sword and then scanned the surrounding faces for the Slav merchant, but the man had vanished. The cunning bastard! Doubtless he had no intention to pay the sum promised, not that Rurik cared for the gold. The merchant had probably used the fight as a screen to spirit away the woman.

"Where are you going?" Arne called out as Rurik stepped over the headless corpse and strode through the gradually thinning crowd, traders and buyers alike returning to their business now that the bloody spectacle was finished.

Rurik didn't answer, his gaze sweeping from one end of the camp to the other. No sign of the merchant or the woman. He was about to begin a search of every tent when he spied a flash of purple silk near the well-lighted docks, and he began to run. Arne huffed not far behind him, grumbling loudly about the witchery of women.

"Hold!" Rurik shouted, not surprised to see the merchant and his burly companion, the woman slung over his shoulder, increase their pace as they headed toward a large river ship that was already loaded with slaves and other retainers. "Hold, I tell you!" When Rurik was almost upon them, the merchant turned back and hastened to meet him while the other man hurried on with his precious load.

"Ah, forgive me, good sir . . . how forgetful of me! Your gold is right here." Smiling tightly, the merchant held out a small leather pouch. "Count it if you must, it's all there. Twenty grivna, the least I could pay for such skill and bravery, such honor—"

"I don't want your gold." Rurik's gaze burned into the man's eyes. "Tell your fat companion to bring the woman here, now, or I will not hesitate to slit your treacherous throat."

"Treachery! What treachery—"

Rurik grabbed the older man and spun him so that he faced the river, his sword resting ominously against the merchant's scrawny neck. "Tell him!"

"As you wish, as you wish! Urho! Bring the slave to me at once!"

"Now talk and quickly, but keep your voice low," Rurik commanded, aware that they were eliciting much observation from curious passersby. "Where did you get that woman?"

"Her parents sold her to me . . . they were poor, needed the silver—"

"You lie! Before that Varangian trader struck her down, she promised me a reward if I helped her. No peasant's daughter would swear such a thing, and no peasant wench would speak with such refinement. Where did you find her?"

"Please, I cannot say or my life may be forfeit!"

"Speak or your life *is* forfeit." Rurik turned his weapon so that the razor-sharp blade rested upon the man's bobbing Adam's apple.

"Very well, I will tell you! Stay your sword! My men abducted her from a wealthy river caravan a day's eastward journey from this camp."

"A caravan?"

"Traveling from Tmutorokan to Chernigov."

Rurik tensed, his instincts alert. Such a caravan might be somehow connected with Prince Mstislav . . .

"How could your men have gotten so close without an alarm being raised?" he demanded. "Surely there were guards—"

"Yes, but what few we found near the girl's tent were slain. It couldn't have gone more smoothly. Everything was arranged in advance."

"By whom?"

"The eunuch of the woman who wished to rid herself of her husband's favorite concubine. The half man paid me much gold to see that the girl's tongue be cut out and she be sold in Constantinople. He said that if his mistress's orders were not followed, she would not rest until I was found and punished."

So the wench was a concubine. Rurik watched as the man called Urho drew near with the limp woman. She was wrapped in a dark cloak with only her head visible, her long sandy-colored hair, more blond than brown, tumbling down Urho's back. Rurik found himself wondering what it might feel like to touch that golden tousled mass, to bury his fingers in it . . .

Rurik snorted. From his own reaction, he was not surprised that she was a favored one.

Her status would explain her graceful speech. She must have been granted an education with the finest tutors by her wealthy master—whom Rurik suspected was a member of Mstislav's senior *druzhina* to afford such a luxury—no doubt fueling the jealousy that had brought her to this trading camp. The woman who had sold her into slavery must have hated her, which meant her master must love her. The hapless wench had promised him a reward, hadn't she? She probably knew that her master would pay well to get her back.

"How much were you paid?" Rurik asked, again pressing his sword against the merchant's stubbled throat. "It must have been a great sum for you to put your own life in jeopardy."

"Two hundred gold grivna."

"A woman's cunning knows no bounds," Rurik muttered, disgusted. This concubine's nemesis obviously wanted her to suffer, otherwise she would have had her killed. To cut out her tongue and sell her to some foreign buyer? He wondered what the witch would think when her beautiful rival turned up once more upon her doorstep, but with a tale of treachery to condemn her before her husband . . . for Rurik had a bold plan formulating in his mind.

"Arne, go to the ship and bring me the money chest," he called to his friend who was standing close by, sword drawn.

The warrior's bushy black brows knit together. "My lord?"

"Just do as I say."

Shaking his shaggy head, Arne sheathed his sword and lumbered away, grumbling to himself.

"If you're thinking to offer me money for the wench, I will not take it," said the merchant stubbornly. "She is not for sale."

"You took a rich woman's gold readily enough—"

"Why not enrich my purse and steal away some boyar's whore?" The man spoke vehemently, oblivious to the cold metal pressed against his flesh. "I'm no warrior. What better revenge could I seek against the scourge that has come upon our land? Those bloodthirsty hordes from Tmutorokan! I lost two sons to that usurper Mstislav's men!"

Rurik turned the merchant so abruptly to face him that the older man almost lost his footing. "Is this true?"

Fear shone from the merchant's eyes, but his expression remained hard. "I have said too much already. For all that I know, you could be one of them."

"I am not," Rurik replied, his voice almost a whisper. "But I can tell you no more. Now answer me."

The merchant studied Rurik's face for a long moment, then his bony shoulders seemed to drop. "I would not have sold my soul for coin. My sons' faces haunt me in my dreams, their voices beg me for justice. If you take this woman from me, I will have lost everything, my vengeance and, one day I fear, my life."

Rurik could see that the older man spoke the truth, and he chose his next words with care.

"Would you sell me the wench if I told you a greater vengeance could be yours? A battle will soon be fought, and your slave may be the bribe I need to sway the outcome to our favor. I can tell you little else, except that you and your remaining family would be safe in Novgorod, should you choose to seek refuge there. This I promise."

Rurik glanced toward the docks, and spying Arne returning with the chest, he turned his gaze back to the silent merchant.

"My man comes with the money. I offer you two hundred gold grivna to match the payment already made to you, good for evil. All I ask is that you do not make me wrest the woman from you by force."

"Keep your gold," the merchant said quietly, his shrewd eyes fixed upon Rurik's face. "But when I return from selling my slaves in Constantinople, I will hold you to your promise. All I ask is that you tell the girl when she wakes that you had to kill me to win her. Perhaps that will be enough to throw that rich she-hound from my scent . . . if it is in your mind to send this concubine back to whence she came."

"Done."

As they grasped each other's wrists in agreement, the merchant asked, "Do you have a name, stranger? I must know where to seek you in Novgorod."

"None that I can give you now, nor is it safe for me to know yours." Rurik unfastened his cloak-pin, a broad silver ring engraved with a snarling beast, from the right shoulder of his bloodstained cloak. "When you arrive in the city, go to the *kreml* and speak to the master of the guard. Tell him you wish to return this brooch to its rightful owner. It will be enough."

The merchant took the brooch, then motioned for Urho to hand his limp bundle to Rurik. "The woman is yours. You are welcome to her. In truth, she has caused me nothing but trouble."

As Rurik sheathed his sword and took the woman in his arms, the lush feel of her body aroused in him an overwhelming sense of possession, but he quickly stifled his reaction. This beauty belonged to another man, an enemy. He intended to make her a pawn: a fact he would do well to remember.

"Be warned, stranger," the merchant added, his gravelly voice low. "Guards may be looking for the wench, though the caravan is yet a day's journey from here. You would be wise to travel swiftly and keep to the west."

Rurik gave a short nod, noting the miniature cross dangling from the older man's neck. "May Christ keep you on your journey to Constantinople."

"And you."

"I take it, then, that the money is no longer required," Arne said dryly behind them.

Rurik turned around as the merchant hurried away. "No, my friend, it is not."

Sighing resignedly, the warrior hoised the heavy chest upon his shoulder and fell into step with Rurik as they strode alongside the busy docks to their ship.

"Ah, well, you already have six concubines at home. What hurt will one more do? There are seven nights in a week. If you could survive the tantrums when you brought back that Khazarian she-cat, I imagine you'll weather the uproar this golden-haired temptress will surely cause." He laughed heartily. "Your good looks are your curse, Lord Rurik. If you were ugly and squat, or flat-nosed like me, your women would not mind so much that you had found another to warm your bed!"

"I'm not keeping this wench for myself, Arne."

The warrior glanced at him in astonishment. "No?"

Shaking his head, Rurik felt keen regret.

"Come," he said, shrugging off the strange feeling. "We will talk once we set sail. Kjell and Leif must also know my plans."

CHAPTER 4

"So you think whoever owns this wench might be willing to part with military information for her return?" Leif asked, his hand firmly on the helm as he kept the thirty-foot river-boat straight upon its course.

"There's a good chance of it." Rurik's gaze shifted from the red-bearded Leif to Arne and then to the youngest warrior, Kjell Thordarson. Each face, illuminated in the pale light of the waning moon, was somber yet thoughtful, each man weighing for himself the decision Rurik had already made. "Once she wakens, we'll find out the name of her master, then when we reach Chernigov, we'll send a message to the man with our demands. Either he gives us what we want, or his favorite concubine will disappear forever."

"You don't mean to kill her!" came Kjell's incredulous response. "I've never seen a prettier—"

"Are you going daft, man?" Arne interjected, exasperated. "We're not blasted murderers!" Softening his tone, he leaned over and elbowed the nineteen-year-old Varangian sharply in the ribs. "I'm sure Lord Rurik will find some use for the wench if Mstislav's man doesn't want her, never you fear."

Rurik made no comment, thinking as his gaze strayed again to the makeshift tent they had erected near the mast that he would decide that issue later. For now, he waited to see that first movement, or hear that first moan, some sign that the woman was regaining her senses.

Other than some purplish bruises on her body, the worst on her left cheek, she seemed whole. He had felt no broken bones. Yet an hour into their journey her eyes still remained closed, her breathing slow as if she was locked in deep slumber. Even when he had discarded the cloak in which she had been wrapped and then exchanged her torn tunic for one of his own, the garment engulfing her slender body, she had not stirred . . . although he could not say as much for himself.

He had seen perfection in women before, but never a form that seemed to tempt his very soul: honeyed limbs of delicate yet shapely porportion, a trim waist so narrow and hips so beautifully curved that he ached to caress them, a taut abdomen with the gentlest rounding, and ripe, upturned breasts he defied the gods to describe. The swiftness of his arousal had stunned him, its near painful intensity disgusting him. Was he no better than that swine Halfdan Snakeeye to lust after an unconscious woman?

Covering her with a blanket, he had quickly left the tent, but his lingering erection had been a powerful reminder that few had so fired his blood. Thank Odin the work of setting sail had finally fixed his mind on other matters.

"I've a demand to add to that message," said Leif, drawing Rurik's attention back to his men. "Now that we know the Severians have been swayed by Prince Mstislav's promises of sharing the spoils of victory, we should ask this boyar how many other Slavic tribes have sworn their allegiance to the usurper."

"None, I hope. Mstislav's armed strength is mighty enough with the Khazar and Kosogian warriors he brought with him from Tmutorokan. The bastard must be gloating to have wooed those Slavs to his banner." After a moment's grim silence, Rurik nodded at Leif. "Your demand is a good one, especially since we cannot traverse the entire southern realm and spy upon each tribe. Not if we're to be back in Novgorod by June, three weeks hence."

As Arne leaned forward and rested his thick forearms on his legs, the narrow rowing bench squeaked beneath his weight.

"Mstislav's battle plans might be in our grasp now as well, my lord!" he said, his voice tinged with excitement. "That would be a fine coup for Grand Prince Yaroslav, and all because some jealous she-bitch hated the sight of her husband's concubine."

"My lord, look to the prow!" Leif cried suddenly. "The wench has climbed onto the railing!"

"What . . . ?"

Rurik was on his feet in an instant. The damned wench must have evaded them by crawling under the back of the tent. He raced to the front of the boat, but he had barely ducked beneath the sail when he heard a loud splash near the starboard side. Throwing off his fur mantle, he shouted, "Bring the boat hard about!" then he vaulted over the railing, the frigid ink-black water of the Desna River closing over his head.

He gasped as he resurfaced, the water's chill so intense it had sapped the breath from his lungs. He looked around him, but he did not immediately spy the woman. Thor help him, if she had gone under he would never find her, not with these demon currents!

Clenching his teeth against the cold, Rurik swam with long, powerful strokes into the boat's wake, his gaze cutting to the right and left. Only then did he see two slim arms flailing wildly some twenty feet away, and he swam as he never had before in his twenty-eight years.

It was not fast enough. When he drew within four strokes of catching her, she went under, her hands eerily clawlike as she disappeared beneath the waves.

"No, damn you . . . you will not have her!" Rurik shouted, spitting water as he cursed the evil river spirits who were dragging her down to her death.

Sucking in a great breath, he dived, his lungs aching as he descended into the midnight depths and groped for an arm, a leg . . . anything. His chest was ready to explode when he suddenly felt something curl around his hand. He clutched at it, realizing he had caught her by the hair.

Rurik yanked the woman up until he held her beneath the arms, then he kicked furiously to the surface, his chest on fire as they burst above the waves. Dragging in huge lungfuls of air, he could not remember a time when it had smelled or tasted so sweet.

"Leif! Arne! Over here!" he shouted hoarsely. Relief flooded him as the woman suddenly coughed and sputtered in his arms, her ragged gasps for breath assuring him that she was alive. Though she clung to him limply, she began to kick her legs. He was astounded that she still had the strength to swim.

"Let me go . . . must escape!" she gasped, trying weakly to push away from him. "Halfdan . . . must escape . . ."

Rurik had no time to reply for the boat was coming alongside them, the woman soon hauled aboard, followed by himself. As Arne released him, he leaned heavily against the railing, fighting to catch his breath.

"By the gods, Lord Rurik, you've turned my beard a lighter shade of gray twice this day! When I saw you dive for the wench—"

"Surely you didn't think you'd seen the last of me." Rurik wiped the moisture from his eyes and gave Arne a wry half smile. "You were the one who taught me to swim, remember?"

"Aye, thank Odin, like a dolphin." The burly warrior jerked his head toward Kjell, who stood in a widening puddle of water, the dripping, exhausted woman in his arms. "Mayhap we should tie the wench to the mast for the rest of the journey, what do you think? She's proving as much trouble as she's worth."

"I'll take her," was Rurik's only reply, sobering as Kjell brought the woman to him. By the light of an oil lamp set upon a nearby rowing bench, he noted with concern that her face was ashen, her teeth chattering, her lips and closed eyelids tinged with blue. If she wasn't warmed and soon, they still might lose her . . . and their best chance to gain some information.

"Set her down, but hold her so she doesn't fall," Rurik ordered. Without ceremony he drew the sodden tunic over her head and threw it on the deck. Ignoring his men's sidelong glances, he lifted her into his arms, grabbed the lamp, and strode with his nude charge to the tent, ducking inside.

"No . . . Halfdan," came a small whimper, the woman burying her face against Rurik's chest as he placed the lamp near the tent's back wall. "Must get away . . . please—"

"Halfdan is dead." Rurik hoped the finality in his tone would reassure her. "He cannot hurt you anymore."

Kneeling, he laid her upon the fur pallet, attempting to ignore her nakedness—impossible task! Hastily he brought the blanket up to her chin. To his surprise, she was looking at him, her eyes the most stunning shade of blue in a face hauntingly pale and marred only by the ugly bruise on her cheek.

"Dead?"

He nodded. She looked so vulerable, the quality in her voice almost childlike, arousing in him a powerful surge of protectiveness. Or perhaps it was simply his own exhaustion. He sat back upon his haunches, determined to get some answers now that she had finally regained her senses.

"The Slav merchant was also killed. You no longer have anything to fear from them."

Rurik was greeted with a blank stare, then a soft query, "Merchant?"

"The one who stole you from your master's caravan."

This time he was answered with silence, and she seemed

confused. Wondering if Halfdan's blow or her ensuing fall might have done more damage than he had thought, Rurik tried another, more direct tact. "Tell me your name, little one."

Oddly, she opened her mouth as if to say something, then her brow creased in consternation.

"Your name," he tried again. "Think hard."

An interminable moment later, she murmured almost to herself, "I . . . I don't know."

"Damn that swine!" Rurik cursed under his breath, wishing it had been his sword that had ended Halfdan's miserable life. The terrible shock must have robbed her memory. Only the image of the Varangian's brutality remained.

"Surely you remember your master," Rurik pressed. "He's one of Prince Mstislav's boyars, isn't he? A member of his senior *druzhina*? You were on your way to Chernigov to meet him when you were abducted."

"Master? I don't know . . ." Suddenly she grimaced. "My head . . . it hurts so."

"Easy, wench, easy," Rurik said soothingly. It was clear he would discover no information tonight. Perhaps she would remember more tomorrow after a comfortable sleep, at the very least recall her name and that of her master by the time they reached Chernigov, three days hard journey from here.

If that failed . . . the thought of taking her home to Novgorod was enticing. Yet he hoped, for the sake of his liege lord and the critical battle to come, that she did remember who she was. There was too much at stake for him to indulge his own selfish desires. She was only a woman, after all, and the world was full of those who could please him.

Rurik ran his palm across her forehead, marveling despite his resolve at the smoothness of her skin. He was pleased to see that some color had returned to her cheeks, and her shivering had ceased. "Sleep now," he bade her as he tucked the blanket once more beneath her chin.

"Yes . . . sleep," she said drowsily, closing her eyes.

"You are safe here. No one will harm you."

"Safe," came her reply, a whispered echo, then suddenly her eyes flew open and she clutched at Rurik's hand. Her gaze was wide and fearful. "You will not leave me?"

"No, little one. I will not leave you."

But he did exit the tent a short while later when he knew from her steady breathing that she was fast asleep and probably would not wake again until the morning. In the night air, his tunic felt cold and clammy, the fabric clinging to his body. Moments before he had barely noticed his sodden state.

Staring at the woman's face—the soft curve of her cheek, thick, sooty lashes so long it was easy to imagine them playing like the finest silk against his skin, graceful gull-winged brows, a patrician nose saucily tipped at the end, and rosy lips so lush and full he longed to press his own against them and tease them open with his tongue—was enough to make him wish she were nothing but a common slave possessing no ties that bound her to another man . . .

"Is she well, my lord?" asked Kjell, interrupting the sensual turn of Rurik's thoughts.

"She sleeps." Deciding the untested warrior was displaying too much interest, Rurik looked at him sharply. He had brought Kjell along on the journey only at the special request of the man's father, another member of Yaroslav's senior *druzhina*, who believed his son needed toughening. Now Rurik could see why. "And sleeping is what you should be doing. The hour will come soon enough when you must take the helm from Leif."

With that, he strode to the prow and stripped out of his wet clothes, his mood growing dark indeed. But he wasn't so much angry at Kjell as he was at himself. He dug in his sea chest for another tunic and a pair of trousers and yanked them on, then throwing his heavy fur mantle around his shoulders, he sat down and stared out across the black water.

By Odin, had madness seized him? He had six concubines

in Novgorod, each one a beauty in her own right. There was nothing special about this wench . . .

"You were a bit harsh with the lad," came Arne's reproachful voice behind him.

"He has the look about him of a lovelorn pup," Rurik said caustically. Running his hand through his damp hair, he did not turn as the warrior took a seat across from him. "Kjell would be wise to keep his thoughts to his duties and not upon fantasies that cannot come true."

"He is young, my lord. Wenches to him are still creatures of fascination and awe, worthy of adoration. He has not yet learned that their fickle hearts are not to be trusted . . . as have some of us."

"It is not only women's hearts that cannot be trusted, old friend. As for the wench, she remembers nothing thanks to her mistreatment at the trading camp, not her name, not her master's name. She's taken on the manner of a child. Only the gods can say when she may recover."

"Yet that is not what's troubling you."

Frowning, Rurik could not see the warrior's expression in the dark, yet he knew Arne looked in sympathy. The grizzled bear could read him as few could; not even Rurik's own father understood him as well. Yet he'd be damned to admit that the woman was behind his irritation. He would be a fool to change his plans and keep her. It would be akin to treason, and let him never, *never* forget that wanting a woman too much held its own dangers.

"Dawn will come soon, Arne. I'll stay on watch while you get some rest."

"As you wish, my lord." He gave a grunt as he hauled himself to his feet. "But rouse me if you decide to go for another moonlit swim. The wench may yet surprise us."

CHAPTER
5

But there were no surprises during the next three days. To Rurik's annoyance, the woman's state did not improve. Sleeping much of the time, she ventured from the tent only to attend to her private needs behind a blanket while he made sure that all eyes were averted. To him, it seemed as if she were ensnared in a strange dreamlike daze, for she showed little interest in anything around her and cared not if she ate or drank. She still remembered nothing when questioned about her identity, and the one time he had raised his voice at her to see if she might for some reason be feigning her malady, he brought on such a fit of tears that he no longer doubted her loss of memory.

She also made no further references to Halfdan, seemingly content with Rurik's explanation that the Varangian trader had been killed. Nor did she ask any questions about Rurik or his men or why she might be with them. In fact, she had spoken very little since that first night. Whenever Rurik questioned her about the name of her master, he had been greeted with the same blank stare.

"Slap her, my lord! That will bring the wench out of it quick enough!" Arne had urged impatiently on more than one occasion, but Rurik had decided that remedy was too severe.

Instead, he hoped that the simple trust she displayed in him would encourage her memory. She clearly viewed him as her protector, a role he knew was useful. Yet they were nearing Chernigov, and she seemed no closer to recalling her name than the first night of their journey.

"The trousers, my lord." Kjell handed over the linen garment as well as a rope belt and a wide cloth sash. "They only reached to my knees, so the wench won't be swallowed up by them."

"They'll do." Rurik strode to the tent, glad for the concealing gray light of dusk. He had purposely adjusted the sail earlier, slowing the boat's pace. He wanted to arrive at the fortified city at nightfall, no sooner.

The men would easily pass as fur traders, but the wench might attract attention, even disguised as a male slave. In the light of day a sharp-eyed individual might discern a female's form so he would take the cautious path, especially since the caravan's searching guards might have reached the city before them.

Inside the tent, Rurik was displeased to see that the woman was resting again, one small hand curled beneath her chin as she lay on her side. He had never seen anyone sleep so much, ill or no! But he supposed it was a form of healing and it had kept her from trying any tricks. The past days she had been as docile as a newborn lamb.

Usually, he preferred women with fire and passion like his tempestuous Semirah, although this woman's tawny beauty more than compensated for her lack of spirit. Looking at her now, the seductive curves of her body outlined beneath the woolen blanket, was enough to rekindle the wanton thoughts he had done his best to repress these past few days—

Thor's blood, man, do not forget she may still remember her name! Rurik berated himself, angered by his wavering self-control. He went down on one knee and shook her by the shoulder.

"Time to wake, little one."

His breath caught as she opened her eyes, huge liquid pools of cobalt-blue that inexplicably fascinated him. Their unusual hue reminded him of the faraway Sea of Marmara on a cloudless, sunlit morning. She yawned prettily and stretched, kittenlike, her slim arms extended in front of her and her bare toes peeking from beneath the blanket. Then she looked up and gifted him with a smile as open and guileless as a child's, a becoming dimple in each cheek.

For a fleeting moment, Rurik could not remember why he had come to the tent. She made such a fetching picture with her wild tousled hair, hanging almost to her waist, framing her face, the oversize wool tunic she wore fallen from one delicately boned shoulder to reveal the soft curve of a breast. Only the sharp scraping of oars outside focused his attention back to his purpose. Cursing himself, he laid the trousers beside her.

"I brought these for you. Stand up and I'll help you put them on."

Without a word she obeyed him and rose, catching his arm to steady herself when the boat suddenly swayed beneath their feet, the waves grown choppy in the stiff wind whistling past the tent. Her unexpected touch sent a charge racing through him like wildfire. Rurik clenched his teeth, warning himself to move fast with what needed to be done. Standing so close to this golden goddess was proving too much of a temptation.

"Lean on my shoulder." While she did, Rurik bent down and slipped first one trouser leg and then the other past her feet. He drew the garment quickly up to her waist beneath her borrowed tunic so that he had little time to focus upon the enticing curve of calf and thigh. Grabbing the rope belt, he secured it around her and then he turned her so she faced away from him.

"I'm going to wrap this sash around your breasts," he told

her, bringing the piece of cloth up under her tunic. "Let me know if I tie it too tightly."

Rurik swallowed hard as his knuckles grazed firmly rounded flesh, and he must have startled her, for she gasped and stepped backward. Instinctively, his arms closed around her and for an instant he reveled in the arousing sensation of her slim body pressed against him.

Surprisingly, she did not pull away but leaned even closer, her bottom rubbing against the hard bulge his flesh had become. With supreme effort he pushed her away, concentrating again on tying the sash. Last, he gathered to one side the extra folds at the neckline of her tunic and fastened them with a plain metal cloak-pin. Her disguise would be for naught if the tunic slipped again from her shoulders.

"It's safer for all of us if you're dressed as a male slave," Rurik explained as he turned her to face him, although she didn't seem the least interested in her garb. "We're very near your new home . . . and your master. Soon you'll be with him again."

She looked at him silently, her tantalizing lips forming no response. Rurik wondered if perhaps he *should* try Arne's remedy. There must be something he could do to shatter the queer spell that gripped her, something that would draw forth her master's name. By the gods, he wasn't one to use brute force against a woman, but in this case . . .

"My lord, we're nearing the city wharf!" came Leif's voice just beyond the tent.

Deciding to wait until they had found their next few nights lodging before attempting a drastic measure that could bring on a noisy flood of tears, Rurik surveyed his handiwork and deemed the woman's attire passable. She made a pretty lad, but with her breasts flattened beneath the sash and baggy clothes, he doubted any would question her sex. Yet he had to do something about her hair, although the thought of cutting those magnificent tresses did not set well with him. He had never seen their like before.

"Could you braid your hair for me, wench?" Wielding a

sword was far more suited to his large hands than such a task.

Rurik was gratified when she twisted her hair into a thick braid as deftly as if she had done so a thousand times.

"Like this?"

He was stunned by her soft query, the first question she had posed to him for three days. Despite himself, he reached out and touched the heavy braid, admiring its silkiness and wondering if she sought to please her master as readily as she had just done for him. He imagined, as a concubine, that she must know many ways to please a man . . .

His imagination firing at the thought, a sudden idea came to him. His blood raced red-hot through his veins.

By Odin, why had he not considered it before? For a woman accustomed to giving pleasure to one man, whose name, then, would she most likely cry out at the height of passion? Surely that of her lover, the hated enemy with whom Rurik hoped to strike his furtive bargain.

A jarring thud suddenly threw the two of them together. As Rurik grabbed the startled woman to prevent her from falling, he realized the boat was sliding against the wharf. Yet this time he didn't push her away. He crushed her against his chest, his lust rearing inside him like a wild thing set free. Why not both satisfy his need and aid his plan? He saw no harm in it, and the quicker he got rid of this far too captivating wench, the better!

Lifting her chin, Rurik brought his mouth down fiercely upon hers, tasting her lips for the first time and finding them as warm and soft and as sweet as he had imagined. He was not surprised when she didn't struggle or twist to escape, instead leaning seductively into their kiss as might any concubine.

When she parted her lips, the moist tip of her tongue touching his, Rurik groaned from the desire shaking him. By Thor, she was eager and willing! Deepening his kiss, his hands slid down her back to squeeze her bottom, and he lifted her against that rock-hard part of himself that ached for the hot softness of her body—

"Harrumph . . . forgive me, Lord Rurik."

Arne's startled yet urgent voice broke through Rurik's impassioned haze. "What is it?"

"Armed guards, my lord, making their way toward the boat. I suspect with the intention of boarding."

Rurik eased his hold upon the woman. There would be time . . . later.

"Find the wench a hat, Arne, quickly!" he ordered. "Her hair must be completely covered." While the Varangian warrior dropped the tent flap to do his bidding, Rurik lifted the woman in his arms and placed her on the furs. He took a moment to stuff her thick braid down the back of her tunic, and noting her flushed cheeks and the anxious frown between her brows, he sought to reassure her. "You must remain here, little one, until I come for you. Do you understand?"

To his surprise, she protested. "No, I want to stay with you!"

Rurik had no time to contend with this sudden and wholly unexpected spark of spirit, although it boded well for her recovery.

"You cannot, wench, it isn't safe. You must remain inside the tent. Do not disobey me."

He had spoken with such sternness that this time she nodded, her eyes very wide. As Arne reappeared with a woolen cap, Rurik rose and brushed past him.

"Put it on her, then meet me outside," he said grimly. "But stay close to the entrance, Arne. It seems our meek little lamb has a mind of her own after all, and might think to join us."

"She'll not get past me, my lord. Have no fear of that."

After casting a last glance at the woman, Rurik stepped from the tent to greet the enemy warriors he surmised were there to check all vessels docking at the wharf. It made sense in this time of war, and Chernigov was the usurper Prince Mstislav's most recently conquered city.

* * *

"For this hole we must pay thirty silver grivna a night?"
Arne held up a smoking lamp to better view the dingy interior of the shack they had rented close to the main marketplace. Tattered furs hung from two narrow windows, the
only furnishings a dilapidated table shoved against a planked
wall and two benches. Cursing under his breath, the husky
warrior kicked at the filthy reeds littering the floor. "Smells
of piss and stale ale to me."

"We're lucky to have it." Frowning, Rurik ignored Arne's
continued muttering. "The city is overrun with merchants
and Mstislav's retainers. If we hadn't chanced down this
street as those other traders were leaving, someone else
would have slept here tonight."

"Aye, and if the prince's watchdogs had only kept us a
while longer with their questions, we'd have missed the
honor!" Arne snorted in disgust. "Are you sure you won't
return to the ship, my lord? I'd trade a pallet on deck for this
stinking hovel any day, and the thought of Kjell and Leif
aboard alone, surrounded on every side by our enemies—"

"Enough, Arne." Rurik's voice was low and firm. "You
know the plan. Leif and Kjell will stay with the ship while
we gather what information we can at the market and deal
with our valuable charge." He glanced at the silent woman
holding his arm, then met the warrior's disgruntled gaze.
"Don't forget that our surly welcome committee granted us a
mere four-day trading pass, then we must leave the city. We
don't have time to waste."

Turning away, Rurik held his lamp higher and pushed
open a door leading to a tiny separate bedchamber. A mouse
squeaked and skittered over his foot into the main room,
causing the woman to start.

"You've nothing to fear, little one," he said as he led her
into the shadowed, windowless chamber. "It's only a
mouse—"

A loud stamping sound came from the other room, followed by a satisfied grunt. "A dead one," Arne announced.

Shaking his head, Rurik set the sputtering lamp on the floor and tossed the large bundle of furs he'd been carrying onto the bed. The straw-filled mattress appeared somewhat fresh, but he would cover it with soft skins anyway. This room wasn't the fine bower his wide-eyed beauty was surely accustomed to, but it was the best available. At least it would offer them more privacy than the tent aboard ship.

"My stomach's yowling like the wolves of Hel," said Arne, appearing on the threshold. "If you'd like, my lord, I'll set up a fine feast in the other room." His gaze raked over the woman. "She looks like she could use a hot meal. She's a bit too skinny for my taste."

"Better skinny than too fat like you." The woman's retort had been uttered so softly that Rurik almost believed he had imagined it. Then he noticed the slight jutting of her chin. Amused by this little show of temper, he glanced back at Arne, who thankfully had missed the insult.

"The wench and I will be eating alone tonight," he said, not offering any further explanation.

Arne stared at him in some confusion. "You will?"

Rurik nodded meaningfully. Settling his arm around the woman's shoulders, he felt the tension in her body subside as he drew her close.

Arne appeared even more confused. "But, Lord Rurik . . . you said you weren't keeping the wench for yourself—"

"I'm not. I have a plan, Arne. Trust me."

The warrior gaped at them for an instant, then understanding lit his eyes and his swarthy, bearded face broke into a lusty grin. "Aye, I'm sure you do, Lord Rurik. When it comes to pleasing the wenches . . ." Chuckling, he turned to leave.

"A jug of wine would be nice, my friend, and half of that fine crusty loaf of bread if you can spare it. And some of that spit-roasted mutton," Rurik called after him.

"There's more than enough." Arne gave Rurik a broad wink over his shoulder. "It'll take me a moment to fetch your meal, then I'll trouble you no more save for my snoring."

Rurik smiled wryly, but he sobered when he studied the woman nestled against him. If she had been affronted a moment ago, he saw no sign of it now. She seemed perfectly content in his embrace, her eyes large and luminous in the lamp's golden light.

Feeling his heart beginning to pound, he hoped Arne hurried with their meal. He was inclined to slam the door shut so they would not be disturbed. He could not remember ever having such a pleasurable task before him, his goal being to drive this woman to such wild distraction that she screamed out her master's name.

He couldn't wait to claim her, to quench within her temptress's body his mounting lust ignited too many long hours ago. Surely when he was spent and satiated, he would be freed from this ungodly fascination. Other enchanting women has ceased to intrigue him when he had tasted their feminine secrets. She would be no different.

Rurik was relieved when Arne's hulking form appeared once more in the doorway, and he left the woman to drag a low, lopsided table over to the bed, indicating with a nod that their meal should be set upon it. As the warrior obliged him, Rurik cut the rope binding the furs and spread some of them over the mattress. The rest he tossed to Arne.

"Sleep well, my friend, but take care that your sword is drawn and ready at your side," Rurik cautioned. "As you said, we've enemies all around us."

"Aye, the usurping dogs," Arne muttered in agreement as he shut the door behind him.

Following his own advice, the first thing Rurik did when he and the woman were finally alone was unbuckle his sword belt and lay it upon the floor within easy reach of the bed. Then he bade the woman to sit upon the lumpy mattress and he took the place beside her.

"Are you hungry, little one?" Rurik noted how prominent

her cheekbones were in a face grown thinner during the past few days.

She smiled her assent, a small curve of her lips that tugged strangely at his heart. He tore off a chunk of bread for her, deciding as she eagerly took a bite that the recovery of her appetite was a good sign. Combined with her recent displays of temperament, he hoped that before the evening was done he would see many more such signs, and thus have a terse message addressed to her wealthy master not long after the first light of dawn.

"Wine?"

As she swallowed another mouthful of bread, she nodded, and he quickly pulled out the stopper and offered her the jug so that she might drink. To his surprise, she took a long draft as if very thirsty, yet it pleased him for her to do so. If she possessed any fears at all about his sensual advances, he hoped they would be dulled by the wine's soothing effect.

"Try some of the mutton," he urged, waiting until she had eaten a good portion despite the fact that the fragrant seared meat had his stomach growling.

It seemed in moments that the wooden platter was empty between them, the bread devoured, and the wine jug empty. He could not help noticing how delicately she had consumed her meal, confirming to him that her manners were indeed refined. Frowning as if trying to remember something, she seemed to look about her for a water bowl to cleanse her soiled fingers, then she sighed in frustration, her hands falling to her lap.

"Would you like to bathe?" Rurik asked, remembering the large bucket of fresh water that the owner of the shack had left them in the other room. At her low-spoken "Yes," he was on his feet and striding from the bedchamber, startling Arne who almost dropped a hunk of mutton as he lurched from the table.

"My lord?"

"Go back to your meal." Rurik picked up the bucket, wishing that he had hot, steaming bathing water to offer the woman. It was easy to imagine how fetching she might look sitting in a tub with her wet hair streaming around her, her beautiful breasts sleek and glistening with moisture.

When he returned to their room, the woman had stripped to the waist, her tunic and the cloth sash lying upon the floor, and she was working at the rope belt at her waist. She must have sensed him standing there, for she looked up and met his eyes, her expression troubled.

"I can't untie the knot."

Closing the door, Rurik moved quickly to her side, marveling that she was so unconcerned by her nakedness. As he deftly undid the belt, she regarded him with such frankness that it took his breath away. Her manner was so comfortable, so trusting, she must look upon him in the same light as her master.

Suddenly he found himself deeply envious of this boyar to possess such a woman. She seemed so eager to please him, almost as if awaiting his next move . . .

"Let me help you," he said huskily, slipping her trousers down over her curved hips and deliciously rounded bottom. When she was standing naked before him, her body silhouetted in gold from the lamp behind her, Rurik doubted he had ever known such desire. She was fashioned so finely. Perfection.

His instincts screamed for him to take her, now, but another part of him wanted to savor the treasure that had been placed in his path. Wadding the sash, he dipped it into the bucket until the cloth was soaked. Then he began to bathe her, first her face, taking care to rub gently over the bruise upon her cheek that was just beginning to fade.

Her entrancing blue eyes never wavered from his gaze, and she stood still for his ministrations as if it were a common thing for a man to perform such a task upon her. Again he found himself filled with envy, but he did not stifle it, the emotion part of the spell under which she held him captive.

Next he slid the wet cloth down her lovely throat, across her fine-boned shoulders, and along slender arms he couldn't wait to feel wrapped tightly around his back. Dipping the sash into the bucket, he brought it to her breasts and squeezed, the coolness of the water that slicked her golden skin causing her to gasp and her apricot-brown nipples to pucker.

Rurik thought for sure that he had endured enough, but he continued to bathe her, down her taut belly, over her hips and between her legs, when suddenly she lost his gaze. Closing her eyes and whimpering deep in her throat, she arched against his hand, her soft woman's curls tickling his skin.

It was too much. Sweeping her into his arms, Rurik laid her upon the bed and leaving her for only a moment, undressed more swiftly than he had ever thought possible. As he blanketed her with his body, he no longer cared about savoring her or taking his time. He wanted her so badly that he was shaking. Believing she wanted him just as much, he parted her legs with his knee and thrust inside her with such vehemence that she cried out . . . not a man's name, not in ecstasy, but in raw pain.

"By Odin . . . ?" Rurik had had virgins before, and in that unsettling instant, he knew the woman moaning beneath him had never known another man. Yet he could no sooner stop his wild assault than the furious hammering of his heart.

"Sshh, little one . . . sshh," he soothed, knowing from experience that soon her pain would pass and rippling pleasure take its place.

Kissing her hungrily, passionately, the wine-scented taste of her mouth driving him into a frenzy, he nonetheless drew back a little and slipped his hand between their bodies. His fingers found the slick, wet heat he was seeking and he slid them into her, teasing the tender bud hidden there that seemed to swell beneath his touch.

He was rewarded at once by her sharp inhalation of surprise, then broken whimpers as she began to toss beneath him, her hips thrusting upward as urgently as he delved within her, neither his fingers or his deepening kisses giving her any peace. He almost laughed in triumph against her lips when her arms curled around his neck to grip him tightly, her panting as hot and breathless as his own.

Then he thought no more, the searing sensation in his loins building to such intensity that he grimaced as if in mortal pain.

From some far-off place he heard her cries of rapture, her incredibly tight, blistering sheath gripping him like a throbbing vise . . . squeezing him, teasing him, until he reached that point where his body stiffened and his breath jammed hard in his chest. As a pure hot explosion of sensation overwhelmed him, more blindingly powerful than anything he remembered, he called out to the woman beneath him, no matter that he didn't know her name . . .

Rurik could not say how much time had passed before he raised his head, but he guessed a good while for the woman's eyes were closed, her breathing deep and regular as if she were asleep. Either that or she had fainted from the force of her passion. He had seen such a thing before. Fearing his weight was too much for her, he rolled over and carried her with him until she was lying on top of him, their bodies still joined.

Loki take him, the wench had been a virgin, he thought incredulously, cursing the devious god of mischief who had wreaked this havoc. A damned virgin! The last thing he had expected was innocence.

Rurik sighed heavily as the woman's gentle breathing stirred the blond curls upon his chest. He hadn't expected the powerful feelings that were crashing in upon him either. Instead of being satiated, he was more intrigued than ever.

A concubine, yet a virgin? An innocent possessing the passionate nature of a wanton? A woman who had looked to him for protection, yet who might now be compromised in value to her master because Rurik had stolen her chastity? An insistent inner voice demanded that he save her from the wrath his defilement of her might arouse, that he keep her safe from harm and take her back with him to Novgorod. He had never felt so strongly drawn to any woman since Astrid—

No, by Odin! For that reason alone, he would leave this wench to her fate!

His actions had been impulsive since the first moment he saw her, but no more! Women were trouble of the worst kind, and he would do well to remember that.

Besieged by bitter memories, Rurik shifted the woman from his body and rose from the bed. To continue touching her, holding her, was a torment he did not need. After covering her with a soft fur, he threw several skins onto the floor and lay down.

Tomorrow morning he would rid himself of her, even if he must abandon his plan to use her for information. He wanted no woman around him that made him feel like this one. He would leave her near the gates of Prince Mstislav's palace, where someone would surely recognize her and return her to her rightful master.

It had to be done.

CHAPTER
6

Awaking with a start, Zora winced at the tenderness between her legs. It wasn't a true pain, but a dull ache, yet she had never felt such a sensation before.

She shifted slightly, amazed that her entire body was sore. She stared in confusion at the raftered ceiling, trying to gather her muddled thoughts. Where was she? Rubbing her hands over her face, she sharply inhaled as she touched her left cheekbone. Ouch, it hurt! Frowning, she ran her fingertips more gingerly over her skin, wondering what she could have done—

"Holy Mother Mary," she breathed in horror, all too suddenly remembering why her cheek hurt so painfully as if a ray of brilliant light had pierced her brain. He . . . he had struck her! That Varangian trader, Halfdan Snakeeye!

Dreadful memories leapt to life in her mind, lurid sights and sounds: Halfdan's scarred face, his leering grin, his terrible laughter . . . and the naked slave women in the tent, all of them writhing, moaning, then the trader throwing her down upon a bench and stroking himself right in front of her!

Halfdan's coarse words flew at her . . . "You cannot escape me, pretty bird. I will have you, here, now, in the dirt!" Then she was running, running, and begging for aid but no one would help her. No one would listen! Fierce-looking Varangians were everywhere, and Halfdan was coming closer and closer. She remembered crying out, "You cannot do this!" then he struck her down and she was falling—

"Oh, no . . ." Zora whispered, feeling suddenly very sick. "Oh, God, no." Rising abruptly on her elbow, Zora flung aside the furs, her hand moving to the place where the dull throbbing was centered. She felt a wetness and gasped in disbelief at the scarlet blood staining her trembling fingers, the same telltale sign smeared upon the inside of her thighs.

He had raped her! That brutish, dung-smelling Varangian had raped her!

A half sigh, half groan suddenly drew her gaze to the floor. She stared wide-eyed, her heart pounding in rage and fear, at the naked man sleeping only four feet away with his broad, muscled back to her. In the dim lighting she could see that he was huge, his hair blond. She didn't need to see more.

Halfdan!

Her first thought was to flee. Then the bright glint of metal near the sputtering oil lamp caught her eye and she drew fresh courage. Focusing with deadly intent upon the sword lying within arm's reach, she decided then and there that she was going to kill him for what he had done to her.

Burning for vengeance, Zora vaulted from the bed, and grabbing the sword hilt, she yanked the heavy weapon from its sheath. She staggered beneath its weight, but clenching her teeth from the effort and fueled by blinding fury, she managed to lift the sword high enough to deal one fatal, hacking blow.

"Now you will pay!" Yet the blade had no sooner begun its downward motion when she was knocked violently to her knees, the sword wrenched from her hand.

In the next instant she was hauled by the shoulders to her feet, coming face-to-face with a man she realized at once was not Halfdan. In fact, she could not recall ever seeing him before, although she guessed from his sheer size and fair hair that he must be a Varangian. She gaped up at him in astonishment, his expression so thunderous that she was swept by cold fear.

"This is something new, little one," he said in a low husky voice that sent strange chills through her. He gripped her upper arms tightly. "I've heard of those who walk in their sleep, but to engage in swordplay? A most dangerous affliction indeed. Someone could have been hurt."

Confused that he addressed her as if he knew her, Zora stared into eyes that appeared black as night in the room's dimness and a bearded countenance made no less handsome by his obvious anger. "Who-who . . . are you?" she finally demanded, her voice hoarse.

"You don't recognize me?"

Again, she was startled. Recognize him? How could she? She had never seen this man before.

Zora shook her head.

Now the blond giant seemed somewhat surprised. "Yet you raised my own sword against me," he said, searching her face. "Why?"

"You raped me! You deserve to die for what you have done, you . . . you filthy pagan!"

Rurik stared at her incredulously, his head beginning to pound. It seemed his docile charge had at last recovered. Gone was the acquiescent child-woman who had so captivated him, and in her place, a defiant avenging angel with apparently no memory of the past few days, let alone the last few hours. Thor's blood, if he hadn't heard his sword sliding from the scabbard, he would have been dead!

"It was no rape," he said tightly. He had never taken any woman to his bed against her will. That might be the sport of other Varangian warriors, but not his. "You did not spurn my advances, wench, but eagerly welcomed them."

"Liar!" Her eyes snapped indignant fire. "I would rather die than submit to a barbarian such as you!"

Suddenly she ground her heel into his big toe with such fury that he released her, cursing. She fled to the foot of the bed, and as if realizing for the first time that she was stark naked, she yanked a fur off the mattress and flung it around herself.

"Say what you like, wench, but you did submit to me and willingly." Undaunted by her insults and her behavior although his toe throbbed in pain, Rurik took a step toward her but reconsidered when she lunged for the empty wine jug and held it poised in front of her like a weapon. Perhaps if he tried to reason with her, he might coax her into cooling her temper. She had already tried to kill him once and then stomped upon his foot. He didn't relish the idea of sustaining any further injury at her hand.

"I didn't know you were a virgin." He used the same soothing tone she had responded to favorably in the past. "If I had, I wouldn't have touched you. It was not my intent to cause any trouble between you and your master—"

"Master?" Zora interrupted, deciding that this Varangian must be mad. He had made little sense since first opening his mouth. She was glad when he picked up a pair of trousers and tugged them on, although she would be the last to admit how disconcerting she had found his nakedness. Keeping her gaze trained upon his face had been almost impossible for what lay below, his physique more formidable than any man's she had ever seen—

Furious at herself for even thinking that this Norseman was remotely attractive, especially after what he had done to her, she spat, "I have no master."

"No? Before I took his life, the Slav merchant who stole you from the caravan told me that you did."

"You killed Gleb?" Stunned, Zora recalled all too clearly that ruthless merchant's plans for her.

"So you remember him."

"Yes," she replied bitterly. "He was going to cut out my tongue and sell me in Constantinople. How could I forget such a man?"

"Then you must remember Halfdan as well."

Zora eyed the Varangian with renewed suspicion.

"Do not fear, little one. He is also dead. I told you all of this before, but you've been ill since I took you from that trading camp. You suffered a severe shock. I'm not surprised you don't remember me, even though you've shared my and my men's company for almost four days now."

Four days?

Unwittingly lowering the jug, Zora wondered if this astounding statement could be true. She remembered the events at that horrid camp so clearly, as if they had happened only an hour past. Yet here she was in a tiny room at some unknown place with a half-naked stranger who was leading her to believe that he had saved her from Halfdan and Gleb.

Saved her? she scoffed, taking the Norseman's measure from head to toe. He had also raped her, and she refused to believe otherwise. Surely even ill she would not have allowed him to steal her honor. This damned Varangian had ruined her!

"Where are we?" she demanded, raising her weapon again when he made a slight movement toward her.

"Chernigov."

Her father's city! So close to her new home, to Ivan her betrothed, and yet this giant was holding her captive for God knew what purpose. Zora lifted her chin, her tone icy. "What do you want from me?"

An unsettling glint of humor lit his eyes. "Only your master's name, little one. I want to release you to his care, but I cannot until—"

"I told you I have no master!" she snapped, infuriated that he would find anything in this situation amusing. "You make it sound as if I am a slave—"

"Not a slave, perhaps, but a boyar's concubine or so I was told. A favored one . . . and obviously without having shared his bed. No wonder the man's wife hated you."

It was on the tip of Zora's tongue to declare hotly that she was no concubine but a princess of the Tmutorokan Rus, and that everything he had been told about her were lies. But something stopped her. She was not certain this man would truly help her. She was nothing to him . . . unless he had something to gain by assisting her.

Smelling treachery, Zora nervously chewed her lower lip, her heart beating a little faster.

Perhaps she was in the hands of an enemy of her father's. Varangian warriors held positions in Mstislav's army, but they were few in number. Unlike Grand Prince Yaroslav who possessed strong alliances with Norse kings and chieftains. If this man knew she had been abducted from the caravan, why hadn't he taken her back?

She was no fool. Her father employed spies against his elder brother. Yaroslav must do the same. Perhaps this man was a spy, and hoped to use her to gain some military advantage for the grand prince. He obviously believed her to be a boyar's concubine; perhaps it was best to convince him.

"What I meant is that I don't look upon Lord Ivan as my master," she said in a much softer tone, giving the Varangian the true name of her betrothed. Ivan would never betray her father, and he was a shrewd man. He would know how to outwit her captor and win her return long before the Norseman discovered her identity. "Nor does he see me as merely his concubine. We are so much . . . more to each other."

"So I thought," Rurik muttered, any amusement he had derived from her pretty display of hauteur vanishing at the image of her even smiling at another man.

Then, angrily reminding himself of his resolve to be rid of her, he demanded, "Where can I find Lord Ivan? I want to send him a message and let him know that you are well."

"Why don't you just take me to him?" Zora countered as guilelessly as possible. "If we are in Chernigov, it would be an easy matter to escort me to the *kreml*. My Ivan is one of Prince Mstislav's most trusted warriors."

Rurik had no intention of betraying himself or his men. It was best she believed he was a mercenary. "It's not that simple, wench." He was determined not to call her "little one" again, forcing himself to think of her as nothing more than a pawn. "There is the matter of ransom."

"Ransom?" came her startled reply.

He laughed, mocking her. "Of course. Did you think I had brought you all this way for charity? When I learned of your value from the Slav merchant, I knew I would profit well by your safe return."

Zora felt her face grow hot as she realized she might have misread this man entirely. So he was only interested in gaining ransom . . . and he was a murderer to boot! She would have felt safer if she were in the hands of a disciplined spy and not some ruthless fortune hunter.

Suddenly her situation felt much more precarious, and Zora decided that she would not wait for any ransom to be delivered. As soon as she saw her chance, she would escape. Then, once she was safe with her father, she would have this coarse Varangian and his companions hunted down and see that they paid with their lives for the unthinkable indignity she had suffered.

"What is your name, wench?"

Zora hesitated. If he discovered that he held a princess, who knew what he might do? "Ilka," she lied, using the name of one of her slaves.

"Ilka. It doesn't suit you." The Norseman's gaze raked over her in a manner that filled her with apprehension. "Beauty such as yours deserves something finer." He gestured to the bed. "Lie down, Ilka."

Zora clutched the fur more tightly around her. "Lie down?"

"We've only a few more hours left until dawn and I want you to look your best tomorrow for Lord Ivan."

Zora wanted to refuse—it was humiliating to sleep in the spot where he had so recently defiled her. But his forceful tone discouraged any argument. Perhaps she had nothing to fear from him, she tried to reason with herself, setting the wine jug close within her reach as she lay down upon the bed and arranged the fur so that it covered her torso. He had been sleeping upon the floor after all—

"Move over."

She stared up at him in disbelief, her heart hammering. "What?"

"I don't trust you, Ilka. You've already proved to me that you can wield a sword. I don't want to wake up to find myself bleeding to death. Or you gone." When she hesitated, he kicked the jug so hard under the bed that it shattered against a corner post. "Move over!"

Her mouth suddenly dry, Zora obeyed by quickly scooting as far to the wall as she could go. She had just turned her back to him when a powerful arm went around her waist. She gasped as he brought her hard against him and threw a heavily muscled leg over her thigh. To her horror, her bare bottom was nestled right up against his hips.

"Sleep well, Ilka."

Sleep well? she thought furiously as his breathing soon became deep and regular.

God help her, she'd be damned if she closed her eyes at all!

CHAPTER 7

To Zora's relief, morning came mercifully swift. Watching sullenly as the Varangian pulled his tunic over his head, she told herself that she held no interest in the immense breadth of his shoulders, so thick with muscle, the bulging contours of his arms, the impressive span of his chest, or the masculine leanness of his waist. She was merely keeping a cautious eye on him.

Amazingly, she felt little fatigue even though she hadn't slept, the heat of his body alone enough to help keep her eyes open. His every movement in sleep, radiating more strength than she imagined most men possessed in their waking hours, had also kept up her defenses.

She suspected that she must have gotten enough rest during the past few days to make up for the lack last night. Since the moment her stern-faced captor had arisen to relight the oil lamp and begin to dress, she had felt alert, eager, and ready for any chance of escape that might present itself.

"Get dressed," the Varangian ordered as he fastened a wide leather belt about his waist. Drawing his gleaming sword from the scabbard, he ran two fingers along one filed edge to the tapered tip and then down the blade's other side as if checking for any damage from its recent mishandling.

To Zora, it looked almost like he was caressing the weapon, the expression on his handsome face somber and reverent. She had heard tales that Norsemen revered their swords, surrounding them with an aura of mystique. Some Varangians even gave their swords a name.

"What do you call it?" She must have asked her question a bit too flippantly for he shot her a dark glare.

"Branch-of-Odin."

"Makes sense for a pagan like you," she muttered, resenting his frown and her own shiver of fear.

He ran the flat of his palm down the three-foot-long blade and then thrust the deadly weapon back into its sheath. "I thought I told you to get dressed."

Bristling at his tone, Zora held the fur she had not let go of since last night more snugly against her body. "In what, if I might ask?"

He picked up some clothes scattered upon the floor and tossed them to the bed.

Inspecting the two garments gingerly, almost afraid to touch them for fear of finding lice, Zora's eyes widened. *Trousers? A man's tunic? Was he mad?* She glanced at him in confusion, but before she could speak the Varangian chuckled in amusement.

"You seem surprised, Ilka. Surely you can see that we couldn't bring you into the city as a woman wearing fine silks and slippers, your beautiful hair unbound and flowing down your back. Someone might have recognized you and we would be dead men." He threw a rope belt and a damp piece of cloth into her lap. "Until you're back in Lord Ivan's arms, you will play the part of my slave"—his voice grew heavy with warning—"and a docile one at that. Do you understand?"

Nodding, she bit back her sharp retort, though the thought

of meekly following this heathen's orders even for a short while turned her stomach.

"May I at least bathe before I dress?" she began in a deceptive flat monotone, but her anger at her lost virginity suddenly overcame her discretion. "Ivan will not be pleased to have the smell of another man upon me."

Her statement was rewarded with a black scowl. She glared right back at him, which seemed to displease him all the more.

"There's water in the bucket," he said tightly. "I used that cloth sash to bathe you last night, but of course you don't remember."

"You did what?" Her gaze skipped in surprise from the wrinkled length of material to his face, which was inscrutable.

"It doesn't matter," he bit off. "Take care that you wring out the sash well when you're finished. Your breasts must be bound with it as part of your guise." Paying no heed to her gasp of outrage, he strode to the door and flung it open, only to pause at the sight of another Varangian who appeared as if he had been just about to knock.

Zora swallowed her pique for the moment, thinking ahead to her escape. She hoped there were not many more Norsemen hiding in the adjoining room. This older man was as dark as her captor was fair, even for the sprinkling of gray in his hair and beard, yet a full head shorter and much wider in girth. His face was round and swarthy, and he had the most peculiar nose she had ever seen. He looked as if someone had punched him good and hard, breaking his nose and squashing it to one side.

"Ah, Lord Rurik, you're awake," the graying warrior said amiably. His gaze flew to the bed and he grinned, which made Zora grip the fur all the more tightly to her breasts. "I trust you and the wench slept soundly."

Lord Rurik? Zora thought, realizing she had neglected to ask her captor his name. Then again, most likely he wouldn't have told her even if she had. She decided Rurik suited him.

A hard name for a hard man. But what of the title? That puzzled her. Since when did mercenary rogues of his sort have titles?

"Not as soundly as I might have wished," Rurik said, casting a meaningful look in her direction. "It's not every night that a man's own sword is raised against him."

"Your sword?" The hulking warrior's grin vanished. He glanced incredulously from Zora to Rurik. "The wench?"

Rurik nodded.

"By Odin, I slept too well! I heard nothing!"

"Don't trouble yourself, Arne. There was never any real danger. Our captive beauty vastly underestimated her opponent. Now come, we have much to discuss and the wench wishes to bathe."

Not missing his sarcastic tone as he shut the door behind him, Zora felt like flinging the damned bucket across the room. Damn his pagan's soul to hell. She couldn't wait to be free of him!

Rising from the bed, she dropped the fur to the floor and proceeded to scrub herself clean, the cold water proving some balm for her temper. A bit of soap would have been nice, but she would just have to wait until she was back in the women's *terem* where she could enjoy a proper bath.

As she gave herself a final rinsing, she squeezed the dripping cloth against her shoulder, relishing the opportunity to wash away any remnant of Rurik's loathsome touch. Sucking in her breath as the chilled water trickled down the front of her body, she suddenly froze as an unsettling flash of memory struck her . . . Rurik, standing tall and broad in front of her, his eyes burning into hers, his knuckles grazing her sensitive flesh as he pressed the soaked cloth between her breasts—

No, that couldn't have happened! she told herself fiercely, cursing that her nipples had grown hard and turgid. He hadn't bathed her! That had been another of his lies!

Flinging the cloth into the bucket with a splash, she dressed quickly although her skin was still damp. She wanted to be clothed, her nakedness an unwanted reminder of her disgrace. Outside, the sounds of activity beyond the planked walls—people shouting and laughing, carts rumbling, horses neighing—spurred her on.

She felt as if she were suffocating in this dim, stuffy little bedchamber, no windows to provide fresh air or an escape. She wanted to see the next room, wanted to know how many other Varangians were in Rurik's band and then weigh her chances. With trembling fingers, she rebraided her hair, then she went to the door and thrust it open.

Rurik was leaning against the wall with his heavily muscled arms folded over his chest, obviously waiting for her to emerge. Her breath caught, for in the bright morning sunlight streaming in from a nearby window, she finally got a good look at his face.

He was more strikingly handsome than she had thought, his short beard and mustache only accentuating his hard, sculpted features. His thick blond hair was longer than she recalled, skimming his shoulders, and gleamed with silvery highlights that mirrored the brightness of his sword. When he inclined his head slightly, she spied a glint of gold and noticed for the first time that he wore a small hooped earring in his left ear, although he bore no other ornament.

But what drew her attention was his eyes. They weren't black as she had imagined them to be, but an intense blue like the color of deep water, or the sky after twilight just before it darkens into night. She found herself captivated by them, thinking they were the most arresting hue she had ever seen . . .

"You forgot the sash, Ilka."

"What . . . ?" As if shattered from some spell, Zora felt a hot blush burn her cheeks as he smiled lazily at her, his teeth a brilliant white against his sun-bronzed skin. Clenching her jaw stubbornly, for she didn't want to wear that clammy cloth against her skin, she muttered, "I did not."

"I'm not blind," he countered, his gaze falling to her breasts. "Your beauty juts free and unfettered for all to see."

Zora wanted to slap him for staring at her so, and to her mortification when she followed his eyes, her hardened nipples were well outlined against the linen tunic. That alone made her rush into the bedchamber, and turning her back to him, she lifted the garment and wound the damp sash around her upper body.

"Do you need any help?"

"No!"

But she did. She sighed with frustration as she struggled with her arms behind her to tie a knot, then jumped when she felt his large warm hands cover hers to take over the task. Shivering at his touch, she jerked her hands away as if stung and, made furious by her reaction, wondered what the devil was coming over her. The man had raped her, let her not forget!

"Come, Ilka," he said when he seemed satisfied that the sash was tied tightly enough. Her breasts were all but flattened, which was quite uncomfortable. "There's food in the other room."

Biting her tongue, Zora followed him from the bedchamber. She made quick inventory of her new surroundings— two narrow windows that she could easily squeeze through, another door leading outside, and best of all no other Varangians in sight except the strapping Arne—while Rurik led her to a bench where he gestured that she should sit. Arne was already seated at the table, ale glistening in his beard as he thunked down his mug and wiped his mouth with the back of his hand.

"Aye, she's got a vixen's gleam in her eye, just like you said, my lord. But I'll watch her well, you can be sure."

Zora shot a glance at Rurik as he set bread, cheese, and a mug of frothy ale in front of her. "You're leaving?"

He nodded. "I've a message to deliver to the *kreml*, remember?" He quaffed his ale standing up as if soon to depart.

Zora's mind raced. Though her stomach grumbled noisily, she gave no notice to the food beneath her nose. If the Varangian gave her name as Ilka, then Ivan might not know it was her and think the message a ruse!

"Are you going to describe me in this message?" she asked Rurik innocently. "I mean . . . it might be wise. Ivan is a suspicious man. He might require some proof that you really hold me, especially since he believes I am safe with the caravan—"

"I had already thought of that," Rurik interrupted.

Before Zora could blink, he pulled a wicked-looking knife from his belt and cut off a two-inch length of her braid. As Arne bellowed with laughter, Rurik's lips curved into a half smile.

"Do you think this proof enough?"

Staring at him in shock, Zora could only nod. Now she knew she was being held by ruthless cutthroats.

"Don't let her out of your sight," Rurik said over her head to Arne, who waved his mug in assent, some of his ale splashing onto the table. "I'll be back soon. If all goes well, we'll have our ransom and the wench will be back in Lord Ivan's arms by sunset. You and I, my friend, are going to leave this city as very rich men."

She'd be gone from here much sooner than that, accursed Varangian! Zora vowed to herself, choking down her bread and cheese as Rurik picked up a bundle of furs and strode from the shack. She tossed back a good swallow of ale, hoping to fortify her courage.

"Aye, drink up, wench." Arne slammed his empty mug upon the table so hard that she jumped. "It'll calm your nerves. You look to be a skittish thing to me." He reached for Rurik's mug, which was still half full, and noisily slurped the contents. "But don't be thinking that I'll be less wary for the ale I've swallowed. Believe me, I'm going to watch you as if I had three eyes in my head instead of two."

"Take that in your eyes!" cried Zora, dashing her ale into Arne's flat-nosed face. As the Varangian sputtered and cursed, she made a dash for the door, wild excitement filling her. Soon she would be free. But her hand barely touched the latch when the door burst open and knocked her backward onto the rush-strewn floor. She landed hard on her backside.

"I had an idea this would happen," Rurik said dryly, ducking his head as he stepped over the threshold.

Forcing back frustrated tears, Zora spouted without thinking, "You loutish pagan! I'll not stop trying to escape until I'm free of you—" Too late, she clamped her mouth shut, but she knew the damage was done when he hauled her roughly to her feet and half dragged her back into the bedchamber.

"Here's some rope, my lord," Arne announced behind them when she was thrown unceremoniously onto the bed. As she lay facedown upon the furs, her arms were forced behind her and her wrists securely tied. Then she was flipped over as if she weighed nothing at all. Tears blinded her eyes as Rurik bound her ankles together.

"I didn't want to have to do this, wench, but you've forced my hand," he said tightly, his expression hard. To complete her humiliation, he tore a length of fabric from the hem of her tunic and used it to gag her. "Nor can I have you shouting for help. Someone outside might hear you."

Then he and Arne were gone, leaving her lying upon the bed like a trussed bird. They had tricked her. As hot tears tumbled down her flushed face, she heard Rurik slam the outer door and she silently heaped every curse she knew upon his head . . . which in truth weren't very many and hardly enough to do his crimes justice.

It was some comfort to imagine the day of his execution. *A hanging?* No, too kind. *An arrow through the heart?* No, too swift. *A tumble into a pit filled with wild dogs?* Yes, now that would suit him! She only hoped her father would allow her to give the signal that would bring about his much-deserved death.

Rurik strode through the crowded market, an odd tenseness dogging him.

He knew he had been too rough on the wench, but she had

pushed him. It had been clear from the mutinous expression in those lovely blue eyes that she planned to escape. After all, she'd tried last night. It was necessary to leave Arne there to watch her.

Foolish little spitfire! She had looked almost comical sitting there on her bottom, her mouth agape in surprise until her chin had jutted at him defiantly, yet laughter had been the last thing on his mind. He should have known she wouldn't cooperate.

That Slav merchant Gleb had been right about the wench. She *was* nothing but trouble! She didn't have a docile bone in her body. Instead she was the most spoiled, disobedient, insolent, and excessively imperious concubine he had ever seen. If one of his women even dared to go so far, he would break her of her bad habits soon enough. Even Semirah, his passionate desert beauty, knew when to silence her tongue.

Lord Ivan was welcome to this woman, Rurik thought irritably. Such impudent wenches served only to ruin a man's existence, and if there was one thing he demanded in his home, it was harmony. To think that he had momentarily believed he wanted to keep her . . .

Cursing his folly, Rurik shifted the bundle of furs upon his shoulder and scanned the variety of colorful stalls for the scribners' section of the market.

He needed to buy paper, pen, and ink to write his message to Lord Ivan. He planned to arrange a secret meeting to discuss his demands, allowing the boyar the knowledge that to thwart him would mean Ilka's death. It was a dangerous scheme, but carefully weighed, and Rurik thrived upon taking such risks. If not, he would never have achieved his esteemed status under Yaroslav, and would still be a lowly member of the grand prince's junior *druzhina*.

Spying at last a stall displaying a wide array of quills, Rurik made his way through a noisy, bustling throng of merchants and eager buyers. The air was filled with spirited haggling in a dozen languages and when he reached the stall, he found the scribe engaged in a heated debate with a foreign customer over the price of some pens.

Impatiently awaiting his turn, Rurik leaned against the booth. His gaze swept a busy market scene that was no different from a hundred others . . . save for the large number of guards who moved through the crowd. At first he wasn't troubled by their presence. Chernigov was a newly conquered city whose occupants had once been loyal to Yaroslav. But then he spied two different sets of guards, four men in each group, moving from stall to stall obviously questioning each trader. Rurik tensed.

"What's the trouble?" he queried the merchant who had finally waved off his previous stubborn customer in disgust, having failed to settle upon a price. Rurik inclined his head toward the nearest group of guards. "You'd think some valuable prisoners might have escaped from the *kreml* for the armed men in this market."

The sallow-faced trader, his skin deeply pitted from the pox, warily appraised Rurik. "You traveling through?"

Rurik nodded, lowering his furs to the counter. "Four-day trading pass."

"Well, you can expect to be answering to the bastards soon enough," said the trader, his gruff tone indicating that he didn't look too highly upon the city's newest citizens. "They were just here, slinging their questions so fast as if to confuse a man. I suspect they'll harry us until they find the wench, be she alive or dead."

Rurik held his voice steady. "Wench?"

"Aye, Prince Mstislav's youngest daughter," the trader spat. His gaze narrowed at the distant *kreml* that loomed on a hill above the city. "Word came just this morning that she was abducted from a caravan bringing her to Chernigov. The guards are ordering everyone to watch for any sign of her. Troops have been sent to search every trading camp along the Desna." Lowering his voice, the merchant leaned toward

Rurik. "The prince has offered quite a reward for her safe return . . . one thousand gold grivna! Any chance you've seen a wench with hair the color of a lion's mane, golden skin, and blue-green eyes? At least that's how they described her. Sounds like a real beauty."

Rurik shook his head, hoping he didn't appear stunned. Loki take him. Ilka, his captive concubine, now bound hand and foot with two inches of her braid hacked off . . . Prince Mstislav's daughter?

The trader grunted his disappointment. "Too bad, my friend. Leading Prince Mstislav's men to his daughter Zora could have made you a wealthy man."

Zora?

Rurik's attention was suddenly drawn to a commotion at one end of the market square, the pounding of hooves growing louder. Shoppers, merchants, and guards alike scattered as thirty mounted guards thundered past the stalls, led by a dark-haired warrior whose countenance was as black as the rumbling storm clouds gathering to the west.

"Lord Ivan, the girl's betrothed!" the trader shouted above the din. "It's rumored that he was to marry her shortly after her arrival." The man coughed on the dust billowing around them. "The guards said a search of all ships was to begin at once, Lord Ivan to lead it. I'd hate to be questioned at that one's hands! He's said to be as cruel as he is arrogant, the *kreml* prison filled with wretches he's marked to die."

Rurik didn't need to hear more; a new plan formed. Yet he took a moment, despite the fierce impatience gnawing at his gut, to buy a quill from the trader so as not to arouse suspicion. Then he left the market by a narrow side street, taking a different route than the mounted warriors. One he prayed would lead him faster to the wharf as he cut between frame houses and down winding alleyways.

He had to get Leif and Kjell off the ship before Ivan reached them. He trusted their loyalty, but torture could drive the truth from the strongest warriors and that would surely be their fate if the enraged boyar found their answers suspect.

Somehow Rurik, his men . . . and his lying little princess had to escape from the city while confusion still reigned.

How swiftly her royal blood had changed their circumstances.

CHAPTER 8

As thunder crashed overhead, Rurik burst in the door of the shack.

Arne lurched from the bench. "My lord, you're back sooner than I—"

"Leave everything here, Arne, we've no time to pack!" he shouted, wiping the rain from his face. Soaked to the skin, he left a trail of water as he strode to the bedchamber.

"By Thor, what's happened?"

"I'll explain later. Kjell and Leif are waiting outside with the horses. Now go!"

"Horses? What of the ship?"

Ignoring him, Rurik pushed open the door to the bedchamber to find the room in darkness. Cursing the unlit lamp, he went to the bed and gathered his captive in his arms. Unable to see her face, he felt her slender body tense. She tried to say something to him, but her words were muffled by the gag.

"Easy, wench, it's me," he said to reassure her, although he imagined that she was less than thrilled to find herself in his embrace. Carrying her into the other room, he was glad to see that Arne had already gone outside. He unceremoniously set the woman down, and severed the rope binding her wrists and ankles.

"The arrangements have been made," he lied, sheathing the weapon as she gasped. He swept her again into his arms. "The ransom has been delivered. We're taking you to where your Lord Ivan will find you."

Rurik could feel her staring at him in astonishment, but he did not meet her eyes as he moved to the open doorway. After glancing up and down the deserted alley, he carried her outside into the pouring rain and handed her to Leif, who was waiting beside a restless roan stallion.

"Lift her up," he commanded after mounting, having already instructed his warrior to do so in such a manner that the woman was seated facing him, a leg on each side and her bottom between his thighs. "Wrap your arms and legs around me," he told her gruffly, not surprised when she didn't respond. Meeting her wide confused gaze, he grated, "Do you want to see your Lord Ivan or not?"

Immediately she hugged his torso and her legs wound tightly around his hips, crossing at the ankles. Pushing her head down low against his left shoulder, he signaled to Kjell, who threw him a large sodden blanket with a ragged hole cut from the middle.

Settling it over his head, Rurik was pleased to see that the woman was completely covered beneath the blanket's voluminous folds. Next came a dripping wet fur mantle over his shoulders that when pulled around to the front further hid the woman from view. Nestled as she was so snugly against him, he only hoped that she could breathe.

"Keep very still," he ordered, bracing his upper arms around her. "Whatever you do, don't raise your head. I promise you, wench, if you thwart me now, you will pay!" With that, he kicked his mount and they set off, his men silent and riding close behind him.

They soon reached a gate leading west out of the city, and

Rurik was relieved to see that the driving rain had chased many of the guards indoors, only a half dozen remaining. Still, if something went wrong now, they would have to fight their way out of Chernigov.

"Remember, wench," he warned in a low, harsh voice. "Keep still and silent or you will not see Lord Ivan again."

"Hold!" came a command from the leader of the guards.

Rurik reined in his horse some ten feet from the gate, his men following his example. Slipping the four-day pass from beneath the edge of the saddle, he held it out to the drenched man who squinted to better see him in the stinging rain.

"We've finished our trading," he informed the leader as the pass was snatched from his hand. Suddenly a huge thunderclap rent the air, and Rurik winced inwardly when the woman jerked against him. Quickly twisting in the saddle to camouflage her movement, he gestured with a nod to his three stone-faced men. "You see, we have nothing left and in only one morning at the market. Our furs have been sold."

"Where are you bound?" the leader demanded, eyeing them suspiciously yet stamping his muddy feet as if eager to escape the storm.

"South to Kiev, to fetch more furs. The trading here is the best I've ever seen."

"Move on with you, then, you're blocking the way!" announced the leader, obviously noticing no more than Rurik had wanted him to see . . . four empty-handed, rain-soaked merchants leaving the city. As the man hurried for shelter, he waved for his guards to open the timbered gate.

Sending a fervent prayer of thanks to the new God, whom he called upon in times of greatest need, Rurik urged his mount onward, and riding two abreast, he and his men passed safely from Chernigov.

Outside the gate that slammed shut behind them with a heavy thunk, they set off at a hard gallop to the southwest. The journey ahead was dangerous. Doubtless Mstislav's troops surrounded the outskirts of the city, but if the rain held, they might keep to their tents and not stop them to ask questions.

It was only a thirty-mile ride to Liubech, their true destination: a northern trading town along the Dnieper River that, as far as Rurik knew, still lay in Grand Prince Yaroslav's hands. As soon as they were well out of sight of the city walls they would veer north. Once in Liubech, they would buy a swift riverboat and sail for Novgorod.

He did regret leaving Chernigov before he had gleaned much military information. Yet he believed Yaroslav would be well satisfied with what they had discovered, and now he and his men possessed an even more valuable prize. The grand prince's own niece, Prince Mstislav's daughter . . . Zora.

The usurper had offered one thousand gold grivna for her return, Rurik marveled. An unheard-of sum! She was obviously beloved. Mstislav might be willing to concede much to his elder brother now that Yaroslav held such a beautiful pawn.

The grand prince didn't have her yet, Rurik reminded himself. His captive had grown very still in his arms although her limbs still gripped him. He hoped that she had enough air to breathe beneath the blanket.

"Are you all right, wench?"

Dazedly feeling Rurik shake her, Zora would have screamed if not for the sodden gag in her mouth. Holy Mother of Christ, he had to be a fool not to know that she was close to suffocating beneath these heavy coverings!

Her face burning and her lungs on fire, she felt him shake her again, this time not so gently. His voice held unmistakable concern as she heard the blanket ripping.

"Look at me, wench! Lift your head!"

Realizing that he must have torn a wider hole for her, Zora obliged him and gasped with relief as he yanked the disgusting gag from her mouth. She paid no heed to the cold rain pelting her upturned face or Rurik's anxious expression as she drew in huge lungfuls of fresh air.

"You . . . you lout!" she rasped, glaring up at him. "Are you trying to kill me?" Surprised by his look of amused relief, she wondered if it was possible that he might actually have been worried about her. But she shrugged off the thought, swearing to herself again that when she was safe in Ivan's arms, somehow this accursed Varangian would pay for his foul treatment of her.

"How much farther are we going to ride?" she added hoarsely when Rurik gave her no reply. "I'll be nothing but bruises—"

"Relax," came his mild answer, although his expression had tightened.

"Relax?" she echoed incredulously. "With this constant jarring and jostling?"

Infuriated when he ignored her, Zora thought back to what she had heard before she had grown so dizzy from struggling to breathe . . . something about them traveling to Kiev, and Rurik fetching more furs, then another male voice yelling for them to move on. Strange talk. Yet she supposed it made sense that they might have passed through one of the city's gates. Perhaps that had been part of Rurik's arrangements with Ivan . . . they would journey for a short way beyond the city to gain a head start and then release her.

Her impatience mounting, Zora blinked against the moisture clinging to her lashes.

"Surely we're almost there," she said with exasperation, but she fell silent when a deep frown marred Rurik's all too handsome features. Odd. He should be elated that he had won his ransom, shouldn't he?

"Soon, wench. I told you to relax. Sleep if you can."

Sleep? Was he mad? The last thing she wanted to do was rest at a time like this, when she was so close to freedom. Yet the moments dragged on and Rurik's furious pace never slackened.

Her limbs growing numb, Zora finally released her hold upon him. The warmth of his massive body pressed so intimately to hers combined with the stifling weight of the blanket was making her sweat in a most unladylike fashion. She could feel moisture trickling between her breasts and down her back, and it wasn't rainwater! The downpour had slowed to a drizzle. Yet despite her attempt to shift away from him, he held her tightly against his chest with one powerful arm wrapped around her waist.

"Damn you, you're hurting me!" she cried, twisting futilely. "Why are you squeezing me so? I'm not fool enough to jump off a galloping horse!" When he didn't answer or ease his hold, she peered around her and saw that they were riding through dense woods, the sky still so gray and cloudy that it appeared almost dusk.

"Maybe you think we haven't gone far enough, but I certainly do," she persisted, struggling anew. "What of your arrangements with Lord Ivan? He won't know where to find me in this forest—"

"No arrangements were made," Rurik interrupted, his voice grim.

Zora felt a telling chill. "No arrangements?"

"Your Ivan is probably still searching the ships along the Desna River. When he and his men reach ours, they will find it deserted. And when he discovers his so-called elite guards allowed four unknown men to leave the city, he'll connect the two incidents and hang the witless fools right then. *I* would do so if they were warriors under my banner."

"You . . . you lied to me!" Zora cried, sickened that she could have allowed herself to be tricked by this black-hearted devil. She should have screamed, struggled, fought him, anything to draw attention to herself! Instead she had clung to him as he had commanded, afraid that if she made a move she would never see Ivan again. "I'll see you skewered alive for this treachery! You damned heathen, you lied!"

"As you did to me . . . *Zora*, princess of the Tmutorokan Rus."

She froze, gaping at him. Fear and incredulity quickly quenched her indignation. May God protect her, he knew!

"Why do you call me by that name?" Zora said in a desperate attempt to confuse him. But she knew it was hopeless. He was too perceptive, seemingly able to read her moves before she even made them. "I'm Ilka—"

"Your name is Zora and you are the youngest daughter of Prince Mstislav, the usurper." Rurik's expression was hard as he glanced at her for an instant and then lifted his gaze to the path ahead of them. He kept his voice just loud enough so that she could hear him above the horses' galloping hooves.

"You were abducted from a royal caravan by a slave trader who was tricked into believing you were a concubine, although for what purpose I have yet to discover. News of your disappearance reached Chernigov only this morning and presently hundreds of your father's troops, perhaps thousands, are searching for you under the direction of your betrothed, Lord Ivan. Your father has even announced a reward of one thousand gold grivna for your safe return." He clasped her tighter, his grip punishing. "But they won't find you, Princess. By sunset, we'll be on a ship bearing north."

"North?" she parroted, her mind unwilling to grasp how close she had come to her father, Ivan, and safety only to have their rescue and all hope snatched from her. "What of Kiev?"

"Another lie," he said easily. "We're bound for Novgorod."

Zora tensed. So her captor *was* a damned spy. Why else would he forgo such an exorbitant reward, instead planning to travel almost five hundred miles? No unscrupulous fortune hunter with a whit of sense would pass up such a sum! This Varangian was fueled only by allegiance, and she could well imagine to whom it belonged. Grand Prince Yaroslav, her father's hated brother. Novgorod was his city, and the seat of his power.

With this startling realization came some comfort, and Zora willed herself to relax.

Her captor could no longer hurt her! If anything, he would be obliged to protect her until they reached Novgorod and she came face-to-face with the liege lord who had sent him upon his secretive mission.

"You're a spy, aren't you?" she accused, not surprised when Rurik briefly met her eyes. "For Yaroslav, my uncle."

He did not answer, but she knew from the way he clenched his jaw that she had guessed the truth.

"And I?" she demanded. "What have I become, Lord Rurik?"

"A pawn."

His blunt reply was horribly final, and Zora was seized by sudden desperation. "Please . . ." she begged, though it galled her that she even found it within herself to do so. "Please let me go. What use can I be to Grand Prince Yaroslav? He must know that I am a—"

"Enough!" Rurik cut in harshly. "It is not my authority to release you. The grand prince alone can decide your fate. I only escort you to him."

Zora held her reckless tongue then. She must keep calm; use her head. It was a good thing that he had interrupted her before she had given away her baseborn status. A very good thing.

If she had revealed to him that she was a bastard daughter, Rurik might think her less valuable and decide that he could still take liberties with her. It was possible. He had assaulted her when he thought her a mere concubine, hadn't he? Usually, bastards counted as no more than slaves in Rus, and even though her father had offered an incredible reward for her, Rurik might hold the more common view.

Suddenly an idea came to her, filling her with nervous excitement and almost bringing a smile to her lips.

Why not make this journey as difficult for him as possible? Since he must protect her until they reached Novgorod, he would be loathe to touch her or punish her no matter what she did to frustrate him. And frustrate him she would! This pagan would wish a thousand times that he had left her in Chernigov!

Now Zora did smile. If she escaped somewhere along the route to Novgorod, so much the better. How humiliating it would be for him to return to her uncle's *kreml* with the news that he had captured her, but she had eluded him! If Rurik was a lord indeed, as his title suggested, her escape would discredit him. A proud Varangian warrior bested by a mere woman! He would be dishonored forever.

Zora glanced furtively at Rurik to find that he was paying her no heed, his expression grim and his gaze narrowed as if searching the forest for signs of danger.

Why not begin? It would make a fine test and maybe, if she was lucky, she would bring some of her father's troops down upon them. They might still be close enough to Chernigov that someone might hear her.

Inhaling deeply, Zora let out such a piercing scream that a flock of blackbirds perched high in the branches above them took to the sky, screeching and cawing in protest. Rurik was so startled that she managed to scream once more, this time right in his ear, before he could clap his hand over her mouth.

"By Odin, woman, what are you trying to do?" he shouted, his face flushed dark with anger. Yanking the gag back into her mouth, he called to his warriors. "The wench might have given away our position. Ride hard, men, as if the black hounds of Hel were upon us! They might be now!"

Zora gasped as Rurik jerked her hard against his chest and kicked his mount into a faster canter, his tone menacing as he added, "And if they find us, wench, I swear—"

"I hope they do find us!" she retorted in spite of her gag, and to enrage him further, she started to laugh.

"Minx! Do you think this a game? Thor's blood, royal princess or no, you'll soon discover that you've more than met your match!"

"So will you, you cloddish pagan," Zora replied under her breath, grinning just for his benefit. "So will you."

CHAPTER
9

Her knees clasped to her breasts, Zora glowered at the tent wall.

Were those swine going to bring her something to eat or not? Her stomach was so wretchedly empty that she felt almost sick from hunger. She hadn't tasted food since the few bites she had managed in Chernigov, yet her Norse captors had the gall to be enjoying a meal without her! Outside they were loudly commenting on how delicious everything was while Arne recounted some ribald tale. She was certain his mouth was full as he spoke. The coarse, unmannered slob!

The boat dipping and swaying beneath her like a flimsy piece of flotsam wasn't helping her hollow stomach either. She had never imagined a river could be so rough, but then again, she'd only traveled smaller routes in the past. They were now on the great Dnieper, one of Rus Land's main trade routes. When she had caught a glimpse of the vast river before she had been whisked aboard late yesterday afternoon, appearing as wide as any three she had ever seen, it was still swollen from the spring thaw, the currents fast and dangerous.

Hearty male laughter erupted outside again. Zora frowned. The Varangians certainly seemed relaxed now that they were a night's journey from Liubech.

Before today the mood had been much darker. The tension resulting from her screaming fit in the forest had been palpable enough to cut and had lasted until well after they set sail. Although it had become clear from eavesdropping on Rurik's low-spoken conversation with his men that the small trading town posed no threat, he hadn't said more than a sentence to her.

He had thrust her inside this stuffy, hastily constructed tent and roughly removed her gag with a terse threat that she had better remain quiet or else. She had been tempted to fling at him, "Or else what?" but had reluctantly held her tongue. His scowl had been fearsome. Obviously his anger toward her had not abated.

Eventually she had fallen asleep, so exhausted from their long ride that she couldn't keep her eyes open. At one point in the night she had half awoken to the unsettling sensation of someone watching her, but when she had rolled over to look, she was alone. She hadn't opened her eyes again until a short while ago.

"Shall I take the wench some food, my lord?" came an unknown male voice. *At last someone had thought of her needs!* "She's probably awake by now and I imagine she's hungry," the voice continued.

"You heard my orders, Kjell. If she wants something to eat, she can come out here and fetch it. I don't want to see any of you waiting upon her. She may be Grand Prince Yaroslav's niece, but I'll not have you taking your minds off your duties to coddle some spoiled, overindulged princess."

Spoiled! Zora thought, outraged. *Hardly!* Hermione had always seen that she remembered her place in the *terem* whenever their warrior father wasn't around, which was much of the time. And if she had known she was free to leave the tent without fear of rebuke, she would have done so earlier!

Rising to her feet, Zora quickly smoothed her hair—the shortened length of her braid blatant testimony to Rurik's cruelty—and adjusted her rumpled clothes. Then she swept from the tent to stand blinking at the bright morning sunshine.

"Ah, Princess Zora. So you've decided to join us."

She shielded her eyes to look in the direction of that familiar mocking voice. Its rich, husky quality had strangely stirred her, she realized to her annoyance. Immediately she skipped her gaze from Rurik, whose wry half smile only fanned her resentment, to Arne, who eyed her suspiciously, then she regarded the two Varangians whom she'd barely gotten a close look at yesterday before that smelly blanket had been tossed over her head.

One of the men, his hand upon the helm, was nearly as tall and immense about the shoulders as Rurik, with curly, flame-red hair and beard, while the other was clearly the youngest of the group and very blond, his youthful face sparsely bearded and quite handsome in a boyish sort of way. He gazed upon her almost with awestruck shyness. This surprised her. She had always heard that Varangians were brutal, bloodthirsty warriors, yet this one, although he had the build of a fighter, possessed the expressive eyes of a poet.

"Are you going to stand there gawking or come and eat?"

With a start, Zora met Rurik's gaze and her heart suddenly seemed to beat faster. His eyes were so devastatingly blue, the sunlight glinting off his silver-blond hair as from a mirror, and there was certainly no boyish youthfulness about him. He was all man, dangerous-looking, powerful, from his arresting features to the hard, muscled lines of his body. To think that she had lain in his arms, that he had touched her so intimately—

What in heaven's name are you doing? Zora berated herself, stunned and infuriated by her thoughts. The rogue was her captor! He'd kidnapped her, gagged her, and practically starved her. Doing her best to ignore his disconcerting appraisal, ignoring all of them for that matter, she lifted her chin and went to the bench where the food was laid out.

Entranced by the graceful way she moved, Rurik drank in the sight of her. Despite his determined resolve to consider her only as a pawn, he was relieved she was wearing baggy male garb. If she could look this fetching in ill-fitting rags, he could well imagine how she might appear in a luxurious full-length silk tunic cut to fit her temptress's form.

Apparently Kjell had noticed as well. The warrior was fairly gaping. Rurik threw the younger man a stern warning glance, though he could hardly blame him. Princess Zora seemed fashioned to turn any man's head.

"There's plenty of food so take as much as you want."

Zora merely glared at him.

Undaunted, Rurik added, "I suggest you take an extra portion of boiled beef. You slept through supper last night, so it's cold. But it tastes good, and we won't have fresh meat again for days."

She gave no reply, but quickly filled a wooden platter. Then she turned away, and determinedly kept from looking at them while she proceeded to the prow where she perched upon a water cask with her back to them.

"Uppity little thing." Arne tore off another generous chunk of rye bread. "Why don't you tell her something of yourself, my lord? I don't see any harm in it. Mstislav's troops will never catch us now. You said she already knows you're a spy, and if she knows your high rank as well, maybe she'll feel herself in better company."

"I doubt anything I have to say will appease her," Rurik muttered, ignoring the sidelong glances his men cast each other.

He only hoped he could appease her uncle. He could imagine the heated accusations that would fly when they reached Novgorod and he presented his indignant captive to the grand prince. Yet he doubted Yaroslav would fault his actions. Rurik trusted that the grand prince would understand his motives, which had been fueled by Zora's misrepresented identity. In time of war, such an excuse should suffice, even though Rurik knew it wasn't the entire truth. Lust had played a part as well.

Since leaving Chernigov, the journey had become a Hel for him. He kept recalling the sleek softness of her skin and the firm rounded beauty of her breasts, the seductive way she had parted her lips to him and the sweet, intoxicating taste of her mouth . . . the way she had moaned in ecstasy beneath him. He had been tempted to caress her cheek last night when he had gone to check on her, and only her sudden waking had sent him quickly from the tent.

"Women," Rurik said under his breath, rising.

"Aye, they're the plague of the world," Arne answered with a grunt as Leif and Kjell looked on in silence. "You're going to speak with her, then?"

Nodding, Rurik filled a wooden cup with honey mead. After studying the distant shoreline for a moment and glancing upriver, he ordered his men, "Keep alert for any trouble." Then he walked toward her. If Zora heard him approaching, she gave no hint of it, not even deigning to look in his direction, which irritated him further.

By Thor, he couldn't wait until they arrived in Novgorod, where he could relinquish his charge of her to Grand Prince Yaroslav! Surely having his six beautiful concubines around him again would chase this all too bewitching woman from his mind!

"I brought you something to drink," he said, holding out the brimming cup.

Flustered by how close he was standing, Zora shifted to the very edge of the cask. "What is it?" she asked suspiciously.

"Mead. Have you ever tasted it before? We Varangians highly favor it—"

"I don't want any," she cut him off, although in truth she would have enjoyed the heady drink. But she refused to par-

take of anything this man said he enjoyed. Her eyes returned
to her meal.

Rurik sighed but he didn't leave. To Zora's annoyance, he
sat down on an opposite cask, facing her.

"It's not poisoned, Zora, or drugged, if that's what you're
thinking."

Swallowing a bit of beef and feeling that she was fast losing her appetite, Zora met his gaze. It unnerved her to hear
him utter her name with such intimate familiarity. At least he
could continue to address her properly as "Princess Zora" or
"my lady," but she doubted he would even if she demanded
it.

"What's on my mind is none of your concern—"

"It is my concern," he interrupted stiffly as if bridling his
temper. "You may be my prisoner, Zora, but you don't have
to fear for your life or your person. Contrary to what you
probably believe, my men and I do not prey upon women."

"Oh, no? After what I experienced at your hands, Lord
Rurik, I would have to disagree. If *rape* isn't preying upon
women, then I must be misinformed."

His eyes took on a dark stormy hue as he leaned toward
her. "It was *no* rape, and this is the last time I will tell you!
How can you say that when you have no recollection of what
happened? You weren't yourself, woman! And you were not
unwilling. I believed that you were a boyar's concubine, familiar with the ways of men and women and experienced in
lovemaking," he stressed pointedly. "I took you to my bed
hoping you would call out your master's name in your pleasure, then I could return you to the man—"

"In exchange for military information, am I not right?"
Zora's cheeks were ablaze from even hearing him talk of
bedding her. It did not matter what he said, she would never
believe him. How could she have given him so easily what
she had wanted to preserve until her marriage to Ivan? She
was no wanton!

After a long moment, Rurik finally nodded, his expression
grave. "You are as perceptive as I had thought. Yes, I knew

when I learned of your value from the Slav merchant that my mission could profit from assisting you."

"I could expect no more from my father's enemy," Zora spat.

"Aptly put, Princess. Enemies, with opposing allegiances. Yours rests with your father and mine with Grand Prince Yaroslav. Eight years ago, I pledged my loyalty to him and for my service, he rewarded me with an honored position in his senior *druzhina*. So you see, you're not in the hands of some ruthless mercenary. And although we're enemies, it is my duty to protect you until we reach Novgorod. I'll honor that pledge with my life if need be."

Despair swept Zora. Since Rurik was talking so freely of his power and position, he must feel confident that her father's troops would never rescue her. Clearly she would be on her own and with no hope of aid if the chance to escape ever arose.

"Tell me something, Zora," he said, interrupting her desperate musing.

She stared into his eyes, noticing the crinkles at the corners and the light brown of his lashes for the first time.

"How did you come to be in that trading camp? The slave merchant told me it was because you had fallen into disfavor with your master's wife, but as you're no concubine, that cannot be true."

"My sister sold me into the slaver's hands," she replied tightly. "Hermione."

"Your own sister betrayed you?" Rurik's blond brows knit into a frown. "Why?"

His question shattered the self-pitying reverie that gripped her, and Zora tensed. She couldn't reveal to him the true story behind her abduction! Then he would know she was a bastard daughter and maybe withdraw his promise of protection.

"She hated me," Zora said bluntly, planning to quickly skirt the topic. "She was jealous of me. It's as simple as that."

"Jealousy? Hatred? Those are not simple emotions. There had to be a cause."

"Hermione believed I held more than my share of our father's affection and favor." Growing more agitated, Zora blurted, "I don't want to talk about it anymore!" She raised her chin defiantly. "Now I have a question for you, Lord Rurik. What made you help me in the trading camp? You couldn't have known when Halfdan struck me down that I was worth anything to your mission—"

"You asked me to help you."

Shocked, she stared at him. "That couldn't be true."

"You did," he replied, his voice grown somber. "You were fleeing from Halfdan and you stumbled into me as I walked from a tent. Don't you remember? I caught you from falling, and you begged me to help you. You even promised a reward."

"A reward . . .?" Suddenly Zora did remember him, not so much his face but the vivid blue of his eyes.

"Yes," he continued. "But when you looked up at me, you cried out and pushed yourself away."

"All I saw was another Varangian trader . . . another Halfdan." She shivered. "It was all so horrible . . . his laughter, the stench of him, those awful serpent tattoos . . ."

"It's in the past," came Rurik's firm reply. "As I told you, Halfdan is dead. I only wish I had been the one to kill him."

"You didn't kill Halfdan?" Zora asked, startled. "If not your sword, then whose?"

"Arne's. He saved my life. I underestimated Halfdan's skill and when he caught me under the chin with his knee, I went down." Rurik shook his head, as if still angry at himself that the other Varangian had bested him. "Arne was there, disobeying my orders, and thank Odin he did that day." His expression grew hard as he regarded her, his eyes angry. "If he hadn't, then you would have been justified to cry 'rape,' Princess. Without Arne's help, I would have been dead and you . . ."

Grateful when Rurik didn't finish, Zora could hardly believe everything that he had just told her. She hadn't considered how Halfdan had met his end, yet now that she knew, the facts were astonishing. Rurik had risked his life for her when he hadn't even known who she was. Or that he could profit from rescuing her. Why, he could have been killed! Aiding an unknown slave woman!

Yet she remained wary. Perhaps he had sensed even then that she was more than a common slave. Perhaps something cued him, her manner of speech, her promise of a reward, anything! To think that he might have felt compassion for her was more than she could stomach.

"If you don't mind, Lord Rurik, I would rather not discuss what happened to me at that trading camp anymore," she said. "Now I'd like to finish my meal before the bread becomes stale and the cheese moldier."

Noting the stubborn set of her chin, Rurik knew the matter was already closed.

"Very well, then. I'll leave you." He rose, setting the cup of mead near her bare feet in case she decided to drink after all. He couldn't quite tell her mood, but it was clear she still did not trust him. He felt he should offer a stern warning.

"If you haven't already realized it, screaming is useless. Unlike yesterday when it might have saved you but thankfully didn't. And if you're considering any more escape attempts, Princess, I caution you against late night swimming. You were lucky that night you plunged into the river, but the Dnieper's currents are far more treacherous than the Desna's. And deadly to all but the best of swimmers."

"You're clearly lying again," she retorted. "I would never have jumped from any ship. I can't swim."

Rurik studied her, amazed. She must have been fearful indeed to dive over the side with no skills to help keep her afloat.

"You did jump overboard, Zora, whether you believe it or not. We were on our way to Chernigov, and this time I was the one who saved you . . . from drowning." Rurik smiled, but he felt no amusement. "You see? There is much you don't remember."

She didn't reply, nor had he expected her to. Her tight-lipped, rebellious expression was answer enough. Thor, but she was obstinate! She had obviously decided to reject much of what he said.

"I almost forgot," he continued. "I bought you some things in Liubech before we sailed." He indicated with a quick nod a brass-bound sea chest. "You'll find some clean garments more to your size, trousers, a tunic, and another sash. I want you to dress like a male slave until we reach Novgorod. The last thing we need is for your beauty to attract any undue attention."

In response, she glared at him surlily.

Rurik sighed with exasperation and turned to go, then added as an afterthought, "I also purchased a brush for your hair and some soap in case you'd like to bathe. As you cannot swim, my men will have leave to draw water for you when you have need of it. But ask them for nothing else."

Astonished that he would have given any consideration to her personal needs, Zora watched as Rurik walked back to his men.

Soap? A brush? She toyed with her disheveled braid, then raised her hand to her cheek, wondering if her skin was smudged and dirty. Had he thought her in need of a bath? She supposed she did look a sight after not washing her hair for days, and she had hardly been able to bathe herself properly without soap—

Stop! she scolded herself, angry that she would care even for an instant about her appearance. The last thing she wanted was for that pagan to find her attractive, and if she was freshly bathed, combed, and wearing more fitted clothes . . . for all his pretty words, he might very well forget himself.

Setting her wooden plate with a clatter upon the deck, Zora knew exactly what to do. She went directly to the chest and, throwing open the lid, gathered up all the items Rurik had mentioned.

She knew that he was watching her. She could feel it, like a strange heat upon her skin. And she knew he'd be furious, but she didn't care. Stifling a tiny glimmer of fear and any regrets about how lovely it would have felt to wash with real soap again, she went to the side and tossed everything overboard.

"Woman! By all the gods . . . !"

Ignoring his roar of outrage, Zora retook her seat upon the cask and calmly resumed her meal. So what if she looked like a rumpled, smudge-nosed witch and stank to high heaven? If it would keep Rurik away from her, she could bear it gladly!

CHAPTER
10

An uneasy stalemate reigned aboard the riverboat for the next few days, Zora attempting to avoid Rurik, which proved difficult in such limited space. Yet somehow she managed. She kept to her tent much of the time, and when she could no longer stand the boredom and needed fresh air, she ventured outside and moved to whatever part of the small vessel where Rurik was not.

Thankfully, he seemed just as disinclined to encounter her. Zora wasn't surprised.

He had been beyond anger. Even furious hadn't done his foul mood justice. Although he had said nothing more to her after his initial outburst, she had seen his temper raging in the way he glared at her when she went to get a second helping of food. His eyes were filled with a cold fury.

Abandoning any thought of continuing her meal, she had fled to the solitude of her tent, where she had remained for most of the day. Her frustration had grown hourly.

How she longed to be free of this accursed vessel and her captors! To be so confined, without any real privacy or the amenities to which she was accustomed—a decent chamber pot, for God's sake—was simply too much!

With her humiliation fueling her, she had created a new plan. She would covertly observe the Varangians and hopefully discover each man's weakness. Such knowledge could then be used against them when an opportunity for escape arose.

Yet much to her disappointment, she had found over the following two days that the ruddy-faced helmsman called Leif had no discernible weaknesses. He possessed both brawn and brains, his skill at steering the boat evidencing sharp instincts. He also obeyed unquestionally everything Rurik said, so there was no help there. As for Arne, he was another of whom to be wary. For all of his grumbling and coarse bravado, she sensed that he had a keen mind, his suspicion easily aroused.

Arne's close relationship with Rurik bordered upon that between father and son. If the story about him saving Rurik's life in the trading camp was true, Zora imagined that Arne had made it his task to watch out for Rurik, his loyalty fierce and as unquestioning as Leif's.

Kjell was the only one who didn't seem to fit into the group. Physically a warrior and appearing more than strong enough to do battle, it nonetheless seemed that his heart was not in his duties. Kjell rarely joined in the laughter after one of Arne's vulgar boasts about his exploits with lusty, big-breasted women, or how much ale the crusty Varangian could consume at one sitting. Sometimes Kjell seemed so detached, Zora wondered how he had been included on what she assumed had been a very important mission.

Kjell seemed most enlivened late in the evening when he recited poetry for his compatriots' entertainment. He told strange mythic tales of long ago battles and heroic deeds that Rurik and the others obviously enjoyed. Kjell's impassioned voice would carry to her inside the tent where she lay abed, and to her amazement, Rurik occasionally joined him, reciting verses commemorating a danger or triumph in battle.

Once, Rurik's eight-line stanza had been a lamentation for a slain friend, Sveinald, who had lost his life because of his love for a woman. The haunting words had moved her more than she wished to admit and shown her a heretofore unknown side of him . . . a sensitive, personal side upon which she had no desire to dwell.

But even though Kjell lacked enthusiasm, she had not discovered his weaknesses, at least until the following evening when she spied him staring at her quite openly. His platter of salted fish and black bread sat in his lap, untouched. Rurik's response was swift and harsh.

"Look to your food, man, and quit gaping at the wench like a besotted pup!"

After that, Zora noticed a dark scowl thrown in Kjell's direction whenever Rurik caught him watching her, and she realized that he must resent the young warrior's obvious infatuation. Was it simply because Kjell seemed more inclined to staring at her then going about his duties? Such disregard for orders would certainly anger any commander. Or did Rurik's reaction have something to do with his promise to protect her? Did he think Kjell might overstep his bounds?

Well, whatever the insufferable lout's reasons, Zora had found her chance. She even went as far as to hope that any discord she fomented between the two men might somehow aid her escape. She couldn't wait to put her latest scheme to the test!

The next morning dawned beautiful and sunny, which lightened her mood all the more. Taking care to avoid Rurik, whom she spared no more than a casual glance when she left the tent, she gave Kjell a surreptitious smile. To her delight, he beamed back at her. He must be attracted to her, she realized. She tried to quell a flash of guilt over using the young man. After all, *she* was a prisoner. Exchanging such smiles the rest of the day convinced her to step up her plan. It would mean forgoing her vow not to wash, but the more appealing the young Varangian found her, the better.

With supper finished, she fetched the bucket that Rurik

had given her to use for bathing—one that had remained
empty since she'd thrown the soap overboard four days
ago!—and humming to herself, she made straight for Kjell,
who stood in the bow with his back to her. He seemed so rapt
in watching the glorious sunset that she doubted he had even
heard her approach.

"Excuse me."

Kjell spun in surprise, almost dropping his mug of ale.
Some of the dark, pungent-smelling liquid splashed upon
her trousers and his expression became stricken, his youthful
face burning.

"Forgive me, my lady!"

"It's nothing," she said lightly, acutely aware that Leif,
Arne, and Rurik had grown silent in the stern, no doubt listening to their exchange. She could almost feel Rurik's gaze
boring into her back, and it made her smile at Kjell all the
wider. "Lord Rurik said that I might ask you for assistance if
I needed some water drawn from the river. Could you help
me?"

"Of—of course." For a moment Kjell didn't seem to
know what to do with his ale, but finally he set the mug upon
a nearby chest and took the bucket from her. "How much
would you like?"

"Oh, you can fill it to the top. I want to have enough to
wash my clothes when I'm finished bathing." As she looked
up at him through her thick lashes, Zora ran the back of her
hand across her cheek, all the while thinking how strange it
felt to be flirting with a man, well, toying with him really. It
felt awkward. She had never done it before. She sighed
plaintively. "I must look disgraceful—"

"Oh, no, my lady, you look beautiful to me! Like a golden
goddess!" Kjell blurted, then he glanced nervously above
her head to the stern. What he saw must have made him
more anxious, for his eager-to-please smile vanished. He
quickly dunked the bucket into the river and then set it with a
dull thud at her feet.

Zora gazed at him with feigned confusion. "Surely you

don't expect me to carry that bucket, Kjell. It looks far too heavy." From his astonished expression, she knew that she had startled him by using his given name. Yet he was pleased, too, despite his concerted attempt not to show it. His hazel eyes gave him away. "I'm sure Lord Rurik wouldn't mind if you helped me." She smiled at him prettily. "Just to the tent."

Again he looked past her, and she surmised that he had been granted some sort of permission for he obliged her, even going so far as to place the bucket just inside the tent. Then he was gone before she could thank him, almost tripping on a pile of rope in his haste to attend to some rigging. Zora could well imagine the black scowl Rurik had hurled at Kjell.

"The filthy idol-worshiper," she muttered as she swept into the tent. She hoped it was loud enough for Rurik to hear.

It was, but he made no reply, his jaw clenched tightly.

Arne, meanwhile, shifted on the bench, his prolonged belch breaking the tense silence. "It seems she thinks you're a pagan, my lord. Are you going to set her to rights?"

Rurik shook his head grimly, wondering what little game Zora was playing now. After looking like a bedraggled ragamuffin for days, why the sudden concern for her appearance? He imagined it was for spite. "She'll get no more explanations from me, my friend. I tried once already."

"Aye, you're right about that," Arne said dryly. "Whatever you said to her, she didn't like it, no, not a bit. I can still see her dumping all those things into the river—"

"Enough, Arne." Rurik's frown deepened. "I was a fool to think she'd appreciate a kindness."

The burly warrior heaved a sigh, then after taking a deep swig of ale, he said, "That wench is a hard one to understand and I pity the man who ever accepts the thankless task! One moment she avoids the whole lot of us, then the next she's talking as sweetly as can be to Kjell, and smiling at him, too."

"You don't have to tell me what she's been doing," Rurik

muttered, angered as much by her overtly flirtatious behavior as at himself for the unreasoning jealousy that was churning inside him again.

Why in Odin's name couldn't he control his emotions? What did he care if Zora found another man to her liking? He had seen the stolen smiles and furtive looks passing all day between her and Kjell. Well, what of it? She meant nothing to him, other than as a valuable pawn, and Kjell was only reacting naturally to a beautiful woman's attention. What man wouldn't?

The cunning vixen! It couldn't be purely attraction that was making Zora act this way. She hadn't paid Kjell any special notice until this morning. She was scheming, that much was plain. But if she was thinking she could pit him and Kjell against each other, or somehow influence the young man to do something rash, she was mistaken.

Kjell might be an unseasoned fighter, but he was no fool. He had sworn allegiance to Rurik for the journey, an inviolable oath that was sacred among Varangians. To break it would bring grave dishonor upon himself and his father's house. He might as well plunge his own sword into his breast, for to his own kind, he would be a man as if dead.

"Kjell!" His shout startled the warrior.

"My lord?"

Rurik lowered his voice, for he didn't want Zora to hear him. "I've noticed lately that you've been paying far too much attention to our prisoner. What say you to this charge?"

Kjell swallowed hard, but he looked Rurik squarely in the eyes, which secretly amazed him. It seemed their reticent poet was finally becoming a man.

"Only that you are too harsh with her, my lord."

"Too harsh?" Rurik quelled his sudden irritation at this unexpected criticism as best he could. "I say you are proving too gullible. Do you truly believe she favors you? She is using you to irritate me, Kjell, to spite me."

"How could she possibly irritate you, my lord?" There

was an undeniable spark of challenge in Kjell's eyes. "Unless there is a chance you might care if she smiles at me or not. If so, perhaps you would rather she share her smiles only with you."

Rurik lunged to his feet so abruptly that the young man, despite his height and warrior's build, stepped back in surprise.

"What are you saying?" he demanded, his voice low and threatening. "Speak up now for after this, you will hold your reckless tongue until we reach Novgorod."

"I'm saying that it's clear you have an eye for the princess yourself," Kjell said, moving so close that they were standing within inches of each other. "Why else would you glare at me every time you catch me looking at her? Perhaps since you already took her to your bed, you feel you've made some claim—"

"By Thor, what madness is this?" Arne interrupted with a bellow, hauling his bulk from the bench to push his way between them while Leif looked on, his mouth agape. "You're growling at each other like two mongrels who've stumbled upon a bitch in heat . . . arguing about the wench as if it made a damned bit of difference!"

"It does when one of my own men denounces me with such a charge." Rurik was so enraged that he could feel the blood pounding in the vein at his temple.

"No, it doesn't, I tell you!" Arne insisted. "Must I remind you that this woman is a royal captive, not some war booty to be fought over? Grand Prince Yaroslav will most likely lock her in some chamber until he wins whatever ransom he asks and then he'll send her back to her father. So what if she smiles at you"—he frowned at Kjell, then fixed a cautioning gaze upon Rurik—"or at you, my lord? Within another week's time, she'll no longer be any of our concern!"

When neither replied and still stood rigidly opposite him, Arne snorted in disgust and hurled a muttered curse at the tent.

"Do not forget that the beauteous Princess Zora is sworn

to another man, Lord Ivan of Tmutorokan, her dreams each night no doubt full of him. If she smiles, surely it is only to deceive. Do not allow yourselves to be fooled." Arne turned to Kjell, his voice filled with somber warning. "Go back to your work, youngest son of Thordar. You've tread in dangerous waters this night. If you value your oath and your life, think well before you seek again to challenge your lord."

As Kjell stalked away without a word, Arne met Rurik's furious gaze.

"Grant him this one error of judgment, my lord, if only for your friend his father's sake. You know that Kjell's sword would be no match for yours, like a cub attacking a rabid bear. If blame should fall upon anyone's head for this night's devilry, condemn the wench. Her false smiles have bewitched him. But I vow, if Kjell defies you again, I will not come between you."

Rurik made to answer, but his words jammed in his throat as Zora suddenly emerged from the tent wrapped in nothing more than a blanket, her long wet hair swept back from her forehead and her dripping clothes slung over one arm. Arching a fine tawny brow at him, her expression smug, he knew then that she must have heard enough to believe that her devious scheme had triumphed.

"I thought I would hang my clothes on the railing," Zora said, actually astonished and a little nervous that things had so quickly reached this stage. She had hardly done more than smile at Kjell, but already he and Rurik were at each other's throat. "They should be dry by morn—"

"Get back in the tent."

Zora shivered, and it wasn't because the early evening air was chill. Rurik's tone was ice-cold and furious.

"But, Lord Rurik, it will only take me a moment—"

"Damn your clothes, woman! You can wear them wet for all I care. Turn around and get back in the tent or I'll . . ."

She retreated into the tent before he finished, her hands shaking as she dropped her sodden clothes at the foot of the fur pallet. Then she took refuge near the back tent wall, almost tripping over the water bucket in her haste to get as far away from the entrance as possible. Her heart pounding in her ears like a battle drum, she jumped when the oil lamp near her feet sputtered and hissed.

Holy Mother Mary, perhaps she had played her part too well . . .

Zora gasped as Rurik suddenly ducked inside the tent and straightened to his full height, his blond head touching the canvas ceiling. He had never entered her sanctuary before, and she was amazed at how small the space suddenly appeared. He was so massive, so broad, that his body blocked out all view of the entrance, making her feel as if there were no escape. From the dangerous look in his eyes, the strong lines of his face set as in stone in the flickering light, she imagined he would prevent her from leaving at all cost.

"What is your scheme, Zora?" The terse question was spoken in such a low voice, it was almost a whisper.

She clutched the blanket more tightly to her breasts. "I—I don't know what you're talking about."

"Then let me help you," he said, advancing toward her.

As the distance between them narrowed, Zora's heart beat all the harder and she tried to take a step backward, but she was pinned in place. Already she was standing flush against the tent. She could only stare at him, his angry eyes searing into hers.

"Your little displays of defiance are annoying, though understandable, but this time you've gone too far. You are deliberately trying to turn my men against me, and I tell you now, Princess, that I will not tolerate it."

"If . . . if you mean Kjell, I only asked him to fill the water bucket and then carry it for me," she said desperately. Rurik was standing so close to her now that she had to tilt her head to look up at him, his scent of wind and sun and sweat disconcerting her all the more. "You said yourself that I could do that!"

"I haven't forgotten." Suddenly Rurik reached out and caught her by the upper arms, his touch like a grasp of iron.

"But what of all those smiles, Zora, and those teasing glances of yours? Do you think I hadn't noticed? It seems you are quite adept at playing the wanton, but I should have known that from the kisses we shared."

"Kisses?" she rasped as he pulled her closer, so roughly that she lost her hold upon the blanket. To her horror, the covering slid from her body to the floor, leaving her standing naked within his arms. "Let me go!" she demanded, panicking. "I remember no kisses!"

"I do," Rurik said huskily. Splaying one large hand over the small of her back, his fingers caressing her bottom, he drew her so close that her breasts swelled against his chest. "Warm, eager kisses that fooled me into thinking you were well accustomed to a man's touch. I remember how you parted your soft lips for me, Zora, and how your tongue swirled around mine—"

"I would never have done that! I'm no wanton!" she cried, trying to twist free and realizing all too quickly that it was hopeless. Her skin puckered into goose bumps as his hand slid slowly up her back, a strange unsettling warmth radiating from some deep, mysterious place inside her to the ends of her toes and the tips of her fingers. Her hardened nipples were rigid pinpoints of sensation, his rough woolen tunic chafing her. Every time she moved against him, she felt a catch in her throat. To her dismay, she realized she was trembling.

"See how your body betrays you, Princess?" he taunted. "You don't have to be a wanton to possess the passion of one. But why try to convince you of this with words when actions speak so much more clearly?"

Zora gasped aloud as his mouth came down hard upon hers. She was so shocked that she tensed from head to toe.

Her worst fears were coming true! Rurik's promises of protection were meaningless! But this thought quickly left her. The warm, demanding pressure of his lips overwhelmed her, like molten heat filling her completely, and when his tongue swept into her mouth, sweet with the taste of honey mead, she felt that she was melting against him.

Sweet Jesus, she remembered this! Suddenly she recalled hungry kisses devouring her . . . the hard, powerful weight of flesh, bone, and muscle covering her body . . . wild, urgent embraces, panting breaths and sighing moans . . . then the sweetest, most agonized ecstasy she had ever known . . .

Her arms snaked around his neck when his kiss grew dizzyingly possessive, her tongue as with a will of its own mating with his, playing and teasing. She felt his hand cradle her breast, his callused palm rubbing slowly against her nipple, and a strange giddiness swelled deep in her belly. She pressed closer, her senses craving more of him . . . She felt drunk from the intoxicating taste of him, light-headed from his touch, the world spinning around her—

"You see, Zora?" came Rurik's ragged whisper against her wet parted lips, his words shattering her passionate vision. "You're a true wanton at heart. I wasn't lying when I said you came to me willingly that night, and by Odin, if I had not vowed to protect you, I would take you again now and you would submit to me just as eagerly."

He released her so abruptly that Zora had no time to regain her balance and she fell backward, slumping to her knees. She was so stunned that for a moment she could not find the words to speak, nor did she think to hide her nakedness.

"Allow me to recall the words for you . . . how does *heathen* sound?" he mocked her, his breathing hard. "Filthy pagan? Idol-worshiper? Barbarian?"

Suddenly Rurik went down on one knee in front of her, gripping her chin so tightly that she winced. "You'll have far worse things to say about me, Princess, if you ever cause turmoil between myself and my men again. That I swear! And don't think your uncle would fault me. My mission is of utmost importance to him, and he would not be pleased to know how you had attempted to thwart it."

Rurik was gone from the tent before she found her voice,

his dark threat ringing in her ears. If she had ever come close to hating a man, it was now . . . not only for what he had just promised, but for the bewildering spell that still lingered within her.

Her lips felt bruised from his kiss, yet still she yearned for the hard pressure of his mouth against hers. She had barely caught her breath, yet she longed to feel again his powerful arms around her, crushing her to his chest, and the wondrous heat of his body scorching her bare flesh through his clothes. Was it possible she might have submitted to him if he hadn't stopped when he did? Considering how strange she felt right now, she feared, incredibly, that it was so. Yet how could that be? Her father's enemy, *her* enemy?

Inhaling deeply to clear her head, Zora wiped her mouth with the back of her hand.

Although she wanted to believe otherwise, she knew now in her heart that he had never abused her. Her hazy, provocative memories evidenced no struggle, only passionate surrender. Yet she would never admit it. Never! She would fight these impossible feelings as surely as she would continue to fight him. Let him wield his threats! Give her time, she would best him. One day he would wish that he had never seen her face.

"And that, *I* swear, Lord Rurik of Novgorod!" Zora vowed fiercely, even as her skin still burned from his touch. She rubbed her arms where he had grabbed her, but the unsettling feeling would not disappear.

"I take it the wench will no longer trouble us?"

Standing in the prow, Rurik did not turn his head at Arne's approach. He continued to stare into the deepening dusk. "Not if she's wise."

Arne left him then, clearly sensing Rurik's mood. His heart was still pounding so hard that it threatened to drown out the sounds of the night coming alive around him, every thunderous beat driving home a realization that made him all the more impatient to be rid of his rebellious captive.

Kjell had been right about Zora, and if there hadn't been truth in his bold accusation, Rurik doubted that he would have become so angry. Yet it was much more serious than that.

He didn't just have an eye for her . . . he was becoming consumed by her. Clenching his fists, he wondered how long it would take him before he would stop shaking.

CHAPTER
11

Shortly past noon the following day they reached Smolensk, a fair-sized trading town, but Rurik gave no orders to stop. They continued on for another few hours, abandoning the Dnieper to veer north along a smaller water route, and only then did he command his men to lower the sail.

"You will stay on board." Rurik's gruff command was the first words he had spoken to her since the previous evening.

"And if I don't?" Zora glared at him as he turned his attention back to his men, dismissing her. "Maybe I, too, would enjoy a chance to walk on dry land again."

"Don't try me, Princess," Rurik muttered as he moved away.

This new threat echoing dangerously the one he had hurled at her yesterday, Zora knew that she would be a fool to press him further. The last thing she wanted was to encourage another incident like the one in the tent. The very last thing.

After the boat was rowed to the shoreline, she watched disgruntled from her perch on the prow as Rurik and his men jumped overboard. Yet her annoyance became amazement as the thirty-foot vessel was hoisted bodily onto log rollers with much grunting and cursing—Kjell and Arne heaving near the front while Rurik and Leif pushed from the stern—and propelled along the short portage trail until they came to another narrow river.

Marveling grudgingly that the combined strength of her four captors accomplished such a massive task, Zora wondered if they might make camp for the night before moving on. Her mouth watered at the thought of freshly cooked meat. And such a stay might afford her an opportunity to elude them.

But when the boat was shoved without delay back into the water, she was keenly disappointed. From Rurik's determined expression as he hauled himself over the railing it was clear he aimed to press onward to Novgorod. No doubt he wished to deliver her as quickly as possible to her uncle.

Her time to escape was ebbing away.

Kjell seemed distant, rarely affording her even a sideways glance. He must have taken Arne's grim warning to heart, and perhaps feared that Rurik might very well raise his sword against him if he took her part again.

In fact, no one seemed to pay her much heed, especially Rurik, although despite his obvious efforts to avoid her, she was convinced from the tense set of his shoulders that he was acutely aware of her presence. He avoided her gaze, too. But whenever their eyes did chance to meet, she never failed to shiver at the forbidding coldness in those vivid blue depths.

He hated her, she was sure of it, which was no less than she felt about him. And when she overheard him talking to Arne that evening about a second portage within another three days journey, she knew it might be her last chance to win her freedom before they reached Novgorod.

She began to make preparations, what few she could. First tearing a strip from her blanket and fashioning a pouch for provisions. Then she started to take all her meals in the tent, eating only a meager third of her dried, salted fish and by now stale bread and stashing the rest.

She would need food once she escaped, enough to last her until she reached the nearest town where she planned to seek refuge at the parish church. Surely the presiding priest would help her return to her father. Tmutorokan was the leading see of the Orthodox faith in Rus, the site of some of the earliest conversions from paganism to Christianity, and Mstislav's lavish support of the Church was well known among the clergy. She could always argue that for the priest to refuse her aid could bring censure upon him from the patriarch of Constantinople, a threat only a fool would take lightly. So she watched and planned.

When they finally reached the portage by midafternoon three days later, her pouch was full. Again, Rurik wasted no time in ordering his men over the side. Zora was ready, too. When he commanded tersely that she remain aboard, she retreated to the stern and sat obediently upon a rowing bench, in false meekness. Inside she was a raw bundle of nerves, her heart hammering.

Be still and be wary! she chided herself, clasping her hands tightly to contain her nervousness. *Watch for the right moment and then seize it!*

She averted her gaze as Rurik stripped down to his trousers, focusing instead on the chirping birds fluttering in and out of the dense trees flanking the portage. But Rurik's bare chest was so bronzed and massive that she couldn't help peeking at him out of the corner of her eye.

It was a good thing she was soon to escape, considering how attractive she found him. Then, she remembered all too well the pressure of those powerful arms wrapped around her, the sleekness of his skin over hard muscle. She frowned, growing angry with herself.

"Excuse me if I've offended your sense of modesty, Princess, but the afternoon sun is warm," he said sarcastically.

Zora swallowed the tart response that flew to her lips. In a

concerted effort to appear as amenable as possible, she offered him a smile.

"It is your ship, Lord Rurik. I would suppose that you can
do whatever you like upon it."

Studying her for what seemed an interminable instant, his
eyes alight with suspicion, he finally muttered, "So I can."
Then he swung his legs over the railing and joined his men
in the shallow water.

Zora exhaled in relief. She was finally alone! She waited
until Rurik and his men were absorbed in pushing the vessel
from the river and lifting it onto the log rollers before she
hurried into the tent and grabbed the pouch, stuffing it down
the front of her tunic. The dried fish was pungent and she
wrinkled her nose in disgust. She hoped that she reached the
church quickly. Surely the priest would feed her well.

Hastening back outside, she was about to retake her seat
when the boat suddenly tilted dangerously to one side. She
barely caught the railing in time to prevent herself from falling. Rurik's sharp commands filled the air, and as Leif
rushed around to help right the vessel, leaving only Kjell on
the starboard side near the bow, Zora knew instinctively she
had found her chance. The boat was barely level before she
had clambered over the side, her feet landing upon a huge
log.

"My lady, what are you doing?" came Kjell's astonished
voice.

Her heart racing, Zora ignored him. She jumped to the
ground and ran for the trees. It seemed that within seconds
she had reached their safety, but she plunged on, prickly
brambles scratching at her, the thick forest before her nearly
as dark as twilight.

The brittle sound of branches snapping caused Zora to
gasp in fright. Someone was crashing through the woods behind her. Oh, God, Rurik? She began to run faster, her panting breaths tearing at her throat and her legs pumping
furiously as she dashed through the trees.

"Princess Zora, stop! It's not safe out here!"

Relief flooded her that it was only Kjell, but she knew that Rurik might be close behind him and she ran all the harder.

"My father has great influence at Yaroslav's court, my lady! You don't have to run away. Come back and I promise that he will help—"

Kjell's words ended so abruptly that she imagined from his sharp inhalation of breath and the dull thud that followed that he must have tripped and fallen. She even dared to believe when she heard no more heavy footfalls behind her that no one else was even near to catching her. As she came to a small clearing, she paused for the barest instant to catch her breath and she shot a glance over her shoulder.

What she saw made her heart lurch. Kjell was lying facedown upon the ground some thirty feet away, a bearded, disheveled man leaning over him. She almost retched when the stranger yanked a bloodied axe from the middle of Kjell's back, then he straightened and grinned at her.

"'Tis a good thing you ran into the forest when you did, Princess," he called out in a strange, guttural voice. "If you'd stayed with the ship a second longer, you would have been attacked along with the rest."

Rurik and his warriors . . . under attack? Was that why he hadn't come running after her with Kjell? It was then that Zora heard the distant sounds of shouting and the ominous ring of metal against metal echoing through the trees. Her gaze, widening in horror, moved from the stranger's face to the dripping weapon in his hand.

Holy Mother of Christ, what sort of men attacked passing ships without first determining if they were friend or foe? Could it be that they held no allegiance but to themselves . . . cared about nothing but their own gain as any ruthless marauders might . . . ?

Zora thought no more, realizing with chilling clarity that she, too, was in grave danger. She spun, only to come face-to-face with four more bedraggled men who had sneaked up behind her. Before she could flee, the closest one grabbed her cruelly by the shoulder and twisted her around in such a way that her back came up hard against his stomach, a knife suddenly at her throat.

"My lady, is it? Princess?" he said in her ear, his breath smelling of rotten eggs. "You'll have to tell us more about yourself, wench. If it's true what the Varangian called out to you before Yurik caught him with his blade, we'll have nabbed a lot more for this day's work than any gold we find on the ship."

"Aye, but what I want to know right now," piped up one of the others, "is why she stinks of fish?"

"It's my provisions! I—I stuffed them down my tunic." Her legs weak with fear, Zora tensed when the man holding her began to grope at her chest. "I was running away!" she added hoarsely. "I—I'm a princess, just as you say . . . Zora of Tmutorokan. The Varangians were taking me against my will to Grand Prince Yaroslav's court in Novgorod. My father is Mstislav, his brother—"

"Silence, woman! Your bawling is making my head ache!" As her captor held the cold edge of the knife more firmly to her throat, he grabbed the collar of her tunic and ripped downward, her pouch tumbling to the ground. "Aye, that's what reeks," he announced. His large, dirty hand slid over the sash binding her breasts. "I'd wager the wench is as sweet-tasting as she looks."

"No!" Zora cried as the sash was torn from her body, baring her breasts to their hungry eyes. She crossed her arms protectively in front of her. "Please, I told you I was a princess. My father has offered a thousand gold grivna for my safe return!"

"There'll be plenty of time to talk of rewards later," growled her captor. His palm was as rough as pine bark as he stroked her, his foul breath hot upon her neck. "After the rest of the band has had a chance to try you. Don't you agree, Yurik?"

"Aye, indeed." The man who had murdered Kjell gazed over her greedily. He wiped his bloodstained axe across his tunic, an evil grin stretching his face. "Why don't we have some fun now, before the others see what we've found? They're busy stripping the ship and those dead Varangians anyway. Aye, let's have her got down on her knees . . ."

Horrified tears sprang to Zora's eyes. She was pushed down to kneel upon the hard ground, the blade still pressed to her throat. She gazed up in shock when the man called Yurik stepped in front of her. He dropped his broadaxe to the grass and began to work at his trousers.

"That's right, swine! Pull out your puny flesh for all of us to see," came a grim voice from the trees. "Then kiss it farewell."

Cursing, Yurik wheeled around at the same moment a spear sailed through the air with deadly force, striking the man holding Zora right through the neck. He teetered lifelessly, blood spurting in a scarlet arc from the wound while his knife fell to the ground. Zora sank back on her heels, so stunned that she couldn't move even when the dead man toppled like a felled tree behind her.

Her eyes were fixed upon Rurik as he stepped into the sunny clearing, his powerful body drenched with sweat and spattered with the lifeblood of his enemies, his stained sword, Branch-of-Odin, in his right hand. His face was hard, harder than she had ever seen it, and when his bone-chilling battle cry shattered the silence and he rushed at his dumbstruck opponents, she knew that she had never witnessed a more terrifying sight. He was no longer a man but a warrior, brutal, invincible. It made her tremble just to look upon him.

Yurik was the second to die, his axe no sooner in his hand than Rurik's sword severed his fighting arm from his body. His piercing screams reverberated around the clearing, and sent two of his comrades to flight. The one who remained stood rooted in terror. He fought for no more than a moment before he, too, met his end, his entrails gushing forth pink and glistening from a hacking blow to his stomach.

Zora bent over and retched then, nearly choking on bile.

Yet her violent heaving was not enough to drown out the horrible screams of one of her captors who had tripped in his haste to escape only to find Rurik bearing down upon him.

"Stand up and die like a man!" Rurik's harsh command was an ominous death knell for his by now incoherently babbling opponent.

An eerie silence fell over the clearing, and Zora didn't need to look to know that the man had been slain. Sickened, numb, and shaking uncontrollably, she clutched her torn tunic to her breasts and waited for Rurik's terrible wrath to next fall upon her.

It never came. She glanced up to discover that he was leaving the clearing, and without affording her even a backward glance.

"What—what if there are more of them?" she cried in disbelief, looking around her fearfully and growing queasy again at the bloody carnage surrounding her.

Rurik stopped, his chest heaving painfully from exertion, and met her eyes, his blinding battle rage having subsided enough for him to answer through clenched teeth. "The last man fled. He will not return."

Indeed, if he believed she was still in danger he would never leave her side, but he suspected that the last robber was a coward and would run until exhaustion felled him. Fighting his overwhelming urge to go to Zora and gather her in his arms, Rurik stood his ground and forced his voice to remain hard.

"But I warn you, Princess, you will find other wandering marauders along your way if you persist in your preposterous plan to escape, and then I won't be there to help you." Staring at her tear-stained face, he threw out his next words like a challenge. "Decide now what you will do. Either come with me to Novgorod or take your chances on foot."

"You . . . you are offering me a choice?"

No, Rurik thought, seeing the amazement in her eyes, *but let her think so*. If she came with him willingly, fearing for her welfare if she did not, then the remainder of their journey might be peaceful.

He couldn't afford to keep chasing her down; he had only two men left now, and Leif had suffered a wound across the shoulder. If she decided against him, he would keep her tied up until he dumped her in front of Grand Prince Yaroslav. Either way, he would win.

"You heard me, Zora. Decide!"

Sensing her uncertainty, Rurik wondered if he might very well have a trussed up, indignant, and acid-tongued princess on his hands for the remainder of the journey. But then he saw her delicate shoulders droop in resignation.

As she rose shakily, he stifled again his desire to crush her in his embrace, and disgusted by his waning self-control, he set out through the woods.

"Aren't you even going to hear my answer?"

"I have other things to do," he said grimly, thinking ahead to Kjell's burial. Finding that the fallen warrior's body was gone, he surmised that Arne must have already carried him to the ship. Anger and regret surged within him again. Kjell had been struck from behind, dying without a sword in his hand; it was the worst fear of every Varangian, Christian or not.

Thor's blood, he should never have agreed to allow the untested boy on this mission! He had known from the start that Kjell lacked the true instincts of a fighter. His weapon was still in his scabbard when Rurik had found him. His sensitive poet's nature had killed him.

The besotted fool might still be alive if Zora hadn't so wantonly misled him, Rurik thought, his resentment flaring. But now was not the time to rail at her for that, not when she was hurrying to catch up with him, branches snapping beneath her feet. When they passed the place where the young warrior had fallen, Rurik saw the black earth stained dark with blood. He heard Zora gasp softly.

"Where is Kjell?"

Her eyes were shining with fresh tears as Rurik turned to look at her.

"So you know that he was killed?"

She nodded, her delicate hand pressed to her lips.

"Arne has taken him back to the ship."

She said nothing for a long moment. Then she whispered brokenly, "I'm . . . I'm sorry, Lord Rurik."

Startled by her apology and touched by its heartfelt sincerity, Rurik nonetheless swallowed the catch in his throat.

"Sorry? Don't tell me that you're admitting you caused this misfortune."

She tilted her chin in defiance. "I'm sorry for what happened to Kjell . . . not for trying to escape."

By Odin, she could rile him like no other! Rurik thought. "The two events were intertwined, Princess. If Kjell hadn't run after you, he would have had the ship to protect his back during the attack. I suggest you save your apologies for his father, Thordar the Strong, another member of the grand prince's senior *druzhina*."

This news came like a double blow. Zora wished desperately that she could turn back time and she hadn't tried to escape, for perhaps this man could somehow have helped her as Kjell had claimed right before he was struck down. If only he had told her sooner! But now there seemed to be nothing she could do but face the wrath of Kjell's father as she must soon face her uncle.

Using her palm to smudge away the last remnants of her tears, Zora glared resentfully at Rurik. "Never fear, great lord, you'll hear no more apologies from me," she said as she brushed past him. "And you can be sure I'll hold on to my thanks for saving me from those men as well! I doubt you'd think it sincere anyway, so why waste my breath?"

Rurik's gaze followed Zora's shapely form as she wended her way through the trees. She seemed not to care if he was coming after her or not. Silently he cursed the strange hold she seemed to have upon him, a hold that was gaining strength despite his every effort to shatter its grip. Yet thankfully it seemed tempered in light of his renewed irritation.

Lengthening his strides to catch up with her, he hoped that she did spite him all the way to Novgorod. As long as he was angry with her, these unwanted feelings could be kept at bay. And if her antics weren't enough, he had only to think of Kjell and her womanly deceit.

CHAPTER
12

Half out of breath, Zora attempted in vain to yank her arm away from Rurik. She was humiliated that he was practically dragging her across the paved courtyard leading to Grand Prince Yaroslav's palace. As they left the imposing timbered gatehouse behind them, she could feel the Varangian warriors who stood sentinel around the fortified compound eyeing her curiously.

"You could have at least allowed me to change into proper clothes first, brush out this braid, wash my face, something!" she gasped out, struggling to keep up with him.

"There wasn't time." Rurik gripped her elbow more tightly. "By now your uncle has received news of my return from the guards who met the ship. He is expecting us . . . that is, expecting me. You, Princess, will be a surprise."

A surprise for you, too, Lord High-and-Mighty, Zora fumed, wondering what Rurik would think when he discovered he had escorted a mere bastard daughter almost the length of Rus.

"Can't we slow down just a bit?" She shot him an angry sidelong glance. "You'd think we were running a race—"

"I caution you to curb your temper," Rurik said, maintaining his pace. By Thor, he would carry her kicking and screaming into Yaroslav's hall if need be, he was so anxious to be rid of her! "You're a prisoner, remember? Despite your blood relation to the grand prince, he will not appreciate your insolence. He can be very quick to anger."

"I could care a whit about what my uncle thinks," came her blatantly defiant reply. "Or you, for that matter! You can save your advice."

Frowning, Rurik was tempted to throw her over his shoulder and give her bottom a good whack, if only to teach her a lesson, but he decided not to let her goad him, which she seemed bent upon doing. Her truculent behavior was certainly a change from the uneasy calm of the last few days, but he couldn't say that he had missed it.

"Suit yourself, Princess, but don't say that you weren't forewarned."

"That's it? No threat?" Gaining courage from his surprisingly cool response, Zora wished she had more time to tell him exactly what she thought of him and the past two weeks of enduring his company, but they had reached the entrance to the massive stone palace. The fierce-looking guards bowed their heads respectfully and stepped aside so that she and Rurik might pass through the heavy double doors.

Her ruthless captor scarcely deserved such homage, Zora fumed. But she was soon distracted by her surroundings. She could tell at once that her father's palace, although sumptuous, was not nearly so large as this one.

Many polished weapons hung from the high, three-story walls, their brilliant pattern broken at intervals by colorful tapestries depicting hunting expeditions and victorious battle scenes. Tall, thick candles lit the cavernous space for there were no windows, while at the far end of the hall, logs the height of small trees burned brightly in an immense fireplace. Although it had been sunny and warm outdoors, spring fading into more summerlike weather, the air inside was chill.

Besides the guards standing at silent attention throughout the room, there was a group of men engaged in discourse near the roaring fire. Zora recognized her uncle at once among the somber quartet whom she imagined must be some of his advisers.

Dark of hair and barrel-chested, with large eyes and a ruddy complexion, Yaroslav resembled her father in all ways save for his height. The grand prince was a short man, standing perhaps a few inches higher than herself. Unkindly, Zora reasoned that he had surrounded himself with such a lofty palace to compensate for his lack of stature.

"So you have safely returned, Rurik Sigurdson!" the grand prince said in a great booming voice, startling Zora when he broke away from the group and strode energetically toward them.

She stood uncomfortably to one side while the two men embraced heartily, confirming that Rurik held a very high place in the ruler's esteem. Then to her surprise they moved away, leaving her standing there alone as if she were invisible. She had never felt so insulted.

"I trust that we've much to discuss," Yaroslav began, his tone sobering as he gestured to the tall chairs placed in a semicircle before the fireplace. "Come, let us sit and—"

"Forgive my interruption, lord prince," Rurik broke in, feeling Zora's indignant gaze boring into his back. Despite the grave seriousness of this meeting, her reaction made him want to smile. Yaroslav's disinterest in her had obviously set her down a notch or two. "There is another matter that first demands our attention."

"Another matter? What could be more important . . . ?" As Rurik gestured for Zora to come forward, Yaroslav focused upon her as if seeing her for the first time. Then he glanced questioningly at Rurik. "This grubby youth has some bearing upon our discussion? A messenger, perhaps?"

Seeing Zora stiffen, Rurik had to stifle again his urge to

smile. "Not a youth, my lord"—he reached out and flipped Zora's thick braid over her shoulder—"but a wench and my prisoner for almost three weeks now. Your niece, Princess Zora of Tmutorokan."

Zora jerked away from him. She was not going to stand there while Rurik toyed with her person and talked over her head! Throwing aside all caution, she rounded upon her uncle.

"Yes, I'm Princess Zora and I demand that you release me at once and return me to my father, Prince Mstislav!" she cried, her outraged voice echoing in the hall. "Such a gesture can only *begin* to compensate for the crimes that this brutal man has committed against me. Before abducting me from Chernigov, he vilely assaulted me and stole my honor, then threatened me at cost of life and limb if I dared to try and escape. He almost suffocated me on one occasion, nearly ravaged me again on another, and has forced me all along to wear this . . . this man's garb! I demand justice! I demand—"

"Silence!"

Her heart pounding, Zora clamped her mouth shut in surprise. She stared at her uncle, who appeared unaffected by her outburst despite his just having to shout to quiet her. Yet his eyes now held a cold glint of hardness.

"You will hold your tongue until I ask you to speak," Yaroslav warned in a low tone. "Do you understand?"

Reluctantly, she nodded.

"Excellent." He turned to Rurik, whose expression had grown dark and angry. "I can well imagine why you thought it important to bring this woman to Novgorod, but first, before you respond to her many charges, I want to know how you came upon my brother's bastard daughter."

Now Rurik looked stunned. Zora felt smug satisfaction at his reaction and smiled tightly when he glanced at her, granting him a slight, mocking bow of her head.

"A bastard?"

Yaroslav uttered a short, humorless laugh. "Born of

Velika, Mstislav's favorite concubine, some seventeen years ago. Am I not correct, young woman?"

Zora was not surprised he knew about her. She had expected as much. "Yes, my mother was Velika."

"Beautiful woman," the grand prince said almost to himself. "I met her once when Mstislav brought her with him to Kiev, our father having summoned us for a meeting of his council. We were rivals even then, long years before we would become the bitterest of enemies." His tone grown cold, he glanced at Zora. "I can see now that you favor your mother . . . perhaps even surpass her in beauty if you get rid of the dirt. Did you not allow her to bathe, Rurik?"

"She refused, my prince."

"Hmmm . . . stubborn and defiant, with a willful tongue to match," Yaroslav said, studying her so intently that Zora began to feel uncomfortable. "Not the wisest of traits for any captive." He turned abruptly to Rurik. "You captured her in Chernigov?"

"Not exactly, my lord, but it is a long story—"

"And one I am most eager to hear. Continue."

Wondering what Yaroslav had meant by his cryptic statement, Zora listened impatiently as Rurik recounted how he had found her in the trading camp, and to her surprise, she learned that the slave merchant Gleb had not been killed, as she had believed. Another lie Rurik had fed her! Then he repeated what little she had told him about Hermione, and at that point the grand prince gave another laugh as dry as the first.

"If this is true, it sounds as if young Hermione has taken on the traits of her Greek mother. I met Canace only once, a year later in Kiev at her wedding to my brother. As lovely to look upon as a vermilion rose, but possessing the prickliest of thorns. Too bad the woman Mstislav married was not the one he loved."

"My lord?" asked Rurik while Zora stood motionless, hearing a family history she knew only too well.

"He wanted to marry Velika, but our father Vladimir

would not hear of it. Only a highborn bride who was cousin to Emperor Basil of Byzantium would do. How it must have vexed Canace to come into a household where a Slavic concubine held the stature of wife." Yaroslav's gaze shifted to Zora. "Yet in time, your mother was banished from the palace, was she not?"

"Yes, shortly after my birth," Zora said softly, feeling Rurik's eyes upon her. "Lady Canace would no longer stand us under her roof. My father visited us in the country when he could, and six years later, when my mother died, he brought me back to Tmutorokan and accepted me publicly as his daughter despite his wife's protests." She raised her chin proudly. "So you see, I may be a bastard, but in my father's realm I am a princess."

"Indeed," was Yaroslav's terse reply. "Go on with your story, Rurik."

Already angered by her uncle's condescending tone, Zora felt her ire mounting as Rurik detailed their short stay in Chernigov and what had happened between them. Just in time Yaroslav threw her a sharp warning glance as if sensing her pique, and she bit back the invectives that had leapt to her tongue. Yet when Rurik finally concluded with their rainswept flight from her father's city, she felt that she would surely burst if she didn't give vent to her feelings.

"Whether I submitted to him willingly or not, this man must pay for what he did to me!" She glared at Rurik, so furious that she stamped her foot. "He has ruined me! Lord Ivan may not even want to marry me now when I return to Chernigov—"

"Who said a word about your return?"

Zora gaped at Yaroslav, wondering if she had been wrong about her value to him. Holy Mother of Christ, why had she let her pride get the better of her? She shouldn't have made so much about her father naming her a princess.

"I—I thought you might send me back . . . surely a bastard can be of little use—"

"Bastard or not," Yaroslav cut her off, clearly irritated that she had abandoned her agreement to hold her tongue, "your father offering a reward of one thousand gold grivna proves your worth to him, and can only mean that he must love you dearly. As Velika's only child, I am not surprised . . ."

The grand prince began to pace before them, his face somber as if deep in thought. Fearing that he might be planning to use her as a political pawn after all, Zora shot a nervous glance at Rurik only to find him staring straight ahead, his handsome features grim.

Dear God, he would not look so serious if some cold, calculating pronouncement wasn't soon to fall upon her head! She began to tremble for the terrible suspense, and when Yaroslav abruptly came to a halt in front of Rurik, she felt her knees growing weak as jelly.

"I give her to you, Rurik of Novgorod."

Zora exhaled sharply, staring at Yaroslav in confusion. Rurik seemed just as confounded.

"If it is your wish that I guard her until you decide what you will do—"

"No, I give her to you as your bride."

Rurik hoped he had heard incorrectly.

Zora felt as if the earth had suddenly been swept from beneath her feet. She was speechless. Surely her uncle must have lost his reason!

"Princess Zora may be my brother's daughter, but she's of no use to me," Yaroslav continued, ignoring her as he addressed Rurik. "Mstislav would never give up his reckless plan of conquest no matter how much he loves her, and I doubt he could offer more than one thousand grivna to ransom her. His coffers must surely be strained to the limit as he prepares for war."

"But, my lord, couldn't you find use for such a sum?" Rurik asked, his voice coming out hoarse.

"Gold is always needed, but I've no time to deal with the details that such a transaction would require. Besides, when the victory falls to me, everything that belongs to my brother will become mine to do with as I like. I give the princess to you for your many years of loyal service." Yaroslav clasped Rurik's arm. "Few have been as faithful as you, Rurik Sigurdson, and you are yet unmarried. Look at her as a well-earned prize captured in time of war but with the blood of my father, Vladimir the Great, in her veins. Someday, that same royal blood will flow through your sons."

Rurik took a deep breath to steady his racing pulse, noting out of the corner of his eye the ashen pallor of Zora's face. He had never seen her so pale, and strangely it cut him deep that she would find the grand prince's proposal so abhorrent. Angrily he shrugged off the odd feeling, and thinking she must be too stunned to make any protest, he decided to spare her any more suffering. He chose his next words carefully so as not to insult his liege lord.

"My prince, you honor me with such an offer, but I must refuse. You know that I have sworn never to marry."

"Why?" Yaroslav dismissed Rurik's words with a brusque wave of his hand. "Because some fickle wench married your older brother instead of you? We have all suffered a woman's deceit at some time or another, Rurik. You are no different from other men. I say it is time you think of heirs for the wealthy estate you have built in Rus!"

"I already have children—"

"You cannot bequeath your entire estate to the bastards you have sired. You may have recognized your illegitimate spawn as your own, but the law limits their inheritance. Will you see much of what you have gained passed back to the state?"

When Rurik did not readily answer, Yaroslav heaved a sigh of frustration. "You were always a stubborn one, Rurik. Very well, if you won't take the wench for your bride, perhaps Lord Boris might want her. Since his second wife died of sickness a few months ago, he's been looking for another. I'll send him a message this very hour—"

"Stop! I'll endure this no longer!" Zora blurted out, finding her voice at last. Her numb astonishment had become blinding outrage. She was so furious that her uncle had so carelessly offered her to Rurik that she was shaking from head to toe. And her pride had suffered no small offense that the brutish pagan had flatly spurned her! "How dare the two of you speak of me in so callous a manner, as if I weren't even here . . . as if I have no say in whom I shall marry? I would rather die than wed some idol-worshiper, and that goes for your Lord Boris as well!"

His ruddy face growing mottled with anger, Yaroslav's voice was deadly quiet. "Lord Rurik is no pagan. Like my father who ruled before me, I demand that every man sworn to serve under my banner is baptized into the Christian faith."

Spurred on by her boiling indignation, Zora challenged him. "If that is true, why does Lord Rurik call so often upon his pagan gods? I've heard him do so countless times, especially when he's angry, and his own sword bears the heathen name of Branch-of-Odin—"

"Old beliefs die hard," Rurik interjected, his resentment at her false charge more than overshadowed by the jealousy ripping him apart. The thought of Boris, a vile, disgusting pig of a man, even casting a sideways glance at Zora was enough to sour his stomach. "If I called upon the gods when angered, it was only because you tried me so sorely, Princess."

"So you thought I should bear my captivity meekly, is that it?" Zora scoffed. "You are more than a fool, Lord Rurik, if you believed I would not try and thwart you—"

"Cease!" roared Yaroslav. "I will take no more time with this! You"—he jabbed a stubby finger at Zora—"will marry whom I choose and believe me, young woman, you have no leave to say otherwise. And if you don't submit to my choice for your husband, you may easily find yourself given as a whore to my entire junior *druzhina* for the insolence you have shown me today. Perhaps that might sway you!"

Zora could only stare at him, wholly astounded by his threat. She couldn't believe that her uncle would really do such a thing to her, but she'd be insane to tempt him. She had heard enough times from her father that Yaroslav was a hard, ruthless man. Now she was convinced of it.

"Good. It seems you have wisely decided to curb your sharp tongue. Since Rurik doesn't want you, and God knows I can see why, I'm certain Lord Boris will be more than happy to accept you as his new bride—"

"I will marry her."

Rurik's firm pronouncement rang in the hall, the words out before he had made a conscious decision to say them. But now that they were uttered, he meant them.

Yaroslav snorted in disbelief. "Are you sure, Rurik? From the ill temper she has displayed, perhaps she is no prize but a bane to any man who accepts her."

"A bane only until she is tamed, my lord. It is a challenge that I see now I can no longer refuse."

She would learn her place within his life soon enough, Rurik vowed grimly as Zora's cheeks flushed pink with indignation, her beautiful eyes filled with dismay. She would serve his needs and bear his children, but she would mean no more to him than any of his concubines, wife or not. *That* would be the first thing he would make sure that she understood. In time, he was certain that his overwhelming desire for her would diminish and so, too, would her hold upon him. No doubt it had been his lust consuming him all along.

"Do I hear any objections?" Yaroslav demanded from Zora like a taunt.

Objections? she thought bitterly, refusing to meet Rurik's gaze. She could raise the roof of this hall with her opposition to this unthinkable match! But with the grand prince's cruel threat ringing in her mind, she said not a word. For now, she would simply endure the outrage that was being forced upon her.

"So be it, then." Yaroslav signaled for two strapping Varangian guards to come forward and flank Zora. "Escort the princess to the woman's *terem* and explain to my wife Ingigerd what you have heard. Tell her to prepare my niece for her wedding. After Lord Rurik and I have finished our business, I will send word to you when I want her brought to the cathedral. Now go, and take special care that she doesn't elude you."

Nudged by one of the guards into motion, Zora held her head high as she left the hall. She could feel Rurik watching her, and she wished fervently that he could read her thoughts. If any man's life was soon to become a living hell, it was his. She would see to it.

CHAPTER
~⁓ 13 ⁓~

Zora sighed with pleasure as gently heated water was poured over her head, rinsing the rose-scented suds from her hair.

"One more time, Marta. We want to make sure all the soap is out before she leaves the tub."

While the slave woman went to refill the bucket, Zora wiped the moisture from her eyes and looked up through spiky lashes at the willowy blond who had just reentered the room. Perhaps ten years older than herself, Lady Ingigerd regarded her with such cool inquisitiveness that Zora decided the haughty Norse beauty was a good match for her ogre of an uncle. She felt like she was being inspected, the woman was staring at her so.

"I'm surprised that Lord Rurik didn't think to provide you with a brush or comb for your hair," Ingigerd commented, arching a thin brow as she came closer. "I've always known him to be a considerate man, especially when it comes to beautiful women."

"He did." Remembering his presents, Zora swatted some suds across the surface of the water.

"Did what?"

"Give me a brush."

"Then you must not have used it very often. It's going to take Marta some doing to untangle all those snarls—"

"I never used it. I threw the brush overboard, along with the clean clothes he bought for me."

"I see."

Zora screwed her eyes shut as another bucketful of water was poured over her head and she missed Ingigerd's speculative look. When she opened them, Marta was standing at the ready with a thick towel, and although Zora would have liked to linger in the bath—the warm water felt like heaven—she rose and stepped from the tub.

Soon she was snug and dry, wrapped in a soft woolen robe and seated before the fire. As Marta began to comb her damp hair, to Zora's surprise, Ingigerd sat down opposite her.

"My seamstresses are altering one of my tunics more to your size. I only wore it once. It's a rich blue brocade that will look lovely with your eyes. And an extra pair of my slippers are being covered with the leftover fabric."

Remembering with bitterness her last such gift, the bolt of cream silk Hermione had given her for her wedding gown, Zora drew her lips together tightly and stared at the dancing flames. She knew she must not appear ungrateful, but she didn't care what she wore to this sham of a marriage ceremony.

"While you were bathing, the guards informed me that Lord Rurik at first refused my husband's offer of your hand in marriage," added Ingigerd, apparently undaunted by her silence. "Yet he reconsidered when Yaroslav mentioned giving you to Lord Boris, did he not?"

Zora cast Ingigerd a sharp sidelong glance, wondering what had brought on such a question. Was her aunt thinking that Rurik had agreed to marry her for some other reason than to enhance his own prestige? Surely not.

"If Lord Rurik changed his mind, it was because my uncle's words finally swayed him," she replied caustically.

"Taking a princess to wife will be quite a coup for a Varangian mercenary who must have started out with nothing but the might of his sword! He's won a royal brood mare to help him secure his precious estate."

Zora wanted to finish by saying that she would be gone long before she gave Rurik any heirs, but she prudently held her tongue. She would be a fool to give Ingigerd any hint of her secret plans.

"If Lord Rurik was so concerned for his estate, he would have married long ago," Ingigerd said almost to herself as if pondering the matter aloud. "He has six beautiful concubines, four of whom have borne him children. Any one of these women would have made a suitable bride, not to mention the daughters of my husband's retainers who've tried for years without success to gain Lord Rurik's attention." She glanced at Zora, her gaze probing. "But instead he chose you."

Wondering again why Ingigerd would be discussing all of this with her, Zora had to admit that she had been surprised to hear Rurik had bastard children, and that he had recognized them as his own. It was a rare man who didn't relegate such offspring to slavery. Perhaps she should have admitted to him that she was a bastard. He might have deemed her not worth the trouble of escorting to Novgorod and now she wouldn't be facing this forced marriage—

A sharp tug on a snarl caused Zora to wince, her irritation pricked not at Marta but that she would waste her time in musing over how things might have been. Her only concern should be how to get herself out of this unhappy mess!

"Gently, Marta," Ingigerd admonished her slave. She rose and stood behind Zora for a moment, then moved gracefully to the carved mantel and faced her.

"Is there anything you want to know about the man my husband has chosen for you?"

Startled, Zora regarded Ingigerd with suspicion. Her aunt's tone, although cool, had not been unkind. "Why would you ask me such a thing?"

"Only because I, too, once faced much the same situation that you do now, and can imagine how you must feel. My marriage was arranged by my father, the king of Sweden, and even though I loved another man I had no say in whom I wished to wed. Yet I am content here with my husband, and I would wish the same for you. In the end, that is the wisest path."

Zora looked at the other woman, now wholly astonished. She could not believe that Ingigerd had revealed so much about herself. Up until now, she had hardly been friendly. But if her aunt was implying that she must simply accept what fate had brought to her . . .

"You wish an impossible thing, my lady," she retorted, resentment welling inside her. "I could never be content with a man who took advantage of me and stole my virginity when I did not have my wits enough about me to say no. A man who continually lied to me and threatened me despite his promises of protection. And during the journey—"

"If indeed he did those things, I'm certain they were for the good of his mission. You seem an intelligent girl. Did you not think of that? But as for your last charge, Lord Rurik is no despoiler of women. You must have provoked him."

Ingigerd's blunt statement took her by surprise. Zora felt her cheeks redden. "I did not!"

"No? You already told me that you dumped the things he had given you into the river. Why else would you have spurned his kindness if not to frustrate him?"

Flushed with indignation, Zora blurted, "All I did was smile at one of his men. Lord Rurik told me I could ask them for their assistance to draw water from the river but the one time I did, he accused me of attempting to turn his men against him. He . . . he came into my tent and . . ." Her skin became gooseflesh as vivid memories of their encounter assailed her.

"And?" Ingigerd prodded.

"He called me a wanton," Zora replied, remembering all too well how Rurik's blue eyes had blazed into hers and how he had pulled her into his arms. As a stirring warmth raced through her, her gaze fell from Ingigerd to the bright orange flames in the hearth. She knew the disconcerting sensation had nothing to do with the fire. "Then he kissed me."

A silence filled the room save for the crackling logs and the soft swish of Marta's comb through her hair until finally Ingigerd said, "I see no ravagement in a kiss."

Admitting to herself that she might have exaggerated, Zora nonetheless jutted her chin. "Maybe not, but he swore that I would be punished if I ever caused trouble between him and his men again."

"And what trouble was this?"

Becoming exasperated by Ingigerd's probing questions and having no wish to open any discussion on what had happened to Kjell, Zora demanded, "What does it matter? That was days ago—"

"It matters in that you have accomplished what many an eligible young woman in Novgorod could only dream," Ingigerd interrupted, her tone miffed. "It's an amazing thing that Lord Rurik has finally agreed to wed, given his wont to spurn *my* every attempt at matchmaking. I would know how it came about."

Heaving a sigh, Zora decided it was best to humor her.

"Lord Rurik and the young man I asked to help me got into an argument. I couldn't hear everything through the tent, but I did hear Kjell say something about Lord Rurik caring that I had smiled at him, then Kjell accused Lord Rurik of having an eye for me . . . of making some kind of claim upon me." She shrugged, wanting to close the uncomfortable subject. "That's all."

Ingigerd again seemed to ponder her words, then she shook her head. "I would never have believed it. Lord Rurik . . . jealous."

"Hardly jealous," Zora scoffed. "He hates me. He couldn't wait to be rid of me."

"Hate? I doubt that. Lord Rurik's a man, isn't he? You're an exceedingly beautiful young woman. He had to favor you to take you to his bed. Perhaps his attraction had already grown to such proportions that he couldn't bear to see you smiling at another man aboard his ship and then today, the thought of seeing you wed to someone else spurred him into accepting you as his bride."

Stunned, Zora found herself wondering if this astonishing theory might be true. Could that be why Rurik had changed his mind about marrying her? Then just as quickly she dismissed the thought. What did she care if Rurik had been jealous, or if he was even remotely attracted to her? His feelings meant nothing to her.

"It's clear you've seen in Lord Rurik only what you want to see . . . an enemy, your brutal captor," Ingigerd continued, ignoring the stubborn set of Zora's jaw. "But I've seen qualities in him over the years that any woman would wish for in a husband . . . bravery, generosity, and honor. It took me many unhappy months after my own marriage to admit that my husband possessed these traits as well."

Zora eyed Ingigerd skeptically. "Your husband also said that he would throw me to his junior *druzhina* if I refused to accept his choice for me. Is that so honorable?"

Ingigerd gave a small laugh. "Yaroslav is not one to be crossed. Yet I do know that he would not have offered you to Lord Rurik unless he believed his warrior was worthy of you. I can see now that you are worthy of him as well . . . an excellent match, I would say. Perhaps you might be the one to ease his heart of the treachery in his past."

Zora was tempted to reply that she would rather see a spear through Rurik's heart, but a firm rap upon the door stayed her. A lump settled in her throat as a female slave entered the room with a garment of shimmering blue draped over one arm, a matching pair of slippers in her hand.

"My seamstresses work very quickly," said Ingigerd, clearly pleased. "Isn't the gown a beautiful color? Now come. Let us see how it fits you."

As Zora rose on wobbly legs, wishing that by some miracle she could be spirited away from this place, this wedding, and, most of all, Rurik Sigurdson, Ingigerd's gaze surprisingly held a glimmer of sympathy.

"You might consider what we've discussed today. Lord Rurik may seem a hard man now, but in time . . ."

At Ingigerd's frown, Zora knew that her aunt had seen the renewed defiance in her eyes. She hadn't needed to say a thing.

The cathedral was empty save for a small group of people waiting at the steps leading to the altar. As Zora walked with Ingigerd into the candlelit interior, she spied Rurik immediately among her uncle and the same four richly clad advisers who had been in the hall earlier that afternoon. How could she not notice him when he stood so tall and straight above everyone else? Her heart began to pound despite her firm resolve to remain aloof, for she had never seen Rurik so magnificently attired.

His jade-green tunic could not have fit his powerful body more snugly, the hem and cuffs of his sleeves edged in brocade, while his matching trousers were tucked into boots of fine black leather. At his neck glinted a heavy gold torque and his belt seemed entirely made of gold, the scabbard holding his sword encrusted with precious many-colored stones. She doubted that many princes possessed anything so fine.

But what made her breath catch and her heartbeat race all the faster was his countenance when he turned to face her, Grand Prince Yaroslav announcing their arrival in his thunderous voice. As she and Ingigerd began to walk down the center aisle, Zora decided that it should be a sin for God to put a man with such looks upon the earth. Freshly shaven, his silvery blond hair swept back from his broad forehead in such a way that his gold earring caught the light, Rurik was truly the most handsome man she had ever seen.

"See how Lord Rurik watches you?" came Ingigerd's whispered aside as they drew closer to the assembled witnesses. "I believe if the sanctuary was full of beautiful women, he would have eyes only for you. Perhaps one day you will thank my husband for this marriage."

Zora did not have to be told that Rurik was staring at her as if seeing her for the first time. His open admiration like a blazing heat upon her flesh, she was grateful for the anger Ingigerd's observation had rekindled in her heart.

How dare he appraise her so in a holy place! Tearing her gaze from his, she walked the rest of the way with her eyes downcast. By the time she and Ingigerd came to a halt at the end of the aisle, she had composed herself sufficiently to face what lay ahead.

At least she thought that she had. When the bishop came forward and placed her hand in Rurik's warm upturned palm, she started as if burned and began to tremble in earnest. She did not dare to glance up at him, but she knew he was watching her. Rurik was standing so close to her now that his clean, masculine scent overwhelmed her. Not wanting to admit how compelling she found it, out of the corner of her eye she was as easily disconcerted by the movement of his taut abdomen as he slowly breathed in and out.

To her relief, the bishop climbing the steps to the altar in a swirl of white cloth and embroidered vestments offered her a distraction, albeit an unhappy one. Once she had looked forward to the beautiful wedding ceremony as might any young woman soon to be married. Now it had become her humiliation, her husband not Lord Ivan of Tmutorokan, her father's choice, but a man whom she swore to escape as soon as the opportune moment arose.

"Come, Zora, we must move forward."

Rurik had all he could do to force his gaze from her. Gone was the grimy-faced urchin in soiled tunic and trousers, his mutinous captive transformed into an ethereal earthbound angel.

She smelled intoxicatingly sweet, like summer roses, and even his wildest imaginings couldn't have prepared him for the sight of her in a well-cut tunic that clung to her lushly curved form, her breasts high and proud beneath a bodice shot through with gold thread. Upon her lowered head glittered a jeweled gold circlet. A gossamer blue veil provided the barest wisp of covering for the cascade of tawny hair framing her face and tumbling down her back.

Repressing his urge to touch a glossy tendril, Rurik began to move forward toward the steps only to feel her resist him, her slippered feet remaining in the same place as if rooted to the floor. Wondering with sudden irritation if she might be considering a final scene of defiance, he closed his hand around her small one and pulled her with him.

"The bishop is waiting, Princess, and our uncle grows impatient. Come."

This time she came willingly but Rurik could see from her trembling chin that the decision had cost her. It was almost unfathomable that such a proud, stubborn young woman might be on the verge of tears, but he feared it was so.

As they reached the foot of the steps, two witnesses coming forward to hold the jeweled marriage crowns above their heads, Rurik loosened his hold and stroked her delicate fingers with his thumb, hoping his gesture might calm her. Instead, she seemed to tremble all the more. Two fat tears slid slowly down her cheeks as the bishop began reciting the service in somber, stentorian tones.

Moved more deeply than he thought possible, Rurik's regret was acute that he was the cause of such unhappiness. Wondering with uncharacteristic emotion if his touch might ever bring a smile to her lips, he whispered, "Is it truly that bad, little one?"

Clearly startled, she met his gaze, her outrage shining through her tears. "So you mock me . . . even now when you have won," she said in a small, hoarse voice. "What kind of heartless barbarian are you?"

Cut to the quick by her words, Rurik riveted his attention upon the bishop, not looking at Zora again until after their vows were said—his spoken with restrained anger and hers barely discernible—and the gold rings upon their fingers. Pronounced man and wife, Rurik could not sign the marriage contract held by the bishop's young assistant fast enough. His jaw clenched all the tighter when after inscribing her name, Zora quickly scrawled three words . . . "against my will."

"Wrong, Princess," he muttered, taking the pen from the wide-eyed assistant and crossing a bold line through what she had just written. "You had a choice."

Ignoring her glare, Rurik took her arm as they turned to face their witnesses. Grand Prince Yaroslav's pleased smile was a sharp contrast to Rurik's ire. He couldn't wait to get his rebellious bride home and teach her his first lesson!

"A feast has been prepared in honor of your marriage, Rurik. Allow my wife and I to escort you to the hall."

"Our thanks, my lord prince"—he turned to Ingigerd, her expression appraising as she regarded first him and then Zora—"Lady Ingigerd, but my new bride is exhausted from our lengthy journey and the hour is growing late. It will be dark when we reach my estate—"

"I feel fine!" Zora blurted. Hoping to delay what she imagined every bridegroom deemed as his marital right, she added, "A feast sounds wonderful, and I'm so hungry—"

"You will have to wait," Rurik said tightly, steering her past their silent witnesses. She knew that no one would interfere on her behalf. Her humiliation complete, she could only try to keep up with Rurik's long strides as he hurried her from the cathedral.

She was not surprised to find Arne and Leif waiting outside in the gathering dusk with three horses. Her dread increasing tenfold, she gasped as Rurik seized her around the waist to lift her onto the back of a huge dappled stallion, but he was stayed when his name was roared out from across the courtyard.

"Thordar the Strong, my lord," came Arne's low announcement after twisting in his saddle to glance behind him. "Some of his men heard of our arrival and came by the ship asking for Kjell. I told them only that he had been killed in battle. They must have carried the news to his father straightaway."

Rurik's expression was grim. He released Zora, and his eyes held a clear warning. "Say nothing while I speak with him, do you understand? *Nothing!*"

She nodded, growing fearful as the stern-faced warrior approached them. Thick-necked and massive, his scalp shaved but for the graying topknot on the left side of his head and wearing a long bushy mustache, Thordar was one of the most forbidding Varangians she had ever seen. She half hid behind Rurik, wondering what terrible things the man might threaten to do to her once he learned of her role in Kjell's death.

"I went to the palace but they said you were here," Thordar said to Rurik as he halted in front of them. So close now that Zora could see the warrior had the same hazel eyes as his son, she was not surprised to find them fierce where Kjell's had been gentle. "Why did you not send me word at once of my youngest son's death, Rurik Sigurdson? I learned of it only an hour past from my men."

"I wanted to speak with you in person, friend," Rurik said. "Not send you such news through a messenger. But first I was bound to speak to Grand Prince Yaroslav about my mission, and then there was the matter of my wedding."

"Your wedding?"

"Yes, to the woman Kjell was defending when he bravely met his end." Hauling Zora out from behind him, Rurik squeezed her arm to remind her to stay silent. "My wife, Princess Zora of Tmutorokan, daughter of our enemy Mstislav yet niece to our lord."

It was all Zora could do to face Thordar as he appraised her, then his gaze swerved back to Rurik.

"You say my son fought bravely?"

"And honorably. Our ship was attacked by wandering thieves at our second portage, and when the princess fled in fear, Kjell went after her. He single-handedly fought off her attackers until just before I reached them, when he took a fatal blow that killed him."

"Then Kjell died with a sword in his hand."

Stunned by the false story Rurik had spun, Zora glanced up at him when he nodded gravely. Yet she said nothing, her heart thundering. She almost jumped through her skin when the stallion snorted restlessly behind her, breaking the heavy silence that had settled over the courtyard.

Roused from some solitary reflection, Thordar heaved a long, ragged sigh. He reached out his hand and Rurik clasped his wrist, the two huge men facing each other squarely for another interminable moment. Then the warrior turned and strode toward the cathedral without uttering another word.

"Does my uncle know what happened to Kjell?" she asked in a nervous whisper.

"We discussed the matter privately and deemed which course it was wisest to take."

"But you lied to Kjell's father!" she said incredulously, yet keeping her voice low. "Why?"

"Because you are my wife now."

Her cheeks flushing warmly under his intent gaze, Zora could not deny the strange niggling of pleasure his words had aroused deep inside her. But before she could say anything more, Rurik lifted her sideways into the saddle and then mounted behind her, one arm holding her securely around the waist as he gripped the reins with his free hand.

"To tell Thordar the truth might have incurred a vow of blood vengeance against my household," Rurik continued, drawing her so close against him that she could feel the heat of his body through his clothes. "The last thing the grand prince needs in this time of war is discord between his senior warriors. Thordar will grieve for his son, but I told him what he wanted, and needed, to hear."

As Rurik kicked his horse into a gallop, Zora felt herself a fool for even thinking he might have lied simply to protect her. His coldly delivered explanation had doused quickly enough any notion that he might be concerned about her welfare now that she was his wife . . . not that she cared if he was or not. No doubt it had been his six precious concubines who had so concerned him, not her!

With his hand splayed beneath her breasts, her apprehension began to mount again like a fever. The hard set of Rurik's jaw was enough to tell her that if he wanted her tonight, there might be nothing she could do to sway him.

CHAPTER
14

Deep twilight had settled around them, and still Rurik urged the lathered stallion on at a breakneck pace, guiding the animal with an expert hand along a road cut between the thickest woods Zora had ever seen. The cool evening air was pungent with the spicy scent of fir and pine. Tall white birch gleamed eerily in the pale wash of light from a half moon just appearing over the highest branches.

The heat of Rurik's body warmed her as his steely arms hugged her against him, yet she wished that Ingigerd had given her a cloak. Then she might not have been so tormented by the passionate memories their closeness evoked . . . memories that filled her not only with anxiety but a strange yearning she couldn't seem to suppress.

As for Rurik, he seemed exhilarated by the night air. Zora imagined that must be because they were drawing nearer to his home, and when he kicked the powerful animal lunging beneath them into an even faster canter, she was forced to cling to Rurik that much more tightly. Her arms flew around his neck and her cheek pressed to his chest as the woods became a frightening blur.

She squeezed her eyes shut, fearing for their lives and certain that at any moment disaster would befall them. All she could hear was the relentless pounding of hooves and Rurik's strong, steady heartbeat against her ear. She couldn't have been more astonished when she heard Arne bellow a command to fling open the gates in the name of Rurik Sigurdson. Wide-eyed now, she watched breathlessly as they burst into a torchlit world of sound and commotion.

"Hail, Lord Rurik!" came exuberant cries of welcome as they rode past massive timbered gates into a fortified compound that stretched into the night farther than Zora could see.

To her surprise, Rurik's estate resembled a settlement not unlike a town. Men, women, and children poured from row after row of longhouses built in the Norse fashion.

Wondering at the great wealth he must possess to support such numbers of retainers, Zora could not help asking Rurik as he slowed the stallion to a trot, "How—how many people are there?"

"In my personal *druzhina*, three hundred seasoned warriors, many with families. Counting slaves and their children, my concubines who have borne me five sons and three daughters and now a new wife who I hope proves as fruitful . . ." He shrugged, his tone brusque. "The number is always growing."

Beset by fresh dread at the import of his statement and wishing that she hadn't asked, Zora said no more as he rode on through the swell of warriors pressing eagerly around them. At first it appeared Rurik was heading toward a huge longhouse near the center of the compound, the building flanked by what appeared to be an assembly hall. But he swerved their mount to the left and rode to another, and decidedly smaller, dwelling with a half dozen guards posted at the door.

"This will be your home." Rurik jumped to the ground and hauled Zora from the saddle.

Noting her heightened color and the apprehension in her eyes, he could imagine what she must be thinking. The same image had been burning in his mind since they had left Novgorod, but his was fueled by desire, not fear. It had been torture to hold her so close for so long, the warmed rose scent of her skin intoxicating him. He wanted nothing more than to take her to his own longhouse and disappear with her for days until his lust was satisfied, but he was determined to give her a very important first lesson.

"These men have been assigned to protect you," he said, practically pushing her toward the wooden structure. "Inside you'll find female slaves waiting to see to your every need. Do you weave?"

She looked up at him in confusion. "What?"

"Do you weave?"

"No—"

"Then your women can teach you. It will keep you busy and out of trouble."

Shoving open the door, Rurik didn't follow Zora over the threshold and he could tell she was surprised when she spun to face him. "Good night, Princess."

"G-good night?"

He nodded, not trusting himself to speak. His throat had tightened just in looking at the ripe fullness of her rose-red lips and her breasts, rising and falling with nervousness, which he ached to caress. Before he could change his mind, he left her and went back to his horse, doing his utmost to keep his resolve firmly in front of him.

Since there were six women he planned to summon to his longhouse before her, Zora would not share his bed for almost a week. It would be a worse torture to wait that long to claim her, yet there was no better way to show her that she held no distinctive place in his life. Just because she was his wife didn't mean he would put her before the others.

Zora could hardly believe her eyes as Rurik rode away in

a swirl of dust without sparing her another glance, his clenched fist raised high in greeting as he gave acknowledgment to the resounding cheers of his men.

Good night? Did that mean, then, that he was not going to force his demands upon her, at least not this evening? Believing it must be so, she was struck by a swamping wave of relief that, unsettlingly enough, held disappointment.

Holy Mother of Christ, what insanity was coming over her? Angered that she would even think she might have wanted Rurik to stay, she grabbed the door and hurled it shut.

"Filthy barbarian!" As shocked gasps sounded behind her, Zora whirled to find two slave women regarding her with widened eyes while another seemed more amused than stunned.

"What are you staring at?" she demanded, although she quickly became distracted by the savory smell of stew bubbling in the iron caldron hanging above the central hearth. It was obvious from the meal cooking that when Rurik had sent for his fine clothes and fancy gold ornaments, he had sent word of her imminent arrival as well. Looking around the large room, she could tell that this longhouse had been prepared for her from the fragrant green rushes strewn upon the floor to the table laid with a white, embroidered cloth.

Her prison, Zora amended, remembering the guards outside her door. Rurik had said they were there for her protection, but she knew better. No doubt he imagined that she might still try to escape, and he was right. But until that blessed day, there was no sense in venting her anger upon the slaves assigned to her service. They had had no hand in her misfortune. Regretting her unkindness, she walked farther into the room.

"Forgive me for snapping at you. It's been such a long and trying day—"

"Aye, I do the same to my Vasili if I've had a bad time of weaving, but he always forgives me," interrupted the slave who had appeared the least startled by her behavior. The comely, thick-waisted woman with wavy brown hair, green eyes, and an engaging smile chuckled as she patted her stomach, which was clearly rounded beneath her woolen dress. "Sometimes too well, the randy devil."

"You're with child?" Realizing she was staring stupidly, Zora lifted her gaze to find only warm humor in the young woman's eyes.

"Four months gone. But don't worry that I won't be able to keep up with my work. My first babe came right on shearing day after I'd helped to herd the sheep." She gave a hearty laugh, but catching her companions' frowns, she suddenly sobered. "Aye, well, enough of me. If you're tired, Princess Zora, I'll be happy to show you to your bedchamber."

"You know my name, then."

"Indeed we do. Word came this afternoon that Lord Rurik was bringing home a royal bride." The slave woman gestured to her companions, who stepped forward a little. "We're honored to serve you, my lady. I'm Nellwyn, and this is Greta and Katerin."

Touched by Nellwyn's earthy friendliness, Zora took an immediate liking to her. The two older women, although reserved, also smiled a welcome. But Zora had already decided that she would soon send them away. One slave was enough to help her with her modest needs, and the less pairs of eyes she had watching her every moment, the better.

Zora winced in embarrassment when her stomach grumbled loudly. "I'd like to see my room, Nellwyn, but first if I could have a bite to eat . . ."

"Aye, you'd better from the sound of it, my lady," came her good-natured response. Suddenly the room was abustle as Zora was led to the table and a steaming bowl of stew placed before her.

Tasting the spiced venison and cabbage, she deemed it far better than an elaborate wedding feast especially since she could enjoy it alone, Rurik not there to plague her. Perhaps he would allow her to eat all of her meals by herself, which would suit her just fine.

It appeared that Ingigerd had been wrong, Zora thought, jabbing her spoon into the bowl. Rurik favor her? Hardly. He had easily and without regret left her alone on their wedding night, proof that he wasn't in too much of a hurry to beget his legal heirs. She hoped that he would take all the time in the world, and when he finally came to her door, he would find her gone!

Zora awoke deep in the night to the feeling that someone was watching her, but the feather bed was so warm and comfortable and she was so bone-tired that she readily fell asleep again without lifting her head to look.

When she did open her eyes with a start much later that morning, however, she remembered the odd sensation as vividly as if she could still feel it. Yet this time the feeling was almost menacing whereas last night she had not felt threatened.

Was it just a lingering remnant of her bad dream? Trying to recall the nightmare that had so suddenly awakened her, she rolled onto her back and gasped in surprise. A lithe, strikingly lovely young woman with the glossiest black hair she had ever seen stood at the foot of her bed, glaring at her.

"Who are you?" Zora yanked the coverlet to her breasts even though she wore a light linen shift. "What are you doing in my chamber?"

"I am Semirah." The woman spoke proudly in a husky foreign accent, her agate eyes fixed upon Zora's face as if studying her every feature. "You are Lord Rurik's new wife, yes?"

Zora nodded, wondering how this woman had slipped past her guards. Then she noticed that the fur covering at the single window across the room was hanging askew, bright golden sunlight spilling onto the planked floor.

"You climbed in my window," she said in disbelief.

Semirah smiled as if pleased with her cunning.

"Why have you come here?"

"To see you for myself," snapped the woman, walking

around the bed with the sleek litheness of a cat until she stopped even with Zora. Caressing the nearest pillow with slim white fingers, her voice became a throaty purr. "What a pity for you to spend your wedding night alone. Lord Rurik spent his with Semirah, a mere Khazar slave, instead of his most beautiful royal bride."

Zora gaped at her. So it had been Semirah on his mind when he left her so abruptly last night! Stung by a sharp and wholly unexpected pang, Zora angrily swallowed it down.

"Did Lord Rurik send you to taunt me with this news?" She drew herself up to a sitting position to better face the woman. "If so, you can tell him for me that I couldn't care one whit if he had spent last night with all six of his women!"

Semirah appeared momentarily flustered. "You . . . you are not displeased that I share your husband's bed?"

"Not in the least and why should I be?" Zora's anger was growing. How dare he allow this woman to come here! "I was forced into this marriage by my uncle, the grand prince. I do not wish to be here but home in Chernigov! Surely as a slave, you can understand—"

The woman tossed her ebony hair. "I rejoiced the day Lord Rurik bought me from slave traders in Kiev and then brought me here. *Rejoiced!* All was well until now, when a wife has come into our midst."

"And I'm telling you that you have nothing to fear from me," Zora insisted. "You and the other concubines are welcome to Lord Rurik. The less I see of him, the better."

Semirah shook her head then, her dark eyes grown hostile. "No, lovely princess, we have much to fear from you, unless . . ." The concubine appeared about to say more, but hearing a noise suddenly outside the door, she fled with agile grace to the window and climbed through it just as Nellwyn entered the room.

"So you're awake," said the slave woman with a cheery smile. "I was just setting up a loom for you and I heard your voice, so I thought I should come and rouse you. Having a bad dream, were you?"

Wondering how Nellwyn could have known, Zora stared at her in confusion.

"You must have been talking in your sleep. Vasili says I do the same thing—"

"Ah yes, a bad dream," Zora agreed, catching on. Grateful that Nellwyn had discerned only one voice instead of two, she rubbed her temple. "But I awoke so suddenly . . ."

"Aye, and just as well. A nightmare is hardly the way to start a bright sunny day like this one. Would you like some breakfast, my lady?"

"Yes, thank you," Zora replied distractedly, mulling over her strange encounter with Semirah as Nellwyn bustled out the door. What could the Khazar woman have been thinking? One moment she was flaunting that Rurik had slept with her, then the next she had seemed startled when unable to rile Zora. Then she had ended with such a cryptic statement . . .

Throwing back the covers, Zora decided not to bother trying to decipher anything. What went on between Rurik and his concubines was none of her concern. She had to concentrate on escape and until she got a good look at the compound, she wouldn't know how best to proceed.

Zora had already changed hastily into the same blue tunic she had worn at the wedding—Rurik had obviously not given any thought yet to her wardrobe—by the time Nellwyn came back bearing a tray.

"I'm going for a walk," Zora announced. Helping herself to a roll drizzled with amber honey, she took a bite as Nellwyn settled the tray on a table.

"A walk? Now there's a fine idea. I'm sure the guards will be happy to accompany you wherever—"

"Without the guards." Pushing aside the fur at the window as the slave woman spun in surprise, Zora peered outside. Seeing no one near, she hoisted herself onto the narrow sill. "Don't look so worried, Nellwyn, I'll be back soon."

"Aye, I certainly hope so, my lady. What shall I tell Lord Rurik if he comes by to ask for you? I've a feeling he might, especially since he stopped here last night."

"My husband was here?" Zora asked, startled.

"Indeed he was, long after you went to bed. He came into your room, but you mustn't have heard him. I scarcely heard him come in the door myself, I was so busy stoking the fire. He near scared the wits from me."

Remembering the sensation of someone watching her in the dark, Zora shivered. Why would Rurik have done such a thing? And had he then summoned Semirah to his long-house, or had he already partaken of his carnal pleasure?

"If Lord Rurik should ask for me, tell him that I'm still sleeping," Zora said tightly, then she jumped to the ground.

"But I can't do that, my lady! I'd be lying and no one crosses Lord Rurik if they've any sense . . ."

Nellwyn's protests faded as Zora hurried to the rear of the longhouse to elude her guards, then she set off at a brisk pace between two more buildings. Licking the sticky honey from her fingertips after finishing her roll, she smiled to herself. It felt so wonderful to walk at will and without Rurik hounding her every step.

She drew stares from those she passed but she had expected as much. Ignoring the Varangian warriors and slaves alike, she set her sights on the impressive timber fortifications that ringed the compound.

She was determined to find a way out. There might be only one or two sets of gates through which to enter, but surely Rurik had created several secret exits for use in times of danger. Her father had them in his palace in Tmutorokan, and in these times of strife, Rurik would be a fool not to. If she kept her eyes open, she might spot one.

Undaunted by the armed men both on the ground and standing sentry on sturdy scaffolding built against the two-story palisade, she pressed on, amazed anew by the compound's size. Occasionally she noticed hints of smiles on warriors' faces, and she wondered at their lack of discipline.

Surely they must know that she was their commander's new wife. How dare any of them look at her so! Then an older, thickset warrior wearing an eye patch came toward her as if about to speak but instead of stopping, he walked right past her.

"I take it, my lord, that you'll wish to resume overseeing the men's training now that you're back?"

Zora whirled, her face hot with indignation as she met Rurik's amused gaze. He had been following her, the rogue! With him standing only some eight feet behind her, no wonder his men had been hard-pressed not to smile. How ridiculous she must have looked to have him dogging her so closely, and without her being aware of it!

"Tomorrow will be soon enough, Nils. Until then, you're still in charge. I expect to see a lively demonstration of my *druzhina*'s battle skills this afternoon before the feast."

"Their prowess will please you, Lord Rurik. If we marched today against the usurper, his men would fall like chaff before our swords."

Braggards! Zora seethed. *Did they not know that no amount of training would save them from her father's fierce warriors?*

She set out again, imagining that Rurik was following her but determined not to give him a second glance. To her dismay, he caught up with her in only a few strides and began walking uncomfortably close to her . . . so close that his hand brushed hers and she started, struck by an undeniable rush of excitement. Damn him! Crossing her arms tightly in front of her, she trod on.

"Are you enjoying your walk?"

"I was until I discovered I had two shadows," Zora muttered, still refusing to look at him. She could not believe it when she heard him chuckle. He may find his treatment of her amusing, but she did not!

"You know, Princess, you could have used the door instead of climbing from your window. The guards are there to protect you and escort you whenever you go outside, not to prevent you from leaving."

"Protect me from what?" she retorted, irritated all the more that he must have been stalking her since she left her dwelling. "Sometimes you're not a very good liar, Rurik. You've put guards at my door because you don't trust me. I'm not an idiot."

Rurik sobered. "You're right, I don't trust you." Amazed that she had addressed him by his given name, yet not wanting to dwell upon how much it had pleased him or how beautiful she looked with her leonine hair still wild and tousled from sleep, he added, "Have you found what you're looking for?"

She stopped to glare at him. "I don't know what you mean. Must there be some motive behind everything I do?"

He sighed, gesturing to the palisade. "You won't find the secret exits you seek, Zora, they're too well hidden. And you'd never come upon one without someone noticing what you were doing anyway. I suggest you abandon your plans for escape and accept your new life here as my wife. It will make things easier for you."

"I care not if my time here with you is easy or hard," she countered, her eyes flashing brilliant blue fire. "All I care is that it is mercifully short."

"It will be hard, then, that I promise you," said Rurik, exasperated by her stubbornness. When she gave no reply and tramped on without him, he stared after her, shaking his head.

Loki take him, how could a woman who appeared so innocent and vulnerable in sleep vex him so completely when awake? And how could this one woman have captivated him to the point where his most exotic concubine had failed to tempt him?

Even the ale he had consumed last night in the hall with his men had failed to spark his desire when he finally summoned Semirah to his longhouse. Never before had he held a warm, seductive woman in his arms only to be consumed with thoughts of another whose lips seemed so much redder, breasts so much more exquisite, and skin so much softer.

Thank Odin that Semirah was proud. He doubted that she would reveal to anyone his lack of interest. And if the same thing happened again tonight with Radinka, his Bulgarian beauty, or tomorrow night with Kerstin, the Finnish mother of three of his sons, he might very well have to change his plan. Perhaps only when he had his fill of Zora would life here settle back to normal. His concubines might be willing to bear his indifference for a time if they believed that he would then welcome them lustily back to his bed . . .

It was an idea, by Thor, and a damn good one! Rurik decided as he strode to catch up with Zora. But he wasn't ready to abandon his most important lesson yet. His imperious princess would know that another woman had lain in his arms last night, and would tomorrow and the next day. Whether he made love to his concubines or not wasn't important. All that mattered was that Zora learn her place. She was just another woman to warm his bed.

"Hold!" he demanded, not surprised when she refused to stop.

Her heart pounding, Zora sensed that Rurik was closing the distance between them but she couldn't have been more surprised when she was suddenly swept up into his arms. His taunting smile astonished her all the more. She had hoped her defiance would have angered him. She had sworn to make his life a hell and she would, too, doubly now that he had just promised to make her life as difficult as possible. But she hadn't expected such a reaction—

"I told you to hold, woman," he said huskily, gripping her hard against his massive chest. "I expect my commands to be obeyed without question."

Flustered by the heat in his eyes, Zora began to wriggle in his arms.

"I'm not one of your warriors who you can just order about, nor one of your concubines who worships the ground you walk on! Do not forget I am here against my will and I plan to act accordingly!"

"Then perhaps if I sling you over my shoulder and walk with you around the compound so everyone can see my new bride with her pretty bottom to the sky, you will come to understand that I will not tolerate such defiance. I had thought the feast tonight a good time to introduce you to my retainers, but this method might make a more lasting impression—"

"Do what you wish," Zora flung at him, thinking that he wouldn't dare to so humiliate her. She was Grand Prince Yaroslav's niece, after all. "I don't care in the least what your people think of me!"

"Very well."

To her horror, Zora suddenly found herself in the position Rurik had described, pitched over his broad shoulder. Unable to speak for a moment while she gasped for breath, she heard hearty laughter coming from the scaffolding and her face burned with embarrassment.

"Comfortable?" Rurik asked amiably as he set out with her along the palisade.

Zora could barely sputter a reply, she was so outraged, one of his hands splayed upon her bottom while the other caressed her upper thigh. "Put . . . put me down!" she demanded, striking his back with her fists. To her frustration, he seemed unaffected by her pummeling.

"Tell me, wife," he began conversationally. "How did you come by making such an observation about my concubines? Or did you simply assume they were content with their lot, as you should be."

"You're mad if you think I'll ever be content with the likes of you," Zora said through clenched teeth, giving up her futile pounding. "Your Semirah may believe that she found paradise when she was sold into your arms, but I never will!"

Rurik slowed his pace, some of his good humor fading. "You spoke with Semirah? When?"

"This morning. You weren't the only one to sneak into my room, though I doubt you came in through the window. Your guards would have given me no protection at all if your Khazar beauty had wanted to smother me with a pillow. She may have spent the night in your bed, as she so gloatingly informed me, but she isn't very happy that you've taken a wife."

Feeling a knot of anger in his stomach, Rurik decided that he would have to speak with Semirah. He would tolerate no trouble between his women. Yet he was relieved to hear that she hadn't divulged the truth about last night.

"So you know—"

"Yes, I know how you spent your wedding night and I don't care!" Zora cut him off heatedly. "I told Semirah the same thing, too. If you're thinking to taunt me with your concubines, Rurik, you only deceive yourself. It doesn't matter to me in the least what you do with your women!"

Rurik lifted her from his shoulder so quickly that he heard her gasp, yet when he set her down hard in front of him, her eyes shone with indignation, not fear.

"Whether you care or not about what I do and with whom isn't my aim, Princess," he said tightly, his earlier humor vanished. "You can see now that I decide who shares my bed and when. You hold no special status here. The only difference between yourself and my concubines is that you bear the legal title of wife. Aside from that, they are your equals."

How hollow his words sounded to him, Rurik thought as Zora's eyes filled with angry tears. He felt like he was trying to convince himself that they were true by saying them aloud, while in his innermost heart, he knew that the more he told himself she meant nothing to him, the more he realized that she did.

Lying to Thordar at the cathedral had proved to him that he would do anything to protect her, for Zora would have been the target of a call for blood vengeance and not his entire household as he had led her to believe. True, Grand

Prince Yaroslav deplored strife between his warriors, but Rurik had been thinking of her alone.

Then standing in her chamber last night after he had left a disgruntled Semirah in his bed, he had almost believed that he might even be falling in love. But, by Odin, that was impossible! He trusted Zora the least of any woman he had ever known. She may be his wife but her allegiance lay with her father, his sworn enemy.

"Come." Rurik took her arm, inwardly cursing the effect her furious, teary-eyed silence had upon him. If she had believed him to be a ruthless brute before, he could just imagine what she must think of him now. "I've sent seamstresses to fit you for some new clothes. They will be waiting for you—"

"Damn my new clothes and damn you to hell!" Zora shouted, his touch igniting like a red-hot spark to tinder the outrage boiling inside her. "I never asked to be your wife!" She swiped at her eyes, refusing to cry again in front of him. "I remember you telling my uncle that you had sworn never to marry and I wish to God you had kept your vow! I've never known a man as hard and unfeeling as you! How could I be cursed with such a husband?"

Jerking away from him, her emotion almost choking her, Zora gave no thought to why Rurik didn't stop her nor did she hear his ragged, half-whispered reply as she fled toward her longhouse.

"Because I want you, Princess. The gods may spite me for a fool, but I want you."

CHAPTER
❦ 15 ❦

Zora would have avoided Rurik the rest of the day, but he didn't grant her a choice. Dressed in a new lavender silk tunic sewn by one of five busy seamstresses, she was escorted from the longhouse by two forbidding warriors.

She could hear the clang of weapons well before they reached their destination, a large barren field on the opposite side of the compound, and she surmised that the men in Rurik's *druzhina* were practicing their battle skills. It made little sense to her that he would wish her to witness such a display. Did he think he might convince her that his warriors could best her father's elite troops? Impossible.

The field was lined by a two-deep throng of men wearing padded leather jerkins and helmets, wives dressed in their finest tunics, and excited, rosy-cheeked children. As soon as Zora approached with her escort, a path opened up for them that led right to the front. Again ignoring the curious stares, she spied Rurik at once, surrounded by three towheaded little boys who were tugging at his mail-shirt.

"Play a game with us, Papa," demanded the tallest boy who appeared about six years old. "We've been practicing!"

"Yes, yes, Papa, a game!" chimed in the two littler ones, each holding a blunt-ended wooden sword.

Laughter rippled through the crowd as Rurik obliged his eager sons by crouching low and parrying their awkward thrusts with his round, gold-painted shield. His delight at their efforts was obvious; he was smiling broadly and laughing, the rich, resonant sound echoed by the boys' happy squeals.

Zora watched him in amazement. So he had some feelings after all. Clearly he loved his children.

Suddenly a little girl with bright red curls came running toward him, and asking his sons to stay their swords, Rurik rose and swept the child high into the air, her chubby arms flying around his neck to hug him tight. Their embrace reminded Zora of how she had used to race to greet her father in those happy times before her mother had died.

Sighing, Zora broke from her reverie. Rurik was studying her, his pretty daughter's flushed cheek pressed to his. Her own face growing warm under his appraisal, she could see that his expression had changed, becoming guarded where a moment ago it had been boyishly open. He had feelings, but they clearly did not extend to her. Squaring her shoulders, she watched as he kissed his child and then set her down, the little girl skipping over to a comely, russet-haired woman.

Another concubine, Zora thought, assailed by that same perplexing pang of resentment. It was then that she noticed for the first time Semirah standing close to Rurik, her chin tilted haughtily, as well as several other richly dressed women with babes in arms or fair-haired tots at their skirts. Strange that she hadn't noticed them earlier.

Was it his plan now to publicly humiliate her by having all of his women and their children around him? Zora wondered as she walked toward him, her head held high. He seemed to be going to great lengths to prove she meant nothing to him. She had never been more convinced of anything in her life.

"You sent for me, my lord?" As he regarded her, she could not help becoming a bit flustered. His eyes were so blue, his intent gaze holding hers captive.

"It is far too beautiful an afternoon for anyone to stay indoors," said Rurik, finding himself more entranced than he wanted to be by the way the sunlight glinted off her hair and how her eyes seemed to catch the light. "I thought you might enjoy the fresh air."

"In different company, perhaps I might. But as I don't care to watch any display of arms, especially enemy forces, I would like to return—"

"You will stay here," Rurik broke in. "You will also accompany me later to the hall for a feast prepared in honor of our marriage."

"Oh, will I sit, then, at a table with your concubines or will I have the honor of a place at your side?" she asked innocently. Glancing around her, she added, "I see that you like keeping your women in packs . . . Not quite the way we do things."

"You will find yourself sitting in my lap for the entire meal if you don't curb your tongue." Rurik smiled just to taunt her. "And don't think I wouldn't enjoy it."

Giving her no chance to reply, he turned to Arne who stood nearby, and taking his helmet from the burly warrior, he donned it as he joined his men in the field. He could feel Zora glaring at him, her indignant gaze boring into his back, but he had other things to occupy him.

Tomorrow he would again oversee his *druzhina*'s training, yet this afternoon he wanted to experience firsthand how some of his newest recruits' skills had improved during his absence. Due to his information about the traitorous Severians joining Mstislav's forces, Grand Prince Yaroslav had decided not to march against his brother until additional Varangian mercenaries arrived from his northern allies. That might take another month, which gave Rurik time to hone his men's skills.

"Wield your weapons as if your life depended upon it,

men!" came the bellowed command of Nils Ulfsson, his senior warrior, as Rurik slid his sword from its sheath. "Soon it will!"

Zora covered her ears as bloodcurdling war cries split the air, but the din didn't seem to bother the rest of the onlookers. The shrieks and howls of the crowd's approval combined with the wild melee. Barbarians! They loved the sights and sounds of battle . . . not just the men, but the women and children, too!

As broadaxes and spears thudded against crude wooden targets shaped like warriors, Zora's gaze moved instinctively to Rurik. He forged across the field, taking on one opponent after another, but this time thankfully it was only in practice.

With a shudder she recalled the blood-soaked bodies strewn across that grassy field at the portage. And she felt fear for her father. If Yaroslav's forces were made up of such powerful men as Rurik, what would be her father's fate? Rurik looked invincible in his silver mail-shirt, which shone brightly in the sun, and a helmet she could only describe as a fearsome mask, the metal nose and cheek guards shielding his face. The ease with which he swung his sword amazed her; she recalled all too well how heavy it had been when she had lifted it against him.

The cheers became even louder when a spear-throwing contest began, and Rurik's exhilarated laughter carried to her as it came down to a match between him and three other warriors who at first appeared equally accomplished. How he was enjoying himself! She couldn't have been more astonished when he grabbed a long spear in each hand and cast them together. And both struck the target, dead center.

Victorious, Rurik gestured to a spear-carrying warrior standing at some distance from him. "Throw it at me," he commanded.

A charged hush fell over the field.

What madness had possessed him to do such a thing? Zora wondered. Surely the man would not obey. Yet suddenly the weapon came hurtling through space, aimed at his heart.

"Oh, God . . ." She gasped as Rurik dodged to one side and catching the spear in midair with a backhanded movement, he swung his arm around in a backward circle and brought the spear up again as if with a single motion. Then he flung it at the warrior who barely had time to duck before it sailed over his head.

Everyone burst again into deafening cheers, the warriors who stood on the sidelines banging their swords upon their wooden shields. "Aye, Lord Rurik's done that since he was a boy!" Arne boasted proudly.

To her amazement, Zora felt herself smiling, but she grew sober when Rurik glanced toward her. *Why, he was showing off!* she realized, looking over her shoulder at his concubines who were broadly smiling. Then she noticed Semirah was standing right behind her, frowning. The Khazar woman leaned forward and whispered, "We must talk!"

Confused, Zora pretended not to hear her. "You want to return to your home, yes?" Her voice was all but indiscernible for the shouting around them.

Zora glanced sharply behind her, but fearing that someone might think her conversing with Semirah suspicious, she turned face front and said in a low aside, "Of course I—"

"Then watch for my signal at the feast. When I stand, you follow a few moments later. Look for me outside the hall."

"But what will I say to Rurik—"

"Think of something, Princess."

An instant later, Semirah slipped away. Hardly able to believe their brief exchange, Zora's tense excitement became nervousness as Rurik strode from the field toward her. Holy Mother of God, had he seen them . . . ?

To her relief, he was smiling at her as he pulled off his helmet and her stomach did a strange flip-flop. Even with sweat trickling down his tanned face, his blond hair damp and flattened against his head, he looked handsome enough to catch any woman's eye. Semirah ran up to him and laughingly caught his arm. The concubine said something to him that

Zora couldn't hear, but it must have pleased Rurik for he laughed, too.

Yes, she wanted to leave this place, Zora thought unhappily, swallowing down the sudden lump in her throat. It bothered her more than she cared to admit to see another woman clinging so possessively to Rurik . . . the same one he had taken to his bed only last night, although why she might feel this way—

Oh, it was too absurd even to consider!

The torchlit hall was enormous and richly appointed, the array of spiced food more varied and plentiful than Zora would have imagined, but she was too distracted to notice much else about either. Rurik's hard, muscled thigh pressed against hers under the table was making it difficult to think, and Semirah's every movement at an opposite table, whether to sample a morsel from her plate or to drink from her pewter cup, was only heightening Zora's nervousness. She hoped the woman would not leave too early, arousing suspicion.

"You're not hungry?"

She glanced at Rurik, surprised to see a hint of concern in his eyes.

"No, not really—"

"You've never lacked for an appetite before, Princess." He regarded her untouched plate, then his blue eyes met hers. Did she see distrust there?

"You seem agitated tonight . . . ever since we left the training field. Something is troubling you. What?" He gave a dry laugh. "Other than what you've already expressed to me, of course."

"Nothing would be troubling me if you would kindly shift your leg away from mine." She hoped that a fit of temper would divert his sharp questioning. He had read her mood too well for comfort. "I'm practically in your lap for how close we are sitting and since I've held my tongue to prevent just such a thing, I'd appreciate it if you would move over!"

"So my nearness is distressing you?" he asked with a roguish smile, stubbornly refusing to budge. "Why?"

Growing exasperated, Zora wished that she could simply scoot away from him but already her hip was hard against the carved end of the high seat that they shared. "Because . . . because it's unseemly!"

"Now there I must disagree with you," he said in a teasing tone that proved he was enjoying their bantering. "No one in this hall would think it inappropriate for a newly married husband and wife to sit so close together. It's expected—"

"Even if they know the bride is unwilling?" she broke in, pleased when she saw him frown. Yet it quickly disappeared as if Rurik wasn't going to allow himself to become riled by anything that she said, and he placed his hand all too possessively upon her thigh. As she sharply inhaled, his gaze grew taunting.

"Perhaps you are not so unwilling, Zora, if it only takes the pressure of my leg against yours to upset you . . . or should I say, *excite* you? Don't forget that I know how it feels to have you melt in my arms and with little provocation on my part. A true wanton at heart like you is one easily aroused."

It was all Zora could do not to slap him for his arrogance, but she kept her hands clasped tightly in her lap, certain that such a response might unleash what the burning look in his eyes seemed to threaten. She shifted her gaze from his face as disdainfully as possible to glance in Semirah's direction.

When in heaven's name was that woman going to give her the signal? Semirah must know some way for her to escape, for surely that was what she had implied when asking if Zora wanted to go home. *Please may it be tonight!* Rurik had made no mention yet of his plans for after the feast, but she feared now that she might be the one next summoned to his bed if only for him to prove his point. *Bastard!*

"A toast for Lord Rurik and his lady!" someone shouted, which caused her to jump.

"May Frey the Fruitful bless them with many children!"

"Aye, happiness and long life together!"

As the hall resounded with similar toasts, slaves rushing between tables with buckets of wine and ale to refill silver-rimmed drinking horns and wooden cups just as quickly drained, Zora refused to meet Rurik's gaze even though she knew he was still watching her. Nor did she drink, for she would not celebrate a marriage that to her was a sham. She sat there silently, her eyes never straying too far from Semirah, and she had to be nudged when Rurik rose to his feet.

"What . . . ?" She stared up at him, confused. His face was somber, an imported goblet of sapphire-blue glass in his hand. In his eyes shone a challenge.

"Stand up."

She did so shakily, wondering what this meant.

"It is customary that we toast each other," he said in a low voice, clearly a cue for her to pick up her own goblet. Despite her trembling hands, somehow she managed it.

First acknowledging his retainers, Rurik raised his goblet to them and then faced her. "I drink to Zora, princess of the Tmutorokan Rus, that she may come to accept her life among us and find contentment."

He took a long draft of wine, his eyes never leaving hers, and Zora felt her cheeks flush hotly. How dare he presume to think that she would ever accept this life?

"It is your turn, wife," he said in a voice grown ominously quiet when she simply stood there, glaring at him.

"Very well." An insult burning upon her lips, Zora looked out across the crowded hall and for an instant her gaze locked with Semirah's. The concubine almost imperceptibly shook her head in warning, and Zora realized like a much needed slap in the face that to humiliate Rurik now might jeopardize her chance to escape. Reluctantly swallowing her retort, she met his eyes and raised her goblet.

"I drink to my husband, Lord Rurik of Novgorod."

She knew at once that she had acted wisely when he seemed to relax. As more good wishes rang out, she took a

sip of wine, grateful when several senior warriors seated farther down their table drew Rurik's attention away from her
with a hearty toast. At that moment, too, Semirah rose and
hurried from the hall, leaving Zora almost breathless with
anxiety and wondering how she was ever going to be able to
follow her. Surely it was too early to make her excuses and
retire for the evening. What could she do?

A male slave coming up beside her to refill her goblet
gave her a sudden idea. She turned sharply into the startled
man, cracking her thick glass vessel against the brimming
wooden ladle in his hand. As vermilion wine splashed over
them both, most of it soaking the front of her tunic, Zora
gasped aloud and purposely fell back against Rurik, who
wheeled around just in time to catch her from falling.

"By the gods, man, how could you be so clumsy?" he
railed at the slave, whose face had gone chalk-white.

"It—it was an accident," Zora stammered, her heart racing from how tightly Rurik's fingers grasped her waist.
"Please don't blame him. I didn't see him standing next to
me and I turned . . ." She looked down at her tunic in mock
dismay. "The stains won't set if the gown is soaked quickly,
but I can do nothing here—"

"Then go change into another." Struck again by her agitation, Rurik added quietly, "But know this, Princess. If you
and your escort fail to return soon, I will come personally to
see what is delaying you."

She didn't answer but simply nodded, then she hastened
from the hall with the two guards he had gestured forward to
accompany her.

Rurik sat heavily and took another draft of wine. "Vixen,"
he muttered, thinking how empty the high seat felt with her
gone. Too empty. Having her so close to him had heightened
his frustrated desire, but by Thor, he would not give in to it
yet!

He fixed his gaze upon Radinka, the shapely, dark-haired
beauty who would share his bed tonight. She smiled at him,

a blatantly seductive invitation that only weeks ago would have set his blood afire, but he felt nothing, not even a stir—

"Shall I call for more wine, my lord?"

Rurik glanced with a start at Arne, who was seated just to his left. The look in the graying warrior's eyes told him that Arne sensed his growing torment as few others could. Yet so far he had held his tongue, and for that Rurik was grateful. He did not need to hear that his life was being turned upside down by a woman. He already knew it.

"A barrelful, old friend."

CHAPTER
16

To Zora's dismay, Semirah was not waiting outside the hall. Trying not to panic, she walked between her two escorts to the longhouse. Had she simply missed Semirah or had the sight of her guards frightened the concubine away?

She began to fear the latter while dressing hastily after sending Nellwyn with the soiled gown from her bedchamber, the slave woman clucking her tongue that the fine fabric might be beyond repair. Zora's frustration intensified when a quick look outside confirmed that a guard now stood sentinel to prevent Semirah from appearing at her window, and for that, she could only blame herself. If she hadn't told Rurik about Semirah's unexpected visit, such an avenue might still be open to her.

Zora's step was heavy as she set out again for the hall; her ploy had been for naught. Then she spied Semirah standing outside a low outbuilding that she had been told housed the privies. Of course! Why hadn't she thought of it earlier? What a perfect way to elude her guards! Feeling a strong resurgence of hope, Zora cleared her throat delicately.

"Could you give me another moment?" Zora gestured to the structure into which Semirah had just disappeared and without waiting for a reply, she hurried to the small building and ducked inside the foul-smelling, dimly lit interior. As she had expected, her escorts didn't follow her but took up positions just outside the door.

"This way!" came an urgent whisper off to her right. Zora moved quickly past several wooden partitions—the spaces between them thankfully empty—to the last one where Semirah was waiting for her.

"I'm sorry . . . I didn't see you when I left the hall and then I had to change my gown," Zora began.

The concubine hissed impatiently, "Sshh, there is no time for much talk! You must listen well to Semirah." Taking Zora's arm, the concubine pulled her deeper into the shadows. "I know a way out, a secret tunnel, but you cannot go until the time is right—"

"When?" Zora broke in excitedly.

"Two days, maybe three. First I must make preparations. There are free workers who come and go who can be bribed to help you. You will need a horse outside the tunnel, a guide to show you through the forest, and gold to hire a boat in Novgorod."

"I have my ring." Zora nervously twisted the wedding band that Rurik had placed upon her finger only yesterday. "And a jeweled circlet."

"Good, but you must have coin as well. I can get you at least ten gold grivna. When all is ready, then I will come for you in the night. Now we must return to the feast, but you go first—"

"How can you come for me?" Zora interrupted, her excitement tempered by her restrictions. "My longhouse is surrounded by guards . . . the windows, too!"

"There are ways," Semirah said cryptically, her expression unreadable in the dark. "Do not fear, beautiful princess. Soon you will be free."

"But what of you?" Zora couldn't resist asking. "What if Rurik discovers that you helped me?"

"He will not. He will think you very clever to have found a way out of the compound, nothing more."

Hoping that that would be true, Zora added, "Yet even so, you risk much—"

"It is not for you that I do this!" the concubine cut her off in a bitter rush. "Until you are gone, Lord Rurik will have eyes for no other woman, desire for no other woman—" She stopped abruptly as if she had said too much and shoved Zora from their dark corner. "Go now before your guards grow anxious!"

Zora wondered about the concubine's explanation as she hurried to the entrance, for it had made little sense. Since Rurik had admitted that the lovely Khazarian had spent last night in his bed, how could Semirah say that he had no desire for her?

Zora pretended to straighten her tunic as she stepped outside to find a half-dozen men and a few women waiting to use the privy. It was clear her escorts had refused to let anyone else in. As she smiled an apology, she was immediately flanked by her guards and from the way in which they hustled her toward the hall, one of them even going so far as to grip her elbow, she could tell that the two warriors had grown impatient to get her back to Rurik.

Yet it seemed that they need not have rushed. Rurik's attention was focused upon the laughing, mahogany-haired woman ensconced upon his lap who had one arm settled atop his shoulder, her fingers caressing the back of his neck. Other than to cast a brief glance in their direction as Zora and her escorts approached the high seat, he paid them no heed.

Watching Rurik bring his goblet to the woman's lips, his answering laughter husky and deep, Zora felt a strange tightness in her breast. She almost screamed in outrage, but she caught herself. She was the princess! She would not be treated lightly.

Aware that every eye was upon her even though the noisy carousing in the hall had not abated, she stopped in front of the head table and stubbornly waited for Rurik to acknowledge her. She'd be damned if she was going to announce her presence. He knew that she was standing there.

It wasn't Rurik who spoke first but Arne, whose light blue eyes surprisingly held the barest glimmer of sympathy.

"If you'd like, my lady, you may have my seat—"

"Thank you, Arne, but I've had enough revelry for one night. With my husband's permission, I would like to retire."

"Granted." Rurik's gruff answer came so swiftly that she started, meeting his eyes. For a man who had just appeared to be having such a pleasant time, why then did his voice have that strange edge to it and his expression seem almost . . . haunted? "Sleep well, wife."

She knew then that she would not be the one sharing his bed that night, and she turned away without saying a word. Now that her chance for escape was so close at hand, she would have to be careful not to rile him. Even though she longed to fling curses at him and sarcastically bid him to sleep well, too, *if* and when he slept at all.

At the huge carved doors she met Semirah returning, and the concubine haughtily refused to look at her. How Zora wanted to tell her that she was wrong about Rurik not having eyes for other women! Against her better judgment, she decided to glance over her shoulder. Why, just look at him sitting there like some god with women at his beck and—

"What? Where did she . . . ?" To Zora's astonishment, Rurik was alone in the high seat and watching her from across the smoky room as a slave poured him another goblet of wine. Feeling a shiver of apprehension mixed with some emotion she could not name, she could not leave fast enough with her guards, praying that Semirah would come for her tonight. Holy Mother Mary, she could hope!

But Semirah didn't come either that night or the next, and thankfully, neither did Rurik.

Nor did Zora see him during the day whenever she ventured outside to enjoy the sunny June weather and take a break from Nellwyn's good-humored attempts to teach her how to use a loom, an activity Zora had originally planned to avoid. Yet she found that the lessons helped take her mind from her troubles. She imagined that Rurik must be on the training field with his men for the air was always ringing with the ominous sound of swordplay punctuated by loud thwacks as weapons struck violently against wooden shields.

Preferring to avoid him, Zora never walked to that side of the compound. The following afternoon, when she did spy him riding toward the main gate with twenty odd warriors, she moved swiftly behind a wagon so he wouldn't see her despite her guards standing in full view.

Attributing her thundering pulse to nerves, she did not resume her stroll until she was sure that Rurik and his men had left the compound, a settling cloud of dust the only evidence of their passing.

"Do you know where my husband is bound?" she asked one of her guards, a lean, lanky warrior who seemed surprised that she had addressed him.

"Novgorod, my lady, to meet with the grand prince."

"But it's so late in the day. Surely he will not return before dark."

The warrior shrugged, his eyes suddenly wary. "I cannot say, my lady."

Deciding it was best not to press him further, Zora wondered if Semirah knew that Rurik might be gone for hours. She wished that she could somehow contact her, but that, too, would be unwise. Instead she returned to her longhouse, resigning herself to another long sleepless night of agonizing over whether the concubine would ever come for her.

"Nellwyn?" she called out when she found the main room empty, the standing loom where the slave woman had been working to unravel the mess Zora had made of her last lesson abandoned. She had gotten so used to having Nellwyn around, enjoying her company and her quips about her husband Vasili, a caretaker in Rurik's stables, that it felt strange not to see her busy at some task. "Nellwyn?"

"Aye, in here, my lady."

Following the familiar voice into her bedchamber, Zora was surprised to find the slave woman laying out a shimmering white garment on the mattress that was far too sheer for a tunic.

"One of the seamstresses just brought this for you. Isn't it lovely? I've never seen a sleeping gown so fine." As Nellwyn straightened, she lifted a delicate sleeve and rubbed it between her fingers. "Hmmm, so silky soft. And just look at how the fabric catches the light! I know Lord Rurik will be pleased when he sees you wearing it tonight."

"Tonight?" Zora croaked, her voice gone hoarse.

Nellwyn turned, her eyes lit with sudden understanding. "Your husband's summons came while you were out, my lady. You'll be sharing supper with him when he returns from Novgorod. I'm to see that you are bathed and dressed, then your guards will escort you to Lord Rurik's longhouse where you will await him."

"No . . ." Zora murmured, barely able to comprehend what Nellwyn had just told her. "He has other women to please him . . . beautiful, willing women—"

"From what I have heard, my lady," Nellwyn interrupted, lowering her voice as if to share a secret, "though it's only the talk of slaves, Lord Rurik has found no pleasure in his concubines and is sending them untouched and unhappy from his bed. Even that haughty desert witch, Semirah, has failed to please him. If you ask me, I believe he thinks only of you."

"No, he thinks only of himself!" Zora countered, even as Semirah's bitter words of two nights ago came flying back at her to echo what Nellwyn had just said. Dear God, could it be true? Was it possible that Rurik hadn't made love to any of his women because of her? Didn't desire his other women because of her?

Swept by sudden elation, Zora was just as quickly shocked at herself. She could care less about why Rurik might be spurning his concubines! This news changed nothing, but it might explain why Semirah was willing to risk everything to be rid of her. No wonder the concubine resented her.

Yet if all this was so, why had Rurik gone out of his way to flaunt his women in front of her since she had arrived? He had made it very clear that she meant nothing to him—

A sharp knock sounding upon the outer door caused Zora to start.

"Easy now, my lady. It's only the hot water for your bath," said Nellwyn, taking a moment to pat Zora's arm reassuringly before hurrying past her. "I'll have them set the tub near the hearth where it will be nice and warm."

Struck anew by what such preparations portended, Zora could only nod numbly. Walking over to the bed, she sank down upon it, her fingers brushing against the sleeping gown.

As if the gossamer fabric had burned her, she snatched her hand away, remembering all too well how miserable she had felt when another garment prepared especially for her had been settled over her head. Her wedding gown, compliments of Lady Ingigerd, who had tried to convince her that Rurik had accepted her for his bride for no other reason than that he wanted her . . .

"Princess Zora, come quickly!"

"Semirah?" Zora vaulted from the bed and after shutting the door against the commotion of slaves preparing her bath in the next room, she rushed to the window and yanked aside the fur covering to find the concubine gripping the sill. "What are you doing? Where's the guard?"

"Talking with the others! Now hear me! I will come for you at dusk. Be ready!"

Semirah was gone before Zora could reply and she whirled from the window, her heart in her throat, as Nellwyn rapped upon the door.

"Shall I help you disrobe, my lady? Your bath is waiting."

Zora had to fight to keep her voice calm. "No, thank you, Nellwyn, I can manage. I'll be out in a moment." Her hands were icy as she brought them to her burning face, her legs weak with relief. Rurik wouldn't see her in that damnable sleeping gown after all!

Suddenly she gasped in horror. Oh, no! Nellwyn had said she was to be escorted to Rurik's longhouse after she was bathed and dressed, which would be long before Semirah came for her at dusk. What was she going to do? Would the concubine know where to find her? Mother of Christ, why hadn't she thought to say something before Semirah had fled?

Caught up in her quandary and pacing the room, Zora didn't hear the second rap at her door. She only looked up when Nellwyn entered, the slave woman's eyes filled with concern.

"Are you all right, my lady? Your cheeks are so flushed."

"I'm fine," Zora began, then she heaved a ragged sigh as an idea suddenly came to her. "No, Nellwyn, I'm not fine. I feel terrible . . . dizzy. I think I should lie down before—"

"Now don't be fainting on the floor!" cried the slave woman, rushing forward to take her arm. She swept aside the filmy gown as Zora sank upon the bed. "You're just overanxious about tonight, aye, I'd swear to it. I was like that myself when I first went to my Vasili's bed, a quaking virgin if ever there was one. He's a good man, but so big that he struck the fear of God in me. Yet he couldn't have been more gentle, and so Lord Rurik will surely be with you."

Rurik, gentle? Willing away all too compelling memories of his steely embrace, Zora said shakily, "Perhaps you're right, Nellwyn." She disliked that she must deceive someone who had been so kind to her, but she had no choice. "Perhaps I'll feel better if I rest for a while. I'm sorry about the bath."

"Don't trouble yourself, my lady. We can heat up the water quick enough when you're ready. Now close your eyes and if you need anything, I'll be right outside."

Zora waited until the door thudded shut behind Nellwyn before she allowed herself to breathe a sigh of relief. It was no more than a few hours before dusk. Surely she could feign her malady at least that long. She must!

"You're going to find a cold empty bed when you return tonight, my lord husband," she whispered, imagining the look on Rurik's face when he realized that she was gone. It was not hard to do. The image she conjured was so grave and menacing, she shuddered and quickly chased it from her mind.

CHAPTER
17

Zora had to be shaken awake, and when she opened her eyes to find Nellwyn leaning over her, she could not believe that she had actually fallen asleep when there was so much at stake. Yet after two sleepless nights, she was not surprised that exhaustion had overcome her.

"You look to be feeling better, my lady. I let you rest a good long time, but it's growing dark—"

"Yes, yes, I feel much better." Zora raised herself on one elbow, trying to shake the cobwebs from her brain. "You said it's dusk?"

"Aye, and according to Lord Rurik's summons, he said he'd be back not long after sunset. We'll have to hurry if you're to be ready in time—"

"Then prepare my bath, Nellwyn."

"I already have, my lady. The water's steaming and I've poured in an extra measure of rose oil just to please you."

Seized by desperation, Zora had to think of some way to get the slave woman to leave her chamber. If it was almost night, Semirah would arrive soon. Zora didn't even want to consider that she might have missed her. "Please, Nellwyn, I need a few more moments alone . . . so I can gather my thoughts. Surely you understand."

Sighing, Nellwyn nodded. "Very well, my lady, but no longer than that. Lord Rurik's not one to have his orders disobeyed." She began to close the door, then paused. "If you think it would help, I could fetch you some wine. A half goblet or so might relax you and I'm sure Lord Rurik wouldn't mind."

"Thank you, Nellwyn, that sounds lovely. But there's no need to bring it in here. I'll enjoy it with my bath."

Finally alone, Zora waited an interminable moment just to make sure that the slave woman wouldn't return. Then she rose and flew to the chest that held her new clothes.

Throwing back the lid, she pulled out a cloak and whisked it around her shoulders, then she snatched up a small embroidered bag that held the gold circlet she had worn at her wedding. Now all she had to do was watch for Semirah. She was barely to the window when she heard men shouting outside and a woman screaming shrilly, then frantic shouts of "Fire! Fire!" split the air.

"Holy Mother, protect us," Zora prayed aloud, wondering if the compound might be under attack. As she flung aside the fur covering she got her first acrid whiff of smoke, carried to her on a strong breeze that whipped her hair about her face. Fearing that her own longhouse might be aflame, she was tempted to jump out the window right then and there.

To her relief, she saw that it wasn't her dwelling but the roof of a distant longhouse that had become a bright orange inferno, thick black smoke boiling into the darkening sky. As warriors began to run toward the building from all directions with buckets of water, she realized at the same moment that she spied a cloaked figure hurrying toward her window that her guards had joined the fray.

"Come! Now!"

Semirah's urgent voice shocked Zora into action. With a racing heart she climbed onto the sill and jumped to the ground, and after covering her head with the hood of her cloak, she clasped the concubine's outstretched hand and dashed with her alongside the building. Men, women, and children seemed to be running everywhere, the confusion and noise like a swirl of chaos around them. Then Zora saw that another roof was burning, the gusty wind having swept the soaring flames onto a neighboring longhouse that was ominously close to the assembly hall.

"You . . . you started the fire, didn't you?" Zora rasped as she and Semirah darted between buildings, keeping close to the walls and well into the shadows.

"How else could I come for you without anyone noticing? Faster now, we're almost there!"

Zora was gasping for breath by the time they ducked into a small storehouse. The musty-smelling interior, its walls lined with barrels, would have been pitch-black if Semirah had not kept the door slightly ajar.

"Over here." Dropping to her hands and knees, the concubine began to claw at the dry rushes strewn upon the planked floor until she had uncovered three heavy-looking iron bolts. One by one she drew them back, grunting with exertion as she then pulled up a trapdoor. "Go! It will be dark, so you must feel your way. You will find a horse and guide waiting for you when you leave the tunnel."

Zora looked from the gaping black hole to Semirah. "How will I get out?"

"When you reach the other side, feel for a latch, then push up hard." The concubine thrust a small, heavy bag into her hand. "Here is the gold! Go! By now the flames may have gone out!"

Only too eager to oblige her, Zora plopped down at the edge of the opening. She had barely swung her legs into the hole when Semirah shoved her from behind.

"Farewell, Princess."

"Oh . . . !"

Zora had never known such a terrible fright as plunging feetfirst into blackness, the wind knocked from her body when she landed hard on her backside. It hadn't been a long drop, perhaps only five feet, and she realized as Semirah slammed the trapdoor shut above her and secured the three bolts that she would have to crouch when she stood or risk bumping her head. Yet the walls were farther apart than her outstretched arms, which made sense if the tunnel had been built to accommodate men the size of Rurik.

"Farewell to you, too, Semirah, but you didn't have to push me," Zora muttered. She could just imagine the bruises she would bear from her fall.

All alone now, she took a moment to catch her breath. She tried not to dwell upon the fact that there were probably rats down here and spiders and God only knew what else, telling herself to think instead about how she was finally going to be free of Rurik. She would never see him again!

Zora was stunned that her excitement could suddenly be dampened by regret. Furious with herself, she focused on getting out of the tunnel. Grimacing as she groped around the clammy dirt floor for the bags holding her circlet and the gold, she was glad when she found them quickly. She rose to her feet, remembering to keep her head low as she made her way down the passage.

It was strange to keep walking forward when she couldn't see where she was headed, the tunnel eerily silent but for the sound of her breathing. Yet she could tell that she was moving in a winding direction and not a straight line, the air growing more stuffy as she moved along. Soon her neck began to ache from hunching over.

As the moments dragged on, she walked faster, one hand extended in front of her so that she wouldn't go slamming into a wall. When was this damned tunnel going to end? She would never have guessed that it could be so long, but then again, the shaft was an escape route.

Although she hadn't seen it for herself, she imagined a wide strip of forest had been cleared around the compound for defense. The tunnel couldn't end out in the open, which would leave one at risk of emerging among enemies who might have encircled the fortifications, but farther away in the trees where those fleeing could exit safely and without fear of being seen.

Telling herself to take deep, slow breaths as she tramped on and the air seemed to become that much thinner, Zora willed herself not to panic. She would be there soon. She *had* to be there soon . . .

Rurik spurred on his stallion, every lunge of the powerful animal bringing him that much closer to Zora. By Thor, it had been a torment sitting through the council of war at the *kreml*, the gravity of events scarcely able to divert him from thoughts of his unwilling bride!

He could well imagine in what mood he would find her, no doubt inspired by his unexpected summons, and it only heightened his anticipation. His frustrating encounters with Radinka and Kerstin had finally convinced him that he could torture himself no longer. He had made his point. Zora knew her place. It was time he quenched this desire that was close to driving him mad.

"My lord, look to the north!"

Arne's cry was almost lost to the wind, the intensity of which had been mounting since they left Novgorod, a summer storm brewing. At first Rurik thought the warrior was referring to the veined lightning crisscrossing the sky, but then he saw an ominous orange haze in the distance that made his heart seem to stop.

"By the blood of Odin, men, ride hard!" he roared, digging his heels into the stallion's heaving sides. He had seen such a glow rising above towns and cities during many a battle and it meant only one thing: fire.

As they approached the compound, the gates yawning open, Rurik could hear the crackling of flames and the resounding crash of timber collapsing. Yet nothing could have prepared him for the sight of an entire row of longhouses ablaze, sparks exploding heavenward as another roof caved in with a mighty roar.

Rurik reined in his horse and was on his feet running toward the worst of the fire before the rest of his men had dismounted. The heat, fanned by the gusting wind, was so intense that he could feel it like a hot blast upon his face twenty yards away. Immediately he took charge, directing his warriors' effort to the assembly hall and commanding that they douse the three-story wall that was closest to the fire.

"What happened?" he demanded of Leif, whose soot-darkened face was streaked with sweat as he came running over to Rurik.

"The first longhouse went up a short time ago, we think from a hearth fire," the warrior shouted above the din. "The wind has done the rest."

Scanning the overcast night sky, Rurik could smell rain through the smoke that was burning his throat, but he couldn't tell if it would come fast enough to save the hall. Right next door was his longhouse, which would have to be doused with water as well.

"Has anyone been hurt?"

"No, my lord, in that the gods have been merciful. Yet I've news that will not please you."

Rurik's gut instincts spoke to him before Leif could say another word. "My wife?"

"Aye, my lord. She is missing. Her slave Nellwyn found her bedchamber empty when she went to tell her of the fire."

"Damn!"

"Thirty men are searching for her, including her guards—"

"Double it! There will be men enough to battle the blaze." As Rurik glanced over his shoulder to the gates that were still wide open, Leif seemed to read his mind.

"There's no chance she could have escaped that way, my lord. The guards have been watching for her."

Then she had to be hiding somewhere inside the compound, Rurik thought as his warrior left him to rejoin those fighting the flames. Surely Zora couldn't have found one of

the secret exits . . . though she had been taking enough walks
of late to make him wonder. She was so keen-witted . . .

"My lord!" came a shout, one of the men whom he had assigned to guard Zora running up to him.

"You found her?"

"Not yet, but we did come upon this hanging from the
door to one of the storehouses . . . the one with the tunnel."
The warrior held out a jagged strip of gray linen. "It was
caught upon a nail. We checked the trapdoor inside but it
doesn't appear to have been disturbed. The bolts were drawn
and the rushes upon the floor looked untouched, yet . . ." The
man shrugged, falling silent as Rurik studied the torn fragment.

"It could belong to anyone," he said almost to himself. "A
tunic, a mantle . . . of whoever was there last." He brought
the linen closer to inspect it further. "This tells me noth—"

Rurik stopped, suddenly catching the unmistakable
citrusy fragrance of bergamot and cedar emanating from the
cloth. He knew only one woman who wore such a perfume.
Semirah. And there would have been no reason for her to be
in that storehouse unless . . .

"Take another man with you and find Semirah, then bring
her to me," ordered Rurik, clenching the linen in his fist.
"Go!"

As the warrior hastened away, Rurik focused his attention
upon the fire, anything to temper the rage that was building
inside him. A few drops of rain hit his face, a clap of thunder
booming overhead. He looked up to the sky as the low-
hanging clouds seemed to open and a steady downpour began in earnest.

Shouts of thanks erupted as with one resounding voice.
Rurik knew that the hall and his longhouse were saved. But
what of Zora, by God? Was she still in the compound or
somewhere in the surrounding forest? The vast tracts of
woodland were dangerous at best to even those who knew
the terrain, but to a young woman raised in a palace with no
knowledge of the wild and its creatures?

Seized by impatience, Rurik could not wait for his warriors to bring Semirah to him. As the rain became a deluge, soon soaking him to the skin, he strode past blackened, smoldering ruins in the direction of his concubine's longhouse only to spy her resisting the men he had sent to fetch her. Yet when Semirah saw him approaching, she stopped her struggles and drew herself up, her gaze unwavering and her chin held high despite the rain lashing at her face.

"This was found at a storehouse known by only a few to have a tunnel." Rurik thrust the telltale fragment of linen toward her. "It belongs to you, woman, and my wife is missing! What say you? Did you have a hand in her escape?"

She shook her head. "I know nothing of your precious wife."

Hearing the bitterness in Semirah's voice, Rurik said simply, "You lie."

"And you are a fool to choose that blue-eyed, sallow-faced cow over Semirah!"

Rurik had never thought to strike a woman but at that moment he came very close. Yet his fury was restrained by pity, for he knew that it was his own disinterest that had provoked the woman. He knew, too, that he would have to pass judgment upon her for her treachery, but for now that would have to wait. He didn't want to think what he might do to her if anything happened to Zora.

"The fire, Semirah. Was that a diversion for your actions?" he demanded.

Her resentful glare was answer enough.

"Escort this woman back to her dwelling and guard her well," he ordered. "Don't let her out of your sight."

"Aye, my lord."

Rurik barely heard the reply, for he was already racing back to his steed. Roaring out names of men to join him, warriors who knew the surrounding forest well, he had mounted by the time they had assembled around him.

"My wife has fled the compound through the tunnel. We

will ride to where it ends and, if need be, branch out. She can't have gone far."

Wheeling his stallion around in a spray of mud, Rurik didn't wait for them to mount their horses. They knew the way. His only thought was to find Zora, before something else did.

CHAPTER
18

Zora gasped as her outstretched palm hit a planked wall, and laughing with nervous relief, she fumbled along the low ceiling for a latch. It took some doing but she finally found it and with all her strength she pushed up. The trapdoor was heavier than she had imagined, but refreshed by the rain pelting her face and a stiff breeze whistling into the tunnel, she was able to shove it backward.

"Hello?"

No greeting came. And there was no horse or guide in sight, at least not from what she could tell standing in the tunnel. Thinking that the man must be waiting for her farther back in the trees, she tossed out her bags and then hoisted herself up.

"Is anyone there?" The steady plunk of rain hitting the earth and branches creaking in the strong wind was her only answer.

Sighing, Zora lowered the trapdoor and re-covered it with wet clumps of moss and pine needles. Then she bent to pick up her bags. Straightening, she winced as something hard landed upon her foot. "Ouch!"

When she heard several more thuds, she realized that the bag Semirah had given her must have come open for it was lighter in her hand. Kneeling to retrieve her gold, Zora found nothing but small rocks at her feet.

"What? Why . . . she lied to me!"

Hugging her damp cloak to her body, Zora looked around her nervously, the dense forest suddenly grown menacing in the dark. No gold grivna . . . no horse and no guide. Damn that Khazar woman! How did Semirah expect her to find her way to Novgorod? The tunnel had been so long, Zora had no idea in which direction lay Rurik's compound, let alone her uncle's city.

Hearing a branch snap somewhere behind her, Zora gasped and spun. Might there be marauding thieves in these woods like there had been at the portage? And surely wild beasts had to abound in this vast northern forest, bears and wolves . . .

"Oh, no, that's it," Zora breathed in horror. Semirah had never intended for her to make it back safely to Chernigov; she wanted something terrible to happen to her out here! Then she would be rid of her forever.

No, I mustn't panic, Zora told herself firmly, clutching the remaining bag to her breast. She still had the jeweled circlet and her wedding ring, and she had made it this far. She could still escape.

All she had to do was find her way back to the compound and then skirt along the clearing to the road. Then once she was in Novgorod, she would find some shrewd merchant willing to risk the perils of a journey to Chernigov not only for the gold she would give him but for the vast reward that would be his upon her safe return—

A sudden rustling too near for comfort caused Zora to jump, but before she had a chance to run, she was collared roughly from behind.

"What have we here?" came a harsh guttural voice as

Zora gasped in terror. Her captor held her so tightly around the neck that she couldn't even turn her head to catch a glimpse of him. "I'm out hunting for a little supper and snare a pretty forest sprite instead. You're a tempting one, wench. Wait till the rest of the lads get a look at you."

"Let . . . let me go!" Zora rasped, scarcely able to breathe for the pressure of her captor's arm against her windpipe. Clawing frantically at his sodden sleeve, she fought the swamping fear that was threatening to overwhelm her. "My husband is Lord Rurik of Novgorod! He will kill you if you hurt me!"

"Nay, wench, the wife to a great lord would never be alone in these woods," he scoffed. To Zora's horror, his hand strayed beneath her cloak to squeeze her breast. "She would know that thieves and cutthroats abound, along with hungry beasts on the prowl for a tender bit of flesh—"

"No! Stop!" Tears smarted Zora's eyes as she struggled against him with all her might. "I have a gold circlet I could give you if you would just leave me alone . . . and . . . and my wedding ring! I dropped the bag when you grabbed me, but I know we could find it—"

"Aye, let's get down on our hands and knees, wench, and see what we can find."

As he began to push her to the ground, Zora began to scream wildly, blindly, kicking her legs and twisting in her captor's grip so desperately that she was hardly aware of it when she was swept up into his arms.

"Let this be a lesson to you, wife, when next you think of fleeing from your home and husband. If such a man as I pretended to be had found you, no amount of kicking or screaming would have saved you."

"Rurik!" Zora had never thought that she could be so glad to see him, and she almost threw her arms around his neck. Yet she was just as swiftly shaken by outrage that he would frighten her so cruelly, and on purpose. She was about to let him know exactly what she thought of him when a host of warriors suddenly came riding through the trees, their smoking torches lighting up the surrounding forest.

"Lord Rurik, we heard screaming—"

"My wife is well, men, just startled."

Startled? Bristling again, Zora nonetheless decided to hold her tongue when she met Rurik's eyes. His gaze was hard, his expression even harder.

"Come, wife. It is time you see the damage you have caused from this night's work."

Realizing that Rurik was referring to the fire, Zora felt a lump of apprehension in her throat as he strode with her to his horse, which had come trotting from the trees at his low whistle.

"I . . . I didn't set it—"

"You might as well have. Semirah wouldn't have committed such an act if you hadn't given her encouragement."

No wonder Rurik had known where to find her! Zora thought, astonished. "How did you learn that it was Semirah . . . ?"

"Her own carelessness," he answered in a grim voice. "And if you haven't discerned it already, wife, there was treachery behind her willingness to help you. She knew the dangers you would face. It is my belief that she hoped you would become food for wolves, and for that I cannot forgive her."

Rurik said no more as he lifted her to the saddle and from the tight clenching of his jaw when he mounted behind her, Zora could tell that his mood was black indeed.

As they set off with his men at a thundering pace through the woods, the rain becoming a cold drizzle, she wondered what Rurik had meant from his ominous statement. Yet she didn't dare to think that he might have said it because he cared about her, no matter how fiercely he held her, his cheek against her wet hair.

As they rode through the gates, Zora had never known such guilt when she saw the damage, a row of still smoldering ruins, all that was left of ten longhouses.

"I never intended . . ." she began, but one look at Rurik's dark expression was enough to silence her.

"Fortunately no one was hurt," he informed her as he slowed their mount to a walk, "but there are families to-night without their homes and belongings. The hall and my own longhouse would have been next if the rain hadn't come."

Zora wisely held her tongue, the strong smell of charred timber making her stomach twist. What could she say? That she was sorry about the fire? She doubted Rurik would accept her apology. Yet at least she could offer part of her own dwelling as temporary quarters for one of those unlucky families. It might help to make amends and soothe her sense of blame.

"The main room of my longhouse is large, Rurik. I'm sure that it could sleep six people—"

"And what of your bedchamber?" His arm tightened like a vise around her waist. "Perhaps four more?"

"I . . . I suppose, but where will I . . ." She swallowed uncomfortably, recalling all too well his unwanted summons. "I mean, you must have a lot to do tonight because of the fire—"

"No more than a few orders will handle," he cut in harshly. "The first one will be that all of your things be brought to my longhouse. Until new housing is built for the people your actions so callously displaced, you'll be staying with me."

Zora was stunned. "But . . . but what of your other women? Surely such an arrangement will only displease—"

"They have no say in the matter, nor do you. The decision has been made."

This last statement was delivered so resolutely that Zora knew no amount of argument would sway him. As Rurik deposited her in front of his longhouse, he gave commands to some of his warriors who reined in their exhausted steeds behind him.

"See that my wife is well guarded and remember, men, she likes to stray, especially through windows. I will return shortly." Then to Zora he said, "Go inside, Princess, and make yourself comfortable. I will send Nellwyn to attend to you needs."

Zora stared at him, trapped. Rurik had told her that outside the compound lurked every manner of danger, yet at this moment, from the look in his eyes that appeared black and glittering in the hazy torchlight, she feared him more. She had the most unsettling notion that he was soon to devour her more hungrily than any beast.

"I said go inside, Zora. Or shall I dismount and carry you myself over the threshold?"

She didn't hesitate but turned and hastened through the door held open for her by a somber-faced warrior. Grateful when it closed behind her, blocking Rurik from her sight, she leaned against the intricately carved doorjamb and pressed her hand over her heart. It couldn't have been beating any faster, like a rabbit's in a snare.

"Is there anything else you'll be needing, my lady?"

Seated at the foot of the huge bed, Zora nervously fingered the embroidered edge of her sleeve. She was tempted to ask Nellwyn for the impossible, that somehow the slave woman might whisk her magically away from what she knew now was inevitable, but instead she shook her head. Bathed, perfumed, and dressed in the sleeping gown she had hoped never to wear, Zora supposed she was ready, if only outwardly, for whatever was to come.

"No, Nellwyn, nothing."

"Then I'll leave you," came the stiff response. "Good night, my lady."

As Zora watched Nellwyn hurry out, she was not surprised that the slave woman hadn't offered any words of reassurance as she had earlier that day. Nellwyn was clearly upset that Zora had deceived her.

Sighing, Zora imagined that everyone must despise her now for her part in the fire, but then again, any other woman in her predicament might have done the same thing! Telling herself defiantly that she didn't care what Rurik's retainers thought about her, she rose from the bed and went over to the chest that held her things.

It had been an awful moment when male slaves had borne it into the room and set it down with an all too final thud right next to Rurik's. Hoping that these Varangians were fast builders so she might soon be able to retreat to her own long-house, Zora pulled a lightweight cloak from the chest and whirled it around her shoulders. She felt naked in this sleep-ing gown, the apricot color of her nipples plain to see through the filmy fabric, and she'd be damned if that was the first thing Rurik saw when he returned.

When was *he going to return?* Zora wondered. Beset again by apprehension, she began to pace the room.

Would he take her at once and have done with it? Glanc-ing at the bed that seemed to dominate the room, the thick headboard carved with grinning beasts and coiled serpents that to her appeared decidedly heathen, she felt a nervous rush of warmth in her stomach. It was too easy to conjure an image of them lying amid the soft furs mounded upon the mattress. She paced even faster.

Perhaps Rurik had found that there was more to be done than he had anticipated, she considered, clutching the ends of her cloak with trembling fingers. He had said he would re-turn shortly, but he had left her hours ago. She imagined the supper that had been set up for them near the hearth had grown cold by now, which made no difference to her. She certainly had no appetite—

A sharp scraping sound from the main room caused her to gasp and she whirled, staring wide-eyed at the door. All the slaves had gone. It had to be Rurik.

Zora waited, her breath caught in her throat. But he did not enter. She wondered if she had only imagined the noise. Then she heard a dull thunk, and another. Her curiosity pricked, she hurried almost on tiptoe to the doorway and peeked outside.

Rurik was just rising from a bench, his boots lying at his feet. He must have sensed her standing there for he looked over at her and smiled. Smiled!

CHAPTER

19

"Good evening, wife."

"H-hello." Flustered by the husky warmth in his voice that matched the heat in his eyes, Zora's cheeks reddened.

What in heaven's name was the matter with him? She had expected him to be angry, gruff, hostile. When Rurik continued to smile at her, his appreciative gaze wandering over her lazily as he unfastened his sword belt and lay it upon the bench, she grew all the more bewildered, her blush creeping up to her scalp.

"Your . . . your supper has grown cold." Then she rolled her eyes. How inane she must sound, and what did she care if his food was no longer edible! To her surprise, he chuckled.

"I suppose it has." He began to pull his tunic over his head, his voice muffled through the fabric. "Forgive my delay, but I thought it good for morale to share some ale with my men, especially after what happened tonight."

"So that's it," muttered Zora, her suspicion confirmed

when Rurik swayed slightly while freeing his arms from the sleeves. She could not help noticing how boyish he looked with his silvery blond hair rumpled about his handsome face, but there was nothing boyish about the powerful span of his chest now bared to her gaze, or the muscular definition of his abdomen . . .

"What?"

Zora started, embarrassed that she had been staring at him so blatantly. "You're drunk."

Rurik smiled at her again, and this time it held a taunting edge.

"Only a little, Princess, and for that, you might count yourself fortunate."

His hands moved to the drawstring at his trousers, and Zora's heart began to thump . . . hard. Thinking desperately that she might be able to distract him with some conversation, she left the doorway, and averting her eyes from him as he undid the knot at his waist, she went to stand by the table where their supper was waiting.

"Fortunate?" she queried lightly, although her fingers were shaking as she fussed with a linen napkin. Hearing movement and the sound of something being tossed to the floor, she didn't dare look up. Yet she could sense that he no longer wore a stitch. "How so?"

Rurik knew exactly what she was doing, trying to delay what had tortured his dreams for weeks. He decided to humor her for a moment, if only because he could see from her flushed cheeks and her trembling hands just how nervous she was.

"Because I haven't come to you angry, Zora, as I might have earlier this night. Ale is a most curious drink. It can either drive a man already pressed to his limit into acting recklessly, and perhaps ruthlessly, or it can calm him. Tonight for me, it seems the latter."

When she still did not look at him, remaining silent as she anxiously chewed her lower lip, Rurik walked toward her.

His impatience to enfold her in his arms was mounting inside him like a fire burning ever hotter, just as his desire for her had been escalating since the first time he had felt her writhe in ecstasy beneath him. Yet unlike that night, tonight he would savor every tantalizing inch of her. Reaching out, he stroked the silken curve of her cheek, her musky rose scent inflaming his senses.

"Come, wife."

Zora jumped and met his eyes, acutely aware that he was naked and fearing to glance down for what she might see. He was so close now that his smell of smoke and sweat made her nostrils flare, but she did not think it unpleasant. Far from it.

"What . . . what of your supper?"

"I'm not hungry."

"Wine, then," she said distractedly as if she hadn't heard the finality in his voice. "Let me pour you—"

"I have drunk enough."

"But—"

Within the blink of an eye he had taken her in his arms and swept her from her feet, startling Zora so completely that she could find no voice to protest as he carried her into the bedchamber. But when he lay her down upon the soft furs and covered her with his massive body, she came alive and began to struggle beneath him, striking his broad back with her balled fists.

"No, damn you! Stop! I don't want you! I don't want . . . this!"

"I think that you do." He caught her wrists easily with one hand and drew her arms over her head. Touching his lips to hers, his warm breath scented with ale, he whispered, "Probably as much as I."

"No, you're wrong!" Zora jerked her head to one side, even as she shivered at the ticklish pressure of his mouth upon her throat. When he turned her chin back to face him, his fingers caressing the stubborn line of her jaw, she cried,

"You may not have attacked me in Chernigov, but tonight that is what it will surely—"

His lips came down upon hers before she could finish, not a feather-light kiss this time but not rough, either . . . somewhere all too disconcertingly in between. His mouth seemed to mold to hers, and as he kissed her like he had all the time in the world, not rushing to force her lips open, Zora felt herself responding despite herself, the tension melting from her body.

It felt so wonderful . . . she could not deny it, and she soon found herself craving more. She heard him chuckle from deep in his throat when she parted her lips beneath his, but to her amazement, she didn't care. All she wanted was an answer to the yearning that was building in some mysterious place inside her, and he gave it to her when his tongue delved into her mouth, his kiss growing possessive and increasingly demanding as if he could not get enough of the taste of her.

How long she was lost to the wet swirling wonder of his kiss she could not say, but when Rurik lifted his mouth from hers, she felt flushed all over and light-headed and grateful that she was lying down. Surely if she had been standing her legs would have collapsed beneath her! She sighed, awash in delicious chills as he first nibbled gently upon her bottom lip, then laved it with his tongue.

"You see, Zora?" he teased in a half whisper, not taunting or holding triumph but in a playful tone that secretly thrilled her. "It's no terrible thing to surrender to desire. I promise that before I take you tonight, you will want me a hundred, no, a thousand times more. You will beg me to end your torment."

"And you, Rurik," Zora said softly when he lifted his head to stare into her eyes, his gaze darkened with passion in the golden lamplight. She did not understand why it was suddenly so important for her to know but she felt that she must ask. "Is that what you are doing tonight, surrendering at last to a desire that has caused you to send three concubines untouched from your bed?"

The change in him was lightning swift.

"Who told you that I sent them away?" he demanded, releasing her wrists to rest his weight on his forearms. "Semirah?"

Seeing the ire in Rurik's eyes, Zora sensed he had wanted to hide this from her. But why? Could it really be as simple as what Nellwyn had said . . . that Rurik thought only of her? Perhaps she meant something to him after all. It could explain so much—

"Answer me, Zora!"

"I . . . I chanced to overhear some slaves talking about Semirah and two other concubines during my walk this afternoon," she lied, not wanting to bring any trouble down upon Nellwyn's head. "But when they saw me, they grew quiet and hastened away."

Rurik studied her face for what seemed the longest moment before muttering more to himself than her, "It doesn't matter what you heard." Then he rose from the bed and grabbing her by the forearms, he pulled her up so roughly to stand in front of him that Zora gasped.

"If you believe that you hold some sway over me, Princess, think again." His voice was harsh as he wrenched the cloak from her shoulders and tossed it away. "Lust can blind a man for a time but once it is satisfied, *everything* will return to what it was before."

Zora was easily convinced of his words for next he ripped the sleeping gown from her body with such force that it fell in gossamer shreds to the floor. Before she could cover herself, he yanked her hard against him, his hands almost cruel in their caress, but when he forced her chin up to face him, she saw in his eyes the same haunting turmoil she had glimpsed there only moments ago. Like a jolt it struck her that if anything, he was trying to convince himself.

His mouth found hers before she could draw another

breath, his kiss savage and punishing as if he wanted to hurt
her. His powerful arms held her so tightly that she feared he
might crush her ribs . . . until she heard him groan raggedly
and his embrace became not brutal but undeniably possessive.

His kiss changed, too, his lips still hard upon hers but no
longer bruising, and soon she was completely lost in the wild
passion of it, her arms winding around his neck to hold him
tight. Time no longer held meaning, and when he tore his
mouth from hers and knelt before her, she was so dazed she
scarcely knew that he had done so until she felt him bury his
face between her breasts, his breath a scorching flame over
her heart.

"Woman . . . woman!" Rurik whispered fiercely, his fury
at his weakness over Zora, at her for taunting him, vanished
in the blazing heat of his desire.

Holding her like this, the woman he wanted above all others in his arms, he could not fight the feelings crashing in
upon him and he wasn't going to try. Afterward, Odin help
him, he would regain his resolve, but for now, let him pretend that she hadn't been taunting him. That she might
care . . .

As Rurik groaned again and pulled her even closer, his
hands worshiping in their caress, Zora felt her skin growing
warmer beneath his wide, callused palms. Yet no sensation
could have been sweeter or more exciting than his mouth
seizing upon a nipple. Inhaling brokenly, she clutched his
immense shoulders when he circled the swollen nub with his
tongue.

"I told you I would make you want me," she heard him
say above her soft moans, his mouth first playing at one nipple, then hungrily searching out the other.

Nor did he neglect the scented valley between her breasts,
his tongue tracing molten trails down one full curve and up
another until she was trembling. Her moans grew louder
when he began to suckle in earnest, his splayed hands grip-

ping her bare bottom to hold her close, and she gasped in pleasure when he nipped her lightly.

"You like that?" came his pleased whisper.

"Yes . . ." Zora entwined her fingers in his hair as Rurik renewed his sensual onslaught, but this time he did so with a heart-stopping difference. With each slow twirl of his tongue at her breast, one of his hands slipped higher along the sensitive inside of her thigh . . . higher . . . higher . . . until at last he found what he was seeking.

Her breath snagging, Zora thought her knees were going to buckle as he slid his fingers gently inside her, and easily for the wetness he found there. Then he withdrew them only to repeat the exquisite torture again and again until she was shaking uncontrollably.

"I . . . I think I should lie down—"

Within an instant she was, for Rurik had pushed her back upon the furs before her words were barely spoken. Yet he didn't join her on the bed. Instead, he remained kneeling beside the mattress and after pulling her hips toward him and spreading her legs, he lifted one of her feet and kissed the delicately raised arch.

"Now, my beautiful wife, do you know what I'm going to do?"

Shivering at the warm huskiness of his voice, Zora could only shake her head. He was so beautiful himself, so broad-shouldered, so bronzed, so handsome, so overwhelmingly masculine, that she could not stop staring at him.

"Fulfill my promise."

With a roguish smile that set her heart to pounding, Rurik slipped his hands beneath her bottom and lifting her to him, he blew softly upon her woman's hair, a deliciously erotic sensation unlike anything she had ever known. But it was nothing compared to when his mouth came down upon her, his tongue slipping into her where his fingers had been only moments before.

"Rurik . . . oh, no!"

She struggled at once, the sensation so intense that she

was certain that she had had enough before he really began. But he held her tightly and if she had hoped to sway him by her outcry, she was mistaken for it seemed only to spur him on. If she had trembled before, now she was quaking, her body arching against him, against the hot wetness of his mouth and the sensual weapon that his darting tongue had become even as she cried out for him to stop.

"Please . . . Rurik, no more!"

Again his response was only to heighten his carnal assault, his focus now upon one point so achingly sensitive that Zora no longer thought to protest for the wondrous pressure that was mounting inside her. Where it had come from she didn't know, but it took over her completely and she found she had no voice left but to whimper.

"Rurik . . . oh, please . . ."

"Tell me, Zora," came Rurik's taunting whisper. "Tell me what you want!"

"I want . . . I want . . . oh!"

The bright burst of ecstasy came upon her so suddenly that Zora grew rigid, her head falling back and her hands clawing at the furs as a pulse of red-hot fire shot through her, radiating to the ends of her toes and the tips of her fingers. She could not say how long she was lost in that searing flush of delirium, but when it had passed she collapsed onto the mattress like a limp doll.

"Sometimes we get what we wish for," Rurik said as from a great distance, lifting her although she could give him no help at all. When she finally opened her eyes, her senses somewhat regained, she was lying on top of him, his flesh, rock hard and insistent, pressing against that still tingling place between her thighs.

"And sometimes, little one," he added, his gaze burning like darkened coals into hers, "it comes to us twice."

Rurik pulled her to him and captured her lips before she could reply, his mouth tasting of rose musk and her sex, his impassioned kiss more possessive than any that had gone before. As his tongue swept into her mouth, she felt him lift her hips and then settle her upon that thick, silken part of him that stood rigid and ready, impaling her when he thrust upward as if he could no longer contain himself.

Zora cried out, not in pain but in surprise, for he was so huge that she could not believe she had accommodated the full-grown length of him. Then he was moving within her, faster and deeper, and so fiercely that she marveled at the fury of his passion. Soon she found herself bearing down upon him to meet his powerful thrusts, and to her amazement, she felt that pressure flaring up inside her like a wildfire sparked once again to flames.

"Rurik . . ." she moaned, their mouths meeting and parting with each lunging motion of their bodies until he plunged his fingers through her hair, fusing his lips with hers.

She didn't have to hear his groans to know that rapture had suddenly found him, for his body throbbed like a thing alive inside her, the hard, rhythmic pulsing keeping time with the waves of ecstasy spreading through her.

For one blinding, eternal moment his panting breath was hers, her ragged breath was his, their heartbeats clamoring together in unison. Then she fell in utter exhaustion upon him as his arms came around to hug her tightly.

It was Rurik who finally spoke moments later, his labored breathing back to normal as if their lovemaking had scarcely taxed him. That alone should have given Zora a clue that the night for them was not over.

"You cannot go to sleep yet, little one," he whispered, sliding his hand along the side of her body until he found the soft curve of a breast.

Zora shivered at the sensation of his fingernails lightly grazing her flesh. "No?"

Her answer came when he rolled onto his side, taking her with him. As he hitched her leg over his hip, she realized to her astonishment that he had grown hard again inside her.

"Rurik . . . ! How—"

He silenced her with a finger to her lips, a rogue's smile

spreading over his face as he teased her with a slow, tantalizing thrust. "Sometimes it comes to us twice. Remember?" He lowered his head and barely touching his lips to hers, his whisper thrilled her. "And sometimes, Princess, even that is not enough . . ."

CHAPTER
20

Muddled from sleep, Zora opened her eyes to bright sunlight streaming through the high, narrow windows. How odd. The bedchamber in her longhouse had only one window . . .

It only took her a quick look around the richly furnished room to remember exactly where she was, and her head fell back upon the pillow as a blush fired her cheeks.

She and Rurik had spent the night together in this huge bed. Holy Mother Mary, she would never have imagined there were so many ways for a man and a woman to—

"Isn't it enough that you've done all those things without thinking about them, too?" she chided herself, trying without success to force the passionate images from her mind. Glancing at the empty space beside her, she wondered how long ago Rurik might have risen. She guessed it was already well into the morning, perhaps even midday, but then they hadn't gone to sleep until almost dawn . . .

"Stop," Zora muttered in exasperation, besieged not only with rousing memories of their lovemaking but by words that had passed between them. Words Rurik had hurled at her earlier in the night that she could not forget . . .

"Lust can blind a man for a time but once it is satisfied, everything will return to what it was before."

Sighing, Zora rolled onto her side and folded her arm beneath her head.

After last night, she wasn't so sure that Rurik merely lusted for her. She had seen the torment in his eyes. Was it possible he might have some feelings for her that went so much deeper, feelings he was fighting because of the deceit he had suffered at another woman's hands? Could he be falling in love with her?

Oh, what did it matter? she fumed, becoming angered by a sudden rush of butterflies in her stomach. If she hadn't asked Rurik about his spurning his concubines in the first place, now she wouldn't be concerning herself with whether or not he cared about her. And even if he did, it wouldn't change anything!

She and Rurik were enemies. All she wanted was to be free of him and home in Chernigov with her father and Ivan, and where she could repay her half sister for the misery she had suffered. It was as simple as that.

Nothing's that simple, came a niggling inner voice but Zora stubbornly ignored it and shifted onto her back in frustration.

What was she supposed to do now? she wondered, staring at the timbered ceiling. Her last escape attempt had failed miserably and until she managed to find some other way to leave, she was stuck here. She would have to be married to a man whose estate was so remote that wild beasts lurked just outside the gates!

Her open defiance of Rurik had also gotten her nowhere; in fact, he seemed to enjoy it. No, there had to be another way . . .

A nervous warmth sluiced through her body at the sudden idea that came to her, one that would perhaps have never occurred to her if not for what had passed between them last night.

Rurik had to know that he had pleased her. She shivered to think of how much. Why not take it further by leading him to believe that she was beginning to accept her marriage? That had been his toast to her after all at their wedding feast. It was what he wanted. Why not make it appear as if she were finding contentment as his wife? Surely then he would let down his guard around her, which could open up any number of opportunities . . .

Seized by tense excitement, Zora drew the heavy fur spread with her as she raised herself to a sitting position.

It was so perfect, made all the more so by the possibility that she meant more to Rurik than he wanted her to believe. Perhaps she could further seduce him into trusting her if she seemed to care for him as well—

"I was hoping I'd find you awake."

Zora's heart leapt into her throat, those same butterflies fluttering like mad inside her stomach as her gaze darted to the doorway where Rurik stood watching her. How could she have been so lost in her thoughts that she hadn't heard him enter? Then again, what had she just been thinking about? All of a sudden, she felt so scattered . . .

"G-good morning," she stammered. Her cheeks grew warm as he took in every aspect of her appearance, her pulse pounding at the air of intimacy that now charged the room.

"Good afternoon, you mean," he corrected her. "It's well past midday."

"Oh." The hard edge to Rurik's voice broke the befuddled spell. Why did he look so grim? Surely there was no crime in sleeping late, especially after what they . . . Remembering all too well the arousing sensation of his hands upon her, she added distractedly, "I didn't hear you leave this morning. When did you—"

"Not long after sunrise." Rurik moved farther into the room but stopped several feet from the bed as if he did not want to come too close. "A journey was required to an estate east of Novgorod . . . that's why I've come to speak with you. I didn't want you to hear the news from any slaves and perhaps create false stories."

Zora was stung by his sarcasm. His present mood contrasted sharply with how he had earlier tenderly kissed the tip of her nose and her eyelids and then bade her in a whisper to go to sleep. Yet she supposed if he was trying to fight his feelings for her—

"News?" she said with feigned lightness, thinking again of her plan. Zora was surprised by the strong sense of guilt that accompanied it.

"About Semirah. I've given her to Lord Boris and he seemed quite pleased with her. She'll trouble you no more."

Zora could not have been more shocked. For a moment she didn't know what to say. She had thought Rurik might somehow punish the concubine, especially after his hard words in the forest about not being able to forgive her, but to rid himself of her by giving her to another man?

"The same Lord Boris who my uncle . . . ?"

Zora was answered with a brusque nod. She stared at Rurik, incredulous.

"Did . . . did Semirah go willingly? I can only believe that what she did to me was because she held feelings for you—"

"Affection had nothing to do with her treachery," he broke in coldly, although his gaze held a piercing warmth that belied the harshness of his voice. "Would you rather I had allowed her to remain here, Princess, where she would be a threat to the mother of my heirs? Aside from endangering your life, the crime of setting fire to my property was enough to warrant my selling her back into slavery, but I spared her that horror by giving her to Boris. He has the coarse manners of a pig, but he's unmarried and rich enough to satisfy Semirah's ambition. I have no doubt she'll have better luck with him."

Stung twice as sharply by Rurik's dispassionate reference to her maternal use to him, Zora had to remind herself to keep calm. But what he had said about Semirah made little sense.

"Ambition?"

"Exactly. I had sensed from the moment I brought her here that she wanted to become my wife because she craved the rank it would give her. Yet when you arrived, she believed that unless she got rid of you, she would always remain a concubine. Her confession led me to think of Boris, for until that moment I was undecided as to what I was going to do with her. Semirah was pleased at my offer to take her to him."

Absorbing this startling news, Zora thought of what Lady Ingigerd had said to her about seeing so much more in Rurik than a brutal captor if she would only give him a chance. It was obvious that he had compassion, even though it would have been well within his rights to deal harshly with Semirah. How swiftly it seemed Zora was learning that Rurik wasn't the coldhearted barbarian she had always perceived him to be!

Suddenly another thought struck her, a troubling one.

"What of your other concubines, Rurik? Perhaps one or two might share a like ambition with Semirah. Must I watch my every step for fear I'll find a knife in my back or poison in my food?"

"My other women have been with me long enough to know their place," came his swift reply, his tone grown no warmer. "They expect no more than I can give them, a comfortable home, safety, recognition for any children they might bear me—"

"No love?" The question was out before Zora could stop it. From Rurik's darkening expression, she almost wished that she could snatch it back.

"That word holds no meaning for me, Princess, and never will." Tight-lipped, he abruptly changed the subject. "My men await me at the training field. Tonight you and I will dine again in the hall so that all can see harmony is restored."

"As you wish, husband."

Her soft response seemed to startle him, his arresting blue eyes alight with sudden suspicion. But if he was going to say something else he thought better of it and strode from the room, slamming the outer door a moment later.

Zora stared at the place where he had stood, stunned that she could miss him when he had just left. Holy Mother Mary, if she wasn't careful, she might find herself fighting some feelings of her own—

Liar, you already are! came that insistent inner voice and this time, Zora could not ignore it.

"Is this to be the way of things, my lord? You come to the training field to vent your anger upon your men? To work them hard is one thing, but to push them beyond exhaustion—"

"I ask no more from them than I demand from myself," Rurik cut Arne off irritably. His lungs hurting with his every breath from the fury of his exertions, he wiped the stinging sweat from his eyes. "If they cannot fight past exhaustion, they are as good as dead men and of no use to Grand Prince Yaroslav in the battle to come."

"Yet this afternoon you were not thinking of that battle," Arne countered bluntly, "but of the woman you have finally taken to your bed. Training your men and yourself into exhaustion is not the answer if you're seeking to rid her from your heart and mind."

"No?" Rurik shot back, vexed that Arne always managed to read him so well. "What then, my friend, is the answer?"

To his surprise, the grizzled warrior who usually had copious advice on every subject, merely shrugged.

"No, Arne, I cannot believe you have nothing to say," Rurik goaded him. "You started this and you will finish it. Speak your piece and have done."

Sighing, Arne met Rurik's eyes squarely. "Perhaps it is an impossible thing and there is no answer, my lord. Perhaps you must simply accept that the gods have thrust a woman in your path who you cannot ignore. I've never seen you so consumed by a wench since Astrid and even though you believed at the time that she was the love of your life, her betrayal thus made all the harder for you to bear, she cannot have meant more to you than your new bride does now."

"And how do you know this?" Rurik demanded unkindly. "You who are such an expert in matters of the heart? You've never married, never loved—"

"Aye, never married you can well say," Arne interrupted vehemently. "But as for never loved, the mother who bore you won my heart the day she came to wed your father as a blushing girl of fifteen! Eva never knew and with my loyalty sworn to your father, I would have died before I dishonored myself. But it was *me* holding her hand when she finally let go of life, broken and alone and with that Welsh whore Gwyneth on the high seat beside your father! If he hadn't sent me to Rus with you, I tell you now, Rurik Sigurdson, though you may be tempted to strike me down for saying so, I would have killed him!"

Breathing hard, Arne glanced to the sword Rurik still held and then back to his face. "By the blood of Odin, are you going to do it or not? You've finally found your chance to silence my meddling tongue forever."

"How could I strike you, friend, when that is why I left Norway as well?" Rurik said quietly, thinking of how terribly Arne must have suffered to see his mother so abandoned, as had he. His throat tight with remembered pain, he sheathed the weapon and then reached out and clasped the warrior's arm, never having felt a closer bond between them. "Forgive me. I had no right to say what I did."

"Aye, you have the right when I presume to know what you're feeling." Arne laughed gruffly as if embarrassed by their display of emotion, yet he quickly sobered. "I only said as much about Astrid because she didn't have to face the barriers you've built inside yourself . . . long held barriers your Rus princess has managed to shatter in a few short weeks time. That alone should tell you something, my lord. And though I'm no good judge of women's hearts, I'd say your comely bride is struggling with herself much the same as you."

Rurik's heart seemed to skip a beat, Arne's unexpected observation triggering the memory of his exchange last night with Zora that he had tried his damnedest all afternoon to dispel. Add to that her unsettling query about love and her soft-spoken words of acquiescence just before he came to the field, and suddenly it was very hard to think rationally. Yet he made himself, all the same.

"How can you say this? Zora may have given in to desire but she despises me."

"Perhaps she did at first," Arne countered, "but I would have had to be a blind man to miss the hurt in her eyes the other night when she spied your dark-haired wench Radinka sitting on your lap. I was tempted to tell you then, my lord, that you were acting the fool . . ." The warrior shook his head. "I'd never have believed after all the trouble she caused us that I would feel sorry for her, but I did."

"Trouble she is *still* causing," said Rurik with no small amount of sarcasm. "What say you of her escape attempt yesterday? That wasn't the act of a woman who might be falling in love with the husband she was forced to marry."

There, he had finally said it aloud, Rurik thought as Arne heaved another sigh. Falling in love. But he wouldn't go so far as to believe that it might be true. He couldn't. Not yet.

"Maybe it was," Arne said heavily as if striking too close again to a painful subject. "After you made it so clear that she meant nothing to you, flaunting your other wenches in front of her, can you blame her for wanting to leave? From what I have seen, wives do not suffer well the concubines of their husbands."

Arne was making so much sense that Rurik was stunned he hadn't thought of this before, or perhaps he had simply refused to see it. Yet if what Zora had told him yesterday was true, she had learned about him sending his women from his bed *before* she had tried to escape—

"Remember, too, my lord, her allegiance to her father.

The struggle she wages within herself cannot be an easy one."

Believing now that Arne could read his mind, Rurik was about to say as much when the warrior added, "There's the princess now, over by the main storehouse."

Glancing over his shoulder, Rurik was surprised to see Zora engaged in conversation with Yakov, the Slav steward in charge of overseeing the details of his estate. Waiting for her off to one side were Nellwyn and the half-dozen guards he had assigned to escort Zora wherever she went. Suddenly suspicious, he could not help wondering what she might be up to, his anger pricked just in considering the endless possibilities.

"So we're back to where we started from, aye, my lord?"

Startled, Rurik turned to find Arne frowning at him.

"What?"

"You've distrust written all over your face. Already you're thinking she must be scheming against you. Well, maybe she is and maybe she isn't, but you'll never have any hope of swaying her loyalty—or her heart—if you storm over there and demand an explanation. Use a lighter hand and a little patience with your new wife. You just might turn the wind to your favor . . . and that's what you truly want, isn't it?"

With that, Arne stomped off, leaving Rurik standing alone on the training field.

But not for long. With her small entourage in tow, Zora made her way toward him. The smile on her face, albeit a nervous one, set his heart racing.

"You win, old bear," Rurik said to himself, aware that the burly warrior had stopped and turned around as if curious to see whether or not Rurik would follow his advice.

Loki take him, he could very well be opening himself up for some treachery, but he was willing to temper his behavior on the chance that what Arne had said was true. Could he dare to hope that Zora hadn't simply been taunting him with talk of love? By Odin, what he would give . . .

"My lord!" came Yakov's high nasal voice as the steward brushed past Zora at the last moment, almost tripping over his own feet in his haste to reach Rurik first. Clearly agitated, the spare, middle-aged man shook a piece of paper at him. "My lord, you must see this! It's a list of things she wants me to buy at the market—"

"If you're referring to my wife, Yakov, then address her properly," said Rurik, sternly rebuking the steward who appeared just as startled as Zora that he had done so.

Taking the paper, Rurik perused the list and saw that it was made up of common household items such as woolen cloth, needles, thread, and so on. Certainly nothing threatening. He lifted his gaze to find Zora watching him, her expression grown anxious, but he turned his attention back to the steward.

"I see nothing here that should cause such alarm."

"Then . . . then I am to do what she says . . . forgive me, what your wife has requested of me?" asked Yakov, his pallid face flushed with indignation. "I thought I should seek your counsel first . . . it's so irregular . . . I mean, I've always been the one to see to what is needed without any interference from—"

"Do you want these things, Zora?" Rurik interrupted him, finally understanding just what the steward perceived his problem to be, a case of someone encroaching upon his duties.

"Yes I do, but not for myself," she answered, her beautiful eyes very wide as if she couldn't believe that he would ask her opinion. "Those items are for the people who lost their homes in the fire. I—I've been around to all of them to apologize and to ask if there was anything I could do to help. The women told me that there wasn't enough extra cloth to be found to make a change of clothes for their families, so I thought perhaps we could buy enough to see them through until more can be woven."

"And you are protesting this?" demanded Rurik, glaring

at the steward who gaped back at him round-eyed as if he didn't know quite what to say.

"Not . . . not that the cloth isn't needed, my lord, but that this woman —"

"For the last time, *this woman* is my wife, Yakov, whose wishes will be obeyed. If she requests something from the market in Novgorod, you need not come to me first. I trust that she is well trained in the workings of a household, however large, and I expect you to respect her judgment in such matters. Are we understood?"

"Yes, yes of course, my lord," the steward said in a nervous rush, his hands shaking as he took back the list.

Rurik turned to Zora, finding that it had given him a great deal of pleasure to speak out on her behalf. "Does this satisfy you, wife?"

CHAPTER
21
❦

Zora couldn't have been more astounded. After how coldly Rurik had treated her earlier this afternoon, she would never have expected him to be so solicitous. Suspicious, yes. Brusque, yes, but to champion her as the mistress of his household?

"Y-yes, thank you. I am well satisfied." Staring into his eyes, she knew that she was genuinely smiling at him as perhaps she had never done before, but she couldn't help it. That Rurik had publicly stated his faith in her, at least as far as domestic matters were concerned, gave her a powerful surge of pleasure that had nothing to do with her plan. Perhaps that was the most startling thing of all.

"Is there any other way I can assist you, then, my lady?" Yakov's eager-to-please tone now lacked the resentment it had held earlier.

It was hard for Zora to tear her gaze from Rurik's, for he seemed just as content to be staring at her as she was at him. Yet the steward's question was a sobering reminder that she *must* think again of her plan, especially now that she feared her growing feelings for Rurik were battling against her. This latest reaction to him proved it! The sooner she took up her duties within the compound, making it appear to all that she was accepting her marriage, the better.

"Yes, Yakov, there is something." Zora hoped Rurik would miss the tinge of desperation in her voice. "I'd like to visit the weaving house if I may, to see if anything else should be ordered from the market, then the cooking house and the storehouses where the foodstuffs are kept, the brewery, the dairy—"

"It pleases me that you've taken an interest in the welfare of my retainers and the needs of my household but it grows late, wife," Rurik interjected, trying to contain the mistrust that had leapt into his mind at this new request. His better judgment was telling him that she had to be nursing some plot, but he was determined to honor Arne's advice. Anything if Zora would smile at him again as she had been a moment ago. "Tomorrow Yakov can show you all of those places, but for now we must ready ourselves for supper. Everyone will be gathered in the hall by dusk."

"But I am ready," she insisted. As if to illustrate her point, she glanced down at the rose-colored tunic that she wore, the shimmering fabric cut to accentuate the lush curves of her body, and then met his eyes. "Does this gown not please you?"

"More than I can say," said Rurik, noting her deep blush, which thrilled him as much as the thought that she might have dressed with his pleasure in mind. "But I have no wish to go to supper with the stink of battle upon me." He held out his hand. "Come. I'd like you to accompany me to the bathhouse."

"I can't go there!" she said, shocked.

Rurik frowned. "Why not?"

She stared at him in confusion. "You . . . you would want other men to see me . . . ?"

Suddenly realizing why she was so flustered, Rurik almost laughed aloud.

"Not the main bathhouse, Zora. True enough, it's probably filled with my warriors. No, I have my own." He took her small hand firmly in his, and drew her toward him. He lowered his voice so only she could hear. "Do not think that I would ever allow another man to glimpse your beauty. It is for me alone. Now come."

Zora could tell from Rurik's husky command that he would not be swayed, and disconcerted all the more by the heat in his eyes, she felt her urgency about her plan melt away. As they left Nellwyn, Yakov, and her guards staring after them, Zora had to walk quickly to keep up with Rurik's powerful strides, but they hadn't gone far before he chuckled and purposely slowed his pace.

"Forgive me, little one. I forget that your legs are shorter than mine."

Little one, Zora thought, undeniably warmed by the way in which he had said it, like an endearment.

Suddenly she recalled another time when he had held her hand, at their wedding only a few days ago. He had stroked her fingers and asked her if it was truly that bad . . . she supposed that he had meant their marriage. She had called him a heartless barbarian, believing he was mocking her, but maybe he hadn't been after all. Maybe he had been touched by her tears. Maybe even then he had cared . . .

Sighing to herself, Zora could hardly believe how much had happened since she had come to Novgorod. Nor could she believe how Rurik's mood had changed from when first she had seen him that afternoon, going as if from night to day.

It seemed that already he was relaxing around her and she had barely set her plan into motion. Was it possible that her simple apology to his people had moved him? Or was it because she had greeted him earlier, not with defiance and sharp words as he might have expected, but in a softer manner? Maybe he had decided he no longer wanted to fight his emotions—

"You know, Princess, you surprise me."

Her heart pitching crazily, Zora glanced up at him. "I do?"

Rurik nodded. "I would never have expected you to call upon the families who lost their homes and tell them you were sorry, and then ask if you could help."

"I would have done more if I could," she said honestly, for in truth her actions this afternoon—other than choosing her gown with an eye toward pleasing him—had been only partially spurred by her plan, but mostly because she felt badly about her role in the fire. "I never intended for such a terrible thing to happen." When he didn't readily reply, she added, "I'm not a callous ogre, Rurik. I have feelings, too."

"I never said you didn't."

Distracted all over again by how intently he seemed to be studying her, Zora looked away.

"I must admit your sudden interest in my household has also come as a surprise."

She kept her gaze trained straight ahead, her heart suddenly pounding. Holy Mother Mary, did he suspect . . . ?

"I don't see why," she answered as steadily as she could. "Surely it is a normal thing for a wife to wish to please her husband—"

Rurik stopped and faced her so abruptly that Zora gasped.

"Is that what you're trying to do?" His demand was strained as he searched her eyes. "Please me?"

Seeing the same turmoil in his gaze, Zora was shaken by the intensity of her guilt. Damn him, why could he make her feel like she was betraying him? The line she was trying so desperately to preserve between what she wanted him to believe and the emotions tugging at her heart was becoming more blurred with their every encounter, a realization both frightening and thrilling.

"Zora?"

She knew that he wanted an answer, but she didn't know what to say, fearing that if she spoke at all she would reveal too much. Then just as suddenly Rurik seemed to change his mind as if he sensed he was pushing her too hard. Squeezing her hand, he set out with her toward a small wooden building that adjoined his longhouse, not speaking again until they were almost there.

"The stones should be red-hot by now," he said, all trace of tension gone from his voice. "I sent word an hour ago that I wanted the bathhouse made ready."

"Stones?" she asked, still unsettled.

"You'll see."

Zora was greeted by a hot blast of air as Rurik opened the door and pushed her gently inside the lamplit, windowless building. She heard him draw the bolt behind her, then he brushed past her to a large open hearth in the center of the room that was piled with smooth rocks.

"You've never been in one of these before, have you?"

Watching as he dipped a ladle into a bucket of water, Zora shook her head.

"Steam baths are a common thing in the north," he explained, smiling at her over his shoulder. "Every house has one. We Varangians swear by them." He gave a short laugh. "Your uncle has a steam bath in his palace big enough to seat his entire senior *druzhina*."

Zora started when Rurik threw water on the hissing stones, steam filling the room. He emptied the ladle again and again until it looked like a dense fog had enveloped them, and only then did he unbuckle his sword belt and begin to strip off his clothes.

"Join me," he said in a low, teasing voice that sent chills racing through her. "I think you'll like it."

It seemed Zora *had* joined him, for already her silk tunic was damp and clinging to her skin, sweat tickling down her back. Yet she grew flustered at the thought of undressing in front of him, despite the intimacy they had shared. Turning around modestly, she gathered the garment to her hips and began to draw it up over her torso.

"Let me help you, Princess."

"Oh!"

Rurik had come up so silently that she hadn't even heard him behind her. She sucked in her breath as he took charge, his splayed hands caressing the tunic from her body. Within the blink of an eye she was standing naked in his arms, even her thin linen underdrawers cast onto a bench near the door.

"Thor's blood, woman, you're so beautiful," he whispered in her ear. He stroked her worshipfully, the curve of her hips, her belly, then his hands glided upward to the soft undersides of her breasts where he gently cupped her. "So beautiful."

Her head lolling back against him, Zora moaned as his thumbs lightly grazed her tightened nipples, circling around and around. Yet the wondrous sensation had no sooner begun when he released her, and she heard him chuckle.

"Not yet, Princess. First the steam bath must be enjoyed. Come and sit with me."

As Rurik took her hand and led her through the billowing steam to a platform set around the walls, Zora could see that his sun-gilded skin already glistened with sweat. Her eyes drifted down his muscled back to the curve of his taut buttocks, her face firing with a warmth that had nothing to do with the peat fire in the hearth. He was so magnificent, his hard masculine body made all the more fascinating in her eyes by the nicks and scars he bore from countless battles.

"Are you pleased with what you see?"

Embarrassed that Rurik had caught her staring at him so brazenly, she could only nod as he turned her around and drew her down to sit upon his lap, her back nestled against his chest.

"Lean your head against my shoulder and close your eyes," he bade her and she did so, sighing within the security of his arms. "That's it . . . now relax and let the steam wash over you." He lightly kissed her temple. "It feels wonderful, doesn't it? So warm, wetting your hair, your skin . . ."

It is wonderful, Zora thought dreamily, but no more so

than the sensation of his steady heartbeat drumming against her back, the added warmth of his breath fanning her cheek, and the way his fingers were toying with the damp hair that streaked her breasts and shoulders. At one point she even felt herself sliding from his lap, the moisture of their bodies a slippery sheen between them, but he only drew her back with a husky laugh and held her that much more closely.

She couldn't have said how many moments had passed, the engulfing steam and the incredible heat of Rurik's body like a cocoon shielding her from all sense of time or place, when suddenly she felt him lift her and stand her upon her feet.

"It was not my intent for you to fall asleep, Zora, but I'm sure this will wake you," he said with amusement in his voice. Supporting her with one arm, he drew something from a basket set near the hearth.

"I'm not sleepy," was all she managed to say just before she felt a stinging sensation cut right across her bottom. "Ouch! That hurt! What are you . . . ?" Now fully alert, she stared in horror from the telltale birch branches he held to the innocent smile on his face.

"It's part of the steam bath," Rurik tried to explain through the laughter threatening to erupt from his throat, Zora's indignant outrage truly a sight to behold. "To get the blood moving. You scarcely feel it after the first few—"

"Blood moving be damned! You will not strike me with those . . . those branches again!" She broke free of his grasp and skittered to the other side of the room. "If you want to lash yourself to ribbons, go right ahead, Rurik Sigurdson, but you'll not have me participating in your strange Varangian custom!"

Her eyes were sparking such fire, Rurik could suppress his mirth no longer.

"It's not funny!" she cried, although he could see that she was fighting hard not to join him, her lips twitching and her dimples beginning to show. "You could have at least warned me!"

"And ruin the surprise?" he asked, actually wiping tears from his eyes. By Thor, he didn't think he had laughed so hard in years. His stomach hurt!

"Some surprise." She swiped irritably at the steam. "I want out of here. I've had enough! From now on, you can enjoy your steam baths and I'll keep my tub, thank you."

"Oh, but we're not through yet, Princess."

Zora glanced at Rurik warily, not liking the enigmatic smile that he now wore on his face.

"Whipping me isn't enough?" she demanded, a giddy excitement fast overwhelming her vexation as he began to stalk her around the hearth. The rogue! She glanced at the door they had entered, but that one led outside and she'd never have enough time to wriggle into her tunic before he caught up with her.

She threw a glance at the opposite door. Surely it led into the longhouse . . . and if she went right now—

Zora screamed as she dashed for the door for at that same moment, Rurik lunged for her. Yet he wasn't quite fast enough for she had it open before he reached her and she rushed inside another room, only to stop right up against a huge wooden tub that was blocking her path.

"What . . . ?" She gasped as Rurik grabbed her from behind and lifting her kicking and squirming into his arms, he stepped with her into the tub.

"It will feel good, Zora, I promise you," she heard him say just before he knelt and then dunked her under the coldest water she had ever felt in her life.

"You're mad!" she sputtered a split second later when she came up for air, her shivering body one giant goose bump and her teeth chattering uncontrollably. Her fingers were so cold that she could barely shove her hair out of her eyes. "Mad, I tell you!"

"Exhilarating, isn't it?" Rurik said as if he hadn't heard her, and letting go of her suddenly, he disappeared for a long moment under the water, so long in fact that Zora began to grow anxious. Yet she needn't have worried for he exploded above the surface with a mighty splash that sent shimmering droplets flying through the room, extinguishing an oil lamp on a table near the tub. His delighted roar shook the rafters.

"By Odin, you can't come any closer to rolling in snow than this! Fresh water from a stream still ice-cold with the spring thaw!"

Zora stared at him incredulously, thinking herself a sorry contrast to Rurik's vigor. He looked like an invincible Norse god rising up from the water, his wet blond hair slicked back from his forehead, his skin sleek and tanned and his face flushed healthily, while she must appear a drowned rat.

"You roll in snow?"

"From October to May, if we're lucky." His broad smile warmed Zora more than she could have imagined possible. "Where do you think we Varangians gain our strength?" Then he sobered a little, beckoning to her. "Come here, Princess."

Inching over to him, Zora wondered what he might be plotting to do to her next in this damnable steam bath of his and she stopped just shy of his reach. "You're not going to dunk me again, are you?" she asked suspiciously, although the water didn't feel half so cold to her now that she had been in it for a while.

"Hardly, wife," came his low reply, but he didn't wait for her to come to him, he came to her. In a single splash, he captured her in his arms, and finding her mouth, his lips were as hot as firebrands upon hers.

Zora was certain she had never felt a kiss more passionate or more incredibly powerful, and within seconds, she no longer felt the cold at all for the seductive weight of his hands upon her body and the wet possession of his tongue as he led hers in a heady dance. Then she felt him cup her bottom and lift her and she was sinking onto fire and steel, the water churning around them.

He took her fast and hard and she let him, her thrusts as relentless and demanding as his own, but never once did their mouths lift from each other's as if neither could bear to breathe alone. And when their climax burst upon them, they shared it wildly, ecstatically, clutching each other as if all joy and life depended upon it for in that moment, it did.

CHAPTER
22

Zora's hair was still damp when she and Rurik took their places at the high seat. She couldn't believe that they were at supper just a little past the appointed hour.

Rurik's hunger for her had not abated after they left the tub, and only the fierce growling of his stomach had been a pointed reminder to him that he should seek some food. Yet he had laughingly hidden his need for nourishment under the guise of building his strength for later that evening, a thought that had filled Zora with dizzying expectation before they had even set foot from his longhouse.

"Good evening, my lady! My lord!" came Arne's boisterous greeting from Rurik's left, the warrior waving a foaming cup of mead. "We were about to give up on you, but it seems the old saying rings true, man cannot live by pleasure alone!"

Was it so obvious what she and Rurik had been doing? Zora wondered, a blush creeping over her face. She touched her hair, wishing it wasn't so thick so she could have dried it faster.

"Don't let him fluster you, Princess," Rurik said in a low aside as if he had known her thoughts. "You'll find that Arne says exactly what leaps onto his tongue. As we've known each other for years, it allows him liberties he deems as his right, I suppose, for putting up with me for so long."

She smiled, appreciating that Rurik had thought to reassure her, then seeing the warmth kindling in his night-blue eyes, she looked away, overwhelmed.

For weeks she hadn't allowed herself to recognize any good qualities in Rurik, and now she seemed to be noticing them all at once. His gentleness, his attentiveness, his humor.

She loved the wonderful richness of his laughter and how exuberant and unrestrained he had been in the bathhouse, giving her a glimpse of the playful boy inside the man. She loved the way he looked at her and the way he touched her. She loved the way he kissed her. Oh, she loved—

Take care, Zora warned herself just in time, her thoughts skirting dangerously close to a precipice she was trying so hard to avoid. She would never have imagined that Rurik letting down his guard around her could make her feel as if she didn't know which direction to turn, but it had! It was all she could do now to remember her plan, and with a start, she realized that she had scarcely thought of it for hours.

"Is anything wrong, Zora? You look troubled."

"No, no, I'm fine," she said, touched by the concern in Rurik's eyes that he made no effort to hide. Suddenly it was twice as hard to think clearly, but she forced herself by finding a matter to which she could turn her hand. "I . . . I was only wondering why the food has not yet been served. You must be so hungry and—"

"Perhaps the preparation has taken longer than the cooks anticipated." He laughed, holding up his brimming goblet. "At least we have fine Burgundian wine to soothe our stomachs. Don't fear, Princess. I will not starve."

"But it's wrong, just the same," she insisted, "and I plan

to speak with them in the morning. I had the chance to over-see several feasts for my father, and this is not proper. I was taught a great lord and his guests should never be kept wait-ing."

"Ah, is that what I am to you now?" Rurik's voice was full of teasing that did not reach his eyes. "A great lord? I thought I was just the husband with whom you've been cursed." As if he didn't want her to answer, he swiftly changed the subject. "What else did they teach you in Tmutorokan? It has occurred to me that I know very little about you other than some family history and that you don't like steam baths."

Zora was relieved to see him smiling again. She remem-bered all too well the angry words she had thrown at him the morning after their wedding, words that she now found her-self wishing she had never said.

"I suppose I learned things that any girl brought up in a palace would," she replied, warmed that he would want to know about her life. "How to embroider . . . Lady Canace never seemed to think we made enough vestments for the Church. How to take care of a household for the day when I would marry"—suddenly thinking of Ivan, Zora was surprised at how easily she could dismiss him from her mind—"and how to make perfume."

"Perfume?"

"Yes, Lady Canace had a passion for concocting fra-grance. She learned it at the emperor's palace in Constanti-nople before her marriage, and when Hermione and I were old enough, she taught us her skills, except Hermione had no desire to learn. She would rather soak in a tubful of rose pet-als than boil them, so she always insisted that I make her share."

"And did you?" Rurik asked gently.

Zora sighed. "If I wanted to live peacefully. But I enjoyed the work, so I didn't mind."

"It must have been hard for you, living in that *terem.*

From Grand Prince Yaroslav's description, Lady Canace and her daughter weren't the most gracious of creatures."

"No, they weren't," Zora agreed, recalling the slights and insults she had suffered at their hands and the worst indignity of all that Hermione had wrought upon her. Yet this time the memory of the trading camp was noticeably tempered, for it was that incident after all that had brought her to Rurik—

Stunned by her reasoning, Zora dropped her gaze to stare blindly at her hands. Yet she had no sooner done so than Rurik lifted her chin so he could look into her eyes.

"But you survived . . . beautifully, which proves your perseverance and courage." He chuckled, caressing the line of her jaw. "Your stubbornness must have helped, too, Princess. I've known few more headstrong than you."

Zora had to remind herself to breathe. Rurik's gaze was so intent that she feared he could see right into her heart.

"My—my mother was stubborn," she said, her words tumbling forth in a nervous rush as she sought to divert the topic from herself. "And proud. My father must have asked her a thousand times to come back with him to the palace, but she always refused. She had been banished once while he was gone from the city and she vowed never to endure the indignity again. We were happy in the country . . . until she became ill."

"What happened?"

"A fever. The climate could be very damp and she liked the out-of-doors so much. She had grown up in a small village before my father found her . . ." Realizing that she was running on and on, Zora sighed softly. "Forgive me. I must be boring you."

"You could never bore me," came Rurik's startling answer, his eyes burning into hers.

Zora found she could not swallow, let alone tear away her gaze even if she had wanted to. Her cheeks glowing, she heard herself stammer, "B-but what of you, Rurik? I know as little about you—"

"What would you like to know?" he asked, although his expression had tightened, his eyes becoming guarded.

Wondering at this change, Zora hoped her question would not upset him further. "Why do you still invoke your pagan gods? I find it a curious thing, considering you are Christian . . ."

Rurik seemed to visibly relax as if this was a topic he did not mind discussing, a small smile coming to his lips.

"To me, the gods are like familiar old friends who linger at the table long after the feast is done, telling long-winded yet fantastic tales that so astound and amaze that all who listen are reluctant to leave the hall even for the warmth of their beds."

"Like Odin?" Zora asked, entranced.

Rurik nodded. "The High One. All-knowing, all-powerful, the lord of battles and god of wisdom. To gaze deep into the well of knowledge, he paid for the privilege with one of his eyes. But he is a fickle god, giving victory to his favorites until he casts them aside for new champions. The fallen become his warriors in death's kingdom, Valhalla."

"Yet I have heard you call out to Thor more often," said Zora when Rurik paused for a draft of wine.

"Fighting men look to the giant god of thunder for strength, for every warrior strives to be like Thor, bold and invincible in battle. Yet as protector of the world, governing the sun and wind and rains, Thor is called upon to give bounty, not only in the fields, but for new brides to be made fruitful."

Zora started as Rurik reached out to caress her cheek.

"Which brings us to Frey, who understands well the needs and desires of men . . . and his sister, Freyja, the voluptuous goddess of plenty who embodies the sensual mysteries of women." Rurik slowly traced his finger over Zora's lips. "She has blessed few with such beauty and passion as you possess—"

"Would you care to wash your hands, my lady? My lord?"

As Rurik frowned at the interruption, Zora looked up in surprise at the young female slave bearing a large copper bowl. Nodding, she was so disconcerted by what Rurik had just said that her fingers were trembling as she dipped them into the water.

"Is the meal soon to be served?" she asked, her voice strangely breathless as she accepted a soft towel and dried her hands.

"I believe so, my lady," said the slave woman, although she really didn't look quite sure.

"This waiting cannot go on," Zora murmured in agitation due not so much to the meal but to the way Rurik was still looking at her. Eager for a reprieve, if only long enough to gather her fraying emotions, she added, "If I may, husband, I'd like to see what is causing the delay."

Rurik's first impulse was to say no, her sudden disquiet reminding him of her suspicious behavior at their wedding feast, but Arne's none-too-subtle jab to the ribs swayed him. Damn if that old Varangian hadn't been listening to their entire conversation!

"You need not request my permission to see to the things that rest in your domain," said Rurik, noting the pink color appearing upon Zora's cheeks. He hoped her blush meant his answer had pleased her. "All I ask, Princess, is that you do not rail overmuch at the cooks. They're a temperamental lot and may choose to retaliate by overseasoning the food."

"I promise to be diplomatic," she replied, granting him a smile as she arose that made him all the more loathe to allow her to leave his side for how much he would miss her. Yet knowing that this would be a good test of trust for them both, however uneasy it made him, Rurik nodded to an entrance-way across the hall.

"The cooking house is just beyond those doors."

As she began to wend her way gracefully through the tables, Rurik was about to gesture for her guards to follow but he changed his mind. Sighing, he leaned back in his chair and twirled his goblet restlessly before taking a long draught.

"She'll be back, my lord."

He turned to Arne, who was raising his cup of mead to him as if in salute.

"Maybe this time, friend, but the battle is far from won."

The warrior snorted, yet not unkindly. "I never said it would be in a day, or two, or even twenty. But at least now you have a chance, whereas before you would have chased her from your arms with your anger."

Rurik didn't answer but took another draft of wine, his eyes fixed upon the doors through which Zora had disappeared.

He could not deny that with her gone the very air seemed to be lacking in excitement, the torchlight grown dim, the buzzing conversation of his retainers grating upon his nerves, and the imported vintage flat and tasteless upon his tongue. He wanted her beside him, in this high seat with him where she belonged, just as surely as he knew now that he loved her.

Loki take him, he had been a fool to deny it to himself for so long, perhaps since the first moment she had looked into his eyes at the trading camp, pleading for his help. But that didn't make him fool enough to admit how he felt about her! Not yet. Not until he was sure that she might feel the same for him.

Call him a coward, but he had been burned once from rushing headlong into the flame and scarred for life by the misery of others to whom love had not been kind. This time, he would wait and watch and though he wasn't the most patient of men—evidenced by the reckless things he had already said to Zora—he would hope that the warmth he had seen shining in her eyes today would one day blaze into a fire.

"You see, my lord, your Rus bride did not run away. Already she comes and look, she has eyes only for you."

It was true, Rurik thought, leaning forward as Zora walked into the hall with a pleased smile upon her face, her gaze meeting his across the vast room as if to assure him that yes, supper was on its way. An instant later, a long line of slaves bearing steaming platters of food began to troop through the doors, only to fan out among the tables of hungry, cheering diners.

"Did the cooks threaten a revolt?" Rurik asked as Zora retook her seat beside him. He knew that his smile was as broad as any green youth's at his sweetheart, but he didn't care.

"Not at all," she answered lightly. Her cobalt-blue eyes sparkled with mischief, her earlier agitation all but vanished. "The food was ready. They only needed a few words of encouragement to load everything onto the platters."

"Dare I ask?"

Smiling, she shrugged. "I told them that great lords deserved great cooks who didn't keep them waiting . . . or else greater cooks could easily be found."

"Very diplomatic."

"I thought so."

As she turned from him to survey the goings on in the hall, Rurik could tell from the heightened rose of her cheeks that she knew he was watching her. And he liked her to be aware of him. He wanted her to be aware of him all the time!

Suddenly an idea came to him, something he had not thought to ask her until now.

"Zora?"

She met his eyes and for a fleeting moment he forgot what he was going to say, she was so beautiful.

"Yes?"

He cleared his throat, yet even then his voice was slightly hoarse. He was not used to tripping over himself when it came to women, yet Zora wasn't just any woman. "Did you have a favorite perfume among those you made?"

"White jasmine," she murmured softly. "But in

Tmutorokan, the flowers were very rare. They had to be brought all the way from Persia."

No more rare than you, Rurik thought. He was determined that if there was a gift he could give her, it would be one that he hoped would remind her of him whenever she wore it.

CHAPTER
23

"Aye, the threads are much straighter, my lady," Nellwyn said encouragingly as she surveyed the crooked piece of blue cloth hanging from the standing loom. "As I told you when we first started your lessons, it takes a fair amount of practice to learn to wield the weaving sword properly. But I'm sure you'll have it mastered in a another week or so."

"You're not a very good liar, Nellwyn," Zora replied with a small laugh. She sank onto a stool set to one side of the loom. "A whole year of practice would make little difference, let alone a few weeks. It's plain that weaving is not one of my strengths."

"I don't know, mayhaps if I took this cloth down and you started all over on a new one—"

"No, no, leave it." Sighing, Zora rubbed the nubbly fabric between her thumb and forefinger. She knew that it didn't look like much, but this length of woolen cloth meant something to her all the same.

During the past two weeks it was to this loom that she had always come to think, every lopsided row, every thread recalling the struggle she had waged in her heart. A struggle that she had finally admitted to herself had been won before it was even begun . . . love having proved the victor.

"I'd like to finish this piece," she added quietly, not surprised to find when she looked up that Nellwyn's expression held familiar empathy.

"As you wish, my lady. Would you like me to fetch you something to eat? It's almost midday and I've need of a bite or two myself." The slave woman grinned as she spread her hands over her growing stomach. "My Vasili swears the babe will be a brawny boy for how much I've been eating of late."

"Yes, that would be nice, Nellwyn, then I should meet Yakov at the main storehouse. He wants to go over our lists one last time. We'll be leaving early for the market." Zora smiled, grateful for the bond of friendship that had grown between them. Nellwyn had forgiven her deceit the day of the fire. "Are you sure there isn't something I could bring you? Some ribbon? A bit of lace? You've been so good to me."

"For the last time, you don't have to buy me any presents," Nellwyn insisted, sobering. "I've thanks enough in seeing that you took my words about Lord Rurik to heart. I've never seen him so happy in all my years here, and you've made him so."

"Do you really think he's happy?" asked Zora, niggling doubts crowding in upon her. "He hasn't said a word to me yet about how he feels . . ." She shook her head. "What if it's as he told me that first night, Nellwyn, when he said all would go back to what it had been after he has his fill of me? What if I've misread everything?"

"That cannot be, my lady. The new longhouses were finished days ago, but you still sleep in Lord Rurik's bed. He hasn't sent you away. And though I wasn't going to say anything until I knew more, I did hear talk this morning that he visited each of his concubines yesterday, yet I see this as a good thing—"

"He went to visit them?" Zora had never known her heart could ache so painfully.

"Only to speak to them for a few moments, don't fear. I wish to God I could tell you what was said, but he swore each of his women and their slaves to silence and no one has dared break it."

His women, Zora thought unhappily. She hated those words! She wanted to be the woman in Rurik's life, the *only* woman.

"How can this be a good thing, Nellwyn?" Zora rose from the stool to pace the floor in distraction. "To visit his . . . his women without saying a word to me, then to swear them to silence . . .?"

"Perhaps he has come to some decision about them that he wants you to hear from his lips alone, my lady. Something that may please you."

Stunned, Zora stopped to stare at the slave woman. "You mean that he might be planning to give up his concubines? How can he when some of those women have borne him children? I cannot believe that he would ever separate mothers from their babes and I wouldn't want him to!"

Now Nellwyn looked nonplussed as if she hadn't considered that issue, while Zora began to pace again.

"No, if my husband went to see his concubines, it had nothing to do with me and why would it? If he hasn't yet said anything to me about whether he cares—"

"Give Lord Rurik some time, my lady," interrupted Nellwyn, a hint of exasperation in her voice. "I'm sure all your questions will find an answer and as for why he hasn't shared his feelings with you, perhaps he is yet shielding his heart. I don't know what he suffered in his past, but it is well known that he swore never to marry. Yet you changed that, my lady, and I have no doubt that one day you will free him of that shield." Nellwyn fell silent for a moment, then asked gently, "Have you told him what lies hidden in your heart?"

Almost to the window, Zora came to a halt but she didn't turn around.

"No, not yet," she admitted, a sudden raw tightness in her throat. "I . . . I don't know if he would believe me. I don't know if he fully trusts me—"

"Aye, but that will change tomorrow. By your going into Novgorod without him, Lord Rurik has given you a chance to show that he can trust you . . . and for you to prove your love. Just think of the joy you'll both share when all the barriers have fallen between you, my lady. After tomorrow, one more will be gone."

"Yes, the joy," Zora said softly to herself as Nellwyn left to fetch her meal. But it was hard to think of such happiness when those barriers sometimes seemed so high.

Faith and trust were precious things not so easily won. She had already done everything she knew these past weeks to prove to Rurik that she could be trusted, that he had no reason to doubt her, but obviously it wasn't enough. She supposed she couldn't blame him after her attempts to thwart him in the past, and he probably still held Kjell's death against her. But if he cared, wouldn't he have forgiven her?

Sighing as she moved to the window, Zora leaned upon the sill and turned her face upward to the warm, soothing sunlight.

Funny. If she chose to crawl out of this window right now, she wouldn't be greeted by a guard as she would have when she first came to the compound. Since the night she had gone to chastise Rurik's cooks, he had allowed her to walk about freely with no escort at all.

She would never forget her elation when she realized that he had not sent guards after her, another good sign that he was willing to trust her. She could come and go as she pleased, and tomorrow she would be journeying to Novgorod with Yakov and a handful of warriors sent along not to watch her but to carry her purchases.

Nor had Rurik ever questioned her again about her interest in his household. It was as if he had simply accepted it, taking almost as much delight in how smoothly everything was running, especially the evening meals, as she derived in pleasing him.

And she wanted to please him! It was amazing how quickly her plan had fallen by the wayside—practically as soon as she had conceived it!—but all she had to do was look in Rurik's eyes to know that she could no more betray him than leave him. Not now. Not when she knew that she loved him as she had never thought possible.

"Yet you betray your father," Zora whispered, unable to make that sharp pang of guilt fade. What would Mstislav say if he knew she had fallen in love with one of his enemies and wished to remain here in Novgorod? One of his hated brother's most famed warriors, the very man she had been forced to wed?

No, don't think of it! she told herself firmly, rubbing her aching temples. Nor did she want to think about the battle that was looming ever closer, although that specter was much more difficult to chase from her mind.

The air seemed forever to be ringing with the ominous sounds of Rurik and his men hard at their training, from dawn to dusk, every day no matter the weather. He had already told her that they would be sailing for Chernigov as soon as Varangian reinforcements arrived from the north, surprising her that he would trust her with such information. And three nights out of the last seven he had spent at the *kreml* in Novgorod, summoned by her uncle to councils of war.

Those were the worst times. Lying alone in that huge bed, her fears seemed to run away with her, the same awful questions tumbling over and over in her mind.

What was the future going to bring? Would her father win, or Yaroslav? She felt herself a traitor for even thinking that her father might lose, but what if he didn't? What if Rurik was captured and taken prisoner, or, even worse, killed during the battle?

"No, no, no!" Zora spun from the window, her heart slamming like a battering ram against her breast. Suddenly she was breathing so hard, she thought she might faint.

Groping for a nearby chair, she sat down and dropped her head to her hands, waiting dazedly for the sensation to pass. She thought she heard a door open but she couldn't be sure, and she felt too dizzy to raise her head.

"Nellwyn?"

Now she heard footsteps rushing toward her, but they weren't those of a woman. She did not have to look up to know it was Rurik who sank to his haunches beside her.

"Zora, what's wrong?"

"Nothing . . . I'm fine," she murmured, daring to lift her head and meet his eyes that were filled with as much concern as his voice. To her relief, the sensation of dizziness was rapidly fading. "I felt a little light-headed . . . but it's almost gone."

"By Thor, woman, you've been working yourself too hard!" said Rurik with more vehemence than he had intended, but unable to help himself for how pale she was. His reaction to this alone only reinforced the depth of his love for her. To see her so was like a sword thrust to his heart. "I was thinking only this morn that you've taken on too many duties, too fast. Usually you wake when I leave the bed but today you slept on as if one dead."

"Perhaps that was due more to how late you kept me awake with your demands, husband," she said softly, sitting up straight in the chair as if to show him that she was feeling better. "I would swear you possess the appetite of ten men, or at least five very greedy ones."

Reassured as much by the sparkle returning to her eyes as her teasing tone, Rurik felt a swell of emotion in his chest that was very difficult to contain. It was all he could do to tell himself that he had only to wait one more day, just *one more day,* before he could allow himself to believe that she harbored no desire to escape.

"I heard no complaints last night, Princess," he countered huskily, thinking that if not for his wretched past, he might have already surrendered to the heated emotion he had glimpsed time and again in those stunning blue depths. Yet some small part of himself still had to be convinced. He had refused for so long to put faith in any woman that his fear of betrayal was almost as strong as the love he carried in his heart.

"In fact if memory serves," he added, reassured further by the saucy tilt of her chin, "I think it was you who coerced me into another—"

"Coerced?" Zora broke in, grateful to be feeling more like herself with each passing moment. Nor was it hard to push all troubling thoughts to the furthest recesses of her mind with Rurik now smiling at her so roguishly. "I only kissed you where you told me you liked to be kissed . . . oh!"

Rurik had risen to his feet and pulled her into his arms so suddenly that her head spun all over again. Yet this time it was wonderfully different.

"If our conversation continues on its present course, lady, I may forget why I came here and seek some other diversion than the one I had intended."

"Why did you come here?" asked Zora, delighting in the sheer strength of his arms as he held her close and the masculine smell of him. "You're usually with your men at this hour."

"I decided to leave Nils in charge for the rest of the afternoon. It's a beautiful day, the warmest one yet, and I thought you might enjoy a swim. I know I'd like one."

"A swim?" Zora pulled back a bit to eye him suspiciously. "If you're planning to get me into that tub of yours again—"

His resonant laughter silenced her and she stared at him in confusion, wondering what he might be plotting.

"Not the tub, Princess. I've a favorite place I'd like to show you outside the compound, especially now after finding you as I did. Fresh air and a break from your labors will do you good."

"But I don't know how to swim," she said, a niggling of fear pressing in upon her. "The one time I tried, Hermione held me under by the hair . . ." She shuddered. "If I hadn't scratched her legs, I wouldn't be here today."

"By Odin, if I ever meet that woman," swore Rurik, having heard enough tales of Hermione's jealous abuses in the last two weeks to turn his stomach at the slightest mention of her name. Sensing Zora's apprehension, he hugged her more tightly.

"You may not agree with me, but I think that's all the more reason you should learn. I'm an excellent swimmer, Zora, so you have nothing to fear. I'd be with you every moment." Feeling her stiffen despite his assurances, he gently stroked her cheek. "It's a lovely spot, Princess. I know you would like it. Let me show it to you."

"But Nellwyn is bringing me some dinner, and then I promised Yakov that we'd go over our lists again—"

"Yakov can check the lists without you," Rurik said firmly, although he was encouraged by Zora's concern for the details of her trip to Novgorod . . . a promising sign that sent his pulse racing. "I already spoke to Nellwyn on my way over here from the cooking house, where I picked up some food to eat after our swim. Now what do you say?"

Staring into Rurik's eyes, Zora felt her reservations fading in the sudden wave of hope that swept over her.

He was being so insistent. Surely it must be for some special reason, for he had never before left the training field early to spend time with her. Dear God, please may it be so! If she at least had some words of love to reassure her before he left, maybe his absence wouldn't seem so bad . . .

"Very well," she murmured, suddenly both excited and nervous. "But if I decide when we get there that I don't want to swim—"

"I would never force you, Zora." He kissed her then so tenderly that it took her breath away, her hope flaring all the brighter.

The winding stream they had followed was beautiful, Zora couldn't deny it, but no more so than the spot where

Rurik finally halted their mount. At its narrowest point, much of the tumbling water had been dammed by huge craggy boulders that looked as if they had been strewn there by some giant's hand, forming a glistening pool that was framed by deep green firs of majestic beauty.

"I call this place Thor's Grove. Do you like it?"

"It's lovely," she said as Rurik slid from the saddle and lifted her to the ground.

"I haven't been here since early April, right before I left on my mission." Still clasping her waist, Rurik looked around him. "The snow was thick then . . . almost as high as that small pine."

Following his gaze, Zora couldn't help asking, "Who came out here with you that time?"

He met her eyes, a curious smile upon his lips. "No one, Princess. I've never brought anyone here before."

Her breath suddenly jammed in her throat, Zora had no idea how she should respond but Rurik solved her dilemma by taking her hand and leading her to the mossy bank. Bending on one knee, he glided his hand across the sparkling, sunlit surface.

"Hmmm, it may not be warm enough for you. Why don't you try it and tell me what you think?"

Zora kicked off her slipper and stuck her toe tentatively in the water. "It's not that cold," she pronounced. Then startled to see some small, silvery blue fish dart by, she grew doubtful. "It looks deep."

"No more than a few inches above my head near the middle—"

"Then a good foot and a half above mine." Zora backed away. "I don't know, Rurik . . ."

"If it will make you feel better," he said, grabbing her hands to stay her retreat, "I'll make sure your head stays above water. You must trust me, Zora. I would never let anything happen to you."

Here he was telling her to trust him! Zora wished that she had the courage to demand of him the same thing. Yet his promise had done much to sway her reluctance. Her nod was greeted by a broad grin, and he released her to begin stripping off his clothes.

"Are you sure no one will see us?" she asked uncertainly, glancing behind her. To reach the stream, they had ridden past tilled fields being tended by slaves and, farther out, cleared pasture where cattle and sheep were grazing under the watchful eyes of armed shepherds ever alert for thieves. She still remembered her surprise when she had found out from Yakov during her tour of the domestic buildings that the compound wasn't wholly surrounded by forest.

"We're out too far," said Rurik as he pulled off his boots. "I told you before I would never risk another man glimpsing your beauty, Zora." In moments, he had yanked off his trousers to stand naked before her but for his gold earring, his battle-hardened body a burnished golden brown in the bright sunlight.

Her heart suddenly beating faster, Zora found she could not stop staring at him, and still she hadn't made a move to take off her own clothing.

"This happens so often, Princess, my undressing before you do, that I'm beginning to think you like for me to help you."

"Perhaps I do," she said playfully, breaking her gaze from his formidable physique to look into his eyes. "You've quite a knack with women's clothing, husband."

With a low growl he drew her roughly toward him, his hands expert as he divested her of every stitch. Then he enfolded her in his arms, not to hug her as she had thought but to sweep her from her feet.

"It will be easier this way," he said as he began to walk into the pool, the water quickly rising from his knees to his hips. Zora gasped, feeling the cold upon her bare bottom, but she shrieked when he suddenly seemed to step off a ledge, the water now covering her to her chin.

"I—it's freezing!" she cried, her teeth chattering.

"But not as ice-cold as the tub."

"N-no," she agreed, wondering how far into the pool Rurik planned to go. He seemed to be drawing ominously close to the middle. "S-should you w-walk out any m-more? It—it might g-get too deep."

"I doubt it. The water seems shallower this year—"

Suddenly Rurik slipped as if the bottom had plummeted from beneath his feet. Zora flung her arms around his neck, terrified.

"Easy, Princess," he soothed her, swimming effortlessly with her back the way they had come. "It's not as shallow as I had thought, but at least I know where the drop-off is." Finding his footing, he stood again, his broad shoulders above the water, his tanned skin beaded with moisture. "Now I want you to hold my hands like this"—tugging her arms gently from his neck, he interlaced his fingers with hers—"and I'm going to push you out just a little—"

"Rurik . . ."

"Trust me, Zora, I'm right here with you. Now kick your legs."

In her panic, she kicked so vigorously that water flew high into the air and all around them. Rurik began to laugh.

"Easy, Princess, or we won't have enough water in this pool to swim back to shore."

Gradually Zora was able to relax and encouraged by Rurik's patient coaching, teasing, and coaxing, she grew braver and even let go of his hands a few times to attempt swimming on her own. It was a bit embarrassing, for she must hardly appear graceful flailing her arms and legs about. But if Rurik thought her ungainly he said not a word.

He didn't let her rest until she had tried swimming not only on her stomach but her back, then as if sensing her limbs were growing tired, which they were, he drew her back to shallower water that came only as high as her breasts. Staring at her lingeringly, he nonetheless released her and moved backward a few steps.

"My turn," he said with a smile. Before she could answer,

he dived away from her so cleanly that he left scarcely a ripple behind him.

"Rurik?"

She rolled her eyes at herself. Of course he couldn't hear her, yet when was he going to come up for air? It felt so strange to be standing there with no other sounds around her than the breeze whooshing through the trees and the water rumbling between the gap in the boulders . . .

He must have read her anxious thoughts for he burst above the mirrorlike surface at that moment and began to swim with long, powerful strokes from one end of the pool to the other. Wondering how many of Rurik's lessons it would take before she might be able to swim so expertly, Zora felt a pall drift over her enjoyment. Would there be many more lessons before he left with his men? Would she ever come here with him again?

Heartsick, Zora watched as Rurik dived once more, but this time the sun was so bright upon the water she couldn't see where he had gone. Standing in place, she began to circle slowly, looking for him and feeling so terribly alone—

"Oh . . . !"

Zora couldn't have been more surprised when he suddenly broke through the surface right in front of her, and grabbing her around the waist, he lifted her high from the water, his laughter resounding all around them.

"By Odin, a river nymph!" Rurik exulted, lowering Zora back down to face him. Expecting to find her smiling, he couldn't have been more startled to find that she had burst into tears.

CHAPTER
24

"Zora? By God, little one, I didn't mean to frighten you . . ."

Hugging her close, Rurik was totally at a loss. Her slender body was shaking with sobs, and feeling her beginning to shiver, he lifted her in his arms and made his way to the bank, where he set her down upon the soft moss. He left her for only an instant to grab the leather bag hanging from the saddle and then he was back at her side, gathering her close again as he pulled out a blanket and whipped it around her quaking shoulders.

"Forgive me, Princess." Rurik stroked her damp hair as her tears soon soaked his chest. "I wasn't thinking. I should have known I might alarm you, but it never occurred to me."

He *hadn't* frightened her, Zora wanted so desperately to tell him as she sobbed harder than she could remember ever having done before. But if she said that, he would want to know what had brought on this bout of tears and she wasn't ready to tell him that either! Not when she still wasn't sure if he would even want to hear how she felt . . . if it even mattered to him how much she loved him, how much she feared for him . . . how much she didn't want him to leave her . . .

"Easy, Zora, it can't be that bad," he said, holding her slightly away from him and tilting up her face. Tenderly, he stroked her tearstained cheek with his thumb. "Sshh, now, everything's fine. We're out of the water and you're here safe with me. Sshh . . ."

Staring into his eyes, her vision blurred from crying, Zora felt herself soothed by his words despite the ache in her heart, and she shuddered in his arms, her sobs gradually lessening. She did feel safe and warm and protected and, with each passing moment, more in control of herself. Shuddering one last time, her hiccup brought a smile to Rurik's face.

"That's it, little one. It was only a small scare. Nothing to cause so many tears."

Zora softly drew in her breath as Rurik bent his head and pressed his lips to hers, the warm pressure of his mouth lulling her more than anything he could have said. Then she hiccuped again, and to her amazement, she found herself giggling when he chuckled against her mouth.

"How quickly the fair lady's feeling better," he teased, his breath warming her lips. "Perhaps another kiss and she'll forget what so upset her."

Rurik's lips this time were not so gentle, his tightening embrace swamping Zora with excitement. Yet she knew nothing that he did could make her forget the anguish lying hidden inside her.

And she didn't want to forget! She would share with him just how she felt but not in words, for she couldn't bring herself to voice what she held in her heart. Yet there were other ways, ways perhaps more expressive than anything she could say . . .

It was Zora who deepened their kiss, her wandering tongue surprising his as she wantonly tasted the inside of his mouth, her hands gliding up Rurik's chest to his immense shoulders where she caressed muscles that were wonderfully hard beneath her palms. If at first he had seemed startled, he soon groaned with pleasure, yet he did not allow her to keep the upper hand for long.

His tongue sought to ravage her mouth as wildly as she had just done, their kiss becoming a passionate dueling that made Zora feel as if she were on fire. Wrenching off the blanket that was only fettering her, she pressed herself that much closer to Rurik's body, for his was the heat she craved. His was the kiss she wanted, and as she slid her hands up the back of his neck, her fingers funneling along his scalp and entwining in his hair, she cried out to him in her mind.

I love you!

She felt herself falling backward as Rurik pushed her to the spongy, moss-covered ground, his mouth burning a blistering path down her throat and across her shoulder while his masterful hands stoked the flames building inside her. She caressed him in kind, his powerful back, his upper arms so thick with muscle, the massive breadth of his chest and the crisp golden curls upon it, delighting in the smooth texture of his skin and the sun-warmed scent of his body.

Then she strayed even lower, wrapping her fingers around silken steel and muscle, exulting when Rurik groaned and called out her name. But she didn't stop, squeezing and stroking him until his body was shaking and he rolled onto his back as if he feared he might collapse upon her. Zora was astride him before he could reach out to her, her lips branding the spot above his racing heart.

I love you!

She moved lower, her hands splayed upon his taut abdomen as she kissed the glistening blond hair trailing to his navel. Then she teased the sensitive hollow with her tongue while Rurik cried out again.

"Woman . . . !"

He tried to pull her up to him but she deftly eluded his hands and found what she had been seeking, his turgid flesh leaping against her mouth as she kissed him and began to stroke the thick length of him with her tongue. Already he was tossing beneath her but she didn't stop, torturing him relentlessly as she drew him with a swirling caress into her mouth.

She tasted a wetness and knew he was very close to release, but she wanted to tease him to the brink of endurance. Her fingers enmeshed for a brief instant in the thatch of blond curls she found so arousing before she drifted lower and cupped him in her hand, squeezing gently.

"Zora, enough!"

Rurik's voice was so hoarse with passion that she knew she could not sway him and she didn't resist when he pulled her up beside him and pushed her once more on her back. Before she could blink he was poised between her legs, his midnight-blue eyes sweeping her with a look of fire.

"Where did you learn such wicked things, Princess?"

Zora gasped as he easily slid his fingers inside her before she could answer and teased her legs wider apart as she arched beneath his carnal caress. She already wanted him so badly, she was trembling from head to toe, and she cried out when he buried himself deep inside her with a ragged groan.

"Hold me, Zora . . . hold me!" came his wild plea and she gripped him with all her strength, her arms flying around his neck and her legs locking at his back.

She felt him stiffen, heard his breath snag in his chest . . . then her own climax came upon her so suddenly that she felt hot tears burn her eyes, but this time they were tears of sweet fulfillment. When she at last opened her eyes heart-pounding moments later, she was staring up into the clear blue sky, Rurik's damp head resting upon her shoulder, his breath warm upon her cheek.

It was so wonderful holding him like this that she wished it could go on forever and she hugged him tightly, willing him to stay. Yet she knew that soon he would roll from her, fearing as always that he might crush her even though she had insisted time and again that she was stronger than she may appear.

Just as she had thought, he shifted and rose onto his forearms but instead of lifting himself from her, he smiled into her eyes. She smiled back, hoping that he could read what she could not yet tell him . . . *I love you, Rurik Sigurdson.*

"You know, wife, you never cease to amaze me," Rurik said gently, struck as ever by her tawny beauty but even more so by the softness in her gaze. By the gods, surely she would not be looking at him like that if . . .

"How so?" she replied, the warmth in her voice only fueling a gut intuition that he wanted so badly to believe. Tempted as never before to admit what lay in his heart, he nonetheless forced himself to think rationally, his fear of betrayal rearing its ugly head like a thing he could not control.

"Tears one moment, passion the next." He shrugged. "You're a hard one to understand."

"Not so hard as you may think, Rurik," said Zora, wondering why he had grown so somber when he had been smiling at her an instant before. "I could say the same about you . . . although I believe there are things you haven't shared with me yet that could explain so much." To her amazement, he suddenly seemed irritated, and rolling to one side, he lay next to her on his back, stone silent as he stared up at the sky.

She had never seen him quite like this before, sensing in him an agitation that was palpable enough to touch.

Usually after their lovemaking, he was open and willing to talk, and so they had, about his childhood and his life since he had left Norway for Rus, his quick rise within her uncle's ranks. About his trading ventures to far-off Byzantium, and even how he had come to be called Beast-Slayer, a story that had convinced her if any wild creatures had come after her in the woods the night of her escape, Rurik would have had no trouble bringing them down.

The only thing they hadn't talked about was the woman who had betrayed him, and she couldn't help thinking that perhaps that was what he feared she was going to ask him now. Well, why shouldn't she? She could hardly ease the treachery from his heart as Lady Ingigerd had said if she didn't know the full story behind it.

Taking a deep breath, Zora raised herself on one elbow to face him. She didn't think to cover her nakedness with the blanket, for their intimacy was such now that she felt completely at ease around him. He knew every inch of her.

"Rurik?"

He refused to look at her, convincing her all the more that he sensed exactly what she was going to say.

"Why did you swear never to marry?"

His expression became grimmer but he didn't get up and walk away, which to Zora was a good sign.

"You already know the answer to that, Princess. You have thrown it in my face once before."

"Yes, I know, and it was unkind of me," she said, watching him for his reactions. "I was hurt that day and I wanted to hurt you back, but I don't think it's true anymore."

He met her eyes. "What?"

"That you're hard and unfeeling . . . that your heart is made of stone."

He sat up so abruptly that she was taken by surprise. Yet he made no comment although his jaw was working as he stared straight ahead of him, his arms propped on his knees.

"What I meant is I've seen you with your children. You love them, I can tell. And in a way, I believe you care about your concubines, too. You could have dealt much more harshly with Semirah, yet you didn't—"

When he glanced at her sharply, Zora fell silent, almost losing her nerve to continue.

"What does Semirah or any of my concubines have to do with my vow not to marry?"

"N-nothing," she said, her heart sinking. It was obvious that he hadn't brought her out here today to explain why he had gone to see his women, but she wasn't going to give up on the other, more important issue plaguing her mind. Not yet, anyway. Sighing, she decided to try another tack.

"What was her name, Rurik? The woman in Norway."

He looked away, his tone grown bitter. "Astrid."

Pained that he could yet feel so much emotion for a

woman who had hurt him so long ago, Zora nonetheless believed that it was all the more reason to persist.

"Did . . . did you love her?"

Rurik exhaled in exasperation, dropping his forehead to his arms. Why was she torturing him with these questions? And as for her observation about his concubines, had she perhaps heard that he had visited them yesterday?

Thor's blood, if he discovered that someone had broken their oath of silence . . . ! *He* wanted to be the one to tell her that he had decided to marry his remaining women to five of his warriors, something to which his concubines had thankfully made little or no protest, understanding what Zora now meant to him. But he would tell her after tomorrow. After he was sure!

"I was young," he finally muttered. He raised his head to stare in front of him again. "I barely knew the meaning of the word."

Then, thinking guiltily that he was being far too harsh and that there was no good reason why he shouldn't share this part of his past with her other than how uncomfortable it made him, he added, "Yes, I believed I was in love with her, but apparently she had only been toying with me. When my brother Rolf's wife died after childbirth, Astrid was right there to comfort him. I suppose a man who one day would be a powerful chieftain seemed far more tempting than a second son who must make his way by sword and by trade."

When Zora did not reply, Rurik turned to find her studying him intently as if she didn't believe that he had told her everything.

"Does my answer not satisfy you?"

She slowly shook her head.

Sensing that this woman knew him far better than he could have imagined possible, Rurik sighed heavily. "May I ask why not?"

"You speak Astrid's name with bitterness, yet I cannot believe that it was only her betrayal that caused you to denounce all women and to deem them worthy of no more a

place in your life than to share your bed and bear your children. No, I believe your hurt goes much deeper."

Her bluntless startled him. Wondering where she might be
leading him with such a pronouncement, Rurik decided to be
just as blunt.

"If my hurt goes deep, it is only because I have witnessed
more treachery in women than loyalty—"

"Is that what happened to Sveinald?"

Rurik was as stunned by her question as hearing his long-
dead friend's name upon her lips. "How did you . . . ?"

"On the riverboat. Late one evening you began to recite
poetry with Kjell and I was still awake in the tent. I heard
you speak of Sveinald as your closest friend, and that he had
lost his life because of a woman—"

"Solveig, one of the loveliest women in the Hardanger,"
Rurik broke in, struck by how much the memory still pained
him after so many years. "She led Sveinald to believe that
she loved him no matter the long-standing oath of blood vengeance between their two families, and he was so taken by
her beauty that he would heed no warnings, not even from
me. One night she lured him to his death, her three brothers
falling upon him with knives when he came to her bower.
They cut him to pieces, then threw his flesh to the dogs."

"How terrible," breathed Zora.

"No more terrible than what happened to my mother because of another scheming woman," he added, his voice as
harsh as she had ever heard it as he turned his face from her
to stare at some distant point.

"I told you some nights ago that I left Norway because I
wanted to seek my fortune, but that wasn't the truth. If I had
stayed, my father's blood would have stained my sword. He
abandoned my mother for his Welsh concubine Gwyneth,
who cruelly harried my mother into her grave while my father did nothing to stop it . . . an aging fool of a chieftain
made blind by fiery hair and a young, voluptuous body."
Rurik snorted in disgust. "The bastard married Gwyneth the

day after my mother died. I hope she has made his life as much a Hel."

He fixed his angry, pain-filled gaze back upon Zora, his shoulders stiff with tension. "Are you satisfied now, wife? Have you heard enough?"

Seeing what it had cost him to reveal so much to her, Zora said softly, "Enough that I understand why you first treated me as you did, and said the things you did. Enough that I would understand if you still blame me for Kjell's death, and rightly. So many times I've wished I could take back the events of that day, that I hadn't run away into those woods . . . that I hadn't misled him as I did. If I can't forgive myself, I don't know how I could ever expect you to."

Rurik didn't reply, yet she could see the strain easing from his face and body as if her words had moved him. When he finally spoke, his tone was hauntingly quiet. "I don't blame you, Princess. Not anymore."

Swept by wild elation, Zora's heart began to beat faster at the way Rurik was looking at her. His gaze no longer held pain but a candidness that made her hope flare bright.

"You don't?"

He shook his head, reaching out to touch a damp curl that clung to her arm. "It was my fault for having brought Kjell along on that mission. If he had been a fighter instead of a poet, he would have known not to rush headlong into those woods without his sword at the ready. Such a simple thing could have saved him. And as for you trying to escape, you only acted as you felt you must. If I ever had a daughter in a like situation, I would want her to fight just as hard as you did."

Scarcely able to believe what he had just told her, Zora shivered as his knuckles grazed her breast. "Then if you've forgiven me," she murmured, finding it very hard to concentrate, "perhaps you don't look upon me as harshly as you once did. After everything you've suffered in the past, I would understand if it might take you a while to admit . . ." Her courage faltering, she glanced nervously at the ground.

"Admit what, Zora?"

His tone was gentle, yet probing. He was scarcely breathing as if hanging upon her every word.

"I . . . I thought that was why you had brought me out here today," she began haltingly, her cheeks flushing with warmth as she met his eyes. "Not just to swim, but because you might want to tell me—"

Zora got no further, for suddenly Rurik gestured for her to be silent while he inclined his head slightly, listening for something. She heard nothing, but he must have for he lunged to his feet and found his belt. His sword seemed to ring as he yanked it from the scabbard.

"What—"

"The blanket, Zora. Wrap it around yourself. Now!"

She obeyed him, watching anxiously as he tugged on his trousers. It was then that she heard it, the unmistakable sound of galloping horses drawing closer and closer. She had no sooner stood, clutching the blanket around her, when three riders burst through the trees. Yet she relaxed when she recognized Arne and two more of Rurik's men, as did Rurik who lowered his sword as the warriors reined in their lathered mounts only a few feet away from him.

"My lord, a message has just come from the grand prince," announced Arne, his bearded face beet-red and sweating. "He has called an immediate meeting at the *kreml*. The reinforcements have arrived."

"At last," Rurik said under his breath, then catching one of the warriors who had accompanied Arne casting a covert glance at Zora, he shouted, "Wait for us beyond those trees!"

Thinking as the three men rode away that he would have to speak to the younger warrior, Rurik turned to find Zora already gathering up her clothes.

"I'm sorry, Princess," he said. But she seemed not to have heard him, moving woodenly and avoiding his eyes as she dressed. Only when he had settled her in the saddle did he try again, holding her close against him after he mounted behind her.

"We will talk later. I promise." Growing concerned when still she did not answer, he prodded, "Zora?"

"Yes, later," she replied in a strange monotone, her body rigid in his arms.

Sighing, Rurik would have liked to say more, but there was no time.

Spurring their mount into a gallop, his thoughts turned to the urgency of Grand Prince Yaroslav's message and the council of war that would probably go well into the night. Yet however late it ended, he planned to awaken Zora as soon as he arrived home. He would hear what she had been going to say . . . words he hoped would confirm the intuition that even now was driving all other matters from his mind.

CHAPTER
25

"My lady, does this cloth not please you? It is of the finest quality, pure Byzantine silk . . . My lady?"

"What?" Startled, Zora focused upon the shimmering bolt of yellow fabric that Yakov was pointing out to her.

"I said does this silk not please you?"

"Oh, yes, it's lovely," she murmured, although in truth she might have been looking at coarse wool for all the enjoyment it brought her. As the steward began to haggle with the merchant over the price, obviously having assumed that she must want some for a new tunic, Zora found her gaze straying once again to the imposing *kreml* that lay directly across the Volkhov River from the marketplace.

Rurik was still there, the council of war having lasted through the night and now continuing into the morning. That could only mean war was at hand. How could she find pleasure in silk and brocade while the man she loved would soon be leaving, perhaps never to return—

No, she mustn't think like that! At least she was here in

Novgorod and close to him rather than pacing their bed-chamber as she had done all night, unable to sleep for those same terrible questions roiling in her mind.

If the meeting ended soon, Rurik might even come to the market to find her. Then perhaps they could talk as Rurik had promised and this time she would not allow anything to stop her.

Deep in the night, she had realized that if she was to free him of his past, she would have to tell him of her love. If she harbored fears, she could imagine what his must be. No wonder he was testing her! It was so plain to her now why he needed to know that he could trust her. True, her life had been touched by treachery, but not anywhere as tragically as his.

"My lady, if you will come this way, I'd like to show you something in another section of the market," said Yakov, his nasally voice once more breaking into her thoughts. "Something that I think will please you."

Puzzled by the steward's enigmatic smile, Zora waited while Yakov handed the wrapped bolt of silk to one of the four warriors who were following them at a discreet distance. Then the spare little man eagerly led her through the bustling market, pointing out various of the brightly colored stalls—a locksmith whom he trusted or a merchant known for the quality of his rubies—until they came to an area that she recognized at once from the cacophony of smells as the perfumer's section.

"Lord Rurik asked me to buy whatever you need to make your perfumes, my lady," Yakov announced, waving his thin, white hand at the many stalls. "Copper braziers to distill the precious oils, flowers fresh plucked from the fields, spices, sweet gums and resins, ambergris and musk to fix the scents, and over here"—he beckoned to her as he moved to a nearby stall, the same secretive smile upon his narrow face—"rare oils from the fabled city of Constanti-nople."

Flushed with pleasure at Rurik's generosity, Zora watched the swarthy Greek merchant who stood behind the counter set a delicate blue-green bottle in front of her.

"What is it?" she asked excitedly, her intuition pricked as Yakov's smile grew wider. She and the steward might have started out on the wrong footing, but since she had made it clear to him that she had no intention of usurping his duties, he had gone out of his way to be kind to her.

"A gift from your husband. Lord Rurik sent men into the city each morning to ask if any perfumers had come from the south, and two days ago, word was brought that this merchant possessed the scented oil you favor. Lord Rurik thought to present it to you himself, but he decided you might enjoy the surprise of finding it here."

"White jasmine?" Zora didn't have to see Yakov's nod to know that it was so. She had no sooner pulled out the stopper than she was greeted with the lush, intoxicating fragrance. She closed her eyes, savoring its beauty.

"You are pleased, my lady?"

"More than I could ever say." Remembering how Rurik had looked at her when he had asked what was her favorite scent, it was all Zora could do to return the stopper for how her fingers had begun to tremble. She clasped the precious bottle to her breast. "I'd like to carry it, Yakov. My husband might meet us here and I want to thank him . . ."

"Whatever you wish, my lady. Now if I may, I'll leave you to choose the things you need while I speak with some of the other merchants. But I'll be back soon to pay for your purchases, and Lord Rurik's men will not be far away if you have need of them."

"Yes, thank you, Yakov," she murmured. She was so absorbed in the fragrant array of Eastern spices at the next few stalls that long moments passed before she realized when looking around her that she had been left completely alone, Rurik's warriors nowhere in sight among the dense throng of shoppers. It dawned on her then that her test had begun, and smiling confidently to herself, she bent to sniff some pungent cinnamon.

"I cannot say that I'm pleased to see how well captivity suits you, my love, but at least you were easy to find."

Zora froze, her heart suddenly slamming in her throat. *Dear God, no, it couldn't be* . . .

"What's this? No fond greeting for your betrothed? Perhaps I've cause to be jealous after all of the bastard you were forced to wed. I sensed as much after witnessing how favorably you respond to his gifts."

Zora slowly straightened, seeing first a tall man wearing the plain brown garb and hood of a monk before she could find it within herself to focus upon his face. She could no more swallow than speak as she met Ivan's cold blue gaze.

"Yes, it's me," he said, keeping his voice very low, "but we have no time to answer your questions. My men are waiting for us at the wharf."

"Y-your men?" Zora's voice was a mere squeak.

"I didn't come alone to rescue you, and from the looks of it," he spat, his tone derisive, "I would almost think that you may not want to be rescued."

"I . . . I don't."

Ivan's angry countenance grew all the blacker.

"I'm sorry, Ivan, but I want to stay here—"

"So it is as I thought," he cut in bitterly. "Wedded and well bedded and now a traitor to her own countrymen. Hardly the news to encourage your father to spare this Lord Rurik of Novgorod if he falls into our hands."

"What are you saying?" blurted Zora, Ivan's ominous words passing like an ice-cold hand over her heart.

"Simple, my love. Come with me and you can plead for your husband's life when the battle falls to our favor. If Lord Rurik is captured, surely you know he will be held for execution, but perhaps your voice raised in his defense will sway your father's judgment. Yet if you stay here, you will have no way to help him, no way to be heard." Glancing around them, Ivan shifted impatiently. "Choose, Zora, and quickly. The time to be gone is now!"

Holy Mother of God, what was she going to do? Zora wondered desperately, her mind racing. She didn't want to leave! Not now! Now when she and Rurik were so close to admitting their love for each other. Yet she could not deny that Ivan was making sense. Damn him for making sense!

She had been tormented for days with thoughts of what might happen to Rurik if her father's forces prevailed, imprisonment, torture, and, if what Ivan said was true, execution, yet now she was being presented with a way to intercede for him. Surely her father would listen to her pleas!

And if he didn't win and Grand Prince Yaroslav retained his throne, Rurik would get her back . . . that is, if he would still want her after her seeming treachery. She had no doubt that he would think the worst of her, yet she could explain everything to him when they were together again. Surely he would understand that she had left him out of love—

"Zora, there is no more time!"

"I don't know . . ." she whispered, never having felt so horribly unsure.

"Do you love him?"

Meeting Ivan's piercing gaze, his expression inscrutable, she nodded numbly.

"Then there is only one thing you can do. I will lead the way and you follow. Our boat is docked by the bridge."

With that, Ivan lowered his head, and folding his hands as if in prayer, he began to move deftly through the crowds, leaving Zora staring after him. But she didn't stand there for long.

Glancing around her and seeing no sign of Yakov or any of Rurik's warriors, she hastened to catch up with Ivan, almost tripping in her haste not to lose sight of him. To her dismay, the bottle of perfume went flying from her hands to shatter at her feet but there wasn't anything she could do.

As tears welled in her eyes, she rushed on, trying not to dwell upon what Rurik would think of her when he discovered she was gone. It was too terrible to contemplate.

Rurik had never known such impatience as he was forced to slow his horse to a walk, the bridge so jammed with people and carts coming and going from the market that he had to wend his way carefully or risk trampling someone.

Thor's blood, he hoped he hadn't missed Zora! The council of war had ended early enough that there was still a chance he would find her at the market; he didn't want to have to wait until he returned to the estate to tell her what he should have said days ago. It was amazing that he felt so exhilarated after being awake all night, but he supposed love could do that to a man.

"Now if that isn't an odd sight," Rurik suddenly overheard someone say as he threaded his mount through the milling throng. "A boat manned entirely by monks, not a sailor among them."

"Aye, must be headed south on some pilgrimage, probably to the cathedral of St. Sophia in Kiev," commented another man as Rurik glanced over to see two merchants eating their morning meal against the railing as they watched the river traffic below.

Looking beyond them, Rurik spied the boat already well in the distance, its white sail billowing in the wind as hooded monks moved about on deck. A curious thing, he had to agree, then he turned his attention back to the busy pedestrian traffic and the market that lay ahead.

Damn, he couldn't wait to find Zora! Had she already gone to the perfumer's section? Maybe if he was fortunate, Yakov had kept her busy elsewhere and Rurik would have the chance to see her face when his gift was placed in her hands. If not, at least he knew that she was thinking about him, perhaps even wearing the white jasmine perfume he couldn't wait to smell upon her skin.

As for himself, Zora had never been far from his thoughts,

nor had their exchange at the stream that had finally convinced him that he had been acting the fool. Why did he need to test her when he could see shining from her beautiful eyes how much she cared? If she hadn't admitted anything to him yet, he had himself to blame. He had only to remember the callous things he had said to her to understand that she might be afraid. By Odin, he would make amends!

She would realize how much he loved her, especially now that Grand Prince Yaroslav's forces would be sailing south within two days. He hoped the battle would prove quick and decisive so he could soon return to her and even more, he hoped that her father's downfall would not drive a wedge between them. If she knew his heart, it might be enough to heal any wounds—

"Lord Rurik!"

Rising in his saddle, Rurik spied Yakov running toward him from the market square and he felt a sudden hard knot in the pit of his stomach. He urged his horse into a trot as he cleared the bridge.

"Lord Rurik! God help us, it is you!"

"What? Why are you shouting?" he demanded, although from the stricken look upon the steward's face, he already knew.

"She is gone, my lord. Your wife! Nowhere to be found!"

Rurik had never known such a terrible moment, but he could not bring himself to believe it. Not yet.

"Did you look everywhere?"

"Yes, yes, and your men are still looking. We've searched each section of the market, even the surrounding churches, but no one has seen her. The merchant at the spice stall where I left her claimed one moment she was talking with a monk, although in such low voices that he heard nothing of what was said, then she was gone!"

"A monk?"

"Yes, my lord, in brown sacking and a hood."

Stung by glaring intuition, Rurik glanced over his shoulder to the river. The boat he had glimpsed from the bridge had vanished. Not even a speck of the sails to be seen.

By Odin, had Zora somehow enlisted the aid of the clergy to see her back to Chernigov? A priest had come to the compound only a few days ago to visit the wife of one of his warriors who was ill with childbed fever. Was it possible that Zora had convinced him to help her, being the daughter of the man who ruled the leading see of the Orthodox Church? She could have told him to have everything prepared for when she came to the market . . .

"Send one of my men back to the estate," Rurik ordered in a voice so ominously quiet that the steward paled. "I want two hundred warriors here within the hour to search every inch of this city. Meanwhile you and the others continue looking, and hire as many men as you can to help. Do you understand?"

Yakov nodded vigorously.

"Then why do you delay?"

"I . . . I didn't get to tell you yet, Lord Rurik, but we did find something she left behind. The gift you gave her, the perfume . . . she must have dropped it. We found the bottle shattered into a thousand pieces . . ."

As his heart was breaking, Rurik thought, finding it hard to breathe for the gut-wrenching pain that was ripping him apart. Yet he willed himself to keep his emotions tightly under control. He had a wife to hunt down.

"Go, Yakov. See to my commands."

"V-very well, my lord. But what of you?"

Rurik didn't answer, veering his horse around so sharply that the startled animal reared, its front legs pawing at the air. This time he thundered across the bridge, giving little thought to the people who had to scatter out of his way or even jump into the river to avoid his mount's pounding hooves.

His mind was upon Zora. By the gods, he would find her, whether she was somewhere in the city or upon that accursed boat heading south! As soon as the grand prince knew that he was taking a ship after her, Rurik would be hard upon her trail.

"And when we're together again, Princess," he vowed fiercely, racing his mount toward the *kreml,* "you'll wish that you had never deceived me."

CHAPTER
26

Sitting alone in a makeshift tent, Zora suspected she had made a grave mistake.

Ivan had thrust her in here so cruelly, threatening to bind her hands and feet if she made a move to step outside, that she wondered how she could have trusted him. She had thought he made sense at the market, but now that she had had more time to consider his words, it made as much sense that he would have promised her anything just to get her to come with him.

"You're such a gullible fool," she muttered to herself, growing more sick at heart with each moment.

She didn't feel well either, her stomach pitching and churning as it had never done the last time she was aboard a vessel. She felt so nauseous that she might have to peek her head outside the tent whether Ivan liked it or not and ask for a bucket. They must have been sailing for an hour already and he still hadn't come back to check on her or explain—

"You can come out if you wish," Ivan suddenly called to her, something that she was now only too eager to do.

Feeling as if at any instant she would retch, Zora clamped her hand over her mouth and burst through the flaps, making it to the railing just in time. When she was finished, she wet her trembling hands in the river and patted her face, never having felt so miserable.

"I'd like to think that you're only seasick, but my guess is that you're probably bearing that bastard's spawn in your belly. Am I correct?"

Stunned, Zora gaped at Ivan, still feeling so queasy that she feared she might be sick again.

Could she be with child? She had considered it fleetingly when she had missed her monthly flow, which should have come a few days after her marriage to Rurik. Yet she had been late before, her body sometimes playing strange tricks with her at times when she was more anxious than others. Those first weeks with Rurik would certainly qualify. But how, then, would she explain her dizziness yesterday and her sudden bout of tears at the stream?

"I suppose I could be," she admitted, wondering if such news would have made Rurik happy. "I was never sick last time I was on the river."

Zora jumped as Ivan slammed his fist down upon the railing and she took a few steps backward, fearing he might strike her. His angular face that before she had always thought handsome was mottled and made ugly with fury, and she remembered suddenly how her father had once described Ivan as an exacting man who anyone would be a fool to cross. Yet until now, she had never seen this side of him.

"By God, woman, I will not foster that Varangian's whelp!"

"No—no one said you must," she said shakily. "I am another man's wife, Ivan. My husband and I will rear our child in Novgorod."

"If I have any say, the child will be taken from you at its birth and drowned," he countered harshly, moving toward her. "You will not be another man's wife for long, Zora, for as soon as we arrive in Chernigov your marriage will be annulled. Your father promised you to me and I will have you for my bride, spoiled goods or no."

"You cannot annul my marriage without my consent," she breathed, horrified by his threat to the innocent babe she carried.

"No? Once your father learns that you fancy yourself in love with his enemy, your word to him will mean nothing. He will be only too eager to end a marriage that never should have been. If you hadn't been kidnapped from the caravan by Yaroslav's spies—"

"Is that what you think happened?" Zora interrupted, startled.

"Why else would my men and I risk a journey to Novgorod if we didn't believe we would find you there?" Ivan shouted as he gestured to the other eight warriors aboard who like him were still garbed as monks. "After hundreds of your father's troops searched every trading camp along the Desna and as far south as Kiev to find no trace of you, it was the only thing left that made any sense. Princess Hermione was the one who suggested your abduction was the work of spies through the messengers she sent to Chernigov."

"Hermoine?" Incredulous, Zora shook her head. "Of course. She believed I was being taken to Constantinople, so she thought it safe to encourage you to search to the north . . . except now her plan has miscarried. She not only engineered my abduction, but without knowing it, she led you to find me."

"You speak nonsense! Your half sister was distraught when she reached Chernigov."

"Hardly distraught! Hermione paid slave merchants to abduct me from the caravan, believing they would cut out my tongue and sell me in Constantinople. It was only because Rurik found me in a trading camp and thought that he could use me to gain military information from my father that I escaped such a fate." As Ivan listened impatiently, his expression incredulous, Zora quickly recounted the story up to her marriage.

"I would never have believed it at the time," she said more to herself than Ivan after she had finished, "but I've Hermione to thank for leading me to Rurik."

"A sentiment as misguided as your half sister's actions," Ivan said acidly. "Yet I cannot believe simple jealousy could have fueled such a crime. There had to be another reason, something that pushed her . . ."

"Rurik asked me the same thing one night after—"

Ivan glared at her and Zora felt her face reddening. Hastily she added, "We talked about Hermione and when I told him that no matter what she believed, our father had treated us equally, he asked me if there was anything I had been given that Hermione had not."

"Was there?"

Zora nodded. "You, Ivan. News of my father's decision that I would become your bride upon our arrival in Chernigov reached us just before we left Tmutorokan, but Hermione never said a word to me about it until the night she drugged me and I was abducted. I can only believe that she's in love with you and wanted me out of the way so she could become your wife—"

"But Hermione has been thwarted for I have found you." Ivan swept Zora with a possessive look that filled her with dread. "I've no doubt your father will punish her soundly for her treachery."

"Didn't you hear me?" Sensing his intent as he began to advance upon her, Zora backed away nervously. "Hermione loves you! Surely you could be just as content with her as your bride! She is a trueborn princess, not a bastard daughter—"

"It is not Hermione I want. You're the woman I chose, the woman I will have."

"But . . . but you never explained how you knew to find me in the market," she blurted, desperate to distract him as he drew closer. "Nor how you learned that Rurik was my husband."

"Simple. After my men and I arrived last night in Novgorod, I had only to mention your name to hear what had happened to you. The common folk of that city seemed to know a great deal about their most famed warrior and his recent marriage, yet it was by pure chance that I spied you in the marketplace when I went to buy food. Obviously you were meant to be returned to me, Zora."

Ivan seized her so suddenly that she had no chance to elude him, his mouth brutal as it covered hers. As he forced open her lips with his tongue, she tried to fight him but he was a strong man, and her struggles were futile. All she could do was endure his loathsome kiss, cursing herself for having been so foolish as to trust him.

"You will be my bride, Zora of Tmutorokan," he said when at last he released her and so abruptly that she fell against the railing. "And don't think that an annulment will be enough to satisfy me. If your Lord Rurik doesn't fall in battle, he will find his death upon my sword, for I'll take no chance that you will ever be reunited."

Tears stinging her eyes, Zora stared at him in horror. "You lied to me!"

His laugh was bitter, but his arrogant gaze held triumph. "So I did."

Unable to bear to look at him, Zora fled to the tent and stumbling inside, she collapsed to her knees. Hugging herself tightly, she rocked back and forth, her anguish so intense that she made no sound as tears coursed down her face.

"Rurik . . ." she mouthed silently over and over, wishing by some magic he could hear her and know where she was. Yet even if he could, would he answer her cries? Unsure, she sank onto the floor in despair.

It was almost dark when Rurik returned to the compound, his two hundred warriors riding silently behind him, none daring to speak. Even Arne had held his tongue, which was a wise thing. Rurik was in so black a mood he was ready to lash out at anyone.

Zora and her accomplices were well on their way to the first portage and there was nothing he could do to stop them. Grand Prince Yaroslav had doused that hope, his words still echoing in Rurik's mind.

"I know it's a hard thing for you to accept, Rurik, but I cannot allow you to leave. Not now. We sail in less than two days and I need you to command your men. But do not lose heart. Upon our victory, you will regain your errant wife."

Do not lose heart. He didn't have one left. By Odin, if he ever so much as thought he might trust a woman again, may he fall upon his own sword!

Dismounting in front of his longhouse, Rurik met Arne's somber gaze.

"See that the men are given a good share of ale, and extend to them my thanks for aiding in the search."

"As you say, my lord." Arne shifted uncomfortably in his saddle. "Do you wish my company? I could bring you some ale—"

"And then what, Arne? We drink ourselves into a stupor and bemoan the fact that we were both deceived by sea-blue eyes and a soft, willing manner? I think not. I can do that well enough alone."

"But maybe you shouldn't be alone, my lord—"

"Believe me, friend, there isn't anything more I want right now."

Rurik turned and entered the longhouse, sighing heavily as he shut the door. He knew Arne meant well, but he had already taken enough advice from him about Zora and he could stomach no more. Moving farther into the main room, he saw that his slaves had seen well to his comfort. A fire burned brightly in the central hearth and he could smell food, yet he wasn't surprised that he felt no hunger.

He was thirsty, though, and he made straight for the table to pour himself a brimming goblet of wine. He downed it and, pouring another, tossed it back as well. Then he shrugged, and leaving the goblet on the table, he sat down in a chair near the hearth and rested the wine jug on his knee.

Why not get good and drunk? If he dulled his senses, maybe it wouldn't hurt so damnably that the gods had seen fit to spite him after all.

He could almost hear them laughing, Loki more loudly than the rest. That wily god of mischief must surely have fashioned this day's wretched events! Yet perhaps none were gloating any more than Zora, wherever she was, for Rurik granting her the perfect opportunity to escape. He couldn't have done a better job than if he had escorted her to the boat himself and shoved it from the dock.

Thor, what madness had seized him to think that he could trust her? She must have been waiting all along for the right moment to escape, her acquiescence and softening of temper toward him just a part of her plan. He had been right about women! They were capable of only the foulest treachery. And he had believed Zora might love—

Cursing aloud the twisting pain over his heart, Rurik took a long draft of wine, almost emptying the jug as he stared unseeing at the flames.

Until this morning he had never thought that he might regret his sworn allegiance to Yaroslav. His frustration that his request to command a ship had been denied was still so acute that even now he was tempted to disobey the grand prince's orders and strike out after her. It galled him more than he could express that Zora was traveling the route he and his men would take in another day's time. The same damned route!

"My lord?"

Muttering an oath against this sudden intrusion, Rurik glanced up to find Nellwyn standing a few feet away from him. He hadn't even heard her enter the longhouse.

"If you're looking for your mistress," he said tightly, "she isn't here."

"I know, my lord, and when I heard you had finally returned from the city, I came at once to speak with you."

"Speak of what?" Rurik gave a short, humorless laugh. "If you're wondering how to fill your time now, you'll have to find yourself some other tasks to keep you busy, Nellwyn, for I cannot say when your mistress will be back. She's on a boat heading home to her beloved father and her betrothed, Lord Ivan." This time Rurik drained the jug, his pain unbearable, then dropping it with a dull thunk to the floor, he lunged from the chair to fetch another.

"That's why I've come, my lord. To speak about your wife, not my duties. I don't know what happened today at the market, but I do know Lady Zora would never have left you for this Ivan."

"And how do you know that?" demanded Rurik, turning on the slave woman so suddenly that she jumped.

"Because she loves you, my lord! She confided in me many times over the past few weeks—"

"You believed her?" Inwardly shaken by the slave woman's emphatic pronouncement, Rurik nonetheless hardened his heart. It seemed that he and Arne hadn't been the only ones tricked by Zora's guile. "She deceived you once before, Nellwyn, the night of the fire. Now she's deceived you again."

"No, she hasn't, my lord, and I would swear to it! If she didn't care about you, she would have slept through the night like a babe, knowing that in the morning she would escape from you. But she didn't sleep at all because she was waiting up for you, waiting and worrying about the coming battle and what might happen to you. Aye, if she did anything today, maybe in her mind it was to help you."

"What are you saying, Nellwyn? That my wife fled the city because she thought by doing so she could somehow protect me? She's gone to Chernigov, while the battle most likely will be fought to the north. What good can she do me?"

"Perhaps more than she could have done here in Novgorod—"

"Enough!" As Rurik's harsh command echoed around

them, Nellwyn's green eyes widened with alarm. "Leave me, woman, and take your fanciful theories of my wife's actions with you! You've already overstepped your bounds."

He turned from her and took a draft of wine, expecting to hear the door close behind her. But when he looked over his shoulder, Nellwyn was still there, standing her ground, her hands propped at her thickened waist and her chin raised stubbornly in a manner that reminded him all too much of Zora.

"You may punish me for this, my lord, but I will have my say! Your lady confided much in me and from what I have heard, I believe you love her as she loves you. Yet you're so willing to think the worst of her, to let your past rule your heart instead of what you can see and feel, that perhaps you don't deserve her love! Why dare to trust, why dare to put faith in another when it is so much easier not to?"

The room went silent for a long moment, Nellwyn's outburst striking Rurik more deeply than he would ever admit. Yet as deeply felt was his hurt and when he finally faced her, his voice was low with warning.

"Are you finished?"

"Aye."

"Then you hear me. What I *see* is that my wife is not with me and what I *feel* is that I am a fool. Now leave me, woman!"

Nellwyn did this time, hastening from the room while Rurik stood there, his heartbeat pounding in his ears. As the door shut with a thud, he hurled the jug with all his might at the wall, dashing it to splinters.

CHAPTER
27

Zora had never known a more miserable five days in her life, her heartsickness growing. Already they had passed one portage and were nearing the second, their rapid progress due to favorable winds and that Ivan and his men never seemed to rest, rowing like demons whenever the sails slackened.

The boat was longer, too, and not as wide as the one Rurik had commanded, which to Zora now seemed like months ago; it cut through the water like a serpent. The only good thing was that Ivan had left her alone, she sensed as much because she disgusted him in her present state as his concentration was fixed upon getting them to Chernigov as quickly as possible.

She had overheard him talking with his men about the scores of warships they had seen in Novgorod docked north of the bridge, and the flurry of preparations that meant that Grand Prince Yaroslav's forces would soon be setting sail. She hoped with all her heart that they had left by now, and that those fearsome ships that she had also glimpsed from the market might overtake this smaller boat. She imagined that was Ivan's fear since he spent much of his time in the stern, scanning the distance for any sign of approaching sails.

"All right, men, let's waste no time!" came Ivan's impatient command outside the tent, telling Zora that they had reached the second portage. Yet she didn't move from her pallet, staring at the bucket that was never far from her side.

At the first portage she had ventured outside to watch them hoist the vessel onto the log rollers, but seeing the woods again where Kjell had lost his life had been so painful that she had quickly retreated to the tent. She had been frightened, too, wondering if another band of marauders might be lurking nearby, looking to prey on passing ships.

That was reason enough why she had made no escape attempts. She had no wish to relive that harrowing experience. Nor had she considered jumping overboard. Her single swimming lesson had hardly left her with the skills to tackle a river's powerful currents, and the thought that the water would be many times over her head—

Zora shuddered. As she felt the boat being lifted from the water followed by a jarring thunk as it was settled upon the logs, her mind raced ahead to when they would leave the river behind to cross overland to Chernigov.

Then she would attempt to escape, for she had no intention of returning to her father's city with Ivan. She would take refuge at a church or with a peasant family and wait for Grand Prince Yaroslav's forces to march past, then find Rurik. He would probably want to send her back to Novgorod, but maybe he might keep her with him. She could hope . . .

"That's it, men, we're almost there, now ease her back into the— By God, men, draw your arms! Behind you! Look behind you!"

Zora sat bolt upright, her hand flying to her breast as a horrifying shriek split the air, then another. It sounded as if the hounds of hell had been loosed upon them. She had never heard such a terrible wolfish howling, which almost drowned out the telltale clashing of swords.

Holy Mother protect them, they were under attack! Yet the boat was still moving and she realized it must have already been shoved back into the water. Had Ivan or any of his men made it aboard?

She screamed when an arrow suddenly came splicing through the tent wall to embed in the bucket, and she hesitated no more. Dashing outside, she somehow retained the presence of mind to keep her head down, and peering over the railing, she thought she was going to be sick all over herself.

Ivan and what was left of his men were surrounded by a horde of yowling attackers, outnumbered by more than four to one. As swords and battleaxes flashed in the waning sunlight, another of his warriors falling in a spray of blood, Zora saw Ivan glance toward the drifting boat as if he was searching for her. Then he suddenly collapsed to his knees, an axe blow felling him from behind. Zora closed her eyes, unable to watch anymore.

"Oh, God . . ." she breathed, having no idea what she should do. "Oh, God, please help me . . ."

Wild, triumphant shouts caused her to lift her head and she gazed in horror at the grisly dance upon the shore. Dismembered arms and legs were being paraded upon spears like trophies, then a severed head was tossed from one sword onto another . . . a head with dark brown hair just like Ivan's—

"No . . . oh, no," she murmured, fear tightening like cold fingers around her throat. She watched in disbelief as ten or twelve marauders broke away from the group and began to run along the riverbank . . . running hard as if they wanted to catch up with the boat that Zora realized to her mounting horror was drifting back toward their side of the shore.

It was the shock she needed. Scrambling on hands and knees to the other side of the boat, Zora ripped her tunic from hem to thigh with hands shaking so badly that she could barely use them. Then, taking care to use the tent as cover, she climbed over the railing at a point where she hoped they couldn't see her and eased herself into the water.

It was so cold and deep, her fear almost overwhelmed her, but hearing the attackers' raucous shouts growing louder and their splashing as they rushed into the river, she willed herself to let go. As the boat floated away from her, she drew as much air into her lungs as she could hold and then dived beneath the surface, using her arms and legs as Rurik had taught her to propel herself downstream.

Fortunately, the currents were strong and that aided her efforts, and swimming until she was sure her lungs were going to burst, she finally came up for air. To her relief, the marauders looked like little figures upon the distant shoreline, they were that far away. Filling her lungs again, she lowered her head beneath the surface and let the currents carry her farther away.

Dusk had fallen by the time Zora dared to consider stopping but she pushed herself onward, sometimes floating on her back to save her strength. She didn't head for the opposite shoreline until it was pitch-dark. With her exhaustion so intense that she feared she might drown before she got there, only by sheer force of will was she able to keep herself calm and her arms and legs moving.

When her feet touched bottom she began to weep with relief, and pulling herself from the water, she crawled into the deep grass and collapsed. She was so weak that her sobs were no more than whimpers, and soon even these grew silent as she closed her eyes against the starry sky.

"The princess, my lord?"

"Aye, I met her only once but you never forget such a face. No wonder my son was willing to risk his life for her, and Rurik Sigurdson to give up his vow and marry her. It's a good thing she didn't crawl so far into the grass that we would have missed her."

"A good thing, too, that we found her before whoever it was that slaughtered those poor bastards upstream."

"Aye, wandering thieves, most likely. Stripped the dead and the boat, right down to the sails. It's a miracle the wench escaped . . . though she might wish otherwise when she's back with her husband. I've never seen Rurik in so foul a mood as when we sailed from Novgorod."

"That's true enough, my lord, but look, she's waking up."

Zora moaned softly, lifting her hand to shade her eyes from the bright sunlight. Still half in her dream, she could have sworn she had heard someone say Rurik's name, but that couldn't be possible—

"Lady Zora?"

She froze, scarcely breathing. Alert now and remembering all too suddenly where she was, the next thing she thought was how absurd that in the middle of nowhere, someone would know her name.

Slowly lowering her hand, she squinted against the light, making out two men who were staring down at her. One she didn't know, but the other . . .

"Oh . . . !" She was swept up into Thordar the Strong's massive arms at almost the same instant she recognized him, her head spinning from the sudden movement. As he turned around, she gaped at the seventy-foot warship moored along the shoreline, fifty armed warriors staring back at her.

"One of my sharp-eyed men spied you lying in the grass," Thordar explained, anticipating her question as he waded into the water. "You're a fortunate young woman to have lived to tell what happened to your friends."

Before Zora could reply, she was lifted into waiting arms and deposited on deck, then Thordar and his companion heaved themselves aboard. As orders were given to lower all oars and push off from the bank, Thordar led her to a rowing bench where he gestured for her to sit. But she remained rooted where she stood, noticing for the first time that farther out in the river another warship was passing them, a long line of ships following as far as she could see.

Grand Prince Yaroslav's army! Surely it couldn't be any later than midmorning, which meant that they had been less than a day's journey behind Ivan's boat, probably advancing upon them with each mile. If only they had come faster, Ivan and his men might still be alive—

So he could then fight Rurik to the death? Zora remembered, shivering. She would never have wished such a violent end upon anyone, yet she couldn't deny that she was relieved Rurik had one less enemy to face.

She sank upon the bench. Simply recalling the events of the past day made her knees feel weak. Or was it because she knew that she would soon see Rurik again?

"Where is my husband?" she asked.

Thordar watched her closely. "Probably not to the second portage. There are many ships, Lady Zora. I'm only glad that we came upon the trail first and buried what was left of the dead. It wouldn't have been a welcome sight for a man anxious about his wife. What happened?"

"We were attacked." Zora shuddered, finding it difficult even to speak about it. "When they were pushing the boat back into the water. If I hadn't been on board . . ."

She couldn't finish, her memories still horribly vivid of what had almost happened to her during that first attack when Kjell was killed and Rurik had saved her just in time. And here she was talking with Kjell's father! Yet Thordar didn't seem half so forbidding now, despite his shaved scalp and the topknot that lent him the fierce look of a steppe nomad.

"Forgive me," he said, clearly sensing her disquiet. "You owe me no explanations. We'll be stopping in Smolensk within a few hours for food and supplies. You'll have to wait for your husband's ship, but you'll be reunited with him there."

Mere hours! Zora could hardly believe it. Yet she felt a sudden surge of nervousness. She could imagine too well what Rurik must think of her, and there was only one thing she could do to remedy it. Surely he would believe her. He had to!

"You have my thanks, Lord Thordar," Zora said softly, his eyes at this moment reminding her so much of Kjell's. "I speak also for my husband."

"For your sake, I hope that is true," the warrior answered. Heaving a sigh, he walked away.

"She awaits you in that storehouse, Rurik. And now since my ships are loaded, my forces must sail. We'll meet again in Liubech."

Rurik nodded at Thordar, his throat so tight that he could scarcely bring himself to speak. He had never known such a moment as when the warrior had met his ship to tell him that Zora was found, and what had happened to the men who had helped her escape. He knew, too, that they hadn't been monks but fighting men, giving rise to more questions for which he would soon demand answers.

"She wanted to wait for you on the wharf," added Thordar as he turned to go, "but I thought it better this way . . ."

"So you were right," Rurik gritted out, looking from the nearby door to the warrior's somber face. "My thanks, friend." They clasped wrists and then Thordar was gone, striding back to the docks where at least fifty warships were moored.

Still more vessels were arriving at the crowded wharf while others, loaded with fresh cooked meat and supplies, were heading downriver on the second leg of their journey, no longer in single formation but four or five abreast upon the great Dnieper River. Soon Rurik's six ships would be loaded and ready to sail, but first he must attend to Zora. With his jaw clenched so hard that it hurt, he opened the door to the storehouse and stepped inside, grimacing at the acrid smell of pickling brine.

It took him an instant to adjust to the hazy lamplight. He spied her sitting upon a barrel, her eyes as wide as he had ever seen them, her hands clasped nervously in her lap. His relief was stabbing and immediate, yet he forced himself to think not of how close he had come to losing her but of how she had betrayed him.

"Thordar told me what little you shared with him, wife," he said tersely, wasting no time on a greeting. "Now I want your explanation."

Zora shivered, Rurik's tone as cold and forbidding as his gaze. It was just as bad as she had feared, maybe worse. She rose, her legs half asleep from sitting so long, and nervously smoothed the linen tunic Thordar had bought for her.

"I—I know what you must be thinking, Rurik . . . that I purposely deceived you, but it's not as it may seem. If it hadn't been for the lies Ivan told me—"

"Ivan? Your betrothed?"

Rurik had interrupted her so harshly that Zora felt as if her heart had leapt to pound in her throat.

"Y-yes. He and eight of his men came disguised as monks to rescue me. He found me in the market and convinced me to leave with him—"

"Convinced you?" Rurik cut in again, his fury boiling all the hotter. How quickly and expertly she was spinning her tale, no doubt fearing his wrath as well she should! "I imagine that you rejoiced at the chance, Princess."

"No, that's not true!" she blurted, taking a few steps toward him. "I told Ivan that I wanted to stay with you, but he said that if I went with him I would be able to plead for your life if you were captured in battle. I was so worried about you, Rurik, and . . . and it made sense. I couldn't have done anything to help you if I had stayed in Novgorod! It was only later when Ivan admitted he had lied to me, that he planned to kill you . . ." She stopped, her expression stricken. "You don't believe me, do you?"

"That it was Ivan, yes, for Thordar told me the dead men had not been clergy, but warriors," Rurik replied, steeling his heart against her no matter that her words echoed what Nellwyn had told him days ago. There could be an explanation easily enough for that. Leave it to his cunning wife to fill her slave woman's head with the same lies just to add credence to her tale!

"But what of the rest?" she asked plaintively. "I swear on my life that it is true."

"You also swore to me once that you wouldn't stop trying to escape until you were free of me." Rurik's bitterness almost choked him.

"That was weeks ago!" she countered, her eyes pleading with him. "How could I have said anything different? I didn't know you for the man that you are. I didn't love you then, but I love you now, Rurik! I love you!"

Rurik suddenly felt as if everything had gone very still inside him, what he had yearned for so long to hear ringing in his ears. By Odin, he wanted to believe her, yet how could he? She had left him!

"I was going to tell you in the market," Zora rushed on, hope flaring that she might have finally reached him. "I thought you might come there to meet me. I wanted so much to prove to you that you could trust me, Rurik, and then Ivan—"

"Persuaded you within a moment's time to leave your beloved home and husband," he interrupted sarcastically, his expression as hard as granite. "Spare me your woman's ploy, Zora. If you love anything, it was only the thought of freedom. And don't tell me next that you're not grieving for Ivan, because I don't want to hear it."

"I'm not grieving!" Desperation seized Zora as she moved closer. "How could I mourn someone who wanted to kill the man I love? Who threatened to drown my baby at the moment of its birth?"

Stunned, Rurik stared at her. "A babe?"

"Yes. I didn't realize it until I became sick on the river. I was miserable."

"I imagine you were," Rurik muttered though deeply shaken. Days ago, such news might have completed his happiness, but now it only heightened his pain. "You must have been wretched knowing you carried my child, not only for your sake but for Ivan's."

"No, you're wrong!"

"I'm right, Zora, so spare me your denials! At least now I know you can produce heirs. I was beginning to wonder how long it would take before you'd be breeding and I could return to my concubines, but I see that once we're home in Novgorod, my life will finally be as it was before I wed!"

Incredulous, Zora's eyes filled with tears. How could he be so blind? How could he say such terrible things? Then another, more chilling thought struck her.

Perhaps she had been the fool all along to believe it might be possible that he loved her. If he cared, he would never treat her this cruelly. Surely he could see that she was telling him the truth.

"Do you love me, Rurik?" she demanded, her voice hoarse with pain. By God, she would know! "Do you love me?"

He didn't answer for the longest time, but when he finally spoke, her heart sank, his tone as biting as the smell in the room.

"I told you once before that the word holds no meaning for me, Princess, and nothing has changed. You've become confused by lust."

"No . . ." Zora breathed, shaking her head. "No!" Rushing at him so suddenly that she caught him by surprise, she struck him across the face with such force that her palm stung, but she didn't care. Nor did she care when he grabbed her by the wrists and shook her hard. "You deceived me!" she cried, anguished tears coursing down her face. "You put trust in me . . . led me to think . . . Monster! You hard, unfeeling—"

"Pagan? Brute? Barbarian?" he finished for her as he swept her fighting and kicking into his arms. "We've come full circle, haven't we, wife? Yet if anyone here has been deceived, it was me and not you!"

"Release me!" Zora demanded through her wracking

sobs, her world crumbling around her. How could she ever have thought she could warm this man's cold heart? Fool!

"Release you?" mocked Rurik, easily subduing her struggles by holding her so tightly that she couldn't move. "I should send you under guarded escort back to Novgorod but I'm not going to let you out of my sight. I'll not grant you another opportunity to escape me, Princess. I've learned my lesson too well."

As Rurik kicked open the storehouse door so violently that it flew with the splitting of wood from its hinges, Zora knew then that he was taking her with him. And despite never having felt so desolate, her heartache a raw bleeding wound, she could not deny that she *wanted* to be with him even as she swore that she would never forgive him for his cruelty. God help her, that made her twice the fool.

CHAPTER
28

Zora refused to speak to Rurik for the entire journey to Liubech, turning her face away from him whenever he addressed her. At first it hadn't seemed to affect him, but by her third day of silence, he could not hide his displeasure, his angry scowl there for everyone to see.

Yet if he had wanted to rail at her, it was impossible on the warship that lacked any privacy, crowded as it was with fifty odd warriors, weapons, and all manner of provisions. She had no tent where they could be alone either, only an open lean-to thrown together with blankets where she slept while everyone else, including Rurik, took shifts sleeping under the stars.

Even when she became ill, which thankfully had been less frequent upon the larger vessel, she refused to answer Rurik's brusque queries about her health. That seemed to anger him the most, yet she stubbornly held her tongue. After the horrible things he had said to her in Smolensk, he didn't deserve to know and what did he care anyway?

Whenever she asked herself that question, she always felt

a niggling that maybe, just maybe he might care, despite what he had claimed. But all she had to do was remember how callously he had denounced her, and the flicker of hope that refused to die would fade back into nothing. Nor did she trust any longer her memories of what they had shared, resigning herself that she must have misread everything no matter Nellwyn's assurances.

By the morning of the fifth day they arrived in Liubech and if Zora had tried not to dwell upon the approaching battle, there was no way to avoid it now.

As Rurik's ships drew into the bustling dock, she overheard him telling Arne that the imposing timber palisade that had been newly erected around the trading town would serve as a line of defense if Grand Prince Yaroslav's troops were forced to retreat. The ominous specter of war was brought that much closer when a senior warrior met them to announce that the grand prince had ordered an immediate march to a point more than halfway between Liubech and Chernigov where they would make camp.

"Why there?" Her growing anxiety caused her to break her silence as Rurik lifted her from the ship. If he was surprised that she had finally spoken to him, he gave no sign of it, his expression remaining as hard as before.

"You didn't think your father would be fool enough to allow us to march to his gates, did you?" he replied, signaling for two strapping warriors to follow as he led her to a place out of the way of the ships being unloaded. "The location of our encampment will ensure ten miles between our armies, unless Mstislav decides to attack during the night. But I doubt he'll stray that far from his precious city for fear he might lose it."

Zora wasn't given a chance to reply as Rurik left her with the two guards while he went to oversee his men. Although the wharf at first appeared a mass of chaos, in less than an hour not only his warriors but all those whose ships had recently arrived had begun to march, slaves and hired freemen bringing up the rear with the provisions.

For a moment, Zora wondered why she and her guards hadn't joined them. Then Rurik rode up on a spirited gray stallion that matched him for size and power.

She tried not to notice how magnificent he looked atop the huge animal, his thick blond hair swept back from his forehead and shining as brightly as the silver mail-shirt he had donned, but she couldn't help it. No matter what had happened between them, he still remained to her the most handsome of men.

"Take my hand," he commanded, his eyes appearing a deep crystal blue in the warm sunlight.

"Perhaps I prefer to walk," she countered, bristling at his harsh tone that reminded her all too unhappily of how cruel he had been to her in Smolensk.

"You have no choice, wife. Do not force me to humiliate you before your uncle's troops."

Thinking that he would probably relish embarrassing her much as he had the time he threw her over his shoulder, Zora accepted his hand with reluctance and he hoisted her up behind him.

"Hold on tight," he ordered. "I don't want to risk your falling off."

You mean you don't want me to threaten your heir with any of my foolishness, Zora thought resentfully, although she couldn't deny that it felt wonderful to wrap her arms around him again.

They had scarcely touched since he had carried her to the ship days ago, yet she hadn't allowed herself to admit how much she had missed it until now. As they galloped to the front of the formation to join Grand Prince Yaroslav and other senior warriors, she could feel the sinewed strength of Rurik's body with his every movement, and she wondered if he was affected in the slightest by having her so close . . .

Rurik cursed to himself. It was all he could do to keep his mind on the grave matters at hand with Zora hugging him so tightly, her womanly softness a seductive warmth against his back.

By Odin, despite her treachery she inflamed his senses like no other! How could one female so sorely tempt him and try him at the same time?

With great effort, he reminded himself of her deceit, which helped to put matters in perspective, if not as much as he would have liked. It seemed the harder he tried to bury his feelings for her, the more impossible the task became, and he had already given up trying to suppress the memory of what had happened in Smolensk.

He still couldn't believe that she had struck him. Perhaps that had stunned him more than anything she had said. Words were easy to discount but actions not so easily. He had never seen such hurt in her eyes, such pain, as if he had broken her heart—

More likely it was despair that her attempt to escape him had failed, Rurik amended bitterly, thinking back on how she had refused to talk to him since that day. She had spurned his every attention, his every query about her welfare, no longer bothering to hide the fact that she wanted to have nothing to do with him or to pretend that she might care.

Yet the moment they had landed in Liubech, he had sensed her agitation and had surmised at once that she was plotting all over again. He would wager a thousand gold grivna upon it! Why else would her first words to him have been a question about where they were bound?

That had sealed his decision to take her with him rather than leave her at the trading town. He wanted to keep her from the battle, but the thought of leaving her somewhere less secure seemed a worse evil.

If Zora was left well guarded at the camp, she would still be there waiting for him when the victory was won, although he imagined that she would try anything she could to return to her father. He would have to warn the men he entrusted with her care to be especially vigilant, for she would outwit them if given half a chance.

"And she said she wanted to walk," he muttered, wondering if Zora really thought him that much of a fool. So she could have escaped into the woods?

"Did you say something?" Her breath was a soft, stirring warmth upon his neck.

"No!"

Rurik heard her sigh but he ignored it, forcing his mind to what lay ahead.

Once a tent had been constructed for her and she had been ushered unceremoniously inside, Zora didn't see Rurik again for hours. When it grew dark, she began to believe that he wasn't planning to come back at all, which wouldn't surprise her.

He had said little else to her during the long ride to the camp other than his last outburst, and she had sensed in him an irritation that she could only suppose was directed at her. Although she didn't know what she had done to deserve this latest display of temper, it really didn't matter. It seemed that hurt was only piling upon hurt between them and there wasn't any way to stop it.

Finally she lay down and turned her back to the two stone-faced Varangians posted just inside the entrance, having grown weary of looking at them and no doubt they of her. There were also a half dozen or so warriors pacing outside the tent. She had watched their shadows moving across the canvas walls all afternoon. She couldn't see them anymore but she could hear the low drone of their voices, an occasional laugh surprising her considering the gravity of their presence here.

These men of the north seemed so confident, so fearless. She already knew they believed that God and right was on their side, victory assured over a foul usurper. To her, the imminent future was too uncertain to even contemplate. She closed her eyes, willing herself to try to get some rest despite the hungry rumbling of her empty stomach.

"You could rouse the dead with that growling."

Rolling over, Zora stared up at Rurik in surprise. In the oil lamp's flickering light he appeared as much a giant as the first time she had seen him, his head grazing the ceiling, his formidable size dwarfing the tent.

Her heart pounding, she noticed then that her guards were gone and she no longer heard men's voices right outside. She realized Rurik must have sent them to help themselves to food for he carried a round loaf of bread under one arm, a wineskin under the other, and in his hands a steaming bowl of something that smelled wonderfully of lamb stew.

"I thought you might be hungry, Princess, but if I'd known how much I would have brought more food." He went down on his haunches and set everything in front of her, then he sat upon the ground and rested an arm on one raised knee. "Go on. While it's still hot."

"Aren't you going to have any?" Zora's face grew warm under his scrutiny. She broke off a piece of bread and dipped it into the stew.

"Not tonight. I never eat before a battle."

Her eyes widening, Zora suddenly didn't feel very hungry. But if Rurik had noticed her reaction he made no comment, reaching instead for the wineskin. She thought he was going to drink but he simply removed the stopper and then handed her the leather bag. She didn't ask if he wanted any, sensing his answer would be the same.

"Eat, Zora. For strength."

She did, understanding his unspoken reference to their child, which for the past days had been the only thing to sustain her spirits.

Whether Rurik loved her or not, she knew in her heart that she wouldn't want to live if anything happened to him, but she must for she no longer had just herself to consider. Yet right now, that didn't make it any easier to swallow the food and she had to wash it down with wine for fear she might choke.

"The guards told me you never strayed from this corner," he said, glancing at the straw pallet on which she was sitting.

"Where else could I have gone?" she asked, wondering at

his sudden frown. Then it dawned upon her that he must still think she was going to try to escape and she gave a sad laugh. "I'm no match for your Varangian warriors, Rurik, even if they lacked an ounce of sense. Those two stared at me all afternoon as if they were afraid I might disappear right from under them."

"You have a history of doing just that, wife." Rurik's jaw tightened visibly.

"So I do," she admitted softly. This seemed to startle him. He had obviously expected her to hurl some retort.

Silence reigned for long moments as Zora ate her meal, but she drank little wine. She wanted to have her wits about her for whatever the next hours might bring. At last when she could eat no more, she pushed the remainder aside and met his eyes.

"Thank you for thinking of me. I feel much better now."

"Good. I suggest you eat the rest when you're able for I cannot say when hot food will be prepared again."

Feeling a chill at the import behind his words, Zora sighed heavily. She was so worried about him. If only he could give her some reassurance. "Are you and your men so confident that you will win?"

"If a man hopes to live, he doesn't go into battle expecting defeat," Rurik replied, wondering why she had asked him such a question. Irritation gripped him as he imagined it was because she feared for her father and his men. By Thor, even with his child growing in her belly, her loyalty to her countrymen had not wavered! "Your father's forces and ours are well matched, Zora, if that gives you any comfort. They have enough men that they will not fall like spring lambs to the slaughter."

"That's not what I meant!" she said heatedly. Then she shook her head, her shoulders slumping. "Never mind, it doesn't matter. You would twist whatever I have to say anyway. I learned that well enough the other day." She rose as if she didn't want to be near him and went to stand at an opposite wall, her back to him. "I'm tired, Rurik. If you don't mind, I wish you would leave—"

"So you dismiss me, Princess?"

Hearing the restrained anger in his voice, Zora glanced nervously over her shoulder to see that Rurik had risen to his feet, his eyes black as coals in the hazy light.

"I—I didn't mean it as it sounded . . ." she began lamely, then her own indignation was pricked as much at herself as at him. Why shouldn't she ask him to leave since he thought the worst of everything she had to say? She had had enough of his callous treatment!

"Yes, I did mean it," she continued, lifting her chin as she turned to face him. "You brought my meal and I have thanked you for it, but I'm sure you have other things to do."

"Nothing that cannot wait, wife." Rurik glared at her as he came closer. "Or have you forgotten that you still bear that title? Perhaps you're already thinking ahead to your father's victory, for surely that is the outcome you hope for in your heart—"

"That's right!" Zora shouted, losing all control in light of his preposterous statement. "That's exactly what I want! Why hide it any longer? You've read me so well, Rurik Sigurdson, I see no reason to keep my true feelings from you. Yes, I hope my father wins and I hope you soon find yourself without a wife!"

He grabbed her so suddenly that she gasped, his fingers tunneling in her hair to yank her head back.

"So this is how I will remember you as I go into battle," he breathed, his gaze ablaze with fury. "Treason like venom upon your lips."

Tears springing to her eyes, Zora could barely answer for the emotion threatening to choke her. "You have made it so, Rurik. You can only blame your—"

She didn't finish, Rurik's mouth coming down so brutally upon hers that it hurt . . . and she knew he wanted to hurt her. His embrace was so crushing that she could hardly breathe and her neck felt ready to snap, her scalp stinging.

But she would not let him hurt her, no, she wouldn't let him! She returned his kiss with a fury that equaled his, determined that he would remember not the lies she had just hurled at him but the blinding truth of her passion.

I love you, Rurik! she cried in her heart as she threw her arms around his neck to hold him tightly, to hold him like she would never let him go.

As if she had surprised him, his embrace eased and became not cruel but wildly possessive, and with a ragged groan he deepened his kiss to ravage her mouth while his hands grew frantic in their caress. She clung to him even as she felt him wrench her tunic over her hips and tear away her undergarment, then lift her and wrap her legs around his waist.

His breathing was hot and desperate against her lips as he yanked at his trousers and she pressed eagerly against him, knowing his intent and wanting it as much as he. She felt his hardness poised for an instant against her moist flesh, then she was riding upon it, his hands gripping her bottom as he thrust inside her like a man possessed, fast, hard, relentlessly, until she was shaking with her need.

She locked her ankles behind him, not caring that the iron mesh of his mail-shirt was biting into her thighs or the insides of her arms as she clutched wildy at his back. All conscious thought was centered upon that wet, throbbing place where they were joined, upon the incredible heat, the friction, the rapture rising up to consume her . . .

"Rurik!" she cried at the dizzying height of her ecstasy, but she heard not a sound, his kiss silencing her as he thrust deeply once, twice . . . then the third time with such ferocity that his whole body shuddered.

"Zora . . ." came his hoarse whisper, his mouth tearing from hers so he could stare into her eyes as his seed burst hot and pulsing from his flesh. And at that heart-stopping moment she knew . . . though she might never hear it from his lips. She could see it shining like truth in his eyes. The pain, the torment . . . the yearning.

He loved her. Holy Mother Mary, if life ended for her now she would need nothing more.

It was that thought she drew on for courage when he suddenly closed his eyes as if to shut her out, his expression growing as hard and angry as before. Then she was standing upon the ground, her crumpled tunic falling around her ankles as Rurik fastened his trousers and strode from the tent.

He was gone without a final word, yet she heard him giving terse orders outside to the men who must have returned. Certain that her guards were soon to rejoin her, Zora walked shakily to the lamp and doused it, then moved through the dark to her pallet where she lay down and drew the blanket over her.

She wanted no one to see her tears.

CHAPTER
29

Zora awoke to the distant sound of drums and she was seized with such panic, she vaulted from the pallet and ran stumbling in the predawn light for the entrance.

"Hold there! Where do you think you're bound?" demanded the guard who jumped up and caught her around the waist while the other man lunged to his feet to block her way.

"The drums . . ." she said distractedly, thinking of Rurik, wanting to go to him. "It's started, hasn't it?"

"Not until they fall still, my lady."

"Aye, and when they do, we should be fighting that usurper alongside our lord instead of left behind in this camp with the slaves and a disobedient wife," the taller Varangian muttered before he was silenced with a sharp gesture from his grim-faced companion.

"Go and sit down, Lady Zora," continued the red-bearded guard who held her, his voice firm. "There is nothing to do but wait." Sighing when Zora refused to budge, he picked her up and carried her back to the pallet and set her down

309

upon it. "Try to sleep if you can. Word will be brought to us—"

"Sleep?" Zora tossed aside the blanket he had dropped in her lap. "How can I when my husband . . . ?" Realizing from the man's frown that she was getting nowhere, Zora willed herself to be calm. "Where are they?"

"Two miles south. Prince Mstislav's army advanced during the night to a village called Listven and Grand Prince Yaroslav's forces have gone to meet them."

No wonder they could hear the drums, Zora thought, rubbing her temples that had begun to pound as insistently. Rurik wasn't so far away, but with these warriors guarding her, she might as well be in Novgorod.

"Your friend said he wanted to be fighting with my husband," she said, trying a desperate tack. "Go if you wish! Both of you! I can wait here alone—"

"Our orders are to stay here with you, Lady Zora, no matter what was said."

As the guard went back to his companion, the two men now watching her warily, Zora knew from their somber faces that she would not sway them. All around her becoming a nightmare, she covered her ears with her hands . . . hating the drums' ominous sound but dreading even more the moment when they would stop.

Standing at the head of his men, Rurik grimly scanned the valley before him.

He had not seen so many thousands of warriors facing each other since the grand prince had defeated his murderous brother Sviatopolk on the plain of the Alta River five years ago. That day the ground had flowed red with blood and today would be no different. Once again, the kingdom of all Rus was at stake.

With the fierce cadence of the drums thundering in his ears, Rurik looked to his right along a hundred-deep line of men that stretched to the distant hills. Then he glanced to his left, the sun's dawning rays streaking the cloudless blue sky with gold fire. Fleetingly, it reminded him of the tawny glory of Zora's hair until the drums abruptly stopped and he thought of her no more.

As a thunderous battle cry tore from ten thousand throats, Rurik yanked out his sword and held it up to the sun.

"Branch-of-Odin, honor me! Defend me!"

Whipping his shield from his shoulder, he began to run with his men toward the enemy . . . the ground made black with their numbers, the air thick with their arrows and spears.

Zora had never known time could pass so horribly slow, each hour dragging into the next and still they had heard no news.

She imagined that she was making the guards dizzy with her incessant pacing, but she couldn't help herself. It was better than sitting and staring at them or the tent walls. Now it was nearing sunset, the sunlight already thinning. She was certain if they didn't hear something soon she would explode.

"Do you think they will go on fighting into the night?" she asked her guards for the tenth time that hour, but before either man could answer, shouts were heard outside the tent accompanied by the pounding of hooves and then horses snorting and whinnying. Zora rushed frantically toward the entrance only to be warned away with a sharp glance.

"Wait here, my lady," came a terse command as both warriors ducked outside, leaving her alone.

"No, I won't stay in here any longer!" Dashing after them, Zora ran straight into a burly warrior who was just about to enter the tent. She would have fallen backward if he hadn't caught her and it was then she recognized him, although the grimness of his expression and those of the guards behind him made her heart lurch painfully.

"Arne!" Her gaze swept him, his clothing stained with sweat and blood, a deep gash on his upper right arm that appeared to have only recently stopped bleeding. "Where's Rurik? Tell me!"

"He is missing, my lady."

"Missing?" Horrified, Zora gaped at him. "How . . . ?"

"This day's battle has been won by your father but by the narrowest of victories. Great losses have been suffered on both sides. I have never seen such terrible slaughter. The dead and the wounded are still being counted."

The dead and the wounded. Holy Mother of God, please not Rurik! Feeling as if she might be sick, Zora forced herself to think rationally.

"Then we must go and look for him, Arne!" She glanced past him to the four men on horseback who appeared to be waiting for them and then back to his dirt-smudged face. "You have horses—"

"Aye, but not to take you to search the battlefield. Grand Prince Yaroslav sent us to fetch you, for he wants you at his side when he meets with your father in Chernigov. He has decided to seek a compromise rather than suffer more bloodshed. If we go on fighting, many more will die for there is still much strength left in both armies."

"But what of my husband?" she cried, helpless tears welling in her eyes. "My husband, Arne! He might be hurt . . . he might need me!"

Although his gaze held pity, the grizzled warrior's voice was resolute.

"Many are looking for him, my lady, and there is always the chance he could have been taken prisoner. Knowing Lord Rurik as I do, he probably ignored the order for retreat and fought on until the last moment, only to become overpowered and captured by your father's advancing forces. We must hope that is what happened, but for now you must come with me. The grand prince is waiting. He believes your presence may help ease the way for talk of peace."

"No!" Backing away, Zora shook her head. "My uncle and my father be damned! If I go anywhere, it will be to search for my husband—"

"Forgive me, my lady," said Arne as he lunged for her and grabbed her arm, pulling her toward him. The Varangian who had so resented being left out of the battle caught her other arm, the two men half dragging her to the horses as she twisted and struggled between them.

"No . . . please! Let me go!" she demanded desperately, but it did nothing but make her voice hoarse. She was lifted into a saddle, one of the men who had accompanied Arne now her steely armed captor.

Arne mounted, then they were galloping past silent, blood-splattered troops just beginning to return to the camp, many shouldering makeshift litters that held wounded men whose agonized moans cut like knives into Zora. Seeing Rurik in each warrior's pain-wracked face, she finally had to shut her eyes against them.

Zora could imagine what a bitter moment it was for Grand Prince Yaroslav as he and his phalanx of warriors were ushered into the great hall of a palace that had once belonged to his viceroy, only to find his brother waiting for them upon a gilt throne. As for herself, any joy she might have felt in seeing her father again was tempered by the horror of the battlefield they had skirted on their way to Chernigov, grisly images she could not shake even as they approached the raised dais.

She now understood why it might be difficult to find someone in such carnage. In places where the fighting had been fiercest, the living had waged battle on top of the fallen until bodies were heaped upon bodies six or seven deep. Yet if she began to believe for an instant that Rurik might be lying at the bottom of one of those lifeless piles, she would go mad—

"Zora!"

She started as her father left his throne and rushed toward her, his thick arms outstretched. Then she was smothered within his bearish embrace until she feared she might faint.

Finally he pulled away to look into her eyes, and in his ruddy face she could see his overwhelming relief.

"So you were in Novgorod all along."

She nodded, knowing he would want a full explanation but feeling too numb to speak. Thankfully, his mind seemed to be upon the pressing matters at hand, and leading her to the dais, he gestured for a chair to be placed near to the throne. She was no sooner seated than he turned his attention back to his somber visitors, his expression becoming as grim as Yaroslav's.

"You were wise to return my daughter to me, elder brother. Any agreement we might reach tonight would have been threatened if harm had come to her."

"I say the same about those men you hold captive in your prison," countered Yaroslav. "If God has been merciful, one of them is the husband of your daughter, Lord Rurik of Novgorod."

An astonished rumble went up from the retainers flanking Mstislav's throne, but he waved his hand for silence and fixed his gaze upon Zora.

"Is this true?"

"Yes, Father," she said shakily, seeing the many questions in his eyes. "My husband has not yet been found and it is our hope that no injury has befallen—"

"*Our* hope, daughter?" His expression tightened. "By such words, I might think you now side with my enemies."

Zora had to swallow against the hard lump in her throat; her father had never before spoken to her so harshly. Yet he must have read in her eyes what he feared. His enraged roar shattered the weighty stillness in the hall.

"If this Lord Rurik is in my prison, bring him to me!"

"There are others whose condition I would know," Yaroslav demanded as Mstislav's guards hastened across the hall to do his bidding. "At least fifteen of my senior warriors have not yet been accounted for, all of them Varangians who would have fought on no matter that a retreat was sounded."

"Very well! Bring however many of these men you can

find!" Mstislav shouted after his guards as he glared at his brother. Then he lowered his voice and leaned forward upon his throne. "Your concern for your *druzhina* is touching, Yaroslav, yet I will not wait for these men to begin our discussion. You stated in your message that you wished to seek a compromise and I agreed to hear you, my promise given for your safety while in my city. Now what have you to offer me?"

As all eyes turned to the grand prince, Zora's were fixed upon the doors through which the guards had disappeared. How she wished she could have gone with them to search for Rurik! But she gasped along with everyone else when Yaroslav finally spoke in his great booming voice.

"Half of Rus, to be divided along the course of the Dnieper River. I will retain the side with Novgorod and Kiev, while everything else will be yours."

Zora glanced at her father to find him pondering Yaroslav's words while his retainers whispered to each other behind him. If at first Mstislav had been surprised, now his narrowed eyes were shrewd.

"Only half, my brother? After my victory today—"

"A narrow victory that could have easily gone to my favor!" interrupted Yaroslav, his face flushed red with anger. "Think carefully before you allow your greed to overwhelm you, Mstislav. My forces are still strong enough to fight, as are yours, yet a lengthy war will only deplete much needed men and resources. Meanwhile our enemies abound, barbaric nomads in the east, neighboring Slavs to the west, and Patzinaks in the south, all of them watching like carrion crows for any sign of weakness so they can swoop down and attack. If we fail to form an alliance this night, neither of us will have the forces left to fight them."

Again a charged silence reigned, everyone waiting upon Mstislav's answer. Zora knew her father to be an ambitious man, yet the wisdom behind the grand prince's argument could not be discounted. Wondering what path he would choose, she was distracted by a side door opening nearby.

Her heart skipped a beat as Hermione entered the hall in a swirl of purple silk.

Their eyes met. From the agitation in her half sister's gaze, Zora realized that Hermione must have heard of her arrival and come at once from the *terem*. Yet Zora found herself abruptly dismissed as Hermione scanned the hall for someone, her porcelain features soon registering her disappointment.

Ivan. She was looking for Ivan, Zora thought, struck by a sudden wave of pity. But it faded when Hermione fixed a gaze of icy hatred upon her as if daring her to say a word about the truth behind her abduction.

"Very well, my brother, I agree to your compromise. Half of Rus, with my throne to remain here in Chernigov."

Zora's attention turned back to her father, who had left the dais to clasp hands solemnly with Yaroslav. As scribes were called forth to prepare the necessary documents, a great swell of conversation erupted among those present that only heightened as the huge double doors at the end of the hall swung open to admit a line of chained prisoners.

Rising shakily, Zora had never known such a clash of hope and fear. Mother of Christ, where was Rurik? She counted five warriors, then eight, but he was nowhere among them. Oh, please, please, tell her it wasn't so . . .

"Rurik!"

Spying him suddenly in a second group of prisoners, his bright blond hair like a beacon in the torchlight, Zora's hoarse cry echoed around the hall. She wanted to run to him but her father's dark glance kept her rooted in place. With her heart pounding as hard as any drum, she watched impatiently as a path was opened for Rurik and the other prisoners. Her eyes drank in the sight of him.

He was limping, dried blood streaking his left leg, but he appeared sound. Even the cold hardness of his gaze could not dampen her joy. Imagining what must be going through his mind to see her standing on the dais, she could no longer heed her father's warning. She hurried down the steps as the prisoners were made to halt in a line behind the grand prince.

"Zora . . ."

Ignoring Mstislav's angry voice, she moved undaunted to Rurik's side, warmed by the astonishment in his eyes. Yet she said nothing to him, boldly facing her father and his retainers instead.

"Hear me, all of you! This is my husband, Lord Rurik of Novgorod, the man I love more than life. I will see no harm come to him!" She glanced at Rurik, her voice breaking. "Can you find it in your heart to believe me now?"

Shaken by her pronouncement, Rurik had never felt more humbled, the plea shining in Zora's eyes chasing all doubt and bitterness from his mind. And here he had been thinking the worst of her up until a moment ago, thinking how happy she must be now that she would finally be free of him!

By Odin, he had not only been a fool, but a blind one! That she could still want him after everything he had done, everything he had said . . .

"No harm will come to him, my daughter, that I swear," Mstislav interjected before Rurik could answer her. "But your marriage to this man must be annulled. I gave my word to Lord Ivan that you would become his bride. He went in search of you to Novgorod. I can only believe that he must still be there—"

"He's not in Novgorod, Father," said Zora, sickened that he would even suggest to end her marriage. "I have so much to tell you . . . I don't know where to start. Ivan did find me and I agreed to return to Chernigov with him, but only because I thought it would be a way to help my husband if he had need of me after the battle. Then Ivan and his men were murdered by thieves at one of the portage trails. I managed to escape but—"

"Ivan is dead?"

Zora spun to find Hermione standing only a few feet away, her lovely face stricken with horror.

"Ivan is dead?" Her voice was shrill and her gaze skipped from Zora to Rurik to her father and then back to Zora.

"Yes. I'm truly sorry, Hermi—"

Her words were cut off by a howl of such rage that Zora felt a shiver of fear.

"You spawn of a whore! Bastard filth! If I've lost my only love, I'll find myself in hell before you have yours!"

Zora saw the flash of a knife at the same moment Hermione lunged wildly for Rurik.

"No!" Without a thought, she hurled herself against him, blocking Hermione's attack with her body even as she felt Rurik trying to shove her out of harm's way.

"By God! Zora!"

Hampered by his chains, he was too late. She met his eyes as the blade sank into her flesh and she screamed once while all around them became confusion. People were shouting, her father and uncle were shouting, Hermione demanding hysterically that her captors release her. Then Zora felt her knees buckle beneath her and she was sinking, even though Rurik held her in his arms. Oh, it hurt. It hurt so much.

"Zora! God help me, Zora!"

She knew he was calling to her but she couldn't answer, her tongue grown thick and heavy. She saw him lift his hand from her side to find blood dripping through his fingers, and his face went deathly pale. Through a ringing that was growing louder in her ears, she could hear Hermione ranting at her as if from a great distance, her piercing voice becoming fainter and fainter.

"Bastard whore! Bitch! I should have poisoned you instead of selling you to that cursed slaver! I should have killed you when I had the chance!"

That was the last thing she heard as blackness rose up to meet her, releasing her at last from the pain.

CHAPTER 30

"Rurik . . . ?" Her eyelids feeling like leaden weights, Zora turned her head to one side and whispered more loudly this time. "Rurik?"

"No, daughter, it's me," came a familiar voice, a large warm hand covering hers.

"Father?" Struck by sudden foreboding, Zora opened her eyes to find Mstislav seated next to the bed, his image blurred and fuzzy. She tried to raise herself on her elbows but immediately fell back, wincing at the sharp pain in her side. "You haven't sent him away, have you? You haven't sent Rurik away—"

"Sshh, Zora, he's in the other room. I finally convinced him to allow the physician to attend to his leg. He's a stubborn one, that Varangian of yours. It's the first time he's stepped away from your bed since we brought you here last night."

"Last night?" She was answered with a nod, her father's face gradually becoming more focused. His expression was somber and he looked weary, as if he had gotten little sleep.

Yet his gray-blue eyes held the affection she had always known there.

"You gave us a scare, daughter, one I hope never to relive. Seeing you lying here so pale, the healers doing everything they knew to help you . . ." Mstislav sighed heavily and fell silent, adding after a long moment, "It reminded me of when your mother fell ill . . . except that time, nothing could be done—"

He seemed to choke and he looked away, but not for long. Meeting her eyes again, he squeezed her hand, a faint smile touching his lips.

"You'll be up from this bed in no time, or so I've been promised. Fortunately the knife did not go deep but glanced off your ribs. Yet you lost a lot of blood—"

"My babe?" Zora broke in, beset by fear.

"The child still thrives within you, daughter," came his reassuring reply. "I only regret that I'll not be there at its birth, for you will be far away in Novgorod."

Her eyes widening, Zora stared at him incredulously. But before she could say anything, he went on.

"I had much time to think during the night and knowing as I do now of everything that happened to you, I cannot in good conscience break apart a marriage that God has ordained. If Lord Rurik had not been at that trading camp, no matter that he had been sent to spy against me . . ." Again, Mstislav had to pause for the quaver in his voice and this time, it was Zora who clasped his hand.

"I love him, Father. More than I could ever say."

He exhaled slowly, nodding. "I know this, Zora. Your courageous act last night could not have proved it more clearly. I loved once, too, but could not marry the woman who captured my heart. It is a pain I have never overcome, and I do not wish such suffering for you. You and Lord Rurik have my blessing."

Swept with elation, Zora could only smile her thanks. Yet she sobered at the thought that suddenly came to her and she asked softly, "What of Hermione?"

Mstislav's expression hardened, but it also held regret. "I've banished her to a convent in Tmutorokan until I decide what else is to be done with her. I cannot forgive her for her cruel treachery toward you, but she, too, has suffered. I never loved her mother, and though I tried to treat both of you equally, Hermione must have sensed that you were the joy of my heart. I've never heard such bitterness as she spewed at me last night. I fear Ivan's death has driven her half mad."

Neither of them spoke for several moments, their shared silence a pained one. Finally Mstislav gently stroked her cheek.

"Your sister's troubles are not your fault, Zora, and I will not have you blame yourself. This is my cross to bear." He gave her hand a last reassuring squeeze, then he rose and moved to the door. "I will tell your husband that you are awake—"

"I already know, my lord." Rurik stepped into the room, not caring that his voice had gone hoarse. His gaze flew to Zora's face. Just to see her conscious again, her beautiful eyes anxious and yet so full of hope, made his chest swell with gratitude. He was certain at that moment that the gods must be smiling. "I've been waiting outside until you finished . . . not an easy task."

Becoming oblivious to all else but her, Rurik was scarcely aware that Prince Mstislav had left them, nor did he recall walking to the bed and kneeling beside it. It seemed that suddenly he was there. Reaching out his hand, Rurik touched her tawny hair with shaking fingers.

"I feared . . ." His voice caught. Swallowing hard, he began again, not caring that his eyes were blinded by tears. "I feared that I wasn't going to have the chance to tell you that I love you, Princess. God forgive me for being such a fool, I love you!"

Zora's heart was too full for her to speak, but she didn't need words. Her own eyes brimming, she took his battle-scarred hand in hers and pressed her lips to his palm.

She knew it had been enough when he smiled, then bent his head and kissed her.

If you enjoyed this book, take advantage of this special offer. Subscribe now and...

⚜ Get a
Historical
No Obligation

If you enjoy reading the very best in historical romantic fiction...romances that set back the hands of time to those bygone days with strong virile heros and passionate heroines ...then you'll want to subscribe to the True Value Historical Romance Home Subscription Service. Now that you have read one of the best historical romances around today, we're sure you'll want more of the same fiery passion, intimate romance and historical settings that set these books apart from all others.

Each month the editors of True Value select the four *very best* novels from America's leading publishers of romantic fiction. We have made arrangements for you to preview them in your home *Free* for 10 days. And with the first four books you

receive, we'll send you a FREE book as our introductory gift. No Obligation!

FREE HOME DELIVERY

We will send you the four best and newest historical romances as soon as they are published to preview FREE for 10 days (in many cases you may even get them before they arrive in the book stores). If for any reason you decide not to keep them, just return them and owe nothing. But if you like them as much as we think you will, you'll pay just $4.00 each and save at *least* $.50 each off the cover price. (Your savings are *guaranteed* to be at least $2.00 each month.) There is NO postage and handling—or other hidden charges. There are no minimum number of books to buy and you may cancel at any time.